# MARY MAGDALENE

# MARY MAGDALENE

## Priestess - Lady –

## Apostol

# EWA KASSALA

ORIGINALLY PUBLISHED IN POLAND IN 2019
BY VIDEOGRAF PUBLISHING HOUSE AS MARIA MAGDALENE
***

TRANSLATED AND PUBLISHED IN ENGLISH WITH PERMISSION.
***

PAPERBACK ISBN: 978-1-7348606-5-8
EPUB ISBN: 978-1-3938621-1-6
***

WRITTEN BY EWA KASSALA
PUBLISHED BY ROYAL HAWAIIAN PRESS
COVER ART BY TYRONE ROSHANTHA
TRANSLATED BY WIESLAWA MENTZEN
PUBLISHING ASSISTANCE: DOROTA RESZKE
***

FOR MORE WORKS BY THIS AUTHOR, PLEASE VISIT:
WWW.ROYALHAWAIIANPRESS.COM
***

VERSION NUMBER 1.00

# Table of Contents

*For my mother, Romana Kassala;*
*Grandmothers: Paulina Kassala and Czesława*
*Stasikowska;*
*Their mothers, grandmothers, great-grandmothers and all*
*other women, with whom I have blood ties and who were*
*before me and who have been on the other side for so*
*long...*

# PROLOGUE

She fell on her face and embraced his feet. They were covered in desert dust, and the sandals were so dusty that their original color could not be seen. He had been walking from afar. He had just entered the city. He raised his hand. The men accompanying him stopped and surrounded her. They looked at her, curious about the master's reaction.

Some of them knew who she was. Mary, lady at Magdala, sister of Marta and Lazarus. Educated in Egyptian temples, a worldly woman, independent, confident, trusting her wisdom, convinced that she can do anything…intriguing, controversial, depraved. Wealthy, rebellious and free. On top of this, beautiful. Until recently.

For several months, it had been said that evil spirits had possessed her. That she was crazy, unstable, mad. She was seen in the desert and on the waterfronts, in the sketchy districts of the city, wandering aimlessly, alternately crying and laughing. She wailed softly and sobbed like a child or screamed, scratching, kicking and insulting everyone who tried to approach her. Raped, beaten, spat on, despised; a low life, an outcast, a possessed woman.

She howled like a badly injured animal. She alternately sprinkled sand on her head, screamed without restraint, tugged at her hair, scratched her face, ripped the remains of her dress. Saliva mixed with foam ran from her mouth. Her bloodshot eyes showed panic, fear, suffering and confusion, but also desperation mixed with resignation and powerlessness.

Her silk dress, once magnificent, was now frayed and stuck to the emaciated body. Mary Magdalene was sore and bruised. Old and fresh wounds covered her skin. Long hair, once so carefully cared for, had not seen a comb or oils for a long time. Matted, tousled and dirty, it completed the picture of a downfall.

The crowd was getting bigger. Those who had thrown stones at her and spat at her, until recently, were now looking at the master. The fame of a miracle worker, healer and teacher had followed him for a long time. Some proclaimed him the Messiah or even the Son of God. Students and onlookers wondered how the one who claimed love to be the most important commandment, would treat the one that should have been stoned long ago.

Mary had no strength. She couldn't keep going any longer. She was running away like a fatally wounded dove, with her wings broken, feathers torn out and her beak beaten. Hunched at his feet, she wanted to run away from cruelty, injustice, lack of understanding and the fate that had long seemed inevitable to her. She was on the edge. Injured to the limits of human endurance, she wanted to die.

At the same time, she had to make the last effort. She owed it to herself. Herself, her grandmother, High Priestess, father, mother, sister, brother, the past and the ideals, to which she remained faithful until recently. The priestesses who had taught her a lot, but did not say how cruel the world can be, how it rejects those who are different and condemns those who do not comply with the rules.

*"Adapt or die - should be the principle they teach the young at temples,"* she thought. She wanted to look in the eyes of the one who was not afraid to live his own way. Just as before, at

Lake Kinnereth, when their eyes met for the first time when she saw in them the vastness of space and freedom that she missed. Now she wanted him to look at her again, touch her, cleanse or reject her, condemning her to non-existence. He was her last chance for a new life or a death, finally ending her suffering.

Jesus bent down. He reached out to her. She knelt. He put both hands on her head. He kept them like that for a while.

"Stand up! You are healthy," he announced.

She rose and looked him straight in the eye. There was not a trace of insanity on her face anymore.

"I found the beloved of my soul, I held on to him and I will not                    let                    go...

# CHAPTER I

# THE PRIESTESS

1.

She was born in a cap, from under which dark and thick hair, quite long for a newborn, appeared. As soon as she was born, the midwife put her by the heart of her exhausted mother. "She is healthy, beautiful and strong, lady," she said. "She'll be lucky in life. A cap guarantees this."

"Can you hear me, baby?" Eucharia kissed the child's fingers.

"There's something else, lady," the midwife made a mysterious face and pointed at the servants bustling in the chamber with her eyes.

"Girls, take the dishes with water, the dirty cloths, and leave," Eucharia ordered, understanding that the woman did not want more people to find out what she had discovered. "Should I worry?" she asked when the door closed behind the servants.

"Quite the opposite..."

"So?"

"The lines on the girl's left hand are arranged so that they form a star," said the midwife triumphantly.

Eucharia opened her daughter's hand. She saw regularly intersecting, strongly outlined lines, indeed arranged in the shape of a star. She knew that for those who received such a sign, it meant not only luck, but also special power, a destiny for higher spiritual purposes or for becoming a leader.

"That's not all, lady." The midwife leaned forward and whispered, "She also has stars on the bottom of both feet!"

"Really?" Eucharia sat up on the bed. "Help me up, I'm very weak..."

The woman raised the girl so that her mother could see the marked places.

"Dear god! Indeed!"

"Yes, lady. In newborn babies, the lines are rarely so clear. And here not only you can see them, but they are also shaped like stars!"

"Don't tell anyone about it," Eucharia said after a moment's reflection. "Give me the black purse from the chest, please. Over there!" she pointed, and when the woman gave her what she had asked for, she took a gold coin from the pouch. "It's for your efforts. And perceptiveness," she put the gold in the woman's hand. "And I am asking you for discretion. It is for the better that no one knows about it. People don't like those who are marked this way. These are wonderful signs." The midwife was surprised. "God gives them only to those who are closest to Him. I would like my daughter to decide about her fate someday. So that no signs would affect how others would treat her and what she would think about herself, you understand?"

"If that is your will, my lady, I will respect it, but at least the rabbi should know. Such a sign is, after all, a mark by Adonai."

"Let her grow up in peace. What is intended for her will happen even if the rabbi does not know about the stars, right?"

The midwife looked at the ceiling, which meant that she was counting on support from heaven, because she did not know what to think. She squeezed the coin more tightly and nodded as a sign that yes, she understood, and she agreed, even though maybe not convinced.

"Well. Let it be that way. But know, lady, that it is the first time in my life that I receive in this world a child with so many stars on hands and feet."

\* \* \*

Syro was kneeling by his wife's bed. The day before she gave birth to a healthy, strong daughter. Their first child together. He was crazy with joy. She was the sun, joy and support for him. He loved Eucharia like no one before, even though she was not Jewish. But he consoled himself that "according to old books," which he liked to quote not always in line with their wording, "you cannot choose whom you fall in love with."

He met her during one of his business trips to Egypt, at her parents' home. Like him, they belonged to the elite of their community because they were very wealthy merchants. He experienced something he didn't believe existed: he fell in love at first sight. His body and mind burned for the first time. As unexpectedly for him, he met with sincere reciprocity. Soon a marriage ceremony took place, despite the doubts and fears of her parents and those he had himself. Together for two years. The birth of their child was supposed to complete their happiness. He had two from his previous marriage. Marta was a 12-year-old, and Lazarus recently celebrated his tenth birthday. God had called to himself their mother, strict and essential, much earlier, before Syro's sad eyes saw the beautiful Egyptian.

Now, Syro held the hand of his beloved tightly. He was scared. He knew it didn't look good. For many hours the midwife could not stop the bleeding. The delivery seemed successful, but something apparently went wrong. Eucharia weakened with every hour. As people say in such situations, she was fading away. *"Has Adonai punished us for uniting without obeying the Moses laws?"* He thought. *"Because I brought a non-Jewish girl into Israel's house? Did he punish me as he once did David, and then Solomon and others?"*

However, there was no time to ponder. It was necessary to act. When on the second day after delivery, the midwife opened her arms helplessly, he immediately called for the best doctor. He examined the new mother, gave strengthening medicine, which at the same time limited the hemorrhage. On leaving, he sighed in resignation, "She has a fever. She is very weak. The blood loss was a lot. The only hope is in God. Pray."

Children and servants gathered in the hall of the household. While awaiting the rabbi, everyone prayed quietly.

"I'm dying..." Eucharia was getting weaker. "Give me my daughter..." With the last of her strength, she hugged the baby to her heart. "Name her Mary," she said. "It's beautiful and universal. I don't want her to change it someday, just like I had to."

"I will, sweetheart." Syro felt his throat tighten.

"Promise me something else," she nodded for him to lower his head. "When she's five, send her to my parents.

"She is my daughter, she should live here," he protested weakly.

He loved his wife and was ready to fulfill her every request, especially since he felt how little time they had left.

"She will always be yours," she assured tenderly. "But do it for me, for yourself and for her. Let my parents take care of her education. Have them send her to Philae. And after 10 years, Mary will decide for herself what her further path will be. Agree, please."

"This is not a good idea..."

"You know Israel. It's not easy for women here. Let her go. Let her know the world and get an education. She will come back here, believe me. And she will always love you."

He looked into her eyes that were getting foggy.

"I am also asking you, when one day you leave this world and I will be waiting for you on the other side, to leave her half of your property."

"Here an estate is inherited by boys..."

"Then write a separate document."

"What about Marta and Lazarus?"

"They'll get the other half. After all they have each other. And when you are no longer around, Mary will be completely alone in Magdala. Such a division will ensure her peace and an adequate life in her fatherland. It will also protect Marta. This is my last will."

When she raised her head with the remaining strength, a streamlet of blood came out of her mouth. "Swear it," she bemoaned.

"I swear it," he promised, stifling his tears. "I will send Mary to Egypt and leave her half the property."

"Swear by your God."

"I swear to Adonai."

Marta and Lazarus stood by the bed and listened to the words of their father. Marta closed her eyes tightly. She didn't want to let tears flow.

## 2.

Mary was an extraordinary child. Ever since she was a baby, she seldom cried. The wet nurses and nannies employed by her father could not stop wondering. She did not wake up at night, she smiled at everyone, she was always babbling in her baby language, she was seemingly happy that she was in the world. She didn't get sick. She could lie in her bed for hours, giving the impression that she was thinking hard. When someone appeared next to her, she greeted them with a joyful squeak. At the sight of her father, she reached out as if she knew that she should show him love and support him in his loneliness and suffering.

"You are a beautiful girl," Marta spoke to her tenderly when no one else was in the room. "I'm not as pretty as you."

Marta didn't like showing emotions. Her mother was reticent. Always busy with important household matters, she loved her children more than anything, but she did not show them her feelings too often. She treated her husband similarly. She was devoted to him and ran the house with a commitment just like other exemplary wives and mothers did. Well organized, helpful, supportive, she got up first and lay down in bad last. She supervised the service, of whom there was always a lot on their property. Her husband thought that she could do with more rest, but she always wanted to personally take care of everything that happened at home.

Marta, even though she had not yet become a woman, was similar to her. She not only inherited raw beauty from her mother but also her character. She was hard-working, conscientious, rarely laughed, and when her mother died, she kept to herself even more. She experienced feminine exuberance and tenderness for the first time only when her father remarried.

He returned from one of his trips, after months of absence from home, with a stranger, whom he introduced as his wife.

"Her name is Eucharia," he announced. "That's how you should call her."

Marta knew only that her father's new wife was from Egypt, a land of depravity and decline.

From the place better not talked about, because it was a hotbed of evil. Many gods were worshiped there, people not knowing that there was no other than Adonai. Women there dressed and behaved like open sinners, and many of them, as Marta once heard by accident during a conversation between her father and the rabbi, had their own estates and could study.

From the overheard stories, she understood that Egypt was something like the old Sodom and Gomorrah, which God punished with destruction for fornication.

However, Eucharia did not seem to come from a place condemned by Adonai. Marta felt that with her. Joy appeared in their house that had never been there before, but also some strange secret, something fleeting, alluring, with the smell of a distant space, disturbing, distant, yet quite close. This elusive something caused anxiety for her heart's, trembling of her voice, a spinning in her head and a longing that could not be described in words.

One night, when Eucharia had already lived in their house for over a month, Marta woke up. It seemed to her that she could hear through the thin walls how her father talked to someone, but using a completely unknown foreign name. Who could be in his chamber at night?

"Who is Aset?" she asked Eucharia the next day.

"Why this question, honey?"

"At night, I thought I heard my father addressing someone with that name."

"What did he say?"

"Aset, I love you."

Eucharia smiled brightly and took Marta's hand, "You're big already. I know that I can trust a wise girl like you. Right?"

"Of course." Marta looked even more serious than usual. She was glad she would be someone's confidante. Especially an Egyptian, someone who certainly had a lot of secrets. She felt grown up.

"When I lived in Egypt, it was my name. But, as you know, it was a long time ago. For the love of your father, I became a follower of Adonai. I have been Eucharia since my marriage. I would prefer, my love, that nobody except your father and you know my former name. People in Magdala don't know that I changed my name, and faith together with it. Will you keep the secret?"

"Of course!" she said eagerly again. She kept her word. For the rest of her life.

The Egyptian woman was completely different from her mother and the women she knew. Not only did she wear colorful, beautiful clothes, but early in the mornings, she sang, danced, laughed and gifted good words to the world. If Marta were to describe her in one sentence, she would say that she is a colorful, tweeting, happy bird. She brought with her a strange cat who did not leave her for one step, made the house full of flowers, took in a stray dog, tenderly stroked her father's face. She also hugged her and Lazarus, played with them, invented games, and Marta particularly liked the one she brought from Egypt. It was called senet.

When her father was not at home, in the evening, they sat on the roof of the house, where a large terrace was located, and played.

"When I was a child, I got it as a gift from my father," Eucharia said, setting the stone box on a low table for the first time. "He taught me the rules."

" Did you play with him?" Marta was in disbelief.

She couldn't imagine her father playing anything with her, or even having a long talk with her. Syro did not look after the children, and if he paid attention to any of them, it was Lazarus. He sometimes took him with himself on trips. He explained to him the intricacies of the world. He sent him to study with the rabbi.

"Of course. He taught me not only the rules of senet," Eucharia assured her, placing the pieces on a stone board. "In Egypt, girls are treated equally with boys. Because, dear Marta, think about it, dear, why couldn't they study, for example? After all, in order to do business, they need to know mathematics, to heal they should know herbs and how the human body works, and to function well in the world, they should know the rules that govern it. Let's play senet because it teaches us how to think and use unconventional solutions. You are very smart, you will learn quickly, you will see."

Marta liked this game not only because she indeed understood the rules immediately, but above all she could spend time with the person who was not only like a new world for her, but also devoted the time to her stepdaughter. She listened to her attentively like nobody else before, wanting to know what the girl was thinking and feeling. She inquired about local customs and opened her eyes wide in surprise, finding out how much the reality in which her husband and his children grew up and lived differed from the Egyptian one.

Eucharia never once told anyone about it, but she believed that Israel, in relation to Egypt, is like a retarded, distant, closed, gray world. Only men rule it. Women don't even have the opportunity to pray to their goddess because she just isn't there. Not only is she gone, there are no temples or followers, or even places where women could study. It wasn't exactly news to her, because her parents, priestesses, and friends warned her before leaving Egypt that she would be going to a terrible place where she would not have much to say. But she thought she knew better. She was in love and nothing else was important to her.

Eucharia spent only two years in Magdala. She died shortly after giving birth, leaving behind despair, sadness, a silent home, trunks filled with colorful dresses and papyri, boxes full of jewelry, box and pawns for playing senet, the cat, fond memories and...the baby.

\* \* \*

Marta became Mary's guardian. Wet nurses and nannies fed her, changed her clothes, put her to sleep, but it was Marta who gave her love. The baby spent the first months of her life in a cradle in the middle of the chamber that belonged to Eucharia.

Her wet nurse laid a mat right next to it, in accordance with the master's ordinance, ready to give breast to the child at her every request. Syro rarely visited there. But when he came, he stood in silence and never took the little one in his arms. He watched. Sometimes tears flowed down his cheeks, not seen by anybody.

When Mary was two years old, thanks to the express request of Marta, Syro decided that the sisters should live in one room. Since then, the wet nurse came only three times a day, and the girl began to eat also other foods apart from milk.

Marta looked after her like a mother. She was 14 already and had had her feminine days for almost two years now. She felt responsible for Mary; she could hug her and stroke her to her heart's content, giving and receiving the love they both needed. They were together, huddled and staring at each other, like two closest persons. Marta behaved like a very young mother in love with a tiny daughter.

As soon as she started to walk, Mary quickly learned the layout of the rooms in the house, the location of trees, bushes and the herb and vegetable garden. During the day, Marta sometimes left her under the care of a nanny, playing in the shade of the trees. She did not like to take her eyes off her, but at the same time, like her mother before, she wanted to take care of everything that was happening in the house. She was always walking back and forth between the kitchen, pantry, utility rooms, living quarters and garden. She was only 14, and she managed the property like an experienced woman. More and more often, her father left the house under her supervision. First for a few days, then weeks, and sometimes even for several months.

One day, when Marta came to check on Mary, who was playing in the garden, she saw her little sister leaning down and speaking to someone in her clumsy childish language.

"What do you have there, darling?"

Marta used the word "darling" only in relation to Mary. She remembered how much she liked it when Eucharia called her this way. She felt special and distinguished then. Eucharia used this term also in relation to her father and Lazarus, no one else. With this word, she marked who belonged to the family and who was closest to her.

Mary looked up. She looked at her sister. "A birdie is sleeping. Sleep, sleeeeep, my little..." she repeated the words of the lullaby she heard every night before falling asleep.

A dead white dove was lying on the grass. Marta sat down next to her. "You're right, she is sleeping. Do not disturb her," she said, knowing that one should not touch dead animals because they are unclean and carry the plague. "Let's go home. It's time to eat something." She wanted to tear her away from the dangerous play. The girl did not react, staring at the bird, so she added encouragingly, "You'll eat something delicious. Yum yum...Come on!"

But the little one did not move. To Marta's dismay, she reached out and put her little hands in front of her and laid them on the dove. Marta froze.

"What if she catches some nasty disease?" she thought.

"Don't sleep," Mary said. "Fly! Fly my darling!"

Then something happened that both Marta and the nanny, who watched the event from aside, later recalled many times. The dove shifted, shook, stretched its wings and flew.

Mary jumped up from the grass, hopped happily and clapped her hands, "She's not sleeping!"

Marta was so amazed at what happened that she didn't even chastise the nanny, who, after all, should not let the child walk one step away. Instead, prior to her watching the miracle, the nanny was taking a nap under the tree.

"You should know that Mary has revived a dead dove," she tried to tell her father about the unusual incident.

He cut her tale off even before she really began it. "Things like that happen, Marta. The bird was only looking dead. As a woman, you have the right to exaltation and fantasy, I know that. But don't mess with Mary, okay? She should have a clear mind and think logically. Don't put rubbish in her head!"

"Yes." Marta gave a word to her father and herself that she would be prudent and rational. She understood well that if the dove were really dead, she wouldn't fly. Father was right. What she saw was just a coincidence. She promised herself solemnly that she would never think magically again. At least she would try.

But it would not be given to her. Not a year passed, and she found Mary in a situation that seemed perhaps not as moving as the incident with the dove. But for her, for very personal reasons, it was much more touching.

It was dawning. The sun was just coming out from behind the horizon. The house was still asleep. She didn't cover the window for the night. At this time of year, bothersome mosquitoes were not flying around yet, nights and days were cold. The light and crisp air made it easy to breathe and sleep. However, in order not to get cold, you had to cover yourself with a thick duvet and put additional warm blankets over it. She woke up and saw that Mary's bed was empty. She thought that maybe it only seems so, and the child was simply buried somewhere under several covers, with which she carefully wrapped her in the evening. She came closer to check it. She stroked the quilt gently, but strong enough to see if there was a small body underneath. There wasn't.

"Oh, Lord!"

She looked around the room. One could hardly see anything in the dark, even though it was already dawning. She slipped her sandals on. She lit a lamp. Looking into every corner was just a formality; she knew that she would not find her there. She ran through the neighboring rooms. Their father was not home, so his chamber was empty, but she also entered there, because sometimes Mary would sneak out at night and go to her father's bed to hug him, to his great surprise. She wasn't there. Their father's bed was empty. Lazarus slept peacefully in the next room. She went down to the servant's rooms. Nobody was up yet. It was early.

She went out in front of the house. Nothing. She looked between the trees, reached the garden through a narrow path. Not a soul. The birds were starting to wake up, the sun was getting up. Then she saw her. She was standing on the roof of the house, on the terrace, where often in the evenings, they spent time waiting on comfortable beds for the night. Her arms were outstretched as if to fly. Marta knew she couldn't scream because she would scare her. She took a breath and rushed to the roof, as quietly as possible, trying not to make noise with her sandals.

When she got on the terrace, Mary was still standing in the position in which she noticed her from the garden. Except that she bent in different directions, pretending to be flying. She was humming.

"What are you doing, darling?" she asked friendly, when she was right behind her, making sure that if something bad were to happen, she would catch her.

"I want to be a bird," said the little girl resolutely. "Like the dove that fell asleep in the garden, remember?"

"And you, do you remember?"

"Yes. It flew away to other countries. I want to fly like her," she confessed with childish honesty. "I'm trying."

"Girls don't fly, you know that?" she laughed, trying not to offend her. "People don't fly. God gave wings only to birds. We walk the earth. We have legs. Look," she pointed to her feet.

"I will fly. You will see!" Mary assured her. "I will soar high. Over there!" she pointed to the sky.

"Maybe..." Marta was happy that nothing bad happened. She still remembered her father's words not to involve Mary in magical or, as he said, feminine thinking, so she didn't want to tease her.

"Let's go, you must be cold?"

"No. I'm here because my mom said you would teach me how to play senet," she turned and walked over to the cabinet.

"Mom, said that?"

"Yes, at night."

"You dreamed about it?"

"I wasn't dreaming. She came, took my hand and brought me here. She showed me that there is a game in the cabinet," she opened the cabinet door, long unused by anyone. She took out a turquoise stone box. "It is here!" she said with joy. "Will you teach me?" she began to set up pawns as if she had done it before.

"Mary, you have just recently turned three," Marta protested in a shaky voice, shocked by what she heard. She wanted to mask her surprise and terror somehow. *For, how could a little girl, her beloved Mary, know the name of the game, and know where it was kept? Did her mother really visit her at night? If not, how did she know something she had no right to ever even have heard?*

"Little girls don't play games," she whispered.

"I play," Mary said seriously. "Will you teach me?"

"Okay, I'll teach you," she agreed uncertainly. "But tell me, please, how do you know the name of this game?"

"I told you, my mom told me. She was in my room tonight, showed me where the box was and promised that you would teach me," she squinted her eyes because the sun had just shone with all its might.

Marta spent the morning teaching Mary the rules of the game. She did not tell her father about the incident. Many years later, she wondered what was more important that morning – Mary's story about Eucharia's visit and learning the Egyptian game, or maybe her assuring that she would fly someday

* * *

Another year passed. Mary grew up to be a beautiful girl. She had the noble, regular features of her mother's face, and her father's pointed chin. She was very smart, learned quickly, talked a lot, was mature beyond her age.

Syro continued to travel. He did business in many countries, brokered trade between Egypt and the world east of Israel. He often spent the night away from home. When he was in his homeland, he most often chose to rest in the house in Bethany instead of his estate in Magdala. It was small but comfortable. With a small garden and orchard, it did not require much input. Syro only kept five servants there. That's where he had peace and quiet. He could cut himself off from the children, no one asked him questions or bothered him. He could be alone. As Marta, although still very young, managed Magdala skillfully, he did not hesitate to leave the property under her supervision. Sometimes he felt that the household members were doing better without him and that they were not looking forward to their master's to return. However, as a father and the head of the family, he felt obliged to be there. Especially that he noticed with joy how well Mary was developing. She was extremely smart, open, direct and cheerful. She resembled her mother in her behavior. He and everyone around him noticed that.

One day, while he was in Magdala, Syro found his younger daughter in his chamber. She was kneeling on the floor, where she arranged parchments and a dozen rolls of papyrus next to each other.

"Mary, don't you think you shouldn't touch my stuff?" he asked, surprised and amused, but also pleased to see how gentle she was and how carefully she looked at them.

"Father, teach me to decipher them," she asked, getting up as if she didn't see anything inappropriate in her presence in this place.

Her father didn't spend much time with her. Most often, he was not at home, and even when he was, he did not pay attention to children. It was as if he didn't notice them.

"You're too small to be interested in such things." To his surprise, he crouched beside her, "Besides, you're a girl. Such activities don't befit girls."

"They do befit!" She liked the word, so she repeated it, "Befit, befit. Will you teach me?" She put her arms around his neck, "Please!"

"Certainly not today."

He was surprised by her direct behavior, but he did not break free from her hug. He was experiencing something pleasant, hearing his daughter's little heart beating so close, and feeling her breath on his cheek.

"Maybe you will?" she whispered straight into his ear. "I'm asking you sooo much! At least a little bit."

"Okay, a little bit," he gave in, not sure why. "So be it. I will teach you a few letters. Come."

He wanted to get up, but she embraced him even more.

"Thank you, thank you!" she covered his face with child kisses. "I love you."

He got up and wiped away a tear so that Mary would not notice. Since the times of his beloved Eucharia, no one had ever used such words with him.

"Father?"

"Yes?"

She nodded at him, asking him to bend down, and when he did, she grabbed him tenderly, but firmly with her small fingers by both cheeks, stretching them as if for a smile.

"Do brrrr," she said.

He was surprised, but he fulfilled her request.

"Brrrr," he made a sound as she wished.

"Very nice, good job," she praised him. "Now we shall see how I will do at reading.

Come."

He sat in a chair at the wide table he usually worked at. She climbed on his knees without asking.

"Alef, bet, gimel, dalet, he, vav," he said the first letters of the alphabet, pointing to them on the written parchment. "Can you repeat that?"

"Say again, only more slowly," she responded.

He sighed heavily, expecting the teaching would not be successful, but he repeated.

She took a deep breath and flawlessly pointed at the letters he had said, "Alef, bet, gimel, dalet, he, vav."

Syro shifted in his chair. He did not believe what he heard and saw.

"Can you do it again?"

She did as he asked.

"Oh, Lord, how is that possible?" he asked himself in spirit.

"Zayin, het, tet, yod, kaf, lamed, mem, nun..." he pointed to the letters, at the same time giving their names out loud.

She repeated flawlessly.

"Samekh, ayin, pe, tsadi, qof, resh, shin, tav," he finished reading the Aramaic alphabet.

With joyful squeaking, seeing the great pleasure she gave her father, she repeated everything, at the same time pointing to the right letters.

"Baby!" Syro raised her high. "God has given you an extraordinary talent!" he called triumphantly.

"Can I read already?" she asked with a disarming smile.

"Not yet, but you'll surely learn very quickly."

He kissed her on both cheeks and set her on the floor.

"Mom thinks so too," she assured him.

"Mom?" he asked in a worried voice.

"She visits me at night and we talk," she confessed.

"Do you dream about her?" he asked hopefully.

"Yes. I dream about her," she replied reassuringly, remembering the impression her confession made on Marta. From that time, she knew that it was better to say that she spoke to her mother in dreams. Why bother your loved ones?

Syro hugged his daughter tenderly. From that day on, they began learning each morning. It went just as he predicted. Reading was not a problem for Mary. After a month, she could do it completely on her own.

"What now?" he wondered. "I won't tell the rabbi that a four-year-old can read. How will I explain this? Of course, she is my daughter, so she must be smart, that's a given. And I taught her how to read myself. But how do I explain to the world that she has such a gift?"

* * *

Lazarus was a quiet child and did not cause problems. Polite and orderly, he stayed away from disputes and conflicts. Since his mother's death, he had fully surrendered to Marta, recognizing her as the one who cares for him and whom he is to listen to. The absolute power was obviously exercised by their father. Lazarus looked up to him and did not question any of his decisions.

He even liked it when his father returned home from one of his distant journeys with the woman he introduced as his wife. He didn't remember his mother at all, so he didn't mind anyone taking her place, especially someone as nice and joyful as Eucharia. He liked her, and because she stroked him, called him "sweetheart", and often played with him, he gave her his childhood heart without hesitation. When she left, he was sad, but he did not despair too much. He accepted God's will just as he had in the case of his mother's death. He accepted the baby's presence without emotion. He didn't mind the little one. He didn't care about her; she didn't belong to his male world.

Following the custom and Syro's decision, he learned to read the Book in the synagogue along with other boys his age almost every day. He traveled with his father and also learned accounting. He was convinced that it was only him who counted for his parent. That he was his natural successor in business and his beloved son. So, when Syro began his morning lessons with Mary, Lazarus felt a twinge of jealousy. Also, when he heard how proudly his father spoke about his younger daughter, and with how much love he looked at her, he understood that she overwhelmed his heart without the slightest effort and that she occupied the space which he, as a boy, should naturally be in. Just as he had been indifferent to her before, he now more and more often looked at her as a rival. However, something happened that changed his perspective.

\* \* \*

"Who did it?" their angry father stood over the broken bust.

It was a valuable souvenir from a trip to Greece. It stood in his chamber in a place of honor among the most important trophies. Marta, Mary and Lazarus stood before their father.

"Who broke Plato?" he repeated.

"I didn't and I don't know who did it." Marta, as always, made things clear.

"You come here most often, Mary. Maybe it happened to you?" Syro leaned over his daughter.

"No, it was not me," she raised her head. "But I guess who could have done it."

Droplets of sweat appeared on Lazarus' forehead. In a moment, it would come to light that he was the culprit. He was sure that this would mean falling out of favor with his father.

He was scared; not of the punishment, but of the rejection, that even this bit of interest and attention Syro gave him, will be taken away. *"She must have seen me,"* he thought.

"Yes? And will you tell us?" asked Syro.

"Yes," she said with a smile.

Lazarus closed his eyes.

"Maybe it's the ghost of the cat," she confessed. "I saw it walk on the dresser. It squeezed between the bust and the vase. Unintentionally, it could have happened to the ghost, father."

Syro looked at her closely," You think so?"

"Yes."

"What if someone else did it, who does not want to admit it?" he asked without looking at his son.

"Maybe this someone is afraid that if you find out that he did it, you will stop loving him?"

Lazarus breathed a sigh of relief.

Syro was speechless. "Who is this child?" he thought. "She reads, speaks and behaves like an adult, and in addition, has such a good heart. It is true that she also has a powerful imagination, but when she grows up, she will probably outgrow it. Children are like that."

He knew that Lazarus had broken his bust. He just didn't understand why he was afraid to admit it. He was already 14, his mustache was showing, he was looking at girls, but he could not admit his guilt? In a single sentence, Mary explained to him why it was so. She was right. Lazarus, like every person, needed love and he was afraid of losing it.

"Go now. And you, Mary, call me next time you see the ghost of the cat. I will have a talk with him," he laughed.

A day later, Lazarus admitted his guilt. Father didn't scream. He didn't even punish him in any way. Instead, he told him about Plato and promised that they would once go to Greece together and bring a new bust from there.

\* \* \*

A few weeks later, something happened that further changed Lazarus' attitude to Mary. It also significantly affected the rest of his life. It was summer, early afternoon. Mary, as every day, was napping after dinner. Marta and the servants took care of the kitchen. Lazarus had just returned from the morning classes in the city. He had not yet entered his chamber when he heard the scream of his younger sister. He threw his bag on the floor and rushed to see what was happening. The girl was curled up in a corner of the room. She covered her head with her hands as if she wanted to defend herself against something. She screamed.

"What's going on?" he knelt beside her, warding off the insects that circled over her.

He was surprised that there were flies in their home. Thanks to the right herbs distributed in the corners and meshes mounted in the windows, flies were rarely indoors. But that wasn't his concern now.

Mary looked up. Her big dark eyes were looking at something in horror. "Black wings!" she pointed at the space above herself.

He looked up.

"They want to take me!" she called desperately.

"There is nothing there. Only a few flies," he noted calmly. "No need to be afraid."

"Black wings want to take me!"

He saw fear in her eyes. "Come to me," he held out his hands to her. "I'll protect you."

She only hesitated for a moment. He felt her face, wet from crying, snuggle trustingly into his neck. He felt grown up. He knew that he could and should protect her against the black wings she invented and against anyone who would want to hurt her. He was her older brother. The blood of one father flowed through their veins.

"Don't be afraid anymore. Everything will be fine. I'll protect you. If the black wings were to take someone, they would take me first, you understand?"

She nodded.

"Hey you, black wings, can you hear? If you want to take Mary, you have to catch me first!" he called, threatening invisible enemies with his fist.

Mary rested her head on his chest. She sighed and closed her eyes. She was now calm, snuggled into her brother. Soon, she began to fall asleep.

Suddenly, Lazarus flinched. His back curved backward unnaturally. He released Mary from his arms. He fell to the floor, and his body began to shiver. Mary stood over him, terrified.

"Nooo!" she shouted with all her might.

Her voice reached the kitchen. Marta heard it, dropped everything she had in her hands and a moment she was with Mary. She found her brother writing on the floor, pushing away a nonexistent opponent, and Mary stood over him and screamed with all her might. Her arms were straight and raised, her fingers trying to capture something invisible.

Marta froze, not knowing what to do. She knelt beside her brother and tried to grab his hands, but she couldn't do it. She had the impression that she was just making things more difficult for him. So, she gave up and looked at what was happening with horror and powerlessness.

Mary finally caught the invisible entity. With her eyelids lowered, focused, she slowly lowered her hands. She raised them above Lazarus' head and began to speak something in a language completely unknown to Marta. She repeated the same formula three times, and finally took a deep breath and blew as hard as she could at her brother. A draft could be felt in the chamber. Marta closed her eyes.

When she opened them, Lazarus was lying calmly with his eyes open. He was all wet. Mary knelt over him and stroked his cheek.

"Thank you. You saved me."

"You saved me," he answered in a breaking voice.

"The black wings came for me. You are my protector."

"And I'll be for the rest of my life."

\* \* \*

One morning, when the daily lessons were about to start, Marta ran into Syro's chamber instead of Mary.

"Father, Mary disappeared!" she called, stopping in front of the table he was working at.

She was agitated. When he saw her, he got up immediately.

"How come?" he grabbed her shoulders and shook her hard. "You haven't watched her!"

She stepped back and proudly raised her chin. "I know that she is your beloved daughter, but maybe she is closer to me than to you!" she said proudly. "She's not here. She disappeared!"

"Where is she?"

He was struck by Marta's self-confidence, and at the same time, by her belief that she was someone much more special to Mary than he was, but he knew it was not the time to focus on it.

"I don't know," she admitted, spreading her hands.

"What do you know?" He got angry. "Do you know anything, woman?"

"You'd be surprised how much," she said softly but feisty.

He didn't listen to her anyway.

"Did you look at home?" He stepped out of the room with a decisive step. He stood in the middle of the hall. "Everyone here!" he ordered loudly. "Immediately!"

"I looked everywhere," Marta said, but he no longer paid her any more attention. "She is neither at home nor in the garden. I checked personally."

"Who saw Mary today?" he looked at his servants.

Silence answered him.

"No one?" He made sure.

The servants had not seen their master so alarmed for a long time - most often, he was calm, did not shout nor even raise his voice. They thought of him as a just and prudent man. They respected him.

Mary was his beloved daughter and everyone's favorite. Now that she was missing, they understood that everyone, as they were standing there, would go search for her, and that's what happened. Syro efficiently divided the service into pairs and ordered who should go in which direction. He and Marta went toward the lake.

\* \* \*

Magdala lay on its shore. The Gennesaret was so extensive that many called it the sea. Others called the lake Kinneret because of its harp-like shape. The Jordan River and many small seasonal streams flowed into and out of it, surrounded by picturesque hills. The waterfront was overgrown with lush, colorful vegetation for half of the year. Flowers bloomed here, trees grew, also fruit ones and the grass on the banks were green, especially after the rainy season. Almost all the plants that Galilea knew grew near the water and on the hills surrounding it. These were olive and fig trees, sycamores, walnuts, almond trees, date palms, evergreen cypresses, rock oaks, pine trees, plane trees, poplars, willows, terebinths and a large number of all others that thrived there, taking advantage of the abundant water resources. Reed and bulrush overgrew the shores, and in the flowering season it was colorful with flowers. Poppies, chamomiles, pyrethrums, buttercups, anemones, and in the gardens lilies, tulips, hyssops and roses, among which ivy meandered, meant that the area of Gennesaret was considered the most beautiful in Galilee.

The lake was known for being wayward. Often, unexpected sharp winds blew over it and the weather changed. However, life was good there.

Apart from Magdala, Bethsaida, Capernaum, Korazin, Gadara, Gennesaret and Tiberias were also situated there. The inhabitants of all these towns lived mainly from trade and fishing. For centuries, merchant routes leading to Egypt had been passing there. It was thanks to them that Syro's fortune was created. He skillfully brokered the trade, and also participated in it himself, like his father and grandfather before. People said that these areas were already inhabited in times not even mentioned by even the oldest papyri.

Syro's estate, the largest and most magnificent villa in the whole of Magdala, was located a short distance from the lake. However, only part of its waters could be seen from the house, and only from the roof terrace.

The Galilean walked very quickly. He was almost running. Marta couldn't keep up with him, but he never turned around, as if he had forgotten that his older daughter was with him. Restricted by a long dress, she jogged as fast as she could. After a while, they saw the reservoir in full glory.

Mary was sitting on the shore, very close to the water. From a distance, she seemed even smaller than she really was. She put her arms around her curled legs and stared into the distance.

They approached her as quietly as possible.

"Mary?" Syro called to her.

Marta stood without a word, a few steps behind her father, surprised by his calmness. She was convinced that he would show his disapproval. However, happy to see his daughter safe and sound, he just sat down next to her.

"What are you doing here?" he put his arm around her small back.

"I look far away," she smiled.

"And what do you see?"

"People who live over there. I want to see them up close."

"We can sail there if you want."

"I want to fly like a dove from the garden."

"What dove?"

"The one who had been sleeping and then woke up and flew to see the world."

Father," Marta interjected quietly. "I once mentioned to you what happened in the garden. Do you remember?"

He remembered the story of the bird miraculously brought back to life, which seemed ridiculous to him. He scolded Marta for it. He ordered her not to tell similar things again. Now, he understood how firmly that experience was stuck in his little daughter's memory.

She put her hand in his. The gesture touched him. She was tiny and so similar to his beloved wife. She had dark hair and eyes that were always beaming, she was joyful, and at the same time calm and balanced. She acted like an adult as if someone else lived in her tiny body, much older, experienced and wise.

"I want to float above the ground, see what is somewhere else. I want to fly."

" My little girl..." his voice broke off because tears welled up in his eyes. "Listen to what I tell you..." She rested her head on his knees. "I loved your mother very much. When she was leaving, I promised her that when you are five, I would take you to your grandparents. We never talked about it because I thought you were still too small. The truth is also that I tried to postpone this day as long as possible because I would like you to be always with me. But it's time.

"Mom also says it's time," she confirmed shyly.

"Have you dreamt of her again?"

She knew that she could not say that they were not dreams, because her mother really visited her. But she remembered the impression such confession made on Marta. So she preferred not to worry about her father.

"Yes, she often comes to me."

"What does she tell you?"

"That you will take me to Egypt."

"It will be so. I'll take you."

They both looked at the calm surface of the lake. There was not a single boat on the shore, all of them went out fishing.

"I'll be back," Mary said, feeling she should calm him down.

Marta, who listened to the conversation, once again in her life concluded that her sister really was not an ordinary child. She spoke and acted as if she were not younger, but much older than her.

43

"Water means the beginning of new things. My dove has flown away, but she will come back here, you'll see her at this lake, Father."

She spoke again as if an adult was speaking through her. When she realized that Syro was looking at her with concern and worry, she babbled happily, just like children do, so as not to worry him:

"I'll come back here too. I'll just need to learn to fly."

She stood up, jumped happily, and started running toward the house, arms spread sideways.

### 3.

"My beloved little one," a beautiful woman called, extending her arms in greeting. "How good that you are finally here!"

She was standing before the great gates of the house, which looked like a palace. She had black, good eyes and long, dark, straight hair. She was dressed in a blue, simple dress and her slender neck was decorated with a menat. Mary saw gold sandals on her feet.

The woman was accompanied by a tall, thin, gray-haired man. He was wearing a white tunic reaching below his knees, girded with a wide leather belt. His sandals were simple, brown.

"They're your mother's parents."

Father ordered the driver to stop the cart drawn by mules.

Jews did not travel by horse. Romans, Egyptians and other nations rode horses, but the Israelites considered horses unclean.

"Peace be with you, Syro," the man said."

"Peace with you," the woman smiled brightly.

"Peace be with you," answered Syro, handing Mary to them and hopping off the cart.

"Our little Aset is finally with us." The woman closed the girl in her embrace. "Thanks be to the gods!"

"I'm not Aset. My name is Mary," the girl looked carefully in her grandmother's eyes.

"Yes, honey, I know." The woman's voice broke, she hugged her granddaughter even tighter and cried.

Mary wrapped her small arms around her neck. "I'm not Aset, but I love you, you know?" she whispered.

* * *

"Your mother used to live here. The bed, tables, cabinets and other furniture, a bathhouse and a terrace, everything is just like it was then," Aida led her granddaughter into a spacious chamber. "Apart from painting and refreshing, we haven't changed anything. It's just like it was seven years ago.

"Very nice," Mary looked around.

"It's all yours now. This is your room."

The chamber looked completely different from the one she occupied in Magdala. It was bright and big. Much more furniture was placed here, and it was different from the furniture she was used to. The legs of the bed, the chests of drawers, and chairs were so curved that Mary was surprised that they were standing at all. They were painted gold, and on the back supports there were colorful paintings depicting figures, animals and plants. The walls were high, each decorated with flowers. Some of them were painted, while others – alive – stood in wide clay pots.

Mary was used to comfort, but her father's estate, the most impressive in Magdala, seemed modest compared to the place she was in. She liked the room very much, but that was not the most important thing. She was glad because the people she knew to be her closest family, received her so warmly that from the first moment she felt that they had been waiting for her with love, just as her father had assured her.

"In Magdala I shared the room with Marta. Who can I live with here?

"You'll be alone. However, not completely. I live close, see," Aida pointed at the small, almost invisible door by the exit to the terrace. "You can come to my room this way," she said, walking to door.

Mary pushed the door open. It opened slightly.

"Go ahead," Aida encouraged her, and when the little girl crossed over, she lowered her head to fit in the low passage and followed her. "It's my space," she explained. "Whenever you want to be with me, all you have to do is open the door. If it is closed, knock and then I will soon come out to you. You can also lock it from your side. There is a latch. If you lock it, I won't bother you. Everyone needs to be alone sometimes, right?"

Aida's chamber was larger than the one meant for Mary and differently decorated. Everything that was carved in heavy wood was richly decorated, inlaid and elaborate. In addition to the huge bed, there was also furniture that Mary had never seen before: a sofa lined with soft cushions, wide chairs lined with shiny fabrics, footrests, a dressing table with dozens of tiny bottles, colorful boxes and multicolored purses, as well as a special wide and long stand on which colorful dresses hung. There were also dried gourds, with wigs in fanciful shapes and in different colors on them. The bathroom area was separated from the bedroom space by a wall made of live bushes and flowers, and a large mirror of polished silver was placed in the place that led to it. The walls of the chamber were covered with paintings depicting, as Mary later learned, gods and goddesses. The central place was occupied by a woman in blue with wings spread wide.

"Who is this lady?" Mary pointed at her.

"That's Isis. The patron of women, the Great Goddess, the giver of life, wife of Osiris, mother of Horus, the one we worship and in whose care we entrust ourselves."

"The only god is Adonai, don't you know it?"

Aida looked at her granddaughter with love and concern. She knew where and how she had been brought up for the first five years of her life. She was also sure that the first day in a new home was not the right time to raise religious topics.

"Certainly we will talk about it many times, I promise," she assured gently. "Now I invite you to the banquet area. Your grandfather and father are waiting for us there. You will meet your teachers, servants and other household members. Besides, it's time to eat something. Are you hungry?"

"Not really."

"At least you can drink something. Caring for the body's needs is our duty and privilege. We got it when we were born, and we should care for it properly."

Mary listened to her grandmother in surprise. No one had ever told her such things before.

\* \* \*

The grandparents' villa had two levels. On the upper one, chambers of family members were located, each equipped with a small bathroom and a large terrace. There were also rooms for guests of whom there were always many at home. A few times a year, the sons of the hosts lived in them, when they came from Alexandria for business purposes, or when family meetings were held on the occasion of the holidays. At that time, the house was filled with cheerful bustle and the screams of children, because the sons of Aida and Karim, both older than Mary's mother, had their families and three children each.

The largest part on the ground floor was a big living room, serving as a place for meetings, play, feasts and parties, as well as daily meals. There was also a kitchen in which dishes prepared earlier in the large and very comfortable main kitchen were finished and decorated. It was in a separate building, located on the side of the villa so that the smells and noises that could come from there would not cause discomfort to the household members. There was also an extensive office downstairs, in which the master of the house received important clients. In addition to comfortable seats and tables for work, there were also souvenirs from numerous travels, as well as papyri, maps, parchments and clay tablets with bills.

The living room opened into the partially roofed garden, whose central point was the blue-tiled swimming pool.

Artificial brooks flowed into it in cascades, flowing through the garden down snake-shaped routes.

Aida and Mary entered the living room, holding hands. Karim and Syro were sitting on wide chairs arranged in the middle of it. They held goblets of colored glass filled with wine. Servants stood by the walls. They waited for the landlady or landlord to introduce them to the newly arrived.

"This is Sithathor, from today your main teacher and guardian," Aida pointed at a beautiful girl in a simple white dress that reached to her feet. "She was a priestess in the temple of Isis. She will teach you Egyptian and Latin."

The girl bowed her head in greeting, and Mary gave her a bright smile.

"And this is Stephanie. She comes from Greece," she indicated to a tall blue-eyed beauty with fair hair pinned at the top of her head. "She usually helps your grandfather with everyday duties, but from today, she will be your second teacher. She can only speak Greek with you. As you probably know, in Egypt the most important language in our spheres is Greek. Your grandfather and I usually use it between us."

"I don't know it very well," Mary confessed, admiring the looks of both teachers. They were refined, taut as harp strings, smiling, and looking very pleased with themselves. She had never seen such beautiful women in Magdala.

"You'll learn quickly," Aida said. "Over the next few days, you will rest and explore the area, mostly with me, but Sithathor and Stephanie will sometimes accompany us. Everyone wants you to feel good here. Once you settle in, we'll decide together what to do next. Do you agree?

"What does "together" mean?"

Aida was surprised by the question, but she tried not to show it, remembering where her granddaughter came from.

"Together, that is you, your grandfather and I. We're a family after all. We make decisions that concern us together."

"I understand and thank you."

Mary looked slightly flustered with information about what awaited her, and the rules that were completely new to her, but she did not want to show how much she was amazed at this world, unusual for her, and how much she liked it already on the first day. She was also delighted that she would participate in making decisions. So far, her father or Marta did it for her.

"Here is your home," added Karim. "You are our granddaughter. The will of your mother, our beloved daughter, was for you to be raised and educated here. We will do everything to satisfy her wish."

Syro, who accompanied Karim since the arrival at the villa while Aida showed Mary her chamber, bowed his head respectfully.

"I admit I will be reluctant to part with my daughter," he said. "I'd rather have her with me in Galilee. However, I would not dare not respect the will of my beloved wife. I entrust Mary to you, also because she will be able to develop and learn under your protection. I also hope that this way, with your help, she will discover even better what is best in her.

"But before you leave her here, you'll stay with us a little, won't you?" Aida was concerned. "We haven't seen each other for several years."

"Yes, I visited you last time bringing the tragic news." Syro's memories returned to his wife's death.

"That was five years ago."

"How time flies..." summed up Karim. He used the words that people around the world usually use on such occasions when they are not sure of what to say and when there are sad topics that need to be addressed. But they are painful for the interlocutors when something irreversible happened when we miss someone we loved. We would like him to be with us, but we know that it is impossible. By saying them, we try to hide the sorrow, sadness and lack of word resources that would convey what our aching heart would like to express.

"I would like to take advantage of your hospitality to take a rest here after the journey, but not too long. Marta and Lazarus are waiting for me at home."

"How long has it been since you left?" Aida worried, looking tenderly at her tired granddaughter.

"Almost 20 days."

"My baby," Aida embraced her. "We are so happy you arrived safe and sound!"

It seemed to Mary that she saw everything as if she were in a dream. Fatigue began to make itself felt more and more. She still heard the beautiful woman who was her grandmother say that she would present her to the rest of the servants the next day and that it was time to rest. Then she felt her father take her in his arms. She snuggled into the source of the smell she associated with stability and security.

\* \* \*

51

Seven days had passed since they came to Egypt. They both had time to rest, and Mary slowly began to get used to the rhythm of the day and the customs in her new home. She slept well in the huge bed with a soft mattress and rollers under her head, filled with swan feathers. She fell asleep immediately and got up at dawn. However, that evening was different. She woke up unexpectedly in the middle of the night. She lay there staring at the flowers decorating the walls, then decided to look into her grandmother's chamber, and as she could not find her there, she went out into the corridor. She heard voices below. Her father was talking with her grandparents.

"I never tried to hide that I wasn't delighted when my only daughter moved to Israel, you know that."

"Grandma wasn't very kind."

"From a country where science and art are valued, where civilization has flourished for thousands of years or more, she suddenly moved to the world of barbarians, shepherds and fishermen."

"Don't exaggerate," father protested, straightening up in his chair.

"She loved you very much and that's why we agreed." Aida didn't give in." However, I imagine the shock she must have experienced when she saw how people lived there."

Mary sat on the stairs. She was surprised by what she heard, but the strangest thing was the way adults talked to each other when they thought she couldn't hear them. It seemed that the beautiful grandmother did not like her beloved dad very much.

"She didn't complain," her father said defensively. "She was well. And above all, she was happy, and this is the most important thing in our life, yes or no?"

"If she were here, she would have survived childbirth!" Aida started to cry. "What kind of medics do you have there? They are best used to look after the sheep! She would be safe here." She wrung her hands," My poor little Aset! I will never forgive myself that we agreed."

Karim felt obliged to soften her words, "Honey, you remember, don't you, that Aset wanted it very much, she dreamed of being with Syro. She wasn't certain of anything in her life more than this. We could not stand in the way of her happiness. Besides, as you know, it's always what is written to be. The gods have their own plans for everyone."

"She converted to Judaism unnecessarily," Aida continued her lament. "Your Adonai is cruel. He has no heart. He is the god of men. Exclusively! Also, whoever saw a god without a wife, who? There is no place for women in your cruel world. Has such strange faith ever existed anywhere? Your poor mothers, wives and daughters," she wrung her hands again. "And my Aset had to live there, without Isis' support, without family. Alone!"

Mary was shaking with emotion. She couldn't understand the meaning of the words she heard. She only understood that her beautiful grandmother was very unhappy that her daughter had married Syro and left with him. But what was wrong with Magdala? What could this pretty lady dislike so much in this heavenly place? What made her so upset? Mary understood that her grandmother suffers and cries because her daughter is dead. But she did not even know her mother at all, and yet she could live with it!

"What did your Egypt offer her?" Syro did not give up. "It's a declining civilization! Who are you? Weak people who have long lost the sense of existence. You seek it in art, philosophizing; you pretend that your world is the best. But you know full well that there is no real sense in it; you live without truth. First of all, you pray to the images of deities. And secondly, you are effeminate, you paint faces, dye your hair and wear wigs, you take care of your body more than brides in my country. Egypt is depraved. A little more and you will be like Sodom and Gomorrah on the eve of the downfall. Or maybe you are already there? There is debauchery, sexual promiscuity, and marital infidelity lurking here at every step. You are lazy, you have lost your homeland, you have surrendered to the Romans and you are not going to do anything about it. There is no God in you because you do not know him at all. You live on memories, talk about past dynasties and their power, but it is only history...In addition, a distant one. Today, Egypt does not exist. You know it well!

"How dare you say such things in the home of the parents of the girl we gave you as your wife?" Aida was indignant. "And this after she died because of you!"

Syro jumped to his feet from the chair he was sitting in, "Because of me?!"

Aida didn't mean to say that.

Karim jumped up too, "I'm sorry for my wife, she is so emotional. We both know well how much you loved Aset. Please sit down."

Syro listened to him. He understood Aida's resentment, even though her words were like a blade embedded in the middle of his heart. He sat down and returned to the conversation, but mainly because of the memory of his beloved wife. He did it also for Mary, who was supposed to spend at least a few years of her life with these people. He didn't want a row; he wasn't going to argue. At the same time, however, he could not allow them to have a distorted picture of the tribe of Israel and to be convinced that Egypt is the greatest place on earth. Because it wasn't like that. At least, according to him.

"I'm leaving Mary with you," he said, almost calmly already. "Please respect that she was raised in the Moses faith. She is an Adonai follower and I would like it to stay that way."

"As she grows up, she will decide for herself," Aida said in a still not very conciliatory, but a much milder tone. "In Egypt, everyone can decide for themselves which god he prays to."

"There is only one God!" Syro got angry again but tried to keep his voice neutral.

"This is, among other things, our superiority over you: we have the right to choose." Aida did not give in, but her expression was so sweet that it would be difficult to accuse her of being upset or of improper treatment of the guest. "I just carried a lively discussion," she later told her husband when he accused her of treating her son-in-law too abusively.

She was a lady from the upper classes. If she wanted, she could control her emotions perfectly. But she didn't always feel like it.

"It's the twilight of the age, that's how countries and nations end!" Syro nodded his head, quite calm already, as sure of his rightness, as of the fact that the power of Egypt had not existed for a long time already. "You are weak, distracted, do philosophy, over-decorate your apartments, drink from glass."

He tapped the goblet in his hand, "You have bathrooms in the houses, cats live with you and you care for them as if they were part of the family! This all would be wonderful if you didn't have other worries. But you do have them. There is no Egypt anymore. It left with Queen Cleopatra. You were conquered by the Romans, whom you say to be barbarians. Maybe they are, but they won with you! You, the greatest civilization in the world! Your world is fading away. We are the future. Because we can live modestly, we are restrained, awake, disciplined, we stick to the rules and clearly distinguish between good and evil. Besides, and this is the most important thing, we believe in one God. He leads us. We will soon win over Rome and the whole world!"

Mary got up and returned quietly to her chamber on her tiptoes, just as she came, unnoticed by anyone.

\* \* \*

"I'm leaving tomorrow," Syro sat on the edge of his daughter's bed. "You will stay in a house where everyone loves you."

It was evening. Mary was lying after bathing, oiling her body and drinking a cup of warm goat's milk with a little honey. Her beautiful grandmother thought that children should get such a drink every evening in order to sleep well at night and grow up healthy during the day.

She pulled back the comforter and moved closer to her father. She knew that she would stay with her grandparents for at least 10 years, because that was the last will of her mother, who was called only by the name Aset in this house. She had long known that she would be in a completely strange place, with people whom she would see for the first time in her life, but she was also sure that she would be fine there because Syro had told her about it many times during the trip.

She couldn't express or understand it, but as long as she remembered, something was always pulling her somewhere further away, calling her, summoning, some internal or maybe external voice encouraging her to go, fly, float – in space or in time? She had an insatiable thirst for the new and unknown, although, as a five-year-old, she couldn't name it. She wasn't afraid of the new. She was not afraid now that her life was about to change so much. She wanted it as if her soul knew well what would happen to her.

"Blood ties are the strongest connection in the world. Know that whatever happens, those whose veins carry the same blood will support each other. They may not like each other or might even fight with each other because that happens too, but blood, blood, daughter, this is something that connects forever. Whether we want it or not."

She listened carefully. She did not always understand her father's words and his arguments; it was difficult for her, but they were deeply remembered, ready to recall should the need arise.

"When you were little, I didn't take care of you too much. I don't know much about children, it's a women area." He justified his former lack of interest. "But when you came to me, demanding fatherly love, I realized that you are the most important for me in the world." He spoke without looking at her. He spoke as if he wanted the world to hear him, or at least his wife, who he was convinced was looking at him, supporting him, directing him from the other world, and waiting for him to join her someday.

"It is not easy for me to talk about it, especially with you, because you are still so little. I loved your mother very much. Know that you are the fruit of great love," he continued. "One that knows no borders and doesn't run away from adversity."

She sat on his lap and patted his cheek.

"I'm sure your mother has given you the greatest gift a human can give to a human: a life full of love, hers and mine. Someone who is born from such a great feeling will give his heart to the world."

He paused. He looked at the white fabric sandals by the bed. Aida gave them to Mary, saying that she was to use them when she would be walking after a bath and ready to sleep, that is in the evening, but she should also put them on in the morning when she woke up. She said people from their spheres do just that. He smiled at the weirdness of Egyptian customs, but he wasn't going to tell his daughter how funny they seemed to him. *"Why do people need separate sandals to wear before sleeping?"* he thought. *"This is one more proof of the demise of this civilization."*

"Make brrrr!" she grabbed his cheeks and stretched them sideways, as she had done before in their home when she wanted to cheer him up.

"Brrrr!" he pursed his lips and let out a breath, snarling.

He laughed; he liked this play. It relaxed the atmosphere and made them feel how close they were to each other.

"Now come with me," he stood up and without waiting for Mary, went to the door leading to the terrace.

He opened it all the way. He went out and looked up. His daughter stood next to him. She had the gift from Aida on her feet.

*"After 10 years here she'll come back an Egyptian,"* he thought, looking at her feet in white sandals. He was not impressed by this prospect, but he decided that, as always, things would go according to God's will. If it is written for Mary to become an Egyptian lady, he will certainly not be able to stop her on this path.

"See how beautiful the world is!" he took her in his arms. "Look at the sky. The same stars shine over Magdala. When I get home, I will look at them every evening and think about you."

"And I'll think about you." She was sad, but she believed that she would be able to contain her tears.

He noticed it. "You know the girls from Magdala don't cry?"

"Really?"

"They are strong, brave and wise. And they don't cry. At all."

"So, what do they do when the tears are coming?"

"They look at the stars."

"Let's look at them together then. You're sad too, I know that."

They stood on the terrace of the estate by the Nile, hugging each other and staring at the stars.

Later, Syro carried her to bed.

"I want to tell you something important," he patted her head. "I want you to remember it well."

"Fine. I will remember every word," she promised, sitting on her heels and looking him in the eye."

"Mary, they'll tell you various things. You will hear about matters that will surprise you. Let your ears be open to listening and your eyes for looking. However, remember all the time that you are the daughter of Israel and you believe in Adonai. They will tell you that there are many gods, that each of them watches over different matters, that there are beautiful and wise goddesses and that you have to pray to them all. But this is not true. Egyptians are like children who don't know yet that there is only one God. Nobody knows what he looks like, because he is not to be looked at. We don't even have the right to imagine him because he is El'Olam, the beginning and the end, the Creator of heaven and earth, he is unimaginable, he is the power by which we exist.

"I know that, father."

"In Egypt, they believe in different gods, but they were created by human imagination. They are just statues that those who have no knowledge of the true God pray to. Remember that. Anyway, you'll find out soon enough. You are a smart girl."

"Father, I will miss you..." She realized more and more that it was not clear when she would see him again after they part their ways the next day.

Her heart was beating very quickly, her breathing became short, and tears welled again under her eyelids. Syro knew that if she would cry, it would be hard for him not to cry, too. With her, as with no one else, he happened to become so mushy at times that he stopped controlling his emotions. This time he swore he could do it. How could such a small person be brave and not cry, if her father could not behave like a man?

"I have something for you," he reached for the purse hanging at his belt. "Something very special."

He untied the pouch. She looked curiously. He put his fingers inside.

"What is it?" She was impatient.

He breathed a sigh of relief. He knew that the tears that might have flown that evening were held back. "You'll see in a moment," he assured her, pretending he couldn't take the surprise out.

"Do you need help?" she offered with a laughter, understanding that her father was only teasing her.

"Indeed, I don't think I can do it myself," he handed her the purse. She reached inside. After a moment, on her open palm lay a gold chain with a wide gold ring on it.

"Beautiful..." She looked at it, her eyes focused on the sign.

"It belonged to your mother. She would definitely like it to be yours."

"What is this?"

"As you can see, it's a ring. But a very special one, because she never parted with it. I thought I would leave it to your grandmother to hand it to you at the right time, but I decided you are wise enough that I can pass it on to you right away. It's still too big for you, so I hung it on a chain."

"Can I wear it around my neck?"

"I think it's best this way. I ordered to make a clasp that does not open by itself."

"Will you help me please?"

"With pleasure."

She raised her hair so that her father could fasten the chain, "Ready! When can I wear the ring?"

"It'll fit your finger when the time comes."

"What is this sign?"

\* \* \*

She opened her eyes and stretched, then touched the chain around her neck and the ring that hung on it. She did this every morning to make sure it didn't disappear at night. She looked at the ceiling and the sky painted there. In the corner on the left was a great sun whose golden rays reached halfway along the chamber. The glorious full moon was the opposite. The paints used for it made it shine silver at night. She knew the picture well already. She watched it every morning for over 30 days.

She looked at the bay window with the door wide open to the terrace. She stared at the green palm leaves that almost entered the room. Then she heard a quiet meow. She sat up. She looked around. The voice came from under the bed. She stuck out her legs and put on the white morning sandals, which she already got to like very much.

"Meow," could be heard again.

She knelt on the floor. Under the bed, in the very corner, was a curled up kitten.

"Aww!" she was delighted. "What are you doing there, baby?"

The cat began to purr quietly. She crawled under the furniture and reached out. "Come here," she encouraged. She looked at it enchanted. He had enormous green eyes, protruding large ears, huge paws in relation to the rest of the body, and he was all mottled. He looked like a tiny tiger.

He sniffed her hand and then apparently decided he could trust her because he started licking her fingers with a rough tongue. "You are beautiful..." She pulled him toward herself and, holding him in her arms, scrambled out from under the bed. She hugged him to her cheek,

"Where have you come from, baby?"

Then, unexpectedly, because she didn't think someone else was in the room, she heard her grandmother's voice, "He belongs to you. He will be your friend and companion. It's mau, a special cat. Faithful, dedicated, intelligent, he can read minds and make wishes come true. You'll see, he'll love you so much that he won't leave you one step away."

"Really?"

"This is his character."

"We had a cat in Magdala, her name was Bastet. Marta said that she belonged to mom and that when she left, Bastet took offense at the whole world and did not want to make friends with anyone. She was sad and was sleeping all the time. And one day, she went out and never came back..."

"Oh, poor thing! Probably nobody cared for her after Aset's death..."

"On the contrary," Mary protested, stroking the cat all the time. "Marta said that Dad fed her personally and tried to talk to her. He let her live in his chamber, while even we could not enter there. Sometimes I saw her ghost there."

Aida decided that the subject of Bastet or even her spirit should not dominate the moment. When Mary got acquainted with her new pet, she wanted her to remember this moment as one that was pleasant.

"Think about what you will call him honey?" Aida leaned forward and petted the cat. "He's a boy, so he deserves a male name."

"I'll get to know him better, see what he is like and then decide, okay?"

"Of course, you have time. The kitty is yours. And from now on you decide on everything that is related to him."

"Can I handle it?"

"Of course! At first, Sithathor and Stephanie will help you a little with his feeding, but soon, this too will be entirely your task. If that will be your will."

"That will be my will," said Mary.

"I am very happy. Your grandpa and I want to make you happy. But also, I admit, we want very much for you to remember that if we take on such a great commitment as being responsible for a living being, then we should care for it. Owning is a commitment."

"I will take care of him," she assured, still stroking the soft fur. "You can be sure, Grandma."

### 4.

Mary had been living in her grandparents' house for a year now. She already spoke Greek, Egyptian and Latin well. She got used to the habits of the house and adopted them as her own. In her way of being, she imitated Aida, who was her ideal of a woman. She repeated her gestures, used the same phrases, moved like her.

She liked the world she got to know and which she became a part of so quickly. If her father saw her, he would probably have difficulty recognizing his Mary, a girl in Egyptian dress and hairdo.

Already in the first month, her long hair was cut so that it reached only to the nape of her neck. Every morning the servants combed and straightened it to make Mary look like her peers. However, despite the oils used, mixed with the white from the swallow eggs, which were supposed to keep her hair styled throughout the day, the hair quickly returned to its original shape, waving and curling. Aida decided that it should be allowed freedom and from that moment, Mary walked around with a head of dark, slightly copper hair, not very long, but curly.

The clothes Aida ordered to be sewed for her were simple – suitable for a girl her age. However, they were made of the excellent, softest and delicate linen. Since the whole outfit was complemented by soft calfskin sandals, decorated with precious stones, anyone who looked at Mary was certain that she came from a wealthy home.

* * *

Leo, because this was the name the cat got, grew up quite well. When he wasn't sleeping, and this was his favorite occupation, he did not leave Mary for one step. One day, when Mary had a morning meal on the terrace together with her grandma and grandpa, Leo ran up to her, holding something in his teeth.

"Oh, it's a bird!" she called, terrified, and jumped up from the bench. "Give it to me immediately! What have you done!"

But Leo, seeing that the gift for his lady had not been appreciated by her, rushed away with the prey in his mouth. Mary ran after him.

"Leo, leave the bird!" she begged.

When, finally, repeatedly called and asked, the cat dropped the bird. It was torn to pieces; it was already dead. Mary stroked and hugged it, not believing that it would come back alive, like the dove in her hands had once done. With the help of Sithathor, crying, she buried the bird in the garden.

"I decided Leo would get a little rattle," she announced to her grandparents the same day.

"But child, a cat is a cat. He should hunt," her grandfather tried to explain the laws of nature to her.

"This is my cat. He gets enough food so he doesn't need to kill innocent birds."

"Hunting is a pleasure for him." he tried to argue but realized that he wouldn't convince his granddaughter's big heart.

"I will attach a rattle to his collar. Its sound will warn the birds that he is approaching. It will be better for everyone." she decided.

From that time until the end of his days, Leo carried a small rattle hanging from his collar.

* * *

"This is Philae Island," Aida said one day as they were exploring the area early in the morning, before breakfast.

She mounted her favorite horse, and Mary, as many times before, sat in front of her, holding the bridle. These trips brought them closer together. They had the opportunity to be completely alone because they were only accompanied by a horseman, who kept his distance from them. They talked then, right after Mary's arrival from Israel, in Aramaic, and later, when it turned out that the girl acquired languages faster than anyone would have expected, they spoke also in Greek and Egyptian.

Aida showed her granddaughter the Nile flowing widely here, the village buildings, as well as the neighboring villas, situated just like their property, on the river bank. They visited some of them, especially those where Mary's peers lived. It was obvious that in accordance with the promise that Syro made to his wife before her death, Mary will soon begin her studies at the Temple of Isis and will have new friends, some of whom were in the neighborhood.

Her grandparents were only waiting for the moment when she would master Greek and Egyptian enough to feel well among her peers. A few months earlier, Mary was six years old, so it was high time she appeared in the world of priestesses.

They did not hurry to send her to the temple, however. They explained to themselves that she was so talented and assimilated knowledge so easily that learning outside the home could wait because if she had any arrears, she would make up for them easily. However, in reality, they wanted to have her with them as long as possible and enjoy her joyful presence. Their home became quiet, calm and empty since the children had left it. Together with Mary, life returned to it.

Aida stopped the horse. "Isis' temple is on this island," she pointed to the place and the impressive buildings in the middle of the Nile. "It is not very old, because it is just 500 years old, and for Egypt, it is not a lot. But it enjoys an excellent reputation. My grandmother, mother and I, and of course, your mother, have all become priestesses in this place. Each of us studied there."

"Will I study there too?"

Hearing hope in her granddaughter's voice, Aida laughed, showing her beautiful white teeth that were her pride. She was almost 50 years old and none of them had ever fallen out, none had to be cured or removed, and it was very rare in Egypt, even among aristocrats. "Would you like to?"

"Very much!"

"Why, honey?"

Mary looked at the tall buildings on the island, "Because I know that my future is there, that priestesses will teach me how to fly because they are wise and they can do anything. That's what my dad told me."

"He said the priestesses would teach you how to fly?"

Mary told her grandmother the story of the white dove, how she seemed to have fallen asleep, and yet she flew away, about Marta telling her before her leaving that she would be able to spread her wings in Egypt. She also recalled that she had always wanted to rise high. She dreamed of meeting people who live far away. She wanted to be in the place where her mother came from.

"l felt here that I wanted to go to you," she put her hand on her heart. "In this place. And my mom said it was time." She looked at her grandma. When she did not see on her face the signs of surprise or fear she saw in Marta and her father when she told them about the mysterious visits, she added," she came to me often. She said you were waiting for me. And she led me to the cabinet in which she hid the senet..." She made sure that she could continue talking. Seeing the approving eyes, she ended," Marta taught me to play."

"Can you?"

"Yes and I really like it!"

Aida decided not to ask her anything else. She knew that if Mary wanted to say something else, there would definitely be time.

"Good that you are here, honey!" she kissed Mary's forehead and kicked her horse.

"Do you know why I also want to study in the temple?" Mary called out as they started.

"Why?"

"Because I want to be like you."

Aida sighed and smiled, looking at the sky. She promised herself that she would do anything to make Mary happy. Then she embraced Mary tighter and stuck her heels to the sides of the horse. They sped forward.

* * *

The High Priestess was standing in the temple courtyard. Adepts were placed in the first row. They were all six to eight years old, had identical blue, long and simple dresses girded with a leather strap, the same sandals, and on their shoulders they had shawls, which, if necessary, could protect their heads from the sun or their back from the cold.

Older girls stood in subsequent rows. Those whose learning was coming to an end, formed a semicircle behind the High Priestess. Teachers, masters and hemet stood on both sides of the Priestess.

"Our temple is a place of worship of Isis," the Great Priestess began in a powerful voice. "We do it not only through everyday prayers. We learn from Isis and for her, for the general public and for ourselves. Because we are a part of her. The goddess is in each of us!"

Mary stood among the adepts. Every year at this time, the girls from the best families started their education in the temple. There were always 12 of them - no less and no more. When one for some reason gave up or dropped out during the studies, no new one could take her place. It had been like that for centuries. Before admission to education, they underwent tests, checks and interviews. They had to show intelligence, prudence and acumen. The candidates were to be independent, responsible and mentally strong.

"You come to us as girls, you will leave as women. Over the years, you will gain new skills. The values that you have been learning in families from a young age, such as commitment, sensitivity, respect for people, the world and yourself, will be reinforced. You will work as a team and individually. If you are not like this yet, you will become obedient and disciplined, and at the same time, independent and creative, as well as accurate, conscientious and punctual."

Mary looked around. There were girls standing on her left and right. She met some of them when she and her grandmother visited neighboring properties. They were her age, and like her, they listened attentively to the High Priestess, looking around in a way such that no one would notice that they were doing it. Each of them knew that from that day on they became the part of an elite world in which they had to show obedience and absolute attention to teachers, and especially to the High Priestess who exercised undivided and indisputable power in the temple and the House of Life. Their fate was in her hands, so they had to and wanted to listen to her.

"Our temple prepares to live in the service of others." The priestess continued her speech. "When you graduate, you will know not only astrology, mathematics, geography, nature, medicine, medicinal herbs, or history. You will master the skill of fighting. You will also learn dance, singing, painting, sewing and other handwork."

Mary's eyes met the blue eyes of another girl. She was shorter than her and smaller. She looked younger, but as it turned out later, they were the same age. Her name was Zoe. Her father was Egyptian and her mother was Greek. They looked at each other only for a moment, but long enough that anxiety arose in the heart of each of them, forecasting something that was to come and would not necessarily be good. Mary pushed this omen away, blowing in the air, and returned her eyes and thoughts to the High Priestess.

The latter was finishing her speech," I am your spiritual friend. I accept you as you are. I give you the strength to become someone better than you think you can be. You will perfect yourself for the glory of Isis and your loved ones. However, first of all, you will become priestesses of the Goddess here. And no matter how your fate goes, you will remain them forever. Whatever you do in life, the power of Isis will be with you. Wherever the gods lead you, you will go there with her strength in your heart. You will walk the path of knowledge, development and love, the path of the Goddess. Today, a new life begins for you. Welcome to the Temple of Isis on the island of Philae!"

* * *

No one knew when and how Mary became a favorite of her friends. Everyone wanted to sit next to her, everyone wanted her attention, smile or praise. They all wanted to be in her circle.

She accepted it with complete calmness, but also with surprise because she did not fight for attention, she did not put any effort into gathering them around her. She was the best student of all; she was brilliant and intelligent, and at the same time modest. She did not exalt herself, was not conceited and she gladly helped others. She radiated light and a bright aura around her. The girls felt it, the priestesses saw it.

Every day at dawn, Sithathor drove Mary to the temple. In the first years of schooling, until the apprentice was gifted her monthly bleeding, Philae rules allowed the students to live outside the walls. Mary belonged to those few who functioned in this way.

In the morning, Sithathor woke her up when it was still dark. All household members were sleeping. Also, Leo, who quickly ceased to be a small sweet kitty, still stretched lazily in Mary's bed, because he preferred to sleep with her despite having his own lair. Seeing his mistress getting up, he looked at her every day with admiration and disbelief and watched her going to the door, only to fall asleep again for hours.

The maid drove her to the wharf on horseback. A boat waited there, which took Mary and other girls to the island. They had to make it to the daily ceremony of waking Amon Ra and bowing to Isis.

When the sun awakened by the priestesses rose, it was a sign that they could start the morning meal. Girls, arranged in a line starting from the youngest, walked with bowls filled with simple, but abundant and nutritious food. It was fruit and vegetables mixed with porridge, a small amount of meat or an egg, and in colder periods, a warm vegetable soup cooked with bird broths was served. There was an order of silence while eating. It was necessary to focus on the food providing the energy needed for prayers and lectures and to ask the Goddess in their mind to let the body make good use of the food provided to it.

After the meal, the study began. Mary absorbed knowledge like a sponge. She listened carefully to the words of priestesses, meticulously followed their orders, wrote, read, counted, measured, mixed, tasted, cut, planted, cooked, prepared, and trained her body and mind.

She liked to study, learn new things, and almost everything was new for her. In Israel, her father taught her how to read Aramaic and Hebrew, at her grandparents' house she learned Greek, Egyptian and the basics of Latin, but it was only in the temple that she was put to the real test by everyday painstaking work.

"Success is achieved by repetition," said the High Priestess, who liked to welcome schoolgirls in the temple courtyard with a new sentence between the morning prayers and meals. "Only practice will let you become champions."

Every day, therefore, in accordance with the centuries-old tradition of the temple, they perfected the body and spirit, learning new things and exercising and repeating what they had learned earlier. Mary was in her element. Learning gave her happiness. She found herself fit in this place as if it had been created for her. As she was liked, praised and admired, she enjoyed every new day. She felt her wings begin to grow.

However, something happened one time she reached for the purse, which she left on her shelf in the place where the schoolgirls kept their outfits change, the tools necessary for study, as well as personal items. She always had a small wineskin with water in it, handkerchiefs, and – in a miniature box – dried sage leaves, which her grandma recommended for her to chew to refresh her breath. She was about to get out one of them when her hand encountered something unexpected. She opened her pouch and looked inside.

"Oh!" She dropped it on the floor. She became paled and stepped back.

"What happened?" the girls said in unison as they stood around her in a circle.

"There is probably...a scorpion there..." she pointed at the sack.

They also took a step back.

"What's going on?" the guardian that was on duty that day stepped in.

"We have a scorpion here," one of them said. "It's in Mary's purse."

"A big one?"

The guardian was calm. Scorpions were rare on Philae – the island was free of them – but they were not unusual in Egypt. They could be dangerous, even deadly, but it depended on their type and size.

They were silent. Apart from Mary, none of them saw it.

The guardian approached the bag and opened it carefully with a long metal cane tipped with a blade," It is dead," she said. " Either you had it there before and without knowing it, you choked it so that it died, or someone made a stupid joke to you." She looked at the faces of the scared girls. "Can I go through it carefully?" she asked Mary.

"Of course, please."

There was a custom in the temple not to look into anyone's private belongings. Only the High Priestess could do so without asking for permission. This law had been respected for centuries.

Adepts could not have any property in the temple except their bags. It was in their bags that they kept what was allowed, necessary and important for them.

"There's no more danger," said the guardian, looking through the bag. "And I will take the scorpion to your priestess. Such issues must be reported."

* * *

Luna was the principal priestess assigned for the youngest group. She was almost 30 years old and had lived in the temple for 25 of them. She was brought up here, and when she finished school, she decided to stay and educate those who came after her. She thought that she owed that to the Goddess.

"A scorpion in an adept's bag?" She was surprised. "If something similar happens again, please let me know immediately. And look carefully at Mary and those around her in the coming days. Pay special attention to Zoe. I have a feeling something is bothering her."

"She's been keeping to herself since she came here. Almost a year has passed, and she still seems scared. Maybe the temple is not a place for her," the guardian suggested.

"It's not up to you to decide that," Luna instructed her.

"Yes, priestess," the girl bowed, understanding her mistake, and left.

A few days later Zoe also found a dead scorpion in her bag. This time she was the one surrounded by the intrigued girls.

"I wonder where it came from?"

"It was first in Mary's stuff, and now in yours, it must be a sign..." they wondered aloud.

Zoe beamed. Suddenly, she was in the spotlight, and everyone's attention was focused only on her. It was very pleasant.

"Maybe Mary and I are scorpion tamers?" she timidly tried to direct the thoughts of her friends. "Maybe we have an extraordinary power that Isis gave us?

Some of the girls looked at her with admiration, while others with doubt. However, all wondered why she, quiet and withdrawn Zoe, with whom no one spoke because she was trying to be invisible, would receive such an extraordinary gift from Isis? Also, why should it be bestowed on both Mary and her, at the same time?

Luna watched them through Horus's eye placed on one of the wall paintings in a place where one could observe and hear everything that was happening among the girls.

When 10 days had passed since the incident with the scorpions, the protector of adepts bowed again to Luna.

"Priestess, Zoe has bruises on her hands. I noticed them during melee classes. According to the rules, I didn't ask her questions, leaving the matter to be explained to you."

"Thank you for watching our pupils closely," she put her right arm straight out on her left shoulder and bowed her head.

It was a sign used by the priestesses as a thank you.

"Do you have any suspicions?"

"Zoe has been acting weird for a long time. She cringes hearing unusual sounds, keeps away from the group, usually stands aside, is reluctant to engage in collective games, and at the same time wants to be in the center of attention. I've seen her bruises and small scratches before."

"Bring her to me."

After a while, the girl stood in front of her and bowed before her properly.

"Show me your hands," the priestess ordered.

Zoe hid them behind her.

"Why not?"

The girl lowered her head and pursed her lips.

"Thank you," Luna turned to the guardian who was still standing by the door. "I won't need you anymore." When she left, Luna sat on a wooden bench by the wall. "Join me," she encouraged, and when the girl did, she asked in a warm voice, "tell me, please, where did the bruises on your hands come from?"

Zoe said nothing. She bent her fingers and bit her mouth.

"I heard you found a dead scorpion in your bag. Do you know how it could get there?"

"I do not know."

"But maybe you have any suspicions?"

Zoe raised a hand to her mouth and started biting her nails.

Luna put her arm around her," Honey, I'm with you. You know that we priestesses look after each other. If anyone hurts any of us, we resist. We are under Isis's protection. All of us. She has great strength. She can defend everyone – you too."

Zoe straightened up. She raised her head, narrowed her eyes and, shaking, confessed," It is Mary."

"What about Mary?"

"Mary did this to me! It's her!" she called out.

"Will you tell me how it happened?" asked the surprised priestess.

"I wanted to pack before leaving for home. I entered the chamber in which we keep our bags. Mary was standing by mine. She rummaged in it. I asked her what she was looking for, and she grabbed my hands and squeezed tightly. She said she knew I had put the scorpion in her bag. And yet, it was her who did it. Her! She tugged my hair and made me keep quiet. She said that if I told someone what she had done, she would kill me. That's why I couldn't say where I got bruises. I was afraid.

"Zoe... my poor, lonely girl..." the priestess hugged her tightly. "Time to get to the bottom of the matter," she decided.

After a while, Mary appeared in her chamber, brought by the guardian.

"Zoe, here's Mary," the priestess stood up. "Stand in front of her and tell us again what happened. How it was with the scorpions and how you got the bruises on your hands. Remember that the Goddess loves you, that she looks at you all the time, that she also looked at the moment when someone hurt you. Isis is in your heart and will always protect you. You have us and we won't leave you alone. The priestesses always support each other and don't let their sisters suffer, right?"

Zoe said nothing.

"Look at Mary," the priestess ordered.

Zoe looked up. When she met her friend's eyes, she began to cry loudly. Tears flowed as if they had been waiting for a long time to be released, and all they needed was a word of

79

encouragement or an event that would cause the dam to burst. Zoe was sobbing, her small body shivering.

The priestess stood firm, and when Mary made a gesture that she wanted to comfort Zoe, she raised her finger, ordering her not to move. She knew that there were times when a man must be alone with his pain, fear and powerlessness and that the tears must flow all the way to their end before cleansing can take place.

When the last sobs stopped shaking Zoe's body, the priestess handed her a handkerchief. The girl wiped her eyes and cleared her throat.

"It's not Mary, it's me," she began, looking at the floor. "I planted the scorpion for her, I also put one in my bag. I wanted to plant another one, but she caught me. I used to tease her all the time, from the beginning, because everyone loved her and nobody loved me. Nobody paid attention to me because I am stupid, thin and ugly. And I wanted to be like her, make them interested in me. I hated her. She took all attention away from me. I thought that if both she and I find a scorpion, she will understand that we are similar and that we should become friends."

Mary stood still. She knew the rules. She knew that she could speak only when the priestess allowed her to. The latter was standing still, carefully listening to the twisted, childish, despairing excuses. She was sure this story was just the beginning. The most important confession was still before them.

"I wanted to put a scorpion in her bag again, but she caught me. It wasn't venomous; it wouldn't do anything to her. I wanted to place a similar one in my bag. I didn't have time. She caught me. She said she could be my friend even without scorpions, but that I should stop doing it."

"Is that right, Mary?"

Mary nodded.

"Did Mary bruise you?"

Zoe lowered her head again.

"We're with you. Tell us," the priestess knelt in front of the girl.

Zoe started to cry again. This time, however, it lasted a short time and looked like a decision to revolt. She clenched her fists to give herself courage and then she took off her dress.

The priestess, the guardian standing by the door and Mary saw her wounded body. Bruises were everywhere. On the back, chest, buttocks and thighs. They had different colors. Some of them had to be created much earlier because they were yellow, others had already turned brown, but there were also many fresh ones which were purple and red.

"It's my father. He does it!" the girl shouted, letting out her pain. "He beats my mother and me. He said that if we tell someone this secret, he will kill us!" she knelt and sat down in helplessness. "Help us…"

The priestess took a deep breath and covered her mouth. Tears appeared in Mary's eyes. Disregarding the temple customs, she did what her heart commanded. She took two steps that separated her from Zoe and embraced her tightly.

"Zoe, honey, I'm sorry, I didn't know."

After a while, they both cried, cuddled up in each other. The guardian was standing by the door, not moving. She behaved as usual. Without the consent of the priestess, she could not make a move. However, she too, so reliable and trained in obedience, could not stop her tears.

Luna crossed her arms on her chest. She knew that she had to tell the High Priestess immediately about everything.

* * *

The High Priestess heard Luna's story. Someone else in the council chamber also became aware of the situation. Hemet Awenger was an avenger and warrior, the punishing hand of the goddess Isis. From an early age, she was prepared to fight. She had all the predispositions for it. Although small-boned, she was tall, strong, perfectly muscled, and at the same time persistent and tenacious. She carried out the orders of the Great Priestess without asking unnecessary questions, and she was completely effective.

"We have long suspected that Zoe is being hurt," the High Priestess turned to Awenger.

"However, we waited for her to confirm it. The future priestess must be able to deal with such a thing or ask for help. Our principles are unambiguous: we do not interfere in matters that we are not sure of what they look like, we do not help if we are not asked, we do not send a hemet, if her action is not necessary."

Awenger bowed her head. She knew these rules. Acting in accordance with them allowed her to sleep undisturbed at night. "What is my task, High Priestess?"

"I give the torturer into your hands."

"How severe should the punishment be?"

"I thought of the heaviest one, but Isis, in her grace and wisdom, enlightened me. Do this…

\* \* \*

That same night, the hemet stood in a man's path. It was dark. He just left the house of pleasure. The narrow cobbled streets echoed the screams of prostitutes, the overly loud conversations, drunken laughs, and cries of those who were arguing, not knowing exactly what about. It was not a quiet neighborhood. Those who lived there because they had no other choice, closed the shutters tightly so that they would not accidentally become witnesses of something they would not like to see or hear.

"Hey, you!" she stopped him.

A shawl covered her face. Only large black eyes with bright whites glowing in the night were visible.

"What?" he growled, concluding that her voice and silhouette indicate that she was a woman, so he didn't have to worry.

"I heard you like to beat people?"

"Go away, bitch, I've already had it today, it's enough for me!"

"I heard you like to beat people," she repeated, jumping toward him.

"You want it?" he straightened up. "I like fighting! I will gladly hit you because I don't want to do anything else with you!"

"You like beating, not fighting," she brought her cheek closer to his face. "Hitting the weak is not a fight; it's violence," she hissed. "And violence is weakness, wimp!"

He pushed her away, "What are you talking about, stupid rag?!"

"You know exactly what," she stood with her legs wide. "First of all, I am sent by the goddess Isis. She told me to punish you for beating the weak. And secondly, I'm not a rag."

"You talking to me?" He didn't believe his eyes. "I'll show you what your goddess can do and you, slut, together with her!"

He set off impetuously, wanting to pounce on her. She dodged him and he ran into a wall. He fell over, but quickly stood up and attacked again. The hemet was calm, moving gracefully, anticipating his every move. He realized that she was incomparably better than him, but he did not give up. He attacked, tried to throw punches, but he was only getting hit. He hit his head against the walls of the buildings and bounced off them, falling into her hands. She hit him like a drum. Regularly, methodically, as she was taught. Focused and without any emotions.

"You can't hit the weaker, you understand?" she asked quietly when he finally collapsed exhausted on the cobblestones. "If you do it again, even if you as much as touch your wife or child, Isis will have no mercy."

He was lying on his stomach. He moaned.

"I want to hear that you understand," she hissed in his ear.

He was silent.

She set her foot on his neck and poked him, and when he still did not answer, she impaled her heel under his shoulder. He howled with pain and fell on his back. "I asked politely if you understand!" she looked into his eyes.

"I understand," he spit through the clenched teeth.

"I hope I don't have to see you again," she said and after a while she was gone.

No shutter opened even a millimeter. The voices of drunkards and prostitutes died down. A night has fallen.

\* \* \*

The next day, Zoe didn't show up at the temple. The messenger brought information that she was sick. The priestesses used their means to learn that the girl and her mother were severely beaten by her father immediately after the bloody and aching man returned from his night trip. It turned out that meeting with hemet intensified his aggression, instead of stopping it.

"Act," commanded the High Priestess, summoning Awenger. "Apparently, the mild means of explanation we have used so far did not work. Isis wants the torturer to never raise his hand again. Do her will!"

\* \* \*

That night, the hemet, unnoticed, appeared in Zoe's father chamber. He was sleeping peacefully. He apparently did not expect the avenger to come back so soon. She stood over his bed. He opened his eyes. But before he could summon the servants, she covered his mouth, at the same time sitting down on him and wrapping her thighs around him with such force that he could not move. In fear, he barely breathed. When she was sure he was gagged thoroughly, she turned him over on his stomach and jumped on his back. Everything happened quickly. He didn't even moan when she twisted his arms back and pulled hard. He got wet with sweat, he began to struggle, but she did not care. She then hit his right forearm with the edge of her folded hands. A crunch of broken bones could be heard. He fainted. Then she also broke his left forearm.

She turned him over.

"Isis protects her pupils," she whispered, making sure he was already conscious and could hear her. "This is the last warning she, in her goodness, gives you. Touch the girls with just your finger, and, acting on her behalf, I will stop being delicate. The goddess gives only two warnings. Then she destroys those who do not submit to her will. Understand this, you bastard, and adapt if you want to live."

He showed with his eyes that he agreed.

"I will free you now. Lie here until sunrise. Don't call anyone, wait for the house to wake up. If you move, start screaming or even moan, I'll kill you before you can blink. Do you understand?"

She deliberately nudged his broken arm. He groaned in pain. "Don't moan, I said!" she nudged him again. "I'm one of those girls who don't have a sense of humor. I think you know that already?"

He nodded. She released his mouth from the gag. He lay still, looking at her in horror.

* * *

Zoe returned to the temple after a week. However, before 40 days passed, the messenger from her father's house again brought information that she was sick and would not appear for some time. They knew what that meant. When their suppositions were confirmed, the High Priestess called Awenger again.

"Finish the matter!" She ordered, making the Goddess mark on her forehead. "I bless you.

Since the last meeting with the hemet, Zoe's father moved around, always surrounded by guards. He was scared. For the first weeks, when the medic put together his broken arms, immobilized his shoulders and forbade any physical exertion, he did not even look at his wife and daughter, certain that Isis's eyes could be anywhere. The truth was also that every move caused him pain. So, for the sake of himself, he preferred not to think about the fact that he should punish his women for what happened to him."

He was an aristocrat – from father to son. He inherited such a large fortune that he did not have to multiply it to live comfortably. He spent days entertaining, traveling, going out and on trips out of town with younger and younger companions. Because the older he got, the more the company around him grew younger. His peers started families, settled down, worked for the glory of the gods and their own families, and he, apart from the fact that, like others, he had a wife and, so far, one daughter, did nothing useful. He felt it more and more and every day he noticed the meaninglessness of his life. He blamed his wife and daughter for what he was like. When he was sick with himself, when he returned drunk, or even just a little buzzed, he beat them with a bamboo rod, reeds or fists, if he had nothing else handy. He also punished servant men and women, and even dogs and cats.

No one dared oppose him. Everyone suffered in silence.

* * *

"Here we meet again," the hemet said in a seemingly sweet voice.

She entered the tiny room in the house of pleasure, where he decided to relax as soon as the medic took off the block from his shoulder and the pieces of wood immobilizing his hands. The fractures healed well.

"What are you doing here?" he jumped up and was now in a sitting position. "Guards!" he called in a voice hoarse with terror.

But no one heard him. Music was playing in the main hall, and the dancing women sang loudly, shaking the sistra.

Hemet put a knife to his throat, "You did it again! You barely started to move your arms, and you beat your wife and daughter.

"I did not want to! I swear! They provoked me!" he cried out.

"There is no hope for you. You will never change. Isis cannot look at you anymore.

"I will change!" he began to cry. "Spare my life!"

"The goddess doesn't take a life unnecessarily. Even from bastards like you."

"Really?" he began to shake, feeling growing hope.

"Really," she handed him a vial. "Drink to the bottom!"

"Is it poison?"

"You won't die from it." She put the bottle under his mouth, "Open your mouth!" He pursed his lips. She knifed him. "Hemets don't lie. I said you wouldn't die of it."

He had no choice. He opened his mouth. She poured all the contents into it. When she was sure he had swallowed, she explained, "It's the potion of oblivion. When you wake up, you won't remember anything about your past life. You will become nobody. You will have the chance to start all over again. The only thing you will only remember from this life will be these words, listen," he was falling asleep because the potion started to work, but he still understood what she was saying to him, "a happy man is not the one who has everything, but the one who enjoys everything he has. This is a message for you to remember. You are getting a chance for a new life. Use it."

He nodded to confirm that he understood.

"Remember also that there are six elements in the world: spirit, water, earth, air, fire and... a pissed off priestess."

He nodded again and fell asleep.

From that day, Zoe and her mother lived alone in the large estate. By Egyptian law, they inherited the property of their lost husband and father. Those who remembered him sometimes said that someone very similar to him was seen at a slave market in a bamboo cage, prepared to be transported to distant countries. Others swore that they met him among the galley slaves. Some claimed that someone very similar to him had become a servant in the temple gardens of Isis in Alexandria.

When her father disappeared, Zoe did not show up at the temple for a while, and when she finally appeared, she looked even thinner than before, but she was calm and seemed self-confident. She ran into Mary's embrace as a greeting.

\* \* \*

The High Priestess was the head of the temple. The fate of each of those crossing the walls of Philae depended on her. She was all-knowing and infallible, inspired by Isis. The master priestesses, who taught and instructed, were subject to her. Many of them were group guardians. Each of them had her own chamber and studio in the temple. The oldest girls took turns being on duty. They made sure everything was in order in their groups and checked if the orders of the masters were properly executed. Philae's financial affairs were handled by a priestess who rarely showed herself to her students. She spent most of the day in her chamber, which was also her workplace. On the high shelves set against the walls, there were scrolls and tablets with recorded income and expenditure.

There were also hemets in the temple. They were independent, reporting only to the High Priestess, and masters in one trade - most often one that required from them an incredible skill and physical fitness. They were fighting avengers. They were called Isis' armed wing. They spied, passed secret information, dealt with matters that were not publicly discussed. There were whispers that they also kill if Isis orders them and that they do it without a twinkling of an eye. Nobody except the High Priestess knew how many of them there are and what they do. The only hemet whose face was known to the students was Awenger. Every day she conducted morning classes with them, right after the greeting of Amon Ra ceremony.

Priestesses and schoolgirls were responsible for housekeeping chores on the island, but most of them were done by servants living there permanently.

Mary had her favorite masters. In addition to the High Priestess and Awenger, she enjoyed listening to the medic Charmion, Yona, a mathematician, as well as Didit, who talked about the history of Egypt, and Agnes, who helped develop the aspects that belonged to the spiritual realm.

\* \* \*

"It isn't my back that hurts, but the burden of life. It is not eyes that hurt, but injustice. It is not a head that hurts, but the thoughts. It isn't the larynx that hurts, but what you don't say. It is not the stomach that disturbs, but what the soul does not digest. It is not the liver that hurts, but anger. It is not the heart that hurts but the lack of love," Charmion, a priestess in charge of healing, stood in the middle of the room with her arms raised.

Mary was in awe of what and how the priestess was saying. She followed her mouth movements, volume of her voice and gestures.

The teacher had long, black, curly hair, always left loose and, most often, a long black dress which flared down. Its sleeves were so wide and had so many invisible compartments that one could hide in them pouches, vials and even medical tools, if necessary. The waist was tied by a belt with bags of powdered medicines and everything that would allow immediate assistance to those in need.

She gave the speech with emphasis and conviction. Not only Mary but also other girls looked at her admiringly. She was elderly. It was said about her that she had lived since forever, because she knew herbs and minerals like no one else, and therefore she never got sick. It was whispered that she had been around for so long that she personally treated Queen Cleopatra. There was some truth in it, but only a small crumb. Charmion was the daughter of Imhotep, the famous medic of the ruler. She was named after her mother, Cleopatra's closest servant.

However, she was born when the queen was no longer in the world. She had accompanied her father at work from an early age, so no one was surprised that she followed in his footsteps.

Listening to the lecture, Mary imagined her mother next to the famous queen and thought that she would like to meet both. Both Cleopatra and her faithful maid.

"Love is the cure for all the pains of this world," said the priestess. "Love is everywhere, in each of us, in the smallest grain of divine dust that we are made of. It is everywhere there is a man. And it always will be. Remember my words. I will teach you for several years about herbs and minerals, you will learn about human bodies and their ills. You will find out how the body works. Who knows, maybe some of you will become medics? However, no matter which path you will follow, remember that love is the first and most important remedy for everything related to man. Also, remember that whoever heals with love, heals truly."

She looked at them to see whether they understood her well and, finding that each one listened to her words with full attention, she added, "In our gardens, we grow herbs that have special properties. Do you know why? Because when we put the seeds in the ground, we sing songs and pray. We do the same thing five times a day every day when plants grow and when we collect them. By this, they acquire special power. The good words and melodies we send, create their structure. What arises from these herbs is sacred and used only during the most important ceremonies and rituals, as well as for healing."

Mary listened and wondered if she could become a medic in the future; try to be like Charmion. Was this the path Isis had planned for her? For now, she didn't feel good enough in any field. She liked everything that the priestesses taught, each lesson revealed new opportunities to her, but none completely devoured her. So, she waited patiently and listened diligently to the teachings. They all fascinated her. With no exception. She was like a desert rose that can wait for years for rain, and when it finally comes, it develops into the most beautiful flower.

When she listened to Didit, she thought that she could devote herself to studying and writing down the stories of the queens and priestesses that had been before them. She wanted to be as wise as Didit, equally precise in giving dates and facts, and like her, diligent in her caring for the past. She listened to her words and believed that it was just as Didit argued: the dead still talk to them, pass them strength and give them power. For there is an inseparable bond between those who were, who are and will be, whether we know it or not, and whether we want it or not.

Didit was revealing a fascinating past to them, and since she looked different from the other priestesses, the girls saw a messenger of goddesses in her. She had very fair skin and the fairest hair Mary had ever seen. It was long, straight, covered her beautiful neckline and round shoulders, always wrapped in a soft light scarf.

"As you know, the last queen of Egypt was the mighty Cleopatra," she said. "We admire her for her extraordinary intelligence, the strength of her spirit, her ability to adapt to the times in which she lived, fighting to the end and her honorable departure. As you know, she chose death, which immediately took her to eternity and united her with the gods. The king cobra, as it is well known, protects the pharaohs, it is their guardian. Do you remember an uraeus on the crowns of Egyptian rulers?"

The girls nodded. Who would not know the famous crown? Even Mary, who had never seen such a sophisticated headgear before, learned what it looked like when she began to live with her grandparents. She admired it, but she often wondered how it was possible to move in something so high, certainly heavy and rather unstable.

"In Egypt, snakes are a symbol of eternal life, rebirth, a repetitive cycle," continued the priestess, looking into the faces of the fascinated girls. "They shed the skin, almost rise back from dead. They belong to the area of our oldest and most secret knowledge. In art and spiritual renewal, they symbolize cleansing. They are like poison and an antidote. Surely, priestess Agnes will tell you more about cleansing, and you probably know something about poisons from Charmion," she smiled, seeing how strongly her stories affect the girls.

"And this is a symbol of Imhotep, a priest, magician and medic," she raised a tablet with a tall staff and two snakes wrapped around it and handed it so that they could see the engraved symbol. "See? Symbol of life, but also of healers. It is said to be the staff of Imhotep, Greeks say of Asclepius or Hippocrates. Oh no! No matter what they think and no matter what people will call this symbol in 1,000 and 2,000 years, we know that the first medic was Imhotep, who created rules of procedures for everyone else. And that all science has its origin in Egypt," she brushed her hair back.

"Remember, too, that not only medical men are famous in the world. Merit Ptah was a priestess whose competences and skills were so great that we still worship her greatness, and Charmion uses her inventions. Do you know that Merit built a chair to help bring children into the world? Well, you will hear about these matters from your teacher one day. I will tell you now about the greatest rulers of Egypt. What do you say? Would any of you like to name five rulers you consider the most powerful?"

Mary was ashamed to see that all the girls raised their hands to tell about their types. She couldn't do it. She heard several times about Cleopatra, she knew about the existence of Hatshepsut, but she realized that compared to other girls, she did not know anything about Egyptian rulers.

"I still don't study enough," she reproached herself. "When I'm at home, I should read books instead of playing with the cat. I lose so much. I waste a lot of time. I have to change it, get a grip and take to something useful!"

She worked constantly. During classes at the temple, she was always very focused, and when she returned home once a month for three, sometimes five days, she also tried to do as much as possible. She talked with her family, visited her grandma's friend in neighboring estates, played senet with her grandpa, at the same time discussing business, caressed the cat, read the books suggested by Aida and The Wisdom of the priest Ptahhotep, which her grandfather gave her, and also looked closely at the home life. She tried to reconcile different currents of life next to each other, soak up as much as possible, enjoy what was given to her, and absorb as much knowledge as possible. But the more she had in her head, the more she felt unsatisfied. It was never enough for her. She wanted more and more.

"There are legends saying that the first queens of Egypt, who were also priestesses, came from the stars." Mary heard Zoe's voice and was surprised that her friend had such unusual information. They came to build a world of harmony. Along with them came the energy of love, as the highest form of cosmic vibration. Queens from the stars associated with terrestrials and had children with them. Mixing their blood with human blood disrupted cosmic energy. It was not good, but it happened. We have to live with it and care for the fragile balance. Each of the queens has left permanent marks on earth and is still talking to us. However, with great respect for all others, Cleopatra, Hatshepsut, Nefertiti, Kiya and Nefertari appeal to me most strongly.

"Exactly," Mary thought regretfully. "This is the advantage of those who are local. The queens have been talking to them since birth. I still have to get to know them. But I'll do it. I will reach the story of each of the great women who ruled this country. I want them to speak to me too. After all, my mother's blood flows through me – she was from Egypt, so I am, too. I will do everything for it to be so," she promised herself.

*  *  *

From the first year of their stay in the temple, students were also taught counting, multiplication, division, geometry and measures. The priestess Yona was not harsh; she gave the impression that she didn't care at all if they were learning anything, and yet each of them quickly mastered the necessary knowledge. They remembered through play, games, drawings and nursery rhymes.

They used white, gray and black stones to help learn counting. Each of them kept them in separate bags. White ones meant units, gray ones – tens, and black ones – hundreds. Units were written as dashes. A picture of a heel meant 10, a rope – 100, 1000 was shown as a lotus flower, 10,000 was marked as a finger, 100,000 was represented by a frog, and 1,000,000 looked like a figure with raised hands.

From Yona, the girls learned about the cosmic structure of the pyramids, sphinxes and even the eye of Horus. This symbol, possessing magical power, was an expression of God's perfection. Well, it turned out, as the priestess very vividly explained to them, that each subsequent smaller part of the drawing of the divine eye is proportional to the previous one, that is, it is a fraction of its size. She also said that from this division, a numerical series was created, maintaining an orderly, logical sequence, which not everyone understood, but they felt that it also meant nothing but divinity. According to the priestess, this was another proof of the power of mathematics and its supernatural origin.

With Yona, they measured distances for the first time in their lives. They walked around the temple square, checking its length in feet and cubits. A commonly accepted measure in Egypt was the unit measured from the elbow to the tip of the fingers. Since this distance varies with everyone, the standard was the royal cubit, accepted so long ago that no one knew when. Half of cubit was called a foot.

Under the watchful eye of Yona, the girls measured, counted and weighed, certain that these skills would be often useful in their lives.

"Tie 10 knots on the rope at different intervals," the priestess instructed.

They loved such games. They worked in groups at such times. If one did not understand something, and this happened sometimes, together it was easier to come to the right solutions.

"Now create a triangle. Let it have 3 knots on one side, 4 on the other, and 5 on the third."

They did what she ordered.

"What did you get?"

They wondered.

"If you ever have to plan something, draw, or build, that's the easiest way to create a right-angled triangle, can you see it?"

They did.

"What will happen if you connect two such triangles? You see? Do you know now how ancient builders built pyramids and temples?"

"Thanks to God's help!" one of the girls replied.

"Exactly," the priestess praised her. "Mathematics, geometry and everything related to it comes from the gods. Thanks to them, we, ordinary mortals, have been and are able to implement plans according to God's intention."

\* \* \*

The High Priestess met all the students for a short time each morning, and the novices for a longer time, once a month. She always had a message for them.

"You should live in harmony, not fight what we have no influence on," she said, sitting on a wide chair positioned so that she could look at all of them and they could see her too. "Let us be happy with the fate the Goddess gives us, but let us also shape it ourselves. The gods give life, but what we do with it depends mainly on us. We have an influence on it. We reap what we sow. So, let's sow wisely. Let's not be afraid of effort. Let's work hard but with pleasure," she uttered the sentences emphatically, slowly, listening to their sound, because she wanted to be sure that they would reach them with the power she intended.

"Let's take care of the body and soul because they are one; they should be fed and nurtured with the same care. In our temple, where so many girls left their footprints before you, we help ourselves improve. Every young woman who leaves our walls and goes into the world as a priestess of Isis to serve people knows that living happily means living honestly. This is what the Goddess teaches us. Live in harmony with yourself, follow the right path."

Mary listened attentively to the priestesses. She looked at Charmion gesturing animatedly, at the wise Yona, the restrained Didit, who stood almost motionless during the speech and looked at the sky, reminiscent of a goddess with long blond hair, at the eyes of the Great Priestess, which seemed to her to focus all the knowledge of this world. She felt that they contained what Goddess had passed on to the priestesses for centuries. She wanted to touch it, feel it; she wanted to possess the knowledge they had. She stared at them and listened to their words with all her might. She promised herself that she would do anything, use all her power to gain access to the old treasury. That she would open herself to the influence of the Goddess, as fully as she could, that she would put all her life at her disposal, would do everything to be able to join the circle of priestesses who pass on the knowledge. She felt more and more that it was her duty and destiny.

"I will be strong," she promised herself. "I will manage everything, overcome weaknesses, laziness and vanity, I will fight adversities, walk the path of good and truth, I will become a priestess. I will be like them: wise, good and beautiful. I deserve the light around my head. I will follow the bright path. And I will never stray from it."

### 5.

She stretched and opened her eyes. It was still dark. Leo was deep in sleep. She patted him. He purred and turned to the other side. She knew that in a moment, Sithathor would enter the chamber, like she did every morning. She will say: "Mary, it's time," which meant that she should quickly get dressed and go to the waterfront to take part in the ceremony of greeting the sun in the temple, as she had always done for several years.

She pulled back the quilt, sat up, and already knew that from that day on, nothing would be the same. Without putting on her morning sandals, she lit a lamp beside the bed to make sure that what she had been waiting for, finally happened. She wasn't wrong. There were red bloodstains on the white linen.

She jumped in joy. Leo raised his head, and seeing her happiness, jumped off the bed and began to spin, chasing his own tail.

"Have you seen it?" she said to him, hurrying into the next room. "Grandma, grandma!"

A small door was open. Aida was asleep. However, when she heard her, she woke up immediately.

Since Mary appeared in their home, she had been sleeping with the lamp on, thinking that you never know when light may be needed with a child at home.

"What happened?" she looked at Mary and didn't have to ask further. She rushed to her granddaughter.

"I became a woman!" Mary announced, proudly straightening up and standing on her toes.

"I'm so happy, honey! Congratulations!" she hugged her.

They stood together, barefoot, with their hair tousled, excited and happy. When Aida, stroking her hair, began to hum a song about a red rose, Mary began to cry. She felt that she had crossed the border that night and entered another world. Soon the gates of knowledge will fully open for her. She will be honored to join the female circle connected by blood. She will be able to enter Saint of Saints, where Isis lives, and draw unlimitedly on the cup of her knowledge. She had just transitioned from the phase of the White Goddess into the Red one. She will get a red dress, undergo initiation and will become no longer an adept, but the truest student of the priestesses of Isis. Finally!

The goddess appeared in three versions. She was White for those whom she had not yet marked with blood, Red for those in full bloom, and Black for those who have experienced enough life to pass on their wisdom.

Aida was moved that she had by her side her daughter's daughter, blood from blood, the girl who had become a woman with her. When she looked at her, when she embraced her, felt her heartbeat and heard her breathe, it was as if Aset was standing next to her. She felt that she was part of the eternal whole and that both Mary and her were inseparably connected with those who had been before them. She cried too, like Mary, but for different reasons.

She felt good and bad at the same time. Bad, because she would love to hear her mother again, smiling and saying, "I'm proud of you," and feel her stroke her cheek again, and she knew that this was not possible. Bad, because she would like her daughter to live, so that she could be here, hug Mary and be happy together with them. Her soul was sobbing with regret that everything passes away.

At the same time, she was proud of her lineage, of the women who came before her and made her exist, of her wise granddaughter and herself. Of the fact that she could and knew how to think, that the Goddess gave her an open mind and allowed her to look at the world with eyes that knew no limits. Of having been given the knowledge that she was part of the cosmic order, and that women before her also embraced each other, felt pride and joy, gave each other strength and together with life passed a little of power. She knew that divinity is a balanced femininity and masculinity, and the eternal pursuit of the world is Maat – harmony. The priestesses taught her that the dance of life is beautiful and it will last as long as humanity lasts.

\* \* \*

As soon as Sithathor entered Mary's room and saw the stained sheet, she knew that there was a turning point. Anyway, many signs had already indicated before that Isis would soon give her ward a monthly blood. The girl already had large breasts, her buttocks rounded, she ate a lot, and besides, it was full moon – that's when the Goddess affects women most strongly. Some menstruate during new moon, others during full moon.

"I will write a message to the High Priestess," Aida answered Sithathor's questioning look. "Tell the servants to take it to the temple. Mary will stay with us for the next few days. We will celebrate!"

Leo lay down at his mistress's feet and raised his head from time to time to enjoy her happiness. He understood that something special had happened. The goddess Bastet watched the world through his eyes. She was alert, especially when she looked at those that would be particularly suitable for her earthly priestesses.

\* \* \*

The same day, her grandfather brought her a red rose. He handed it to her at breakfast," Congratulations!" He kissed her forehead. "I heard you became a woman."

Mary remembered a similar day in Magdala. When Marta was blessed with blood, it was strangely quiet, as if on the one hand something sublime and necessary had happened, but on the other it was unclean and enclosed in conspicuous silence. Marta was locked in her chamber and her sister was separated from her. The maids whispered in the corners. Her father asked a midwife to come to their house and explain to Marta how she should behave and what new obligations regarding cleanliness she had from that moment on.

"Nida." This word silently circled all corners of the house then. Nida meant seven days of uncleanness. Who touched the menstruating woman or even sat down in the place where she previously rested, was tainted just like her. He had to clean himself and wash his clothes. After seven days, as the custom proclaimed, the woman was obliged to take a ritual bath in the mikvah to return to the community.

In Israel, menstruation was associated with mystery, uncleanness, punishment for sins, and penance. In Egypt, it was an occasion for joyful celebration, especially the first one.

Mary remembered one of the classes with Charmion when she explained to adepts what the monthly blood was.

"The moon is a woman," said the medic. "And a woman is like the moon. We are connected. We operate according to eternal life cycles, remember that. Monthly blood is the matter from which the universe originated. The primordial seeds of existence are hidden in it; it moves them through time. We are her priestesses. It gives us power and authority. When we are included in the cycle of existence, when we change like the moon, passing from new moon to full moon, we are goddesses. When Isis gives us blood, she includes us in her circle. We give birth to new life also through her."

The adepts listened to Charmion enchanted. Each of them was waiting for the day of this gift. Everyone knew that one day it would come, and looked forward impatiently.

"Moon blood is an effective remedy," continued the medic. "It can put dying people back on their feet, restore strength, renew the body. It is an aphrodisiac and helps in love magic. All you have to do is add one drop to wine, and your chosen one will give you his heart," she stared at the girls listening to her like to an oracle.

"On moon days, your spells gain exceptional power and are effective like at no other time," she raised her finger to draw their attention even more. "It's your moment of transition! It may be painful or uncomfortable, but they are or will be, for each of you, for you, for you and for you..." she pointed to several of them. "...the days of exceptional power and openness to the voice of the Goddess. It may happen that your legs or stomach are swollen, your head hurts, maybe you will even vomit. It does not matter. The passage, rejecting the old and entering the unknown sometimes hurts. You will be reborn with new strength, even more beautiful, wiser, with refreshed body and spirit, even more attractive to the world and yourself. Monthly blood is a gift from the Goddess!"

They listened, fascinated.

"When this joy comes to you, accept your body, it is beautiful and perfect. Always!" Charmion was finishing the lecture. "Respect it, love it, surround it with love and care, because it is a garden for your soul."

\* \* \*

The priestesses were standing in an even row in front of the entrance to the main temple. They were in blue, long, simple dresses. On their shaved heads they had identical wigs made of evenly trimmed black hair. Their bodies were thoroughly depilated. Hair removal was the daily duty of every priestess and priest in Egypt, no matter what god or goddess they served and in what temple. Only the most important ones, of

105

exceptional status, had the right to not shave their heads. It was enjoyed by the High Priestess, but also by Charmion, Yona, Agnes, Didit and several other mistresses.

Behind the priestesses stood women from the adepts' families. They had similar dresses, but their heads were not bald. Each of them was once a student at the temple, but later they chose a different path. They got married and left for different parts of the world. Nevertheless, each of them, no matter what she did in her life, was still a priestess of Isis, because whoever became one, remained so for the rest of her life.

Older students lined up behind them. They also had depilated bodies. Their hair, as was the custom, could reach at most to the shoulders. They wore blue dresses.

Before important ceremonies, the priestesses and older students underwent a ritual purification of spirit and body. They also submitted to strict fasting. It lasted seven days for priestesses, and three for students. At that time, they drank only water.

Before them, opposite the closed gates of the temple, stood the students. However, not all of them, only those that had been blessed with the privilege of blood in the last year. They wore white dresses, girded with an accessory ending with the Anch symbol.

Mary was among them. She stood with her head raised, excited, her face flushed. The gate was to open soon, and she and others should enter the temple. For the first time in their lives, they would be honored to cross this threshold. She was trembling. She hadn't eaten anything for three days. Fortunately, the nausea she felt yesterday had subsided, so she was light and unencumbered. She felt as if she could rise like a bird and fly any moment. She glanced at Aida. Her beautiful grandmother, upright and elegant, stood among other distinguished women.

Their eyes met. They were proud of each other.

When the sounds of the sistrum flowed, the temple gate opened and the High Priestess appeared in it. Her head was adorned with an intricately pinned hairstyle, crowned with goddess symbols: cow horns and a solar disc. The holy golden cobra "ureaus" seemed to come out of the sun disc, sticking out its divine tongue. In her left hand the priestess held Isis's staff with a silver serpent, in her right was a tit sign made of red stone, also called Isis's blood or Isis's knot. She was in a black long dress. A wide, colorful menate decorated her neck.

She struck the cane on the floor three times, and when the women waiting in front of the temple bowed deeply before her, she turned and walked toward the statue of the Goddess. They followed her. They were accompanied by the sounds of sistra, harps, flutes, pipes, drums and trumpets.

She stopped in front of the statue that stood in the center of the temple. Further behind it, there was only a small door covered with gold metal sheet, leading to the Saint of Saints. The High Priestess bowed her head, the other women knelt and their foreheads touched the electrum-lined floor. As they stood up at her sign, a song flowed from their lips. They knew it well, it was performed at all the festivities dedicated to Isis.

*Oh you, the saint and eternal protector of humans,*
*you, who always embrace with your generous protection the*
*mortals*

*and sweet mothers, you who have compassion for the misery of
the unhappy!*
*There is neither day nor night, not even the tiniest moment,
that would be devoid of your benefactions.*
*You shield people on land and seas,
you stop the storms of their lives and give them your saving
hand,
the hand which unravels the unsolved threads,
with which you silence hurricanes,
with which you neutralize the disastrous revolutions of stars.*
*You are worshiped by the celestians,
the inhabitants of the Underworld bow their heads before you.*
*You give movement to the world, brightness to the sun,
the universe molds under your hand,
Underworld lies under your foot.*
*Your voice is answered by the stars,
processions of times return at its call,
the gods' joy depends on it, the elements humble before it.*
*At your command, the winds blow, the clouds draw their feed,
seeds germinate, vines climb up.*
*The air birds, beasts in the backwoods, snakes crawling on the
ground
and sea monsters tremble before your majesty.*
*Our spirit is too mundane to be able to glorify you,
to honor you with the sacrifices you owe
we don't have enough words to tell what we feel before your
majesty,
nor a thousand lips or as many languages would be enough for
that,
or an endless, bottomless stream of pronunciation.*
*And therefore let it be our concern,
what is the only thing left to pious people:*

*that we would forever keep in the deepest secrets of our hearts*
*your divine face and grace, and your greatest majesty,*
*and that we may be eternally conscious of them.*

Mary sang along with others. The words that were breaking from her heart flowed towards the one who loved them, who gave them strength, embraced them with boundless love, indicated them the direction, called for their growth, assured that they could do everything.

Mary felt her power especially on that day. Like other adepts, admitted to the group of Isis's students that day, she had fasted and spent time praying and cleansing. She was happy, excited, full of faith. She brimmed with pride. Finally, in just a moment, she was going to enter the Saint of Saints. What she had been waiting for so long was finally going to happen.

She thought about the past years – about Marta and Lazarus, her father, her coming to Egypt, meeting her grandmother, the High Priestess, and about starting her education. So much had changed in her life since leaving Magdala! She felt how much she had grown up, how good she felt in the place where she was. How, finally, she fully felt that she was on the right path, although she still did not know where it would lead her.

After the song was finished and the gifts were laid at the foot of the statue, the High Priestess again struck the floor with the silver cane. It was a sign that the most important part of the ceremony was about to start.

They formed a line. Each of them held a lit oil lamp. They were warned that the place they would soon enter would be dark because of the lack of windows and openings that would let the sun in. This place symbolized the beginning of life, the temple of the female womb, from which monthly blood flows, so it was an inscrutable and secret space. No man could enter there, and among women – only the priestesses or disciples of Isis, and only those whom the Goddess gave the moon gift.

The High Priestess started to walk. Adepts followed her in focus and silence. After a while, they were inside. The room was almost empty. There was only a hearth on the tripod in the middle, with a large, silver, shiny cauldron next to it, and a round sacrificial table. They stopped. Soft music flowed from everywhere, with a rhythm reminiscent of a heartbeat. It could be heard clearly, but soon, muffled by the sound of footsteps, it became just one of the elements of what surrounded them. Other women appeared around them: schoolgirls, priestesses, initiated members of their families. They were all naked. They left dresses and accessories in the main hall of the temple.

The High Priestess struck her staff for the third time. It was a sign that the adepts should take off their dresses. When they did so, she also took hers off. The music stopped and she dipped a ritual silver goblet in the cauldron. After she filled it with the goddess's drink, she lifted it above her head.

"This is holy blood!" she announced, holding it high. "Thanks to Isis, this drink fills our bodies and gives life. It is the beginning and the treasury of humanity!

She put the cup to her mouth and took a sip, "Lady, please accept our gift!"

She tilted the container, pouring the contents into the hearth. A flame burst out.

The adepts took a step back reflexively, but almost immediately returned to their places. They knelt. Mary looked sideways. Her friends humbly touched the shiny floor with their foreheads.

"Lady, come to us! Honor us with your presence!" cried the High Priestess, raising her hands high.

The women in the room repeated her gestures and shouted as loudly as she did. "Come, come!" They called.

Their bodies bent sideways, back and forth as if they were dancing. They lost themselves in their requests. At first shy, because it was the first time they were taking part in such a ceremony, after a while the adepts behaved like the others.

As time disappeared, a powerful voice rang out. It came from heaven. "Here I come, entreated by your prayers, I, the matrix of the universe, the lady of elements, the primeval source of all ages, I, the greatest of deities, I, the queen of underground shadows, first among the heavenly, me, whose face is the face of all goddesses, whose beckoning governs the luminous vaults of the sky, the healing breaths of the oceans, the desperate silence of hells, I, whom the whole world worships in many shapes, in different rites and under different names. I, called Mather, Minerva, Venera, Diana, Proserpine, Ceres, Juno, Bellona. I am here with you, I, the queen of the world, Isis!"

They fell on their faces. They were praying. Each of them submitted her pleas to the Goddess. They assured her of their devotion, loyalty and willingness to serve. They humbly begged for granting of what was most important to each of them.

Later, they formed a circle again. The High Priestess was no longer in its center. She stood among them. A luminous flaming ball appeared in her hands, created by willpower.

Mary looked at it admiringly. It looked like a glowing piece of the sun. She wanted it with her whole heart. The High Priestess held it for a moment by her heart, then passed it on. The flickering light gave a pleasant pulsating warmth. It was changing hands. Light as a feather, unreal, but true. A concentrated bright energy.

The high priestess said, "Here is the eternal fire. It burns and never goes out. It is in me and in your hearts. It ignites the senses, gives strength, encourages to do the deeds. It is in every man and woman who walks the world, it is in the earth, sky, sun and wind. And in all creation, because it comes from the Source. It embraces and encompasses everything. It lasts forever and is an eternity. I give it to you when you go into the world, you give it back to me when you return to me. Carry it like those who did it before you and those who will come after you. May the flame in your hands be even and strong."

\* \* \*

Agnes wore colorful dresses. She had a lot of them. Among them were green, blue, red, purple, yellow, multi-colored. They had different shapes and lengths. The girls wondered where she got them from and how the one who created them obtained such intense colors. When it turned out that Agnes dyed the fabrics herself, using natural plant dyes, their admiration increased.

She also liked jewelry. She had plenty of it. It adorned not only her neck and wrists but also ears, arms, fingers and toes, calves and ankles. She even had it in her nose and mouth. Her hair was copper in color and waved in the wind. She never tied them.

Agnes often asked them questions. "Sit down comfortably," she once asked at the beginning of the lesson. "I will now address you individually." When everyone sat in a comfortable position while she sat opposite them cross-legged, she said, "Now, close your eyes. Have you closed them? Well. Imagine that you have become fully grown-up, you are a priestess, you have left the temple or decided to stay. Can you see yourself? What is your dress like? Do you have anything on your head? What are you carrying in your bag? What do your shoes look like? Do you see yourself?"

They nodded and smiled at the imaginary picture.

"Now think about who you are helping and how you are helping. What is your strength? How do you become a source of power for someone? What emotions do you give people? Who is your authority and why? How would you like others to feel with you? How do you make those around you feel well?"

They were sitting with their eyes closed.

"Don't open your eyes. Think about the answers to these questions. You have time. You won't open them until you hear a gong."

Sometimes, they sat for a long time. Minutes went by, the sun was higher and higher and the gong sound did not come. They had time.

"What is my path?" Mary wondered. "What does my soul want? What is my life mission? Which way should I go?" Weeks and months passed, and she still couldn't find the answer. The masters helped her in her search. They asked additional questions, guided her, but never gave a ready prescription.

"A priestess is a woman who decided to be faithful to herself and to follow the voice of the Goddess," Agnes explained. "To hear it, we need our own space, peace and time. So, let's learn to cultivate loneliness. We need to be able to calm down and focus in even the largest crowd. It's difficult, but you can learn it. Our bodies, hearts and minds are the temple. Let's get the ability to lock ourselves in it so that no one could bother us. If need be, let's go to the desert, find a cave, let's lock ourselves in the cave. This will allow us to hear more clearly. When we make contact with our inner voice, we will be able to connect with the whole world and even become it. And someday... maybe one of you will become a Priestess of Light."

"A Priestess of Light?" Mary was curious.

"This is the highest possible level of brightness that we can achieve on earth. An absolute union with the Goddess. An enlightenment."

"Are you a Priestess of Light?" Zoe liked to ask questions directly.

"I would like to, but few can achieve this status."

"How will we know that we have succeeded?" Mary inquired further.

"When that happens, you'll have no doubt." Agnes's voice sounded kind but sure. "You can feel it with all of yourself. You will have the ability to understand others and empathize. You will be able to look at the past and future, read minds, understand dreams, enter into the dreams of others and shape them. At every step and in every deed, you will feel the support of the Goddess, those that were before you and that are around you. Because you will become a Goddess and all that she is. The world will be on your side. You will have visions, you will not be afraid of changing reality for the better, you will see people as they are, and that is why you will love them. You will become harmony, goodness, beauty, wisdom and light. You will know and feel everything."

"I want this!" Mary said loudly.

"Let it be so!" Agnes bowed humbly and made the triple mark of the Goddess.

### 6.

"What have you made of her?" Syro wasn't going to hide his indignation anymore.

During the day, emotions had been accumulating in him from the moment he saw Mary and hardly recognized his beloved daughter in her.

The official reason for his visit to Egypt was business. However, he came, of course, primarily for Mary. When he left her there a few years earlier, he promised his in-laws that for her sake, he would not visit his daughter too often, so as not to hurt hers and his heart, to let her develop peacefully and get educated without a burden of his approach to the world, and his harsh customs. Besides, after the last visit and the sharp exchange of opinions about the civilization differences between Israel and Egypt, he somehow was not eager to meet his in-laws.

He and Mary wrote letters to each other all the time. He was moved when he read them. However, something had changed in recent years. When he wondered when it happened, he concluded it probably was when she became a woman. It was from that moment that her words began to be more subdued, polished, full of polite but, as he thought, meaningless phrases. He thought Aida was raising her to be a restrained Egyptian lady, which could mean she would be growing more distant from him. At the same time, he wondered what the term "too often" meant when referring to the number of visits possible, and when he felt that enough years had passed that his visits would not be perceived as frequent, he set off on his way.

Mary waited in front of the house gates, together with her grandparents. He noticed from a distance that she looked similar to her grandmother, and when he saw her closely, his heart froze – she reminded him so much of Aset from the period when he met her.

"Father," she greeted him in Aramaic and bowed her head.

"Peace be with you," Aida and Karim also spoke in Aramaic.

He was surprised and disappointed that she did not throw her arms around him, she did not hug him, and later, in the reception room, she behaved like Aida. She sat upright, smiled, made restrained gestures and carried on a conversation. That's right: she carried on a conversation!

She no longer talked as before. She did not speak with so much delight and emotion as she once did. She was refined. She became someone else. It bothered him the most. This is what he wanted to complain about to his in-laws in the evening, when Mary, as she announced, "retired for her nightly repose" because she would have to return to the temple the next day at dawn. She was released from it for one day only, on the occasion of her father's arrival. However, when she was already in her room and ready to sleep, snuggled into Leon's soft fur, she decided that she would go downstairs again. She wanted to tell her father that she had decided to ask the High Priestess to allow her to accompany him during his stay in Egypt and not return to the temple during those days. She put on the white sandals and stopped at the stairs. Syro's agitated voice came from below. She felt like in her childhood, when she witnessed a similar conversation in the same place. The adults didn't know then that she could hear them.

"What have you made of her?" he cried outraged. "She was supposed to grow and you killed her spirit! What happened to her authenticity, spontaneity, and delight in life?"

"Oh, my dear," Aida opposed gently, "calm down. She's just changed. You left a little girl here and you found a young woman. In Israel, and even among the poor in Egypt, girls her age get married and give birth to children, don't they? She is almost an adult."

Seeing that Syro was thinking about what she said, she smiled a dignified smile. "Indeed, she's different from what she was like. How many years has it been? Let's see," she spread her fingers and began to bend them. "Right, it's been eight years already she is here!"

"Seven!" he corrected.

"Almost eight. But seven or eight, what's the difference..." Aida was unusually agreeable.

She felt satisfied. Their granddaughter was similar to her; she quickly found herself in their culture and adopted it as her own. She became an Egyptian, a student of Isis and a young lady. Aida had no doubt that this was due to her efforts, which

117

she admitted were not huge because the little girl absorbed everything with the joy and openness of a child's mind.

"You were supposed to take care of her education. This is what I promised to Aset when she was dying. I brought her here. I kept my word. And what have you done?! You made her..." he thought for a moment "... an Egyptian!"

"I understand you don't like it," said Karim. "Is that right?"

Syro shifted in his chair and nodded. Aida always seemed exalted to him. He preferred to talk to his father-in-law. He was factual and concrete. Syro liked to do business with him – it was always based on the integrity of both sides, and it was similar in their private conversations.

"Please correct me if I'm wrong, but I don't think that you expected a different outcome when you left her here. We are in Egypt, and we propagate traditional Egyptian, eternal values in our home. You knew it from the beginning. You are a wise man after all. Who did you expect to find? Mary is your daughter and our granddaughter. We all want the best for her."

Mary decided that this time it would not be like it was in her childhood. She would not return to her room to think about what she had heard. She walked down the stairs. Leo was running next to her.

"Father, I missed you so much," she sat down next to Syro and took his hand. "I haven't said it before, but know that I love you very much." She rested her head on his shoulder. He was silent, surprised. Aida and Karim didn't say anything either. "I will ask the High Priestess to let me be with you the whole time you will be in Egypt," she announced. "We haven't seen each other for so long, I have so much to tell you! I missed

118

you terribly!" she called, getting up. "I'm going to bed because at dawn I will go personally to ask her for a release. Of course, if you don't mind, father..."

She leaned over and kissed his cheek. Her appearance in the room surprised him as much as the others, but he already pulled himself together. He smiled. Aida and Karim also just understood what they witnessed. The atmosphere lightened in an instant.

"And besides, I'm not at all the lady you see in me. Not yet," she embraced her father's neck. "I really missed you so much. And finally I lived to see you!"

She grabbed both his cheeks with her fingers as she did when she was a child, and stretched his lips. "Do brrrr!" she commanded as she did when she was five years old.

"Brrrr!" he complied with her request.

She kissed him again. Then she kissed Aida and Karim on the cheeks.

"Good night," she said with distinction in Egyptian, bowing her head. "I love you," she called out on her way out.

She clicked to call Leo, and when he brushed against her legs, she turned and walked calmly to her room. Only when she was already upstairs, she threw herself on the bed, pleased with herself. She kicked her legs and the night white sandals soared to the ceiling.

"I don't think I'm quite a lady yet. I still need to work a lot on myself before I become one. Or maybe I will never be one," she sighed with a smile.

\* \* \*

"Here they believe that Atum is the father of all gods. Look," she pointed at a painting on the temple wall to Syro.

"Right. In Egypt it is shown as a snake. For us, the snake means the original sin. A symbol of old beliefs."

Mary invited her father to the island of Philae. She proudly showed him the temple buildings. Some were reserved only for priestesses, others for priests, but passages, courtyards, roads, squares and marinas were intended for common use. She showed him the soaring columns and high porticos in the temple of Isis, the temple of Hathor, the gate of Ptolemy II and the great courtyard.

They entered the temple of Asclepius. Atum, who created the earth and everything that exists on it, looked at them from the heights of the blue walls in the form of a mighty original snake enveloped in fog. His divine body was arranged in interpenetrating weaves that formed a kind of regular winding ladder resembling the symbol used by scholars dealing with medicine and magic.

"Do you know that Atum created the world by taking his own semen in his mouth?" she laughed because she suspected that her father might be embarrassed by the conversation about the Atum's semen. His expression confirmed that she was right. "When he spat, the god of air, Shu, and the goddess of water and moisture, Tefnut, were born," she continued, unabashed. "The divine siblings set off to explore the world. They did not return for a long time, so one day, anxious Atum sent his eye to look for them. It penetrated the whole earth for a long time and finally found them. Happy that the children rejoined him, Atum shed many tears. A human being arose from each of them.

"Quite a nice story. But you don't believe in it, do you?"

"Look at this. See there?" she raised her hand. "The divine siblings conceived another heavenly pair. Geb, or the god of the earth, and Nut, the goddess of heaven. They had two pairs of twins: Set and Nephthys, Osiris and Isis.

"I've heard this story." He decided not to hide his knowledge of Egyptian gods. "But just because I know their names, doesn't mean I believe in them."

"Of course, father," she laughed.

"Geb made Osiris and Isis the first rulers of Egypt." He was now the one pointing to the next drawing, "There, the royal couple are sitting on the thrones of the pharaohs. And to show you that your father really knows something about the history of the place where his daughter is raised, I will tell you that Set, the jealous brother of Osiris, did not like it at all. In short, Set deceitfully killed Osiris and quartered his body. He scattered all parts around the world so that nobody could find them. However, loving Isis did not give up. She searched for a long time until she found all the pieces."

"Not all...the penis was missing," she said.

"What are they teaching you here, child!" he shook his head in disbelief. "In Israel, girls your age don't know how to pronounce this word. Well, of course, you are right, the penis was missing. There, the picture shows Isis shaping it from clay

"I know these paintings well, Father," she said. "I also know what a human body looks like. Also male one. The medic Charmion teaches us that."

"What kind of place I have sent you to!" he laughed, already quite relaxed, because he realized that his daughter had already gone through many levels of study in the temple and one could talk to her like to an adult. Anyway, when she was small, she also spoke mostly like an adult, except that she didn't then have the knowledge she had gained in recent years.

She also laughed. She was glad that the conversation about Osiris and Isis, specifically about the penis of Osiris, meant that she could already talk to her father normally. They made a connection again, as before. Except that it was now at a completely different level.

"As we both know, this story ends well, because Osiris miraculously regenerated himself," concluded Syro. "Later, he and Isis lived happily ever after, as it happens in this type of myths. Different peoples around the world have similar stories of the risen gods. The Egyptians are not unique in this."

"I like this story," Mary watched the paintings with admiration, almost not paying attention to her father's amusement. "It's magical and timeless. It shows love that overcomes everything. It's worth living for such love. I would like to love this way one day, so that nothing but my beloved would matter to me..." she sighed. "I understand and admire Isis. I would like to be as strong as her and love like her with all my heart and without borders. You know, love conquering all obstacles, present despite death, and even overcoming death!"

"Overcoming? What do you mean?" he stopped.

"Well, that it neutralizes it. Deals with it. Makes it not important, it can oppose it, make it non-existent."

"Your mother and I were connected by a great love," he sighed. "Aset left behind the world she knew for me. She traveled far with me and... stayed there forever." He lowered his head," And yet probably, I'm almost sure, she would like to come back to Egypt. Meet her parents and, above all, meet you and be with you. Apparently, God had other plans for her."

His mood changed, but he knew they only had a few days for themselves, so they shouldn't be sad.

"You are the fruit of this beautiful love," he added, his good mood almost back now, and kissed her forehead. "You are a gift from heaven."

"Father, I'm glad you came. I missed you so much!"

They were walking around the island. He told her about Marta and how well she was doing with running both estates – both at Magdala and Bethany. That when she persuaded him to remarry and he decisively refused, she decided that she would not get married either and that she would focus on supporting her father, managing the estate and helping her brother. Lazarus, unfortunately, had become sickly since the incident called by the household members "a meeting with black wings." Her father did not write about it in his letters so as not to worry her, but her brother was sometimes so weak that he did not leave the bed for a month or two. Then the disease would disappear and he functioned normally again. He even thought about getting married. Many ladies were interested despite his weaknesses. After all, he was the son of the richest merchant in the area.

Mary told her father how good she felt with her grandmother, about science, about her fascination with priestesses, about their principles, knowledge and openness.

"We're not as open as they are. We have rigid rules and stick to them. Well, and above all we have one God. The true one." He wanted her not to forget about her homeland. "When we parted years ago, I asked you to always remember who you are."

"Of course, I remember. And I always will. Also, be sure that I will come back to you and Magdala," she assured him. "And I wear my mother's ring on a chain all the time. I've got it, look," she reached to the neckline. "It's still too big. It already fits the index finger, but I want to wear it on the ring finger."

"It will fit when the time comes," he reassured her.

"Yes, I know. I am waiting for it."

"And I'm waiting for you at home."

* * *

When her father left, Mary threw herself into her studies. She repeated Greek words and phrases, verses of poems, old Egyptian hymns, and expressions and proverbs of Ptahhotep even more intensively than before. It pleased her that she could easily speak and read Aramaic, Hebrew, Latin, Egyptian and Greek. Each of these languages was almost her first. She used Hebrew and Aramaic least often, but since her father's visit, she decided that she could not neglect them, because, when she would return to Magdala one day, they would be indispensable for her, and certainly not at the child level at which she once learned them. She asked her father before he left to send her the Torah. She wanted to study it, be up to date with the language, but also to learn the principles of the religion that was dear to her father.

"This book can only be studied under the guidance of a rabbi," Syro warned her. "And I haven't heard of women doing it."

"I want to try to do it. On my own. Can I?"

He remembered how quickly she learned to read. He had always known that she was capable. Besides, he loved her very much. Could he deny her anything?

"I will send it to you."

That's what happened. Several months have passed since his departure, and shortly thereafter, the valuable parcel was delivered. It was carefully wrapped. The scroll was in a chest, which was wrapped in palm leaves, and finally everything was wrapped in canvas.

She took it out and unrolled it. She started reading. She slowly put letters together.

בְּרֵאשִׁיתבָּרָאאֱלֹהִיםאֵתהַשָּׁמַיִםוְאֵתהָאָרֶץ:וְהָאָרֶץהָיְתָה
תֹהוּוָבֹהוּוְחֹשֶׁךְעַל־פְּנֵיתְהוֹםוְרוּחַאֱלֹהִיםמְרַחֶפֶתעַל־פְּנֵי
הַמָּיִם:וַיֹּאמֶראֱלֹהִיםיְהִיאוֹרוַיְהִי־אוֹר:וַיַּרְאאֱלֹהִיםאֶת־הָאוֹר
כִּי־טוֹבוַיַּבְדֵּלאֱלֹהִיםבֵּיןהָאוֹרוּבֵיןהַחֹשֶׁךְ:וַיִּקְרָאאֱלֹהִיםלָאוֹר
יוֹםוְלַחֹשֶׁךְקָרָאלָיְלָהוַיְהִי־עֶרֶבוַיְהִי־בֹקֶריוֹםאֶחָד:

\* \* \*

Every day after the ceremony of awakening Amon Ra and greeting the sun, even before breakfast, the students had classes strengthening the body. They trained under Awenger's watchful eye.

"The sun is the light of your life!" she called so loudly that if one of them was not awake yet, it happened then, quickly and abruptly. "It is its food, a reflection of joy, a source of brightness that you carry within you. When the sun shines, your soul rises excitedly. When the sun covers its face, your heart dies. You need light to live and you feed on it. Today, now, thank the sun, the life, joy, power, the source!"

They learned the right posture, as well as walking, sitting and gesturing appropriate to the given situation. However, first of all, they swam, paddled, jumped long and high, shot a bow and arrow, used a spear, a javelin and various types of short melee weapons. They also learned hand-to-hand combat. The hemet slowly revealed to them the advanced skills, depending on their predispositions. The assumption respected in the temple from the beginning of its existence was that every priestess should not only be educated, wise, good and sensitive, but she must also be able to fight and certainly be able to defend herself.

Mary wasn't the best in martial arts. She was poor at defense, and attack classes were her least favorite. She comforted herself thinking that nobody was good at everything. Although she practiced with fervor, neither she nor Awenger were happy with her progress.

* * *

One night, when the whole temple was asleep, a warning whistling from the guard point could be heard first, and then alarm gongs. The girls jumped up from the beds. A whole group of 12 of them slept in the big hall.

"Alarm! Alarm!" Awenger shouted, striking the gong with all her might.

Panic broke out, but the hemet quickly controlled it.

"Do you remember what to do in an emergency?"

126

"Follow orders from your superiors," Zoe was the first to regain her cool.

"Exactly," Awenger stood on her legs wide apart, in a fight-like position. "We must evacuate as soon as possible. We have information that enemies are coming to the island from two sides. They want to kidnap you. You must save yourself."

The girls were so scared that they didn't ask any questions, they just stared at Awenger

"You will take the most necessary things and go to the eastern harbor together. No one can notice you. The temple must give the impression that we do not know about the planned attack. The boat will take you to the east side of the Nile. From there, you will be taken to a safe distance on horseback. You will continue to move in twos – a group would be suspicious and it would be easy to be tracked down. Your goal is to reach the Temple of Isis in Luxor as quickly and safely as possible. We will meet there. Do you understand?"

They nodded, waiting for further orders.

"I won't come with you, I have to take care of the adepts because they are also under the threat of kidnapping. You are old enough to do it on your own. Remember, you have skills that will help you get to Luxor. Be strong. See you soon. May Isis guide you!" she made the triple sign of the Goddess, bowed, and without waiting for their reaction, ran towards the hall of the adepts.

Years of exercise were not wasted. They rushed for their belongings and after a while, they stood at the gate, fully dressed and with bags slung over their shoulders. "Are we all here?" Mary counted them with her eyes. "Let's go then. Just be quiet! We're going together, and it's best to split already into pairs now."

For years, Mary was the one their eyes turned to, and whose words their ears wanted to hear. Without soliciting it, she somehow became their informal leader, a smart and delicate one at the same time. Not selfish, but supportive and sensitive, moreover intelligent and pretty. Most people wouldn't like such a person, but they liked her, because despite the fact that they felt that she was someone special, she herself did not think so, or at least did not let anyone feel this way.

"Let's stick together. A group means strength," she laughed to cheer them and herself up. "And maybe, let's take the knives out of our pouches and put them behind the belts. It's better to have them handy. Who knows what can happen to us today?"

They searched in bags. After a moment, the blades shone in the moonlight.

"Zoe, will you come with me?" Mary could not imagine that she could be in a pair with anyone other than her.

"Sure!" Zoe was proud. "You are clever, I am experienced being under attack, we can do it!" She remembered the old days and since she could make fun of it, it was obvious that she managed to draw strength from the violence she had once experienced from her father, even though years later and probably with the help of a miracle, but still effectively.

They ran quietly under the walls of the Temple of Isis, carefully ran around the main courtyard, crept past the Temple of Asclepius and reached the marina unnoticed by anyone, as Awenger had commanded. There was a boat waiting for them.

"It's strangely quiet on the island," Mary said as she boarded.

"Probably each group has a different escape route," Zoe explained, pleased that Mary had chosen her for the pair. "The priestesses are experienced. As we can see, also in escapes. They perfected everything."

"Let's stop talking and run away," one of the girls urged.

"Indeed, maybe you can discuss it when we get to a safer place?" another one reproved them.

Zoe waved her hand in resignation. She had long come to terms with the fact that rarely someone wanted to listen to her.

Mary looked around again, "I am telling you, it is strangely calm."

"It is better for us, isn't it?" Zoe thought she should calm her down. "We are lucky, the Goddess is with us."

As the hemet announced, horses and guides were in fact waiting for them on the other bank to take them to a safe distance.

"I suggest the Black Cat inn for the first meeting place. It's easy to find – it's just before the southern entrance to Luxor. Let's get together there and get to the city in a group. If either of you fails to get there, the next place is the temple of Isis," Mary, like all others, was already sitting on the horse. "Isis is with us," she said. "Sisters priestesses, before you leave, let each of you make a sign of the Goddess!"

They were not priestesses yet, but the disciples of Isis. However, after her words they felt as if they were ones. She really made them feel strong. Even those that trembled with fear and uncertainty, calmed down and straightened up. They felt that they could make it because they were adults and could do everything. They stopped the horses that were getting ready to run. Their thighs squeezed their sides and they pulled their bridles. They bowed their heads, and like soldiers before the battle, they made a traditional gesture of worshiping the Goddess, solemnly touching their forehead, mouth and solar plexus. Then they joined in their thoughts.

"Yours is the blood, Isis, yours is power, Isis, yours is magic," all of them uttered the words important to them, loud and confident.

They bowed again three times and set off on their way. As Awenger had commanded, each pair, led by a guide, went in a different direction.

"You're a safe distance from the temple. The Nile and the nearest port for you is there. Get to a ship to Luxor," before leaving them, the guide showed the way to Mary and Zoe.

"How far is it from here?"

"You could arrive on horseback before noon, but you will go on foot. I'm taking the horses."

"How come?" they asked at the same time, surprised.

"Get off the horses, young ladies," he ordered, instantly turning from a nice guide into a thief.

"If I sell them, I will have a few pennies for taking you to a safe place. I am entitled to it."

Surprised, they did what he ordered. He took the horses by the bridle and rushed away.

"He didn't even say goodbye," Zoe sighed. "What shall we do?" She expected Mary to have a ready plan, as usual. However, she was wrong. They were standing, both equally stunned, in the middle of nowhere, on the edge of the desert, without horses and without water.

"It's good he didn't take our bags," Zoe noted.

"Yes, indeed, a very decent man," Mary laughed.

"You know, he could have done it."

"Well, I'm saying I'm impressed with his kindness."

"Stop joking," Zoe sat down on the sand. "What shall we do?"

"Let's think about it," Mary suggested agreeably, seeing the beginnings of panic in her friend's eyes.

"So, you do not know?" She was surprised. "But you always know."

"Zoe, we were able to deal with worse situations, right?"

"I guess."

"What would Awenger do in our place?"

"She would surely handle it."

"So we can handle it, too. What do we do in difficult situations first? Let's remember the rules."

"We run away!" Zoe laughed, but seeing that she had not amused Mary, she added, feigning remorse, "I was making jokes now."

"So, what do we do first?" Mary did not comment on her lack of seriousness.

Zoe was convinced that also this time Mary would find a way out, create a plan, and she would just adapt to it. Then, when they start implementing it, everything will be fine. She calmed down and closed her eyes. She remembered one of Awenger's early morning lessons.

"We sit in a comfortable position and open ourselves to the support of the Goddess," she recited from memory. "That's number one. If we don't know what to do and we have time, we delve into ourselves and look for a solution. The answer will definitely come. Then we plan our actions step by step, considering all pros and cons, we analyze weaknesses and strengths. Then we implement them, systematically and calmly. At the end we achieve the goal."

Satisfied with herself, she opened her eyes.

"I remember everything!" She was happy. "Now we know what to do."

"Well done," Mary praised her. "We will do exactly as you say."

"Oh. Meaning what? Because I don't know after all."

"Let's start by choosing a comfortable position and thinking about what awaits us," Mary crossed her legs and straightened up. "Do the same, close your eyes and think. Let's create an action plan."

\* \* \*

After seven days of travel, Nefer and five other girls met at the inn near Luxor, where they had set their meeting place. They arrived there by boats and barges on the Nile. As it turned out, none of them had anything to pay the guides with, but they all made it. Some sold a decorative pendant, others convinced the ferryman that their rich parents would pay for them, Nefer made a bet with the ferryman that she would defeat him in arm wrestling and she won, for which he allowed them to board the ship, and Mary and Zoe did palm reading for the travelers on the barge for a small fee, and collected the necessary amount. They were tired, hungry and not very clean, but happy with themselves.

"We'll wait a day or two for the others," Nefer ordered.

She was the one who knew strategy. Best of all, she knew how to fight, and with her appearance and strength she resembled a big man. They liked her despite her roughness and sharp character. Most often, she would say what she thought directly, and would often blame them for being too delicate. However, she helped each of them, especially during difficult morning classes with Awenger.

"Let's stick together," she added. "I can see only shadowy characters here. I'm pretty sure they'll attack us when we're sleeping. When I shout "attention!" all of you have to be ready to fight. Have your knives on hand. You will need them. Look also around for equipment and tools you will be able to use in battle. Do you remember what the hemet said? Stools, brooms, pots, cups, skewers, dishes – everything that is on hand can be used to defend and attack."

Indeed. There were not very friendly looking men sitting around them. They glanced at them greedily. It was obvious that they were up to something. They gathered in a close group and arranged themselves by the wall to sleep while waiting for the others. Nefer decided to stay awake.

"You are indestructible," Mary admired her. "Where do you have so much strength from?"

"How come you don't know?" She was surprised. "You know everything."

"It only looks like this." Mary enjoyed the kind words, but as she had heard similar words several times, she knew that the praise was exaggerated. "Nobody knows everything."

"You have something in yourself I can't name. It's power. But you act like you don't want to acknowledge it. You are modest. It is praiseworthy, but it seems to me that it stands in your way to open up to the possibilities that you have."

"Maybe it will come with time? Now I know that I hardly know anything. When I listen to priestesses, I see how much I have to catch up with, how much I have to learn, how much to get to know. And how much to live through. They are so wise and experienced!"

"You are like that too. Like them. You have peace, humility, wisdom and patience. You look with your heart. I see it when I open up to you. You impress me very much. I don't have feelings or visions, but I feel that I should protect you, take care of you and make sure that nothing happens to you."

"Nefer, it's an honor for me," Mary put her hand on her right shoulder, just like the priestesses did, and bowed her head before her.

"It's my honor, Mary."

"You are like Awenger, please give orders and make us reach Luxor in one piece. You know how to do it and what to do."

In this way, Mary transferred the management of the group's affairs to Nefer. She had never formally had it herself, but it had long been established that she was the one who made the most decisions. Now, in an emergency situation, she handed the reins to Nefer.

It was late evening. Some of the girls were sleeping. Nefer remained alert, even when she was talking to Mary. Yes, she looked into her eyes, listened to what she was saying, but at the same time she looked around. She did it so that no one who was unfamiliar with martial arts would notice her focus and readiness to defend a possible attack.

"Attention!" she called at one point, leaping to her feet. "Attention!"

She grabbed a long dagger and before the girls could get up, she had already hit one of the attackers.

"Get in the circle!" she shouted.

They carried out her order immediately. Awenger's exercises had done their part. In emergency situations they reacted automatically. They stood side by side, leaning forward, with knives held toward the attackers. They bared their teeth threateningly and snarled like wild cats preparing to attack.

Not expecting this turn of events at all, the men stopped at first. The one Nefer wounded, looked with surprise at the wound inflicted on him. However, the consternation did not last long.

"It's just girls," he called. "Go at them!" encouraged his companions."

To give themselves courage, because they had not expected the girls to have weapons and be able to use it skillfully, the men moved at them shouting loudly.

"Attack!" Nefer called out.

The girls, screaming at the top of their lungs, rushed at the attackers. Stools, tables, dishes and whatever was at hand were put in use. At exactly the same time, the gates opened and the other girls entered the inn. Seeing what was happening, they threw themselves at the men, maybe not in full agreement with the rules that Awenger taught them, but effectively. They jumped on their backs, punched them, bit them, and scratched, and because the ones in the circle were also doing well, the attackers soon began to give way. It turned out that the girls not only outnumbered them but, under Nefer, they won. The attackers fled.

They stood sweating and panting after a short but intense fight, amazed that they had succeeded.

"The goddess brought you here at the right time," Nefer concluded, glad that their friends had come to their aid.

"We can handle everything," Mary smiled. "They say that miracles are coincidences that occur in a very specific place and time, favoring the ones chosen by gods. I think we just witnessed one of them, or at least that's how we can explain what happened."

She closed her eyes and tried to get to the heart of the event with her mind. It was hard to believe that it wasn't some kind of a planned game. She wanted to get to the truth. She strained all her senses to see it. She imagined herself looking at the matter, pulling away layers of curtains. However, she saw only

136

blurred space. It seemed to her that for a moment she saw Awenger's calm and smiling face. She sensed that what was happening had been carefully planned by her, but it seemed as if the teacher was taking care that this thought would not reach Mary. After all, the priestess would not put them in jeopardy. That's exactly what Mary should think, according to Awenger. But in an emergency, her extraordinary talents and the ability to look into areas invisible to other people began to manifest.

\* \* \*

Soon, they stood before the gate of the Temple of Isis in Luxor, which was the destination of their journey.

"You did very well," the hemet greeted them. "You've all arrived here. I am proud of you! You will return to Philae tomorrow."

"Separately?" Nefer flexed as if she was already ready to leave.

"You'll come back together, but of course without me," the hemet cooled down her enthusiasm. "As you can see, you can travel unattended, you are doing great" she said it with such pride that they understood that for them and for her, this trip was a test of what she had taught them in recent years. "Now you have time for thanksgiving prayers and preparation for the road," she added, bowed to honor them, and left.

7.

Every year, when the Nile was rising, the students left the island for three months. Most often, they went together with their families to urban estates. Mary's grandparents went to Alexandria. They went by boat. They had a smaller house there than in the countryside, but equally comfortable and convenient. Mary liked to go there. At first, the city overwhelmed her a little, but it did so less and less so with every year. The regular layout of its streets when she saw it on the maps, delighted her. She knew from the priestesses that the city was built according to the plan of Dinocrates, who designed the roads along the north-south and east-west axes. Regularity, repetition and order had always been characteristic of construction in Egypt and Greece, where the master came from. The heart of the metropolis was the royal quarter. There, in the Ptolemy palaces, which occupied almost a third of the center, lived the prefect of Rome. The most important, richest and widest street in the whole city and the world of Alexandria was the Canopian Road. It led through the center, where the main square, the most important temples, the palace, the white marble gymnasium, the theater, the most famous library, and many amazing monuments, fountains and columns were located. West of the city walls was a place for gardens and cemeteries, while the Egyptian district occupied the eastern part. The inhabitants were proud of the lighthouse on the island of Faros, connected to the city by a road over an artificial dam. The building measured 430 feet and was crowned with a giant statue of Poseidon. The fire burning at the top could be seen as far as 25 miles away from the shore.

Mary's grandparents' house was built a short distance from the royal quarter. It was designed perfectly. Comfortable, multi-story, spacious, it allowed the household members to enjoy all comforts. The floors on the ground level were covered with beautiful mosaics. The bathhouse at the back of the house was furnished in a modern Roman style, and the patio with a tree provided a place where one could rest in a shade even at noon.

Lying in her chamber, Mary could clearly see the royal palaces through the window. Maybe that's why she sometimes thought of Cleopatra. She was the last ruler of Egypt. She allied with the two most powerful Romans of that time, first Julius Caesar, and when he was murdered, with Mark Antony. She was connected with them not only through the political alliance but also a great affection and children born from these relationships. When it became certain after losing the battle of Actium, that the power in Rome would be taken over by Octavian August, the enemy of Mark Antony, she committed honorary suicide. Thus, the Ptolemy dynasty ended and Egypt came under the rule of Rome.

Mary knew from her grandfather that over 40 years of Octavian August's rule first brought new orders to the empire, then the customs that were more stringent than before, but at the same time, also political stability. Rome did not have a governor in Egypt, as in other conquered countries. A prefect exercised power on behalf of the emperor. This was the case during Octavian Augustus rule, and nothing changed in this matter in the time of his successor, Tiberius.

Karim did not talk about this with Mary, but for anyone who knew at least a little about politics, it was clear that the prefect's task was, first of all, to watch over the regular supply of grain to the capital of the empire, and to collect taxes. The prefect also made sure that gold and precious stones mined in the conquered lands would end up in the imperial treasury, as well as trade revenues. Egypt was the only country having access to both the Mediterranean and the Red Sea, and its ports were among the largest and most developed in this region of the world. For centuries, the country had brokered the trade between Arabia, Asia, Europe and Africa, so it was also extremely rich, and the Romans were not shy to use its resources to their heart's content.

The Ptolemaic dynasty came from Greece, so during their reign, their countrymen enjoyed numerous privileges in Egypt and held key positions for centuries. The official language was Greek and everyone who wanted to achieve something had to know it. The Romans not only maintained the state of affairs found after the Ptolemaic dynasty but also cherished the Greeks and made it even more difficult for native Egyptians to advance in society.

For some time now, the prefects of Rome had changed frequently. Alexandria counted four of them in three years. First was Quintus Fabius Maximus, followed by Lucius Seius Strabo, who ruled for a very short time. He was replaced by Aemilius Rectus, and then it was Gaius Valerius' turn, and it seemed he would settle in Egypt for longer.

The party they were invited to was taking place at the prefect's palace. Karim and his wife were guests there for years because Karim did business and traded with the Romans, including brokering the supply of wine and food to their army. The contract he had was lucrative, so he tried hard not to lose it. Karim was so efficacious that both the Romans and him were happy with the cooperation, so each subsequent prefect invited him to the party.

This year, for the first time in her life, Mary was also invited to the palace. She was too young to be granted such an honor before.

She was excited. Until now, she had seen the palace, which once belonged to the famous Cleopatra, only from the outside. The entrance was always guarded by Roman soldiers, but even if they were not there, it would probably never occur to anyone to try to get to the prefect's home.

She was curious to see what the places where the strong energy of the famous ruler looked like. Aida warned her not to expect too much because the prefect and his predecessors had arranged the palace entirely in Roman fashion, besides, the queen had lived there almost 70 years earlier. The perfumes she used, even though they were said to be of the best quality, had long dissipated.

When they considered the outfits they should wear, Aida did not hesitate. "We're from here," she said. "Nobody expects us to dress as Roman women. Anyway, that would be in bad taste. Let's be ourselves. They admire us for that."

Mary was touched by her words. "We are from here," she said with such conviction as if she had no doubt that Mary was also thinking that way. This was indeed the case more and more often, even though deep in her heart arose a kind of vague mist of a feeling that she would soon return to Magdala.

\* \* \*

Mary was convinced that it would never happen to her. She was so prudent after all. Maybe somewhere in her soul she hoped it would be different, but she told herself that no, probably not, it would not be given to her.

The yearning of the heart, sighs, shiny eyes, yes, it was great with her friends. She envied them. She looked at them with pleasure when they talked about their infatuations and first loves, but she was afraid that if she admitted to herself that she would like that too, this feeling would never be given to her.

Sometimes she looked into the eyes of boys and young men, and they stared at her eyes or mouth, sometimes very insistently, but she did not see any of the symptoms with herself that the girls talked about. That evening, however, she trembled, something tickled in her stomach, her legs buckled and she sank into his eyes. So these stories about wings, swirls and soft knees were not exaggerated? Did something like that happen to her too? She could not believe it. Yet it was happening. For real!

"I'm Marcus. Prefect Gaius Galerius is my great-uncle," he introduced himself. A young man stood before her, a little over 20 years old, with a beautiful, long, noble face, a pointed Roman nose, and – just as in the stories of her friends – a bright look of his blue eyes. He waited for her to give him her name, too, as was customary.

She stared at the unusual blue and did not know what was happening to her.

"Mary, our granddaughter" Aida answered for her, considering that the silence prolonged improperly.

Mary came to her senses. She nodded.

"Can I show Miss Mary the property? I'm almost at home here. The prefect is my mother's brother, I was invited by him." Marcus specified his position neatly, and as a well-behaved young man, he directed the question to Aida, because if it went to Mary, he could not be sure that she would answer. He saw what was happening to her, and his vanity was pleasantly boosted.

"Mary?" her grandmother did not want to help her make the decision, although she was sure that the girl would not refuse.

First of all, Mary knew how much Karim cared about good relations with Rome, so a walk of their granddaughter with a close member of the prefect's family would definitely be a good idea. Secondly, and it was obvious that it definitely became a decisive argument, she saw how Mary reacted to the offer. Her burning cheeks said it all.

"I haven't seen a more beautiful girl since I came here..." When they came out onto the patio, he looked deep into her eyes.

She was intoxicated by the sound of his voice and seemed to be in paradise. She felt stunned, but to her own surprise, the words she put together sounded quite reasonable, "Have you been here long?"

He was glad that besides being beautiful, she could also speak, and in his language to that.

"Over half a year."

"Have you seen many girls?" she laughed, feeling her lost balance return slowly.

"Lots of them!"

"Have you been anywhere outside of Alexandria?"

"Do you have anything besides Alexandria here?"

"I can understand now why they call you barbarians." Returning to her almost regular heartbeat, she said the words with such a wonderful smile that he took it as a compliment.

Anyway, he would be delighted with anything she would say. He noticed her immediately as she entered the room where the reception was being held. She was so fresh! It seemed to him that a bright glow was emanating from her, and when he looked at her closer, he thought that he had never met such a beauty before.

"Do you know that Egyptian civilization is the oldest and most developed in the world? The pyramids stood here at a time when Romulus and Remus had not yet been heard of in the place where Rome is now."

"Where are such beautiful and outspoken girls born?"

Although she did not admire his homeland, he liked what she said and how she said it. She was confident, feisty, and at the same time modest in some strange way. He also hoped that she was submissive, like most women he knew. He liked her very much.

"Go to the province, you will find all kind of beauties there!"

"Where are you from? You don't look Egyptian."

"My mother was from here, but I was born in Galilee."

"Oh, a Jew. That's why you are so beautiful!"

She was surprised. She did not know that the descendants of David were considered beautiful by the Romans. What he said meant just that.

"My grandparents, especially grandmother, think I'm from here."

"Have you lived here for long?"

"I will only be in Alexandria for two months, then I will return to the temple."

"A temple? Are you a priestess?" He was surprised. He took a step back, inspected her with amusement, "You don't look like one."

"Not yet. I have a few years of effort before I can take my vows."

"Do you want to serve in the temple? With your beauty and temperament? You're kidding! You are born for a worldly life. You should go to parties, light them up with your presence, receive homage."

She pulled away. She had mixed feelings. For the first time, she met someone who treated the future priestess without any respect, telling her at the same time with delight that she was beautiful.

She didn't know what to think. On the one hand, she was accustomed to the fact that priestesses enjoyed great attention in Egypt, and on the other, she had never heard words assessing her appearance so unambiguously and with such great and credible admiration. True, she had always known that she is not ugly. She had heard from Marta in Magdala more than once that she was beautiful. However, no one in her environment apparently thought it would be important to her, because it was not often emphasized. In the temple, the priestesses taught that the most important thing about a woman is what they know and what they have in their hearts. The appearance was important because it affected the condition of the spirit, but certainly not of most significance. They were to be clean, tidy, depilated and look properly. In this way they expressed their respect for the Goddess, themselves and the world. Yes, they looked in the mirrors while learning the temple makeup or draping a dress, but beauty was never what was considered the most important thing there.

"Do you like me?" she asked, wondering at her own directness.

"Do I like you?" He was surprised. "I'm delighted with you. You look like a goddess!"

She was happy about what he said, but she wondered how many girls he had said something similar before. How many did he charm? How many did he seduce? How many cried because of him? He was so handsome!

"Will you show me the palace? Maybe Cleopatra's spirit will tell me how to treat you. She knew how to deal with strong Romans."

He laughed, delighted by her sense of humor again that evening, and showed the way.

\* \* \*

Her grandparents didn't mind her acquaintance with Marcus.

"Mary will meet excellent company," Aida said. "His friends are the most significant young people in the area, and she should spend time in the best environment. She cannot limit herself only to priestesses from the temple. It is possible that soon enough we will start looking for a husband suitable for her. Who knows what she will decide when she faces the choice of what to do next?"

\* \* \*

When he kissed her for the first time, the ground parted under her feet. The world ceased to exist. Her head grew dizzy, her wings spread and she felt she was flying. She knew that nothing could be compared to this feeling. Then, in Alexandria, at the time of the Nile flooding, she fell in love. It happened unexpectedly for her and was so strong that she intended to not return to the temple but to go to Rome with him and become his wife. In her mind, she saw herself at his side. She imagined his parents, especially his mother, and their first meeting. She was sure they would like each other. She thought about a wedding and a beautiful, long life together. However, she did not share these dreams with anyone. She talked about them only to Leo. She did it quietly and at night, when the whole house was asleep, while she tossed from side to side, thinking about her beloved.

She told the cat how Marcus kissed her, hugged her, how he brushed off invisible dust from her hair, how he helped her get on the horse, passed her a cup, or put pieces of tangerine on her open hand, and later ate it out himself. Leo listened patiently, sometimes yawned widely, showing a black palate. The wise eyes of the goddess Bastet looked through him, and she had watched such falling in love closely many times before.

Mary sighed. She was tired because she didn't sleep at night, but she looked more beautiful than ever. However, although she was absolutely happy and dreamed to announce it to the whole world, something told her to keep the visions of a future life with Marcus to herself.

Her grandparents watched her with joy, but also with worry. They enjoyed her delight with her first love, but at the same time, they realized better than anyone the very little chances of survival of what they thought was a beautiful, youthful crush.

By discreetly watching over the development of events, they approved the new acquaintance of the granddaughter, thinking that it would end as soon as it began. They thought that when they would leave Alexandria, their granddaughter would forget about Marcus.

Mary joined the group of joyful young people, friends and colleagues of Marcus. They were called "golden youth" because they were wealthy and everything they surrounded themselves with was always of the highest quality. They had resources to draw on because their ancestors belonged to the richest and best-known families. They started going on trips together, sightseeing the area, seeing old temples, meeting with close and distant friends, visiting places, including those that did not enjoy the best reputation. These were especially tempting for the young people.

Delighted with the novelty, after years of rigor in the temple, daily rituals, learning, discipline, obedience, Mary suddenly felt another world open to her. Pleasant, lazy, filled with pleasures; a space where no one ever was in a hurry, and everything that was happening was done in the pursuit of fun. The new friends were joyful, cheerful, focused on learning new things. They saw no problems and took big mouthfuls of life, convinced that they deserve the best of everything.

She accepted their habits happily and treated their approach to life almost as if it were her own. She was absorbed in a new world for her, a wonderful world of carefreeness, fun, and a lack of any duties. She felt a part of it.

"Tomorrow our group will be on a night trip following in the footsteps of Antony and Cleopatra," she announced to her grandparents one day. "I need a maid outfit. We will dress in disguise like they did, and we will visit port pubs and various forbidden places."

"What a ridiculous idea," Aida objected.

"A magnificent idea! Marcus came up with it and everyone loved it. Me too."

"Maybe you'd better give up? I don't know if it's the right entertainment for a young lady."

"Grandma, I certainly don't have a chance for such an adventure in the temple."

"No doubt about it."

"So?"

"Are you sure you want this?"

"I'm sure."

"Go then. Have fun, and if anything makes you worried, come back. Sithathor will be somewhere around and at your service all the time."

"I won't need it."

"Of course, I know that you are mature and very independent, and you are safe in Marcus' company. But Sithathor will be there anyway. Just in case."

\* \* \*

When it became quite dark, everyone appeared at the entrance to the port district, as they agreed. There were 10 of them. Four Romans, two descendants of old Egyptian aristocratic families and four girls, including Mary. All young, beautiful, happy, eager to explore the world, carefree, with hotheads, everyone to some extent unconsciously vain and slightly conceited, as is often the case with children raised in prosperity.

Mary stood out among them. She was slender like Egyptians, but tall in comparison to them. She had dark hair like them, but her hair was curly. She inherited her straight nose and fair skin from her father. That evening, she was also distinguished by the color of her outfit. She had a gray dress and a black wide coat to be inconspicuous, but at the same time, at her grandmother's request, she put a red headscarf over her head, so that Sithathor could see where she was in the crowd.

Everyone else also adopted the convention proposed by Marcus. They put on simple clothes that servants wore every day. Just like Cleopatra and Antony over 50 years before them, they felt that they would blend more easily in the crowd with a disguise. They wanted to visit the premises, considered by their parents and grandparents as suspicious and absolutely unsuitable for young people with their origin and position. However, they did it, of course, with their knowledge and consent.

The port district was not considered the safest. It was full of sailors and sketchy characters from all over the world. Although Alexandria's glory days were already behind it, it still remained one of the most important, and certainly the largest ports in the Mediterranean. In the waterfront district, there were plenty of bars and cheap places where you could rent a room, take a bath, have a haircut and a good massage after a sea trip. There were also pubs giving better and worse food, and of course, houses of pleasure with women from all over the world.

The narrow streets were filled with street vendors. They offered everything from beer, wine and juices, through fruit, little snacks, powders and miracle mixtures to heal even the most dangerous diseases, to shoes, clothes, scrolls of magical papyri, and even weapons. Aromatic smells of cuisines from all over the world mingled there, as well as the stench of sewage, cesspool and stinking waste.

Mary kept close to Marcus. They had been seeing each other for over a month now, and they were enthralled with each other with the same strength as on the first day. They both seemed to float slightly above the ground. They admired each other's beauty, intelligence, openness, defiance, feistiness and fresh views of reality. They were like two different worlds, curious of each other, eager to infiltrate each other. She admired his maturity, experience, distance and gentleness. He was delighted with her exterior, which harmonized with her spirit in an unusual way. She was like the quintessence of the mystery and charm of Egypt, of which he had heard so much in Rome. He saw in her what he had dreamed of, and what he expected from the land of ancient kings and wise men, from a place ruled so recently by secretive, wise and, as his countrymen thought, promiscuous Cleopatra. The one who turned the heads of Julius Caesar and Marcus Antony. He often wondered who she was and what she had in her that let her control the two greatest leaders of Rome with such power. He was fascinated by the queen and her times, also because he knew the nicknames she was given in his country. For his countrymen, she was a slut, harlot, poisoner, hag, murderer, power-hungry witch, the one who did not hesitate to use the worst tricks to achieve her goal. As a strong woman who knew what she wanted, she intrigued him.

"If she hadn't been beautiful and intelligent, she might have been able to seduce both chiefs for a short time, but since she subordinated them so strongly, she must have had a lot more in her," he thought.

He was also attracted to her due to the fact, that a little bit of blood of Julius Caesar, Antony and several other great leaders, flowed in his veins. His family was not wealthy, it did not belong to the immediate surroundings of the emperor in Rome, but both his mother and grandmother often repeated that he was almost the grandson of two of the most eminent Roman families: Claudiuses and Juliuses, and that royal blood flowed in him. Ever since his childhood, he wanted to believe it strongly, just like the women in his family. When his grandmother's brother became the prefect of Rome in Alexandria and invited him to his house, his dream came true.

When he met Mary, she became the embodiment of his ideas and dreams of this place. He imagined her as Cleopatra and himself as Julius Caesar, or better, Marcus Antony, and he was glad to finally find her.

They entered the first bar they encountered. The smell of strong drinks hit them. Liquor was treated seriously here. Sailors were sitting by the wide tables. The hour was still early, so many were tipsy but not drunk yet.

"Oh, look who honored us?" one of them called, pointing his finger at the newcomers. "Young masters seeking excitement? In disguise? Very nice," his loud laughter boomed.

Mary hid behind Marcus's back. Neither he nor his colleagues were afraid. They were raised in Rome, where every boy was said to be born a warrior.

"Can we join you?" with confidence, Marcus threw a few coins on the table by which the one who recognized that they were in disguise was sitting. "Host, wine for everyone!"

This generous gesture made the sitting guests move to make room.

"What are we celebrating, Roman?" the sailor wanted to know.

"We're celebrating life!"

The host and his helper almost immediately fulfilled Marcus's wish, placing clay cups on the tables and filling them with pale wine.

"Let it be that way!" the other agreed. "Life is worth everything. Let's drink to it!"

They clicked the cups.

Tff! Marcus spat on the floor. "Give us the best wine you have!" he shouted at the host. "Life is too short to waste it on drinking water!"

The sailor patted him on the back.

"Well, man, so young and already so clever," he praised him, feeling that in his company and with his deep pouch, there was a chance for decent drinks that evening.

The host appeared with a corked jug, "This is excellent Greek wine. Expensive." He squinted his eyes, expecting a specific reaction.

Marcus threw him a few coins. "I hope its taste will be worth it," he picked up the mug of fresh wine.

Mary did the same. They others followed. They drank.

"Not bad," Mary praised it.

Then she sensed someone standing behind her. She turned her head to look.

"Give me your hand, lady, I will tell you the future," she heard.

Behind her was a little woman with a wrinkled face. She could have been a hundred years old or even older.

"Once, here, in this place, I predicted the future of Cleopatra," she assured, showing a toothless smile. "I'll tell you what awaits you."

"Who are you?" At the sound of the name of the ruler, Marcus got interested in the old woman.

"A priestess."

"Maybe you were once, but probably a long time ago?" he laughed, and his friends joined him.

"Who was once a priestess, will always be one," she answered calmly.

"Marcus, let her tell you what awaits you," one of the boys called. "You never believed in sorcery!"

Marcus shook his head, "I still don't believe in it. Magic is good for barbarians. We, Romans are rational.

"What do you care?" His companions decided that as he was already after a cup of wine if they insist strongly, they would manage to convince him. "You are not afraid, are you?"

Right. These words almost always worked on young, ambitious, but not always completely confident men, so they were also effective now.

"Come here, woman!" he gestured. "And tell me, what does await me?"

The old woman spat three times and rubbed the saliva into the threshing floor.

"Give me some wine, I'll rinse my throat," she ordered confidently, settling on the bench next to him.

"You are cheeky!"

"I have nothing to lose," she laughed. "And put a coin on the table!"

When he did, there was laughter in the inn.

"Marcus, you'll know everything in a minute!" one of the boys said.

"Well, it's all over for you!" another shouted.

"We'll see what is written for you!" one more snickered.

The boys had a great time. At least, they wanted it to look like this. In reality, they tried to hide their fears of the unknown, to dismiss from themselves the belief that the Egyptian world and what they knew about it, was for them a dark, intriguing secret, one that they tried to tame by mocking and ridiculing it. In fact, however, they knew that this old world, the holy cats, crocodiles, priests, priestesses, sphinxes and pyramids conceal a spirituality and mysticism that they will be never able to know. They felt respect for it.

"Wow, there is a lot of life ahead of you," the old woman said, looking at his hand. "I need some light here!" she demanded, and when the lamp was placed in the spot she indicated, she continued. "You'll get far. And you will have a happy life. Honors await you in your country. You won't complain. I see three children and it looks like two wives."

"Simultaneously?" someone called out, laughing.

"No. The first one will die. You will remarry."

Mary stiffened. It got quieter in the inn.

"Keep talking, witch! Go ahead, I'm not afraid," Marcus added himself some courage.

"I see love here. Big one."

"Keep talking, I need that," with his free hand, Marcus reached for the cup with wine.

The woman fell silent, then tilted her head back and everyone saw her eyes with the whites turned upside down. She began to speak as if she were reading someone else's words.

"Don't fall in love with a woman who reads, who feels too much, who writes. Don't fall in love with an educated woman, with a sorceress, a priestess who thinks and has faith in herself, who can rise and fly. With one that laughs or cries when she makes love. Don't fall in love with the one who is funny, brilliant, rebellious, contrarian and impudent. Do not fall in love with such a woman, because if it happens, whether she will be with you or not, whether she will love you or not, you will never go back from such a woman. Never." She sighed deeply, then took a breath with a whistling sound, let it out loudly and concluded, "You will recognize her by her wings."

There was silence. Nobody dared to speak first. The old woman's eyes returned to their normal appearance.

"Well said," Marcus raised his hand and looked at it closely. "Homer wouldn't have expressed it better."

"Exactly," a sailor nodded.

Marcus looked at him incredulously.

"What, master brat? You don't know that every sailor knows the author of Iliad and Odyssey?"

"My respect," Marcus bowed his head before him, still surprised.

Had he not had the old woman before him, he would probably have liked to continue the subject of familiarity with Homer's works among sailors, but telling the future from his hand seemed to him more worthy of attention at that moment.

"Tell me one more thing, woman, have I met the one with wings?" he asked.

"Happy is the one who knows that nobody has the answers to all questions," she said mysteriously and laughed, as she took the coin from the table.

"Let it be your way, philosopher," he gave up. "But I want you to also look at the hand of this beauty," he pointed at Mary.

The old woman eyed the girl.

"Show me, child, what the gods are preparing for you," she said gently, parting her fingers.

Mary bowed her head and asked as quiet as she could so that nobody but the old woman could hear her.

"Why did you leave the temple?"

"Love caused my undoing," she also replied in a whisper.

"Can love cause that?"

"Oh, it can, it can. We don't always give it to the ones who deserve it."

"Everyone deserves it."

"Oh no, child. Not everyone. And may you never have to find out."

"What are you whispering about?" Marcus interrupted them. "Look at her hand and say what you see. Here you have a coin!"

The old woman strained her eyes. She looked at her hand again and again. She put it right next to her eyes.

"Give me the lamp!" she ordered, intrigued.

She ran a dirty fingernail down the marks on Mary's palm. She looked up respectfully and fixed her eyes on her.

"You are the chosen one," she said softly.

Only Mary could hear her.

"What are you mumbling there?" Marcus urged her, reaching for his cup.

"I won't tell the future for her," the old woman stood up. "She is too young! Take your money and leave me alone!" she pushed him away.

"You don't want money?" He was surprised.

"Leave her alone," Mary said gently. "Let her go."

She took the rejected coin and pushed it in the woman's hand. Then old woman gestured at her to lean closer. "You are the one with wings," she whispered in her ear. "You'll fly the highest! Following love. Strange, heavenly love."

She patted Mary's hand, which she had seen a moment ago, spat on the floor three times, turned and walked away.

"Crazy!" someone summed up.

"But she did take the money, so she is probably quite reasonable in this madness," added another.

"Let's go. Enough fortune telling for today!" Marcus exclaimed.

"Have fun, brats!" the Homer expert called after them.

\* \* \*

They wandered the streets pulsating with nightlife. Nobody paid any attention to them anymore. They sang, commented on the fortune-telling of the old woman, shook their heads with admiration at the uniqueness of the world, thinking of the sailor who knew poems. They laughed and shouted. They were tipsy as much as others who visited this place at this time, and as amused as most of them.

Only Mary walked a little away from everybody. She thought about what she heard. "The first wife will die. You are the chosen one, you have wings. You will fly the highest. Following love."

"We're going inside," she heard before she could start making order of it in her head.

Two big, burly men were standing in front of the entrance to a building, not very tall but fenced with a solid wall. One glance was enough for them to let the guests inside. They recognized those who have money without a mistake.

"Are you sure we want to come in here?" Mary tugged Marcus's sleeve.

"Do not be afraid. We are safe."

"Have you ever been to such places?"

"It happened," he replied evasively enough for her not to feel offended, but with some pride, because such a declaration confirmed that he knew life much better than she did, but all in all it was only expected because he was a man. "Come, priestesses. I will certainly not lead you to such a place. Maybe it's worth seeing what this side of life looks like?"

That convinced her. After all, what did she have to lose? What could happen to her at the house of pleasure? She knew Marcus was right. There was no chance to visit such a place with priestesses. So, maybe it was the first and last time in her life to see something like this. Besides, she realized it with relief, still, at a safe distance, she felt the presence of Sithathor. She was glad that the guardian was with her.

The first room resembled an inn, like one of the many they visited that evening, except that the men did not sit by the benches, but on richly decorated mattresses or poufs, leaning on cushions scattered everywhere. They drank wine and beer, which did not run out from their cups and goblets because someone was always pouring it for them, and watched the women dancing and walking between them. Some of them enjoyed the caresses of girls that they called to themselves.

"Where can we find a place for young people?" Marcus casually asked the owner who was bowing before him. He held Mary's hand. He felt her trembling. He liked it.

"If you let me know you have had enough, we can leave at any moment," he assured her.

"The lord and his companions can choose any place they want for themselves. We have girls of the first class," assured the host, rubbing his hands. "If necessary, we also have attractive boys from exotic countries." He looked at the company, looking for those who might like homosexual love, and not noticing anyone like that, added, "Maybe one of the noble ladies would like to try?"

"Bring us wine," Marcus demanded.

They settled in different places, in groups of twos or threes. There was not much free space. Mary still clung to Marcus. She wasn't afraid, but, squeezing his hand, she felt more confident in this world, so foreign to her.

"How did they get here?" she wondered, looking, almost as if hypnotized, at the women seeking the guests' attention.

They came from all over the world. Tall and short, slim and plump, with different hair colors, of different ages. One of them was so fat that she needed the help of two people to get up and go with the client. There were dark-skinned girls from the hinterland; there were fair-skinned from the North. Most, however, looked like Egyptians.

"Many of them are slaves bought at the market. I think they are fine here, you can't see them complaining," Marcus calmed her down. "It's a job. A profession like any other."

"I am not sure..." Mary was skeptical.

After a few moments, when the bottom showed in the cups, a short girl of classical shape approached them

"Sit here?" she asked in broken Latin.

"Sit down," Marcus showed her place, amused.

"You want me?" she asked with a hard accent, placing her hand on his thigh.

"I'm with her," he nodded at Mary.

"Do you want together?" the girl licked her lips and put her other hand on Mary's thigh. "Very beautiful."

"Where are you from?" Despite the fact that the situation embarrassed her, Mary tried not to show it. After all, nobody dragged her here by force. She herself wanted to know this place. In addition, she wanted to be thought of as an adult, so nothing should surprise her.

"From Gaul," she replied, waving her hand dismissively as if she wanted to push away the old memories stuck somewhere in her head.

"Have you been here long?"

"Forever," she smiled. "This is my place," she said eagerly, feeling the owner's eyes on her.

"Will you show us the house?" Marcus had enough of sitting.

"Owner," she pointed at the man who greeted them at the entrance.

Marcus nodded at him. "We want to see your house," he said when the owner bowed before him. "The lady is here for the first time. She is interested in this place." He slipped a coin in his hand.

The man glanced at what he had received. He appreciated the value and bowed down, "Of course, sir. I will guide you."

"She will show us," he nodded at the Gallic girl.

"As you wish," the host bent again and showed the direction in which they should go, instructing the girl what to show to the guests.

They found themselves in a long corridor. There were doors on both sides, almost one right next to the other. There were groans, sighs, grunts and other sounds, unlike humans, coming from behind them.

"There love," the guide explained.

"These are rooms for guests," Marcus said, watching Mary's reaction. "Girls go there with those who chose them."

"Paid service is not love," she objected because she did not like how the girl called what was happening behind the door love. "I'm sure of it."

"Don't be indignant. I told you this is a profession like any other. And apparently, much needed. You see? All rooms are occupied."

The guide opened one of the doors and gestured at them. They looked through a narrow crack. On the floor lined with soft mattresses lay a fat beauty that they had seen a moment ago. A man put his head on her abundant breasts. He embraced her, greedily sucking one of her breasts, and cried. The woman stroked him tenderly.

"Regular customer," the girl explained. "He always takes her. We call her Mom."

"Do they do something more?"

"Rarely. He likes cry and Mom hug," she explained not too grammatically, but they understood her easily.

She opened the next door. Disturbing moans and cries came from behind them.

"Is she beating him?" Mary couldn't believe her eyes. A short girl with a short whip in her hand stood above a naked, strongly built man lying on his stomach. She beat him on his buttocks, and he moaned, pleased.

"More, more..." he repeated after each hit.

"People have various needs," Marcus explained as if he were a regular in such places and had already seen everything.

"That's why there always were houses of pleasure, they are and will be. Everywhere and always."

They stood in front of the next door. They looked through the crack. They saw a man and two girls. One lay beneath him with her legs spread wide, and the other kissed his lips and knelt in such a position that Mary covered her eyes and stepped back.

"I don't want to watch this."

"Virgin?" their guide nodded understandingly.

"Let's go to the next one," Marcus did not comment on her words.

"It is medicine," the girl let them into a small, empty room hidden behind the last door of the corridor.

"Medicine?" Marcus was surprised for the first time that evening.

"Cure. Help," she explained.

She pointed at bottles, jars, powdered specifics and herbs hung at the ceiling. There were also healing stones, healing bath bowls, bamboo tubes, dried reptiles and amphibians.

"Not have children?" she pointed at a small vial and made a drinking gesture. "No problem! It hurts and burns," she pointed at dried herbs, "it will help! Blood?" She put her finger on the dried sea sponges and small scraps of canvas, "Medicine, you understand?"

Marcus nodded.

"Where did you get it from?" Mary wanted to know.

"We've got it!" the girl cut short, whether because she did not find the right words or simply did not know the origin of the specifics. They had always been there. She didn't have to figure out where they came from.

This place reminded Mary of the Charmion's studio at the temple. It wasn't that big, but you could find here the remedies that women need most.

"Let's go!" the girl gently pushed them, carefully closing the door behind her. "Come on!"

They entered a small patio. A tree grew in its center, and below it was a pond and a small fountain. Someone neatly spread colorful pillows around it. It was empty here.

They went over to the other side. The girl opened a low but wide double door and let them inside. It was dark inside. At first, they could hardly see anything. Soon, however, it turned out that the room was full of people. They were in pairs, triangles, quadrangles, smaller and larger groups. They were illuminated only by tiny lamps hung at several points by the walls.

They stopped.

"Oh no!" Mary could not believe that she saw with her own eyes, live, what she had so far only seen on old vases, the walls of temples, and in medical scrolls. What was happening before her eyes was a huge sex orgy.

Marcus probably did not expect such a view either, because his eyes widened not only because of the darkness but above all, because of surprise.

People present there acted as if they were under the influence of intoxicants. They had slow, soft movements, from time to time there was a chuckle, a sigh or a grunt.

"What is this?" Marcus grabbed the girl's hand.

"You paid, you watch," she explained. "Pay more, you'll join there," she pointed encouragingly at the fornicating companies.

"I cannot look at this," Mary retreated toward the door. "I won't stay here any longer. This is disgusting!"

She turned to leave. Then her eyes met something unexpected. There was a small figure sitting, or basically squeezed into the corner of the room.

"Is it a child there?" she could not believe it.

"She learn," the guide explained.

Mary came over to the little one. The girl cringed in fear and covered her head as if she wanted to shield herself from blows.

"Don't be afraid," she held out her hands to her. "Marcus, help me."

He reached for one of the lights hanging on the wall.

"Who do we have here?" he brought the light closer to the girl's face.

Big, scared eyes looked at them. Mary crouched down.

"No! She learn," their guide protested firmly, sensing what it was about to happen. "Boss angry. Don't touch!"

"Come to me," Mary reached out to the little girl again, disregarding her words.

She was curled up like a scared animal. Not paying attention to the now very clear protests of the guide girl and her assurance that the boss will be very angry, Mary took in her arms the little one, who did not protest. She was just shaking. Probably out of fear and cold, because as it turned out, she was wearing only a thin sleeveless shirt.

"We will have a problem," Marcus said, but at the same time he seemed confident that he would be able to handle it.

"I'm taking her home. She is still a child!" Mary was already heading for the exit.

They came back the same way they got there. Except this time, it took them much less time.

"What's that supposed to mean!?" the owner protested, seeing what was happening.

"You keep little children here?! Barbarian!" If it wasn't for the fact that her hands were occupied, Mary would come at him with her fists. "Earth should not carry people like you!"

"I don't do anything illegal," he protested.

"And here I would have a different opinion," Marcus stood with his legs spread wide. "Don't you know Roman law?"

Marcus's companions, the whole group, including the girls, immediately found themselves next to them and stood like a wall behind him.

"She is my property!"

"Not anymore!" Marcus pushed the man and threw a purse under his feet. "And I better don't find a child with you again, because you'll face a grim outcome."

"She just lives here. I took in an orphan," he changed his tone, collecting money that fell out of the purse. "Take her if you want. She was of no use anyway. I only incurred costs. I fed and dressed her out of kindness."

"We're leaving!" Mary hugged the girl tighter. "I won't stay here one more moment!"

8.

The girl saved from the house of pleasure lived at the estate on the Nile. She was given a separate, small chamber and was in the care of Sithathor. Scared at first, she quickly noticed that she was in no danger. She began to eat, learn the language, and later also laughed. No one understood her language, and the color of her skin and hair indicated that she came from some distant countries in the North.

One day, when Mary was on the property, the girl first pointed at the cat.

"Leo," she said, pleased. Later she pointed at herself. "Dobrawa!"

Mary hugged and kissed her happily. She knew that from now on, every day of Dobrawa's life would be a reward for what she had suffered earlier.

* * *

Mary returned from Alexandria changed. She had grown up, became serious, and at the same time, she was so happy that to those who were in her company, it seemed she was not walking, but hovering above the ground, that she was more beautiful and stronger than ever.

She studied even more, more willingly and faster, she was humming from morning to evening and, which had never happened before. She giggled and babbled with other girls belonging to the group of initiates, who were in love for the first time, just like her. She did not want to talk too much about her chosen one – she was more eager to listen to the confessions of others – but she did not hesitate to tell how handsome Marcus was, how bright his eyes were, how much he cared about her. However, only Zoe knew that he bought out

Dobrawa, because Mary did not want anyone besides her to know that she was at the house of pleasure. Such a confession would certainly cause an avalanche of questions, and she preferred to avoid it. Although quite a long time had passed, she still thought about that place with horror. But fortunately, other memories covered that one.

She was thinking about Marcus all the time. She uttered his name quietly while falling asleep and waking up in the morning. She had his image under her eyelids. Her lips still remembered his hot kisses, and her skin – the touch that caused anxious chills. One day the messenger brought a letter with his seal.

"I don't want to wait any longer. I will come visit you soon. Be mine. I love you. Marcus," it read.

She put the papyrus scroll to her lips and kissed it. She felt closer to him – after all, he had it in his hands so recently.

"Leo, did you hear that?" she asked the cat. "He will be here soon!"

The animal raised its head, stretched and yawned.

"I see you are very excited!" she laughed.

Immediately afterward, she rushed to her grandparents to tell them the good news. They were sitting in the big hall downstairs. It was almost dinner time.

"What does his arrival mean?" Aida knew that to be properly prepared to receive a guest, you need to have as much information as possible about the reason for his visit.

"It looks serious to me," Karim looked at things from a man's perspective. "He wouldn't travel that far just to say hello to us."

"Well, I am not sure it would be to us..." Aida had no doubt what was driving Marcus, but she wanted to hear it from her granddaughter.

Mary, however, did not intend to say anything more, and they tactfully did not ask.

"How do we receive him?" Mary wanted to know.

"In the same way we would receive any other Roman whom we like, and who is also the grandnephew of the governor." Karim had no doubt how sensitive the matter they were dealing with was.

"Well, but...How?" Mary wasn't sure how to feel.

"What do you mean: how?" Aida knew the rules. "Don't expect us to ask him anything. We will patiently wait for him to reveal the purpose of his visit. He is a well-behaved young man. He will know that this should be done so as not to cause unnecessary anxiety."

"Yes. I would definitely be grateful if he didn't cause unnecessary anxiety," Karim repeated his wife's words and laughed.

He loved her, her style, exaltation, manners and elegant choice of words, always appropriate for the situation.

Mary decided that her grandparents were making fun of her beloved. She stood up abruptly. When she later considered her behavior; she did not understand it herself. She did not know what upset her, but she felt blood rushing to her head.

171

"I want you to know that I love him," she said ecstatically. "He is the love of my life! And I will follow him to the end of the world!" She stomped her foot, turned and ran upstairs, slamming the door in her chamber loudly.

"Yeah," Karim nodded understandingly. "It got her."

"We have to wait it out, my dear. This will be the best."

\* \* \*

At night, when Mary was sleeping, Aida came to her husband's bedroom. "What's going to happen, my love?" she lay down next to him. "How should we behave in this difficult situation?"

"We'll just have to wait and see." He was in a good mood.

"Do you understand the seriousness of what is happening?"

"Maybe even more than you think," he patted her on the back. "Governor's descendant, even if just a grandnephew...it is not good, in fact, it looks like trouble."

"And you are saying this now?" she jumped up, outraged. "Where have you been when your granddaughter ran around Alexandria with him?"

"In the same place you were!" he also sat down. "You don't remember? We saw nothing inappropriate in it. We thought it was a momentary attraction, which would pass along with the time of the Nile flooding. You said yourself that once Mary would return to the temple and her daily duties, she would forget about him."

"And what did you say then? Well? Shall I remind you?"

"Please do!"

"You said, my love, that youthful love is like a storm between the dry and rainy season. It comes suddenly, is intense and short."

"Because that's the way it is!"

"What if he comes here to marry her?"

"What's going to happen? You don't know?"

"No."

"Really, there is something you don't know? Woman...you know it, you just don't want to say it out loud."

"What will happen then?"

"If it really is so, we'll be in trouble."

"Why do you think so?"

"Will the grandson of the governor of Rome, not in a direct line, but still a descendant, you understand, Aida, will he marry a granddaughter of merchants? A girl, in whose veins the blood of Israel and Egypt flows? Can you imagine this? It is rather impossible."

She went silent. She knew Karim was right. She started crying, "What are we going to do now?"

"Don't cry, wife. Mary is even smarter than everyone thinks. She will get through it." He wiped her tears, "And we? We have handled worse situations."

\* \* \*

A few days later, the expected guest appeared before the gates of the property. Karim immediately sent a messenger to the temple to inform Mary. They had agreed with her that they would do it as soon as Marcus would appear in their home. She came home when he was resting after the trip.

"What did he say?" She was impatient.

"That he had a tiring journey and would gladly take advantage of our hospitality," her grandfather explained. "We put him in the chamber upstairs. His servants are in the garden house.

Mary kissed Karim and turned to rush upstairs.

"Don't you dare!" Aida stopped her.

"Grandma, I want to see him so badly!"

"Be reasonable," she took her hand. "Go to your room, take a bath, anoint the body, put on a beautiful dress. You rode a horse. You are in a simple temple attire, your hair is tousled. It is better he does not see you like that."

"Grandma, I love you very much, even if you are so old-fashioned!" she kissed her and then, embracing her waist, tried to spin her as if in a dance.

She was happy.

"I'm running upstairs," she announced, then burst into her room, combed her hair, washed her hands, wiped her face and, without changing her dress, stood at the door of her beloved, "Marcus, it's me!"

He opened immediately. He pulled her inside, closed the door and hugged her tightly. She was shivering and could not or did not want to control it.

"You are here, finally you are with me..." he whispered.

"I couldn't wait to see you."

They kissed like never before. Greedily, without restraint.

"Be mine, please..."

"Yes, I want it too. I am yours and I will always be."

"I love you!"

Suddenly there was a knock on the door. Sithathor stood behind them. When Aida found out that her granddaughter did not fully follow her advice, and moreover, that after smoothing her hair she ran straight to the guest's chamber, she immediately sent Mary's guardian upstairs. Little Dobrawa accompanied her.

"Dinner is ready," Sithathor announced in an official tone and loud enough for them to hear.

"Dinner is ready," repeated Dobrawa, who was still at the stage of learning the language.

Mary jumped away from Marcus as if she just realized that she had done something that did not befit a lady. Not only did she not look properly, but she was in his room and, moreover, they were kissing and without restraint!

"I couldn't help myself," she said remorsefully. "Forgive me."

He pulled her close again.

"I love you, you know?"

He kissed her.

"Dinner's ready. Please join us," Sithathor repeated in a firm voice.

Mary adjusted her dress and opened the door. Sithathor and Dobrawa looked at her anxiously. The little one could feel the mood of others perfectly. That was because she did not yet fully understand the meaning of all words, so she focused on observing the emotions.

"We're coming. I wanted to say hello to the guest," Mary explained, leaving the room with her head down, like a guilty person.

However, her eyes said that she did not feel guilty in any way. In this house, she has heard many times that love explains everything, that it is the most important thing in the world and will overcome all obstacles and borders, if only it is a true love. Her and Marcus' feelings were like that – she was sure of it.

Dobrawa put her hand in Mary's hand.

"Do you recognize me?" Marcus leaned over to greet the girl.

When she realized who he was, the ghosts of the past probably came back to her, because she pulled away and cringed in fear.

"It's Marcus," Mary reassured her. "He saved you."

"You saved me," Dobrawa declared resolutely, hugging Mary that was leaning over her, seeking support and assurance that everything was good and that the events from the past would never come back.

"Don't worry, my love. You'll always be safe here."

\* \* \*

During the meal, Marcus did not present the purpose of his visit, as the hosts had expected. This disappointed Aida and

176

confirmed and even reinforced Karim's fears. He only said that he felt honored to be able to visit his friend from Alexandria, whom he liked very much, as well as her whole family. He added that he would like to believe that he would be able to confirm his commitment soon, but he was not ready for that yet.

Later, as Aida and Karim analyzed his words, it turned out that each of them understood them differently.

"It was a marriage announcement," Aida said.

"Even if this is his honest intention, he knows that his family will not agree. They claim to be descendants of Claudius and Julius. They would not allow him to get involved with an Egyptian with the blood of Israel flowing in her veins. I bet he already knows that. He is not a stupid boy, he knows life."

"It is obvious that he loves her! Can't you see it? Really?"

"Did I say he didn't love her? I said that he probably knows that his family would never agree to marry someone like that. That's what I said. And I don't know how, but we should do everything to protect her from some crazy move."

* * *

The night was difficult. Only servants and little Dobrawa slept in the entire estate. The others could not or did not want to shut an eye, for various reasons. Aida and Karim were vigilant so that their granddaughter would not think of visiting a guest in his chamber, or so that he would not go to hers, though they were almost sure he would not dare do it. Sithathor was tasked with staying up all night and watching that the door of one of the chambers does not open at night without justification.

Mary and Marcus did not sleep because they could not. They were immersed in love. They suffered that there were walls and corridors between them that they could not pass.

The next day, after breakfast, Marcus politely said goodbye and went towards the marina together with his servants, intending to board a boat sailing to Alexandria. Mary returned to the temple, unhappy, but accepting the fate.

\* \* \*

That same evening, the temple maid brought her a note. Mary unrolled it with trembling fingers.

It read, "I will be at midnight waiting in the marina. Come. We will escape. I love you. M."

"What happened?" Zoe worried, seeing Mary pale.

"Oh, Zoe, I think my prayers brought on what's happening now," she confessed quietly, sitting down on her friend's bed.

It was evening, they were preparing to go to bed. All of them had already put nightdresses on. After an eventful day and an almost sleepless night at her grandparents' house, Mary appeared in the temple excited and very secretive. She did not say anything, and the unwritten rule of the temple advised not to ask about private matters of someone who did not want to talk about them. So, although they saw that something unusual was happening, the girls were tactfully silent, hoping that Mary would tell them herself in due time.

"Marcus offers me a meeting tonight," she confessed quietly. "He's here, he didn't leave."

Zoe covered her mouth with astonishment.

"What are you going to do?" she asked after a while in a conspiratorial tone.

"I do not know. Really."

The other girls in the chamber pretended not to notice their whispers. They glanced at them from time to time, trying to guess what was going on.

"I want to go to him."

"Really?" Zoe was afraid of her courage. Her surprise was so strong and loud that the other girls had no doubt that something was happening that they had to know about. Right now!

"Why don't you talk about it?" Nefer spoke up first.

She was the biggest straight shooter of all and did not like strict social rules. She thought that rules were invented by people so that those who knew them, could break them with pleasure or without pleasure, but always with a thrill.

Without asking for permission, she sat next to Mary on Zoe's bed, "Will you tell me what's going on?"

"I'll tell you, come," Mary decided.

They all converged in an instant because they were just waiting for it.

"Go ahead!" Nefer encouraged.

"But don't tell anyone," Mary started.

"Let them swear an oath," Zoe decided to further secure her friend's secret.

"Good idea." Nefer knew, as each of them did, that in such situations an oath would not hurt.

They knew no one would break it. The priestesses could ask, and they, bound by the necessity of keeping the secret, could not say anything. These were the rules. If someone wanted them to reveal the secret, all they needed to answer was "I am bound by the oath of silence." It explained everything.

"What will we make it to?" Nefer was practical.

"Isis!" Zoe had no doubt.

"Is the matter so serious?" Nefer was surprised.

"It's more serious than you think," Mary looked at them in such a way that they were sure they were about to learn about something really worth swearing by the most important of the goddesses."

"If any of you doesn't want to be here, leave now and forget what you heard" Nefer demanded.

None of them moved. They all sat around Mary, ready to take the oath.

"Let's stand up then," Nefer decided to finish the matter. "Let us pay the triple respect to the Goddess."

They all bowed three times, intently touching their foreheads, lips and solar plexus with their fingertips.

"Yours blood is the blood, Isis, yours is the power, Isis, yours is the magic," they recited at the same time.

"I swear by Isis' power that I will not reveal to anyone what I am about to hear. If I don't keep my vow, let the Goddess take all the blessings away from me. Repeat three times."

They repeated her words unanimously.

"Let it be so," she concluded solemnly.

"Let it be so," they repeated three times.

"Now, speak," she encouraged, as they sat around her again.

Mary didn't omit anything that seemed important to her. They listened in absolute silence, without interruption as she spoke.

"And now I got this," she finished, showing the note from Marcus.

They passed it from hand to hand like an almost sacred object.

Earlier, they told each other stories, talked about infatuations, feelings and emotions that bothered them or made them happy. However, none of them had ever opened the gates to her heart and thoughts so wide. They admired Mary. They felt how real she was in her fears, worries, obligations, doubts, in being torn between duty and the wish of fulfillment. They understood her need for love.

"I love him most in the world. I feel like I could follow him wherever he would lead me," she sighed.

They still said nothing.

"Will you go to him?" Nefer was the first one to speak again.

"Maybe you need to consult the High Priestess?" Zoe suggested timidly. "She can help in the most difficult situations."

They laughed. All of them, except Zoe, who pursed her lips, pretending to be offended.

"What an idea!" Nefer criticized her. "Don't you know that sometimes it's better not to say a word than to say too much?"

"And you are so smart?" she put her hands on her hips. "Then tell Mary what to do!"

They all began to talk simultaneously. One over another. Everyone wanted to speak. They were excited and aware of the gravity of the moment. They understood that one of them – the greatest, the wisest, one that all of them liked, respected and appreciated – could leave forever that night. She could leave all these years behind: studying, endeavor, effort, expectations for the future, and follow her beloved. Leave the path to the priesthood, become a wife and probably go somewhere far away.

In class, their masters also taught them history, geography, strategy and political thinking. A priestess had to be educated in every field, so they knew a lot about the world and its social conditions. They understood that the relationship with a Roman, especially one of such a noble lineage, could take different turns, and even, in fact, may not be finalized at all if his family disagrees. What will Mary do then? Where and how will she live? Will Marcus withstand the pressure? Will love be stronger than everyday problems? Won't Mary be suddenly alone, somewhere in a distant world, at the mercy of who knows who? Supposedly, love is the most important thing in the world. It is worth living for it, you can leave behind everything that you have for it. "But how do you know which love is real and for life?" they wondered aloud.

Those, who, without knowing them, would see these well-behaved, polite and obedient girls, might have the impression that thinking is alien for their minds. How wrong would they be! The future priestesses of Isis not only looked and behaved perfectly, but were intelligent, wise and well-educated. They understood a lot, learned quickly, comprehended the world with all their senses. Some of them read the thoughts of others, could look into the future, had visions, communicated without words, healed with touch. Others had the talent or ability to count, look at stars, build, manage, or even fight. They could live with each other without competing and comparing; they knew that other women could be their inspiration. They accepted others, especially their right to make their own choices. They were aware of their strength, knowledge, wisdom and skills, and because they were reticent, modest and innocent, few of the ordinary people knew of their powers.

"Thank you for listening to me," Mary bowed her head before them. "Thank you for your words and support."

She got up. They did the same. They watched in silence as she put the most necessary things in the bag, threw the shawl over her head and left.

"May Isis guide you," Zoe said her goodbye.

As she disappeared behind the door, they all bowed three times and made the triple sign of the Goddess.

* * *

He was waiting at the marina. Giving him her hand, she entered the tiny boat without a word. She sat next to him, focused and tense, for she knew that her future depended on what would happen that night. She did not want and could not go wrong in choosing a path. It wasn't until the oarsman sailed far enough that the temple lamps no longer illuminated them, that she dared to look into his eyes.

"I love you," she heard. "And I want to always be with you."

"I love you," she whispered.

The boatman turned his head away to not see their passionate kisses.

After a while they reached a larger boat.

"At dawn we will go to Alexandria. We are alone here, this boat is at our sole disposal," he announced, inviting her on board. "Come on, let me show you our place."

The chamber at the back of the ship was comfortably equipped. There was a bed in the middle. Next to it were tables filled with bowls full of treats and jugs with liquors. Beautiful flowers were arranged by the walls.

"It's all for you," he pointed around.

They were alone for the first time without the watchful eyes of the family, friends and acquaintances. They stood opposite each other and looked into each other's eyes.

She reached out to him, "Come on, I'm ready."

* * *

She opened her eyes when it began to dawn. What had happened the previous day and night seemed a dream to her – the morning farewell to Marcus at her grandparents' house, the return to the temple, the oaths and the conversation with the girls, the night escape, the boat. The place where they were, the bed with soft bedding, flowers, and even Marcus by her side, all seemed unreal. She felt sore, but light and fulfilled. As if what had been accumulating in her for a long time, suddenly found an outlet. The unknown was discovered, and the dreamed of and expected – fulfilled.

Marcus looked at her with admiration, leaning on his elbow.

"I love you," he said. "I want to be with you."

"I will always love you," she patted his cheek. "And I'll always be with you."

He sat up. He sensed a note in her voice that worried him.

"We will sail to Alexandria, you will be my wife. We will have children. I will love you until the end of yours and my days because you are the woman of my life."

"You know I am all yours," she also rested her head on her arm, bent at the elbow.

They were lying opposite each other now, completely naked, beautiful, connected by a luminous thread of love.

"I will wait for you. And I am asking you to wait for me," she was speaking calmly, holding his hands. "Go to Alexandria, talk to your family about us. I will be here. I have one more year left. Wait for me. A year is not much. The true love not only knows no boundaries, but time does not matter for it, either."

He was surprised. He came to Philae convinced that they would sail to Alexandria, that he would introduce her to his family as a wife, go to Rome, live together, and with time when children would appear, even those who might be against his marriage, would change their minds. He was proud of his decision, courage and determination. He was as sure of the rightness of his choice as he had never been before in his life.

The only thing that worried him, were the words of the old fortune-telling woman in Alexandria. She said that his first wife would die. At that time, he, of course, thought of Mary. Even at that time, already he wanted to be with her, but the prospect of her death obviously frightened him. He chased the thoughts of it away then, but something made the bad memory come back to him. Because of this, when he heard what Mary said, he was surprised, but he also felt relief somewhere deep in his rational Roman soul.

"Let it be as you say," he said sadly. "The year will pass quickly. Know that I am only yours and it will always be so. I love you immeasurably. I will overcome every obstacle so that we can be together because you are the one I've always been waiting for. And I'll be waiting."

* * *

In the morning, Marcus sailed to Alexandria, and she got on the horse and rode to her grandparents' house. When she came inside, almost everyone was still asleep. She went to her room, washed and changed.

The goddess Bastet looked at her through Leo's eyes. She was disappointed. She hoped that beautiful Mary would abandon Isis, stay with Marcus, and when he would leave her, she would become her priestess. It was quite a possible way for this smart and beautiful girl. The goddess had long watched her path and wanted to have the girl on her side. At the Bastet temple in Alexandria, a woman like Mary could become a high priestess. However, apart from watching her through Leo's eyes, she couldn't do anything else. Because who would dare to oppose the will of Isis, the greatest of goddesses?

When she was ready, she quietly opened the small door to her grandmother's chamber. It seemed huge to her once, and now she had to lower her head to pass through it. Right now, she realized it with pleasure. A lot had changed in her life since she came here. Also, the door size.

Aida was still asleep. Mary carefully pulled back the cover and quietly slipped into the bed, settling beside her grandmother.

Aida opened her eyes. "My love," she hugged her and patted her tenderly.

Mary reached for the chain hanging from her neck for years, "Can you unpin it, please?"

They sat up. Aida leaned over her granddaughter and a moment later, Mary's mother's ring rested on her hand. "I feel it'll fit me now," she slipped it on her finger.

It fit as if it had been made for her.

Aida kissed her forehead.

"Aset got it from us when she married your father."

"She loved him very much..."

"Yes. You are a fruit of a great love."

They embraced and cried almost simultaneously.

"He left" Mary confessed after they wiped their tears. "We gave ourselves a year. I love him, grandma. And he loves me. He said he was ready to leave everything for me and stand up to his whole family if the need arose. He has his fortune in Rome;

we would have something to live on. Because he would like us to go there and live together."

Aida listened. She knew exactly what had been going on since Marcus left their home. Sithathor watched their actions from a safe distance. However, as requested by Aida and Karim, she did not interfere at any stage. Even if the boat would sail to Alexandria with Mary on board, she would only watch. Both Aida and Karim believed in the wisdom and prudence of their granddaughter. At the same time, they knew that there was no greater element than love. They were also convinced that Isis was watching over her chosen ones and whatever would happen would be good for Mary.

She could guess what had happened on the boat. Then she looked into her granddaughter's eyes, she was certain of that.

"I was quite close with him," Mary confessed. "As close as possible. And it was beautiful."

\* \* \*

"High Priestess, thank you for letting me appear before you," she bowed.

Nothing had changed since the last time she was there, that is when the issue with Zoe was happening many years ago. Even the wide leather chair stood in the same place as it did then. Seeing the chamber completely unchanged for years, she felt safe. The High Priestess gave the impression that she had been sitting in this chair from the beginning of the world. This observation also gave Mary a sense of stability.

"What brings you here?"

"I broke the temple rules," she confessed.

The High Priestess looked at her inquiringly.

"In what way?" she asked without the slightest emotion.

Mary thought that it probably was not the first time the Priestess heard such words, and thus they did not make any impression on her, and yet during all the years she had spent in the temple, she did not remember hearing that anyone of the students had done something similar to what she did. So she didn't know what would await her. She was most afraid that she would have to pick up her belongings and leave. It would be an unbearable defeat for her. By deciding to go to the Great Priestess, she risked a lot. She didn't have to do that. She was sure that her friends, bound by an oath, would never betray her. However, she believed that in order to continue functioning in a world with such transparent and clear principles, she should live following them herself, and above all, in harmony with herself.

"I left the temple without the permission and knowledge of the guardians," she said.

"That's not good," said the Priestess, still without emotion.

"But that is not everything."

"Yes?"

Mary looked into her eyes, and in a moment, without thinking much, she was next to her, she fell on her knees and embraced her legs. "I spent the night with the man I love," she confessed as honestly and simply as she could.

Then the words flowed on their own. She spoke about how she met him, how her head was spinning, how beautiful, smart and good he is, that she loved him like no one else in the world, that she wanted to be with him forever. She told about her

189

doubts concerning his Roman family and that she was a little afraid of what might happen to her in a distant city. She felt that she couldn't abandon her grandparents who raised her and whom she loves very much. She couldn't do something so terrible to them. She even said what had been on her mind since she met the old woman in the port tavern – that Marcus's wife would die, so maybe she would rather not be the wife because she wanted to live. Very much. After all, she had a lot to do in life. Anyway, when the old woman saw the lines on her hand, she told her something else. That she is the chosen one, that she has wings. That she will fly high. Mary did not know what these words could mean, but she always sensed that she had a mission to accomplish, but she still did not know what it was. She prayed fervently to the Goddess, asking her to show her the right way, and it was probably Isis who put Marcus in front of her. She let her know the taste of love. She is grateful to the Goddess for this. She loves with all of herself. She would follow him to the end of the world. She was ready for this when she left the temple at night, but her inner voice told her to come back. That her place is here. That she was supposed to stay in the temple. That she would decide next year what path to follow. Now she is here.

She kneels before the High Priestess and does not know what will happen. She entrusts herself to her wisdom with faith and trust. She leaves herself at the priestess's disposal. She doesn't know if as one who has met the taste of a man, she has the right to be here. Whether Isis embraces with her wings also ones like her – at a crossroads. In love.

The High Priestess patted her head, "Freedom is the highest value, but only for those who are responsible for their own decisions and actions. You are still looking for your way. And so be it. My child, remember that whatever path you choose, you will always be the daughter of Isis. You loved very much. As a priestess, you have the right to do so. You can stay in the temple, after all, you are one of us."

\* \* \*

The last year in the temple had always been a time of recapitulation and decision making. The girls, or rather young women, who were graduating, became the priestesses of Isis, and they remained ones forever, in every situation, for the rest of their lives. Some got married or decided to serve the Goddess in one of the many temples, others applied themselves to one of the beloved fields. Some became mistresses and taught, but it was very rare, and an even smaller group had the predisposition and the desire to become hemet and to fulfill Isis's will in the most difficult matters, for as long as they had enough strength. Others went somewhere far away and sometimes all the trace of them disappeared; no one knew what and where they were doing.

However, each of them, regardless of the chosen path, left the temple educated and prepared to live and serve the Goddess in the best possible way. They were the elite.

"Think about everything you've learned so far," they heard from their mistresses. "Review it, look at it carefully. Confront your inner voice and reject what is not in harmony with it. Listen to it carefully. It will warn you of danger, show solutions, point at opportunities and perspectives. If you go astray, you will find with its help the path of truth again, which is the divine light. You received it coming into the world. Follow it.

"Can anyone say that there is only one right way of thinking and acting?" They heard questions that made them think about everything they had learned before. "Open yourself to the feelings and thoughts of others, appreciate their life effort, do not judge, do not value. Everyone comes into the world for some reason and it depends on them what they do with the power given to them. Everyone is needed because he is a part of the divine whole. He is here because he was supposed to be here. We owe respect to everyone.

"A priestess is a creativity, creation and inspiration," they heard. "She's empowering yourself and others, she's a trust in life and yourself. The priestess is full of inner light. She loves herself and others in good and bad times, in joy and sadness, in successes and failures. She loves her body and cares for it, knows its strengths and weaknesses. She can be alone but can draw on wise relationships, appreciate the strength of the mistresses; she is inspired by other women. She bows to the Goddess in all her forms. She appreciates the beauty of herself and of the world around. She is here and now, but she can also connect with the past and future. She feels a bond with those who were before her and those who will come after her. She is one with them, draws strength from them and passes it on.

"What is needed to achieve anything we care about are emotions and faith in what you do. Real strength comes when your presence, your actions and words awaken something in other people; when they affect them and change their soul. When you are yourself and surrender to the purpose of life which is assigned to you. When you accept the truth about who you are – the good and the not quite pleasant. When you remember whose arms you are standing on. When you open up to others and when you intuitively think of someone, because it may mean that he needs support. Learn to obey the intuition, don't be afraid of making new mistakes. And remember that for those who meet you, you are a reflection of the face of the Goddess. Stay strong and share your light."

Mary felt that she was getting closer every day. That the gates would soon fully open for her, that she would see the light more clearly than ever before. She couldn't wait for this moment."

## 9.

It was a full moon. The only one of the kind in the year. A red moon. The goddess never gets as close to her followers as at this time.

Saint of Saints, the most important place in the sanctuary of Isis, had been prepared for this event for several days. Each year, before the initiation, the room was thoroughly washed and incensed three times. New, never used lamps were brought in and placed against the walls, forming a circle. Dresses, bags, ritual knives, and gift-filled crates were prepared for each new priestess. It was made sure that the seal with the sign of the Goddess was in good condition. On the last day, a hearth was prepared, and myrrh, incense and gold were collected at the sacrificial altar. Herbs and vials with mixtures to be used during rituals were arranged around.

Those to be ordained had been fasting for seven days. They thoroughly cleansed their bodies and prepared themselves spiritually. They prayed all together and each one separately sang songs, recited hymns, danced and played instruments.

Finally, the long-awaited day came, followed by the night. The one they had been waiting for years.

* * *

They were standing in a circle in the main hall of the temple – the High Priestess, mistresses, teachers, hemet and those who were to be initiated. There were 12 of them, among them, Mary in a long, simple blue dress, without decorations or jewelry, dressed in the same way as her friends. Each of them was holding a wreath, made with the most beautiful plants she managed to collect. They were to give it as a gift to the Goddess, however not in front of her statue in the temple, but in the waters of the Nile.

This was because Isis appeared most often in open spaces, especially on full nights. She liked when her priestesses danced barefoot to the moon, and the sacrificial altar stood under the open sky. She valued forests, meadows and gardens. She felt good among the flowers, on the sand, by the water. She liked nature.

The girls bowed to the High Priestess and the mistresses. Then each of them lit a lamp standing against the wall and raised it. They were ready to leave.

"Yours is blood, Isis, yours is power, Isis, yours is magic!" the High Priestess cried out.

They repeated her words three times.

The mistresses, teachers and hemet went first, followed by the girls in a line. As they walked, they sang hymns.

A bonfire was lit on the Nile to celebrate their holiday. It was big. They stood around it.

"Goddess, accept our gifts and sanctify today's night with your presence," asked the Priestess, thus indicating that they could lay wreaths on the water.

Dedicating the wreath to Isis, each of them, quietly or loudly asked her for a blessing.

"Choose the best path for me, lady," Zoe asked.

"I will do everything you command me, please, let me be the best at what is written for me," Nefer knelt by the water and sent her wreath.

"Lady, let me carry the light," Mary asked, "and let my footprints outlive me."

Each girl, in turn, put flowers on the water, sending with them a request to the Goddess.

Immediately after this part of the ceremony, they returned to the temple. Fragrant incense was placed on the tripod, and the room was filled with smoke, but it did not irritate the eyes or scratch the throat. It came from the best quality herb blends, used only for full moon ceremonies.

"Every woman carries a part of the Goddess in herself" Agnes recited. "And the priestess tends for the balance of the male and female element in the universe. It is her duty and mission. Without it, there is no harmony, Maat disappears, the world descends into chaos."

Airborne substances were slowly starting to work. Week-long fasting, prayers and concentration, combined with magical smoke, made them see the reality more clearly, and at the same time it became more fluid, swaying and colorful. Unknown hues of colors appeared before their eyes, new particles appeared in the air, life revealed its smallest elements, previously invisible to the naked eye. They could smell better, they could see and hear more intensively. Their sense of touch was also enhanced.

Agnes's voice flowed to them as if from behind a transparent curtain. However, they not only heard it clearly but also understood the meaning of each word perfectly.

"Every woman carries two roses of the Goddesses in herself. One is our own heart and the other is the womb, the eternal garden of life. By drawing power to these two points, we are able to destroy the negative energies of the world. Only priestesses can do that, and each of you is a priestess today. Let's do what we have practiced many times now, try to use what you have learned."

The students, mistresses, teachers, hemet, and even the High Priestess followed her instructions, "You will now breathe the light. Take your positions."

Breathing light was what Mary and each student always wanted to do. They learned the basics, knowing that they wouldn't be honored to fully know the path until the night of the full moon that would be their initiation, and that's how it happened.

"Come into your heart's field. Let the sign of infinity appear there," Agnes ordered.

She knew that each of the girls needed different time to get ready. So, she waited until they were all in the right dimension.

"Now the rose of the heart is the focal point for you," her voice went straight to their open minds, despite the fact that the priestess did not speak words, but only sent a thought to each of them. "Send a sign from there, in front and behind you.

Draw infinity with your eyes, so that the heart is its center point. Throw behind what is bad, send the white energy of light into the future. Your heart has cleansed it. Can you see? This is how infinity arises. Meditate, focus, let your soul dance. Let your breath be the energy of light. A woman's heart has a fractal structure. It is the same as a rose, the flower of the Goddess. It can turn evil into good."

They were breathing deeply. Some of them swayed back and forth or sideways, others made small circles with their torso, or did not move at all.

"Now do exactly the same with the womb fractal. Let the second rose be activated. Let it join infinity. Let your souls perform a dance of light in the second fractal" Agnes did not speak, but rather kept sending thoughts to each of them.

They did what she asked, so they heard her, received her intentions without even knowing it. After a while, a blissful smile appeared on their faces again, and drops of tears flowed from under many eyelids.

"Our tears have the power to heal the world. They contain medicinal substances and carry the energy of love with them, and this is the highest form of vibration of the universe. Remember: only love counts. Your concern is taking care of the good energy of the world and cultivating female strength in it. You are priestesses, so you bring love to the world. It should guide you in everything you do. It should construct you and always be your signpost. Love is life."

This part of the ritual was over. The High Priestess got up and bowed to Agnes.

A delicate, but more and more noticeable scent of roses began to float around. It meant that the Goddess was with them. She came to her priestesses to accompany them. She looked at them from above, she was in them, next to them. The fragrance of these flowers had always been an inseparable sign of her presence.

"It is time for blood sacrifice," the High Priestess ordered.

The mistresses placed cages with exotic birds in front of her, which were brought from afar especially for this occasion. They had been gathered throughout the year in various parts of the world on behalf of the students, to grace the night of the initiation. The goddess received them as a special gift.

For centuries, each of the girls that was to become a priestess placed the bird she had bought on the sacrificial altar. Following an old custom, long used only on that one night of the year, the High Priestess then pierced its heart with a special double-edged knife made of iron with the addition of glass; so it was supposed to be this time.

Mary was going to be the first one to make the offering. She approached the cage in which her colorful bird was waiting to be offered. It shimmered with thousands of colors. It looked as if it came from paradise. It was beautiful. Like the others, it desperately tried to flap its wings and shouted loudly, sensing the approaching death, but it was tied up and had no chance of escape.

For the ritual to be complete, a blood sacrifice was needed. The goddess had demanded it since the beginning of the world. A long time ago, in times that no one remembered anymore, virgins of flawless beauty were laid on the altars. Later, when the Goddess forbade human sacrifices, animal hearts were pierced. They had to be big, healthy and strong. Gifts for Isis were given in order to satisfy and propitiate her, and receive her support. The sacrifice of the most beautiful birds that could ever be found, was a part of a long tradition and was supposed to cause that the new priestesses would receive the favor of the Goddess.

Mary took the bird and, kneeling, placed it on a low stone altar, before which the High Priestess was waiting, holding a ritual knife in her hand. The victim could not be tied, so Mary untied its immobilized wings.

She looked at it and cried. It was lying on the altar and, held by her, did not even try to break free or shout, as if it gave in to fate.

Everything around her was rippling. She no longer knew if she was really taking part in the initiation and kneeling before the altar, while looking at the knife raised by the priestess, or was it all her imagination? Suddenly, a light flashed in her head. She saw that the bird was not colorful at all. It was the white dove she remembered from her childhood, from the garden in Magdala. The one that flew away, warmed by her hands. She could see her clearly now. The dove was lying on the altar, and she stroked her soft feathers, felt the warmth of the blood pulsing in her, and her heartbeat.

"No!" she called out.

The priestesses looked up.

"No!" she repeated strongly.

She stood up and hugged the bird to her chest.

"The goddess doesn't want blood sacrifices anymore," she said firmly. "Sacrificial blood will henceforth belong to the past. We will cease blood sacrifices in every temple and in every place where we worship Isis. The Goddess wants love. Only love."

She heard her voice and was surprised. It wasn't her who spoke. That voice came from within her. It was like a clean breath, like the bright energy that she fully sent to the world today for the first time.

She stood upright, hugging the bird. The voice she received was a voice given to her from above. She was it. She felt fully herself – for the first time with such power. The scent of roses intensified. A light appeared in the temple and soft sounds came from everywhere, entered their heads and filled their hearts. It was the music of the Goddess.

Those of them who were still contemplating began to raise their heads. However, just like the High Priestess, they were not surprised at all by what was happening. The goddess revealed her will in different ways. Anything could happen during the red full moon at the initiation. They were looking at the High Priestess. It was her decision how the words that had just been spoken, would be received.

She put the knife down on the altar. She stood up. She took two steps towards Mary. She put her hand on the girl's shoulder and remained silent for a long time. She absorbed her energy, listened to her heartbeat, learned her secrets, looked into her life, her past and future. Then she bowed her head respectfully before her, "Goddess speaks through you. We hear her words, we understand her will. Let it be done!

"Let it be done," the priestesses repeated in chorus.

"Let it be done," Mary repeated.

She looked at the bird. It was no longer a dove. It was shimmering with colors again and probably sensed that it was spared because it lifted its head and stared at Mary. She lifted it, opened her hands and watched it soar to the top of the temple and fly out through the hole through which the night sky could be seen.

She had never noticed before that there was a window at the top of the temple's vault. Now she was looking at the stars. The other girls came to the cages and each of them released her bird. They watched them open their previously bound wings, spread them wide, and fly. They all found their way to freedom without fail. They flew out to the red moon.

Dazed and under the strong action of herbal vapors in the air, the girls were happy with the decision of the Goddess. They didn't want a blood sacrifice either. They thought it was terrible, but they also knew that certain things are being done because they are sanctified by tradition, and this should not be changed without a reason and without the clearly proclaimed will of Isis.

The full moon was extraordinary not only because of the decision of the Goddess to stop the blood sacrifice and the fact that she passed it through the lips of Mary, who after all was not entirely a priestess because she did not yet have her seal. The ceremony was also different because a moment later when the would-be victims were released, the High Priestess had a vision. This rarely happened during initiation. Most often her visions came when she was among the most initiated, or when she talked to Isis alone. This time it was different, also because the vision was about one of those present, and it really happened extremely rarely.

"She's coming." Unexpectedly, also for herself, the High Priestess opened her arms and turned them palms up.

The others fell on their faces before her. Those who had previously participated in her visions knew what was about to happen. The Great Priestess came into contact with the universe. Everything seemed to indicate that Isis decided to speak to her here and now. With everyone present, including those who were just becoming priestesses.

"The end of time is coming," her voice sounded as if made of silver, metallic, but soft and gentle. "Time will stop and then start again. Let's tremble, because this is the end of everything we know. Let's shiver, but don't be afraid. The old will disappear, but the new will appear in its place. The Divine good will come, a new but eternally lasting force sent from the heights. It will be a signpost, a wide path that will be created from blood and suffering. The one who brings with him boundless love will come down here. He will come as a man and make the closed gates open. He will destroy the old world, and will forever control a new one that will be born in pain. The old temple will collapse, and the light that will be love, will shine. Let us tremble, waiting for opening the gates, which will happen because of his sacrifice."

The great priestess lowered her hands. She opened her eyes.

"Mary, stand up," she ordered after a moment of silence.

Mary was kneeling with her forehead by the floor, like the other women. When the Priestess said her name, she did not understand at first that she was being addressed.

"Mary, I'm talking to you!"

She raised her head shyly. The High Priestess reached out to her, "Mary, the guardian of the light, come over!"

She was stunned but soon stood opposite her.

"Kneel!" the priestess ordered gently and put her hands on Mary's head. "You were chosen and marked at birth already. Your path is not straight. It has led you here and will lead you further, to your destiny. With the distinction given to me, I give you strength, I give you power, I give you light. Follow the feminine path, it is your duty. Go in the name of the Goddess. Take care of her particle part in the time to come. Your paths will not be straight, you will descend into the darkness, touch the abyss, go to the bottom, but you will not be afraid. This is your mission. Fulfill it for centuries. Give women strength to last."

Mary felt a bright light flow into her body, roses bloom in her, the energy of the Goddess fill her. She felt one with her. She united with the High Priestess, and through her, with the eternal Goddess. She was the sun, moon, air, fire, water and earth now. She was everywhere. She disappeared. She melted into the world, merged with it, felt being it. She felt good. She wanted to stay there, but she had to come back to become herself and feel her body again, to follow her path. To fulfill what she was called to do.

She rose from her knees. She was breathing freely. She had power. She was ready to carry anything she was predisposed to. She felt strong as never before, powerful and tough, and at the same time delicate, sensitive and aware of weaknesses. She was a woman, a priestess of the Goddess, a guardian of the gate of light. She returned to her place and knelt among the others.

She was one of them. She drew on their strength and gave them hers, forever united with them.

\* \* \*

It was beginning to dawn. They waited intently for the last ritual. They were kneeling, and the High Priestess stood in the middle. They bowed their heads before her majesty and brushed the hair away from the back of their necks. A priestess in a blue moon-shaped bonnet, crowned with cow horns, entered the circle, bowing to her superior. It was a symbol of Isis. She bowed and kneeled before each of the girls. With a skilled move, she put a ritual seal with fine needles high on the nape of their necks, where the hairline began. The thin blades were soaked in blue ink. It was obtained from the plants from the temple garden, mixed with ink from special types of squid. Applying the seals was painful, but everyone waited for them and treated the pain as distinction and honor. Like for many women who had been before them, the seal stamped the symbol of the Goddess on their skins. They were to wear it for the rest of their lives.

After each one was marked, they rose and held hands.

"You are entering a new day as priestesses," the High Priestess announced. "From now on, wherever life paths lead you, you will always be one. Stand up. Let the gates be opened before you. Go and carry out your mission."

\* \* \*

Each of the newly ordained priestesses was received by the High Priestess before leaving Philae. A protector could also attend the meeting. A protector was a woman from the family, most often a mother or grandmother, who was once educated in this place herself, or another wealthy guardian, responsible for recommending the girl for the studies and her constant support, while ensuring appropriately valuable offerings to Isis. Thanks to generous donors, the temples on Philae could function as well as they did in the times of their greatest glory, that is, in the times of the Ptolemaic dynasty.

During her farewell conversation, Mary was accompanied by Aida.

"Some time ago, on the way to Luxor, we confirmed that we are doing well in a group and we can support each other, that we can cooperate and we can fight. Even me. It was a big challenge, but already then the matter seemed a bit suspicious to me..."

Mary was bothered by the case from many years ago, and she wanted to explain it before leaving the temple. She looked at Awenger questioningly.

"High Priestess?" the hemet made sure she could now tell the secret.

"Tell her, she's a priestess. She can know everything we know."

Aida smiled elegantly, awaiting her granddaughter's reaction when she would hear the methods used in the temple to properly prepare the students for life.

"Your intuition wasn't wrong," Awenger looked at Mary appreciatively. "It was an exercise. The idea was to put you in an emergency situation and in an unknown area."

"Everyone except us knew that, right?" Mary wanted to be sure.

"But you guessed it, didn't you? And a few other girls didn't quite believe in the threat either.

"Oh no! I remember that night very well, we were all terrified and overwhelmed. We didn't suspect it was exercise. And in Luxor, when bandits attacked us, even if any of us had doubts about the authenticity of the threat before, she stopped having them then.

"Indeed, the priests were very authentic," Awenger laughed.

"They were priests?

"Well, we would not have sent real robbers after our beloved students!

"Grandma, did you know what was going on?" Mary could not believe that distinguished Aida was also initiated into the case.

"Of course, honey. All the guardians fully trust the High Priestess and believe in the effectiveness of the methods used here for centuries. Anyway, let me tell you that I experienced something similar in my youth. To, this day I have a thrill while remembering those events."

"Each of us must be able to fight and cope in extreme situations," concluded the High Priestess.

"It may happen that you will never be forced to use these skills and may it be so, but we want and must prepare each of you for such an eventuality. Love is your weapon, but life is not only the neat, flourishing gardens on estates on the Nile, it's not only our temple. We live here in a closed world of order, righteousness and light. It can be different outside. Anyway, you've probably noticed this many times before?"

Her all-knowing gaze penetrated Mary's memories. She saw in them a little girl reaching out to her savior.

"How is Dobrawa?" she asked as if she knew the issue perfectly well. "Has she managed to learn the language? Did you help her chase away the evil ghosts from the past?"

Mary looked at her grandmother. Her eyes said, "No, I didn't tell the High Priestess about the little one, but you know she reads in our hearts and heads, she knows everything."

"How do you do it, High Priestess?"

"I'm connecting with Goddess. I listen to her voice. You can do it too."

"There must be still a lot of learning ahead of me," Mary said hopefully.

Unfortunately, although the priestesses claimed that she was fully ready, she did not yet find the ability to connect with the Goddess every day. Yes, during big ceremonies and rituals, after cleansing the body and spirit, she did enter the Divine energy, but these were exceptional situations. On a daily basis, despite her efforts, she could not do it at all.

"As the ancients used to say, everything has its time and place," said the High Priestess. "When the right moment comes, you will connect. You will call for her and she will appear. The power and skills that you received here may never reveal themselves fully, they may also strengthen your light gradually and slowly, or burst one day, all of a sudden, unexpectedly and with such force that you fall on your face."

"So everything is ahead of me," Mary summed up. "For now, I feel like a jar that had been filled for years, which turned out to contain not precious wine, but water. Transparent, clear, but only water nevertheless."

"You say only water?" the high priestess laughed. "Only? There is no life without water! And if we believe strongly, there comes a moment when water becomes excellent wine. That's how it can be with you. Turning water into wine, why not? We call such situations miracles."

Mary felt she was a priestess. She obtained the knowledge, skills and character traits she had always dreamed of. Her dreams of flying came true. She soared high, but she still was not satisfied. She was getting impatient. She would like to be like her mentors already, like the High Priestess, like a hemet. She would like to be wise, beautiful, lit up by the inner calm light. Her glow was already a little radiant, but she still didn't feel it was full. She was overwhelmed by anxiety and doubt whether this was what the world was proposing to her, what the white dove had promised, what she had strived for in recent years. The state she reached was beautiful, but she felt perfectly well that it wasn't the top. She still had capabilities to use. They did not even start to be used!

The High Priestess seemed to read her mind again.

"We want you to know something else," she said, penetrating Mary with her eyes again.

Mary looked at Aida. Both the hemet and her were staring at the High Priestess.

"You've been given signs. You have them in three places. They are stars," She drew the shape in the air with her finger. "One is on your hand and the other two on your feet. Know that this is very rare. They say that the person who is born with them is destined for unusual goals."

Mary knew about the star on her palm. She looked at it many times. But on the feet?

"Each of you was checked very carefully before entering the temple, remember?"

Mary remembered the tests, conversations and examinations from years ago, including the moment when she stood and then lay naked in front of Charmion on a special high table. At one point, the medic whispered something to her helper. A moment later, not only Charmion was bending over her, but also the High Priestess and Mistress Agnes, of whom she did not yet know that she was dealing with magic. They examined her body thoroughly. Perhaps they stopped longer by her feet? She didn't remember. The examination lasted so long that at some point she did not care anymore who and at what they were looking.

"We didn't tell you so that not to influence your attitude and your choices" Aida explained to her and feeling that maybe, as a grandmother, she should have told her, she added: "These are the rules. We don't want one's behavior to be determined by the awareness of the marks."

"So I have signs indicating that I'm chosen one, but no one can say what my destiny is?"

"It's the right of youth to be impatient. You will learn everything in due time. You have special marks, that's for sure. They predispose you. But marks alone, without your actions and the choice of the right path, are still just a suggestion. It's up to you how you make use of it."

The High Priestess nodded slowly. This meant that the meeting was over. The women knelt and touched the floor with their heads, thanking and honoring her. She made a threefold sign of the Goddess over them and then over Mary's head.

"You are a priestess marked with stars. The chosen one. This is a great commitment. Remember that. Go! Bring love to the world, be the keeper of light."

### 10.

"Your time on earth is limited," her grandfather hugged her tightly. "Like for all of us. Don't waste it. Don't get trapped in trying to meet the expectations of others, even if your sister or brother or even your father demands it. I know he is sick. I also know that he loves you very much. However, remember that the decision on the path you choose must be yours. Whatever you decide, be sure of it. And be careful in Galilee – you don't know this world. Listen to what people say, see how they live, what is important to them. Remember that they have only one god and everything is subordinated to him. Do not boast of being a priestess of Isis, they may not accept it. Get to know them, try to understand, but do not let the noise of their opinions drown out your inner voice. And most importantly, as before, always have the courage to follow your heart and premonition. Remember that you are a free human. Don't let anyone enslave you."

"Yes," her grandmother added. "Don't mute your inner voice. This is what we have tried to teach you. But also remember that following this voice does not mean that you have learned the absolute truth," she laughed. "Yes, my smarty pants!"

"I will remember that" she assured her.

"Sithathor, watch over my granddaughter, you are responsible for her!" her grandfather said to the most faithful guardian standing aside, who was to accompany Mary on the journey. "You are experienced and not a youngster, so I expect you to send me letters often, in case Mary could not do it for some reason."

"Yes, sir," Sithathor bowed her head.

"And one more thing..." Aida opened her purse. "I have something for you here," she spread a shawl made of thin, delicate but strong fabric before Mary. It was crimson.

"In the country you are going to, women cover their heads. It may thus be useful to you. Wear it.

"It's beautiful, thank you!" Mary threw the present over her shoulders.

"And scarlet is the color of power."

"I will wear it," she kissed Aida on both cheeks. She said goodbye to her grandparents, but at the same time she looked around. She expected to see Marcus. She hoped he would come to say goodbye to her. She sent him a message as soon as she decided to go to Israel. He should be here. She looked in all directions, convinced that she would see him at any moment. But he wasn't there.

They were standing on the waterfront in the port of Alexandria. Soon, in a moment, she was supposed to set off to go to her father. She said goodbye to her grandparents' Egypt, which was in fact the only world she knew and where she felt well. She was coming back to her roots, to the places of her childhood, remembered with great nostalgia. She was worried about her father's condition, excited about the journey, and saddened by the fact that Marcus was not with her. She hoped so much she would see him again. She missed him with the powerful force of the first love. She kept looking around.

Aida saw her searching eyes and understood her. She remembered the time when she was in love for the first time. The sleepless nights, constant waiting for the beloved and the signs of him thinking about her. Counting flower petals and the divinations whether and how much he loves her. Elations, swirls, butterflies in the stomach. She remembered her tears when she thought she had lost him. Fortunately, Karim became her husband, so she had her beloved with her, and when she thought about Mary, the experience told her that her granddaughter would not be with Marcus. And she didn't feel sorry about it at all.

Mary had the journey first by ship and then by land ahead of her. Her grandparents thought it would be the most convenient and fastest way, and it was necessary to hurry. The situation was an emergency. Almost immediately after her initiation in the temple, a message from Magdala arrived. It was concise. Delivered by pigeon, the most expensive but also the fastest way of communication in the world. Marta wrote that their father was very ill and she urged her sister to come home as soon as possible.

So she left almost immediately.

"Come back to us," her grandmother shouted when Mary was already on board, and the ship was departing from the shore.

"I love you!" she tried to shout over the sound of waves, with her eyes still searching Marcus, a scarlet scarf covered her shoulders.

# CHAPTER II

# THE LADY

## 1.

A huge red sun was setting on Lake Gennesaret. Mary looked at the first buildings of Magdala appearing in the distance. She was coming home. Sithathor, already very tired by the long journey, and a big, experienced guardian – a Greek named Ben – were with her. The Greek was chosen and paid for by her grandparents. He was to take care of their granddaughter's safety and deliver her safe and sound to Magdala. It was Ben who chose carriers and porters in Ptolemais.

They had enough stuff to transport. Crates, jute sacks and large saddlebags were placed on donkeys and carts pulled by mules. Everything was filled with clothes, shoes, cosmetics, colorful fabrics, small everyday items, and even three small rugs, papyrus rolls, treats and gifts that she brought for her family. There was also a large and comfortable basket for the cat because Leo was traveling with his lady. He had a collar set with small precious stones and a leash, previously useful when traveling by boat to Alexandria, and now necessary for the sea voyage. His basket, strapped to the back of a donkey, was padded with a soft pillow.

"Let's stop for a moment," she ordered Ben.

"Lady, your father's estate is already near," he protested. "If we hurry, we'll be there before it gets quite dark."

"You're right. Go," she agreed. "I'll stay here for a moment and will catch up with you later."

The donkeys and mules were heavily laden, so they rode slowly. Ptolemais was a port situated quite close to Magdala. If they traveled without load and on horseback, the road would take them several hours, instead, it was already the second day of their travel. Mary rode a horse, so even if she waited where she was standing now until the sunset, she would still get to Magdala before them. Ben knew that he would be able to keep an eye on her from the road leading to the city, so she was safe. He nodded in agreement and started off.

She watched them leave for a moment, then jumped to the ground. She stretched her arms. A sheet of lake stretched out before her. Many times in Egypt, thinking about her home, she wondered if the lake actually has the color she remembered. It turned out that it was so: its waters really shone with pure azure. Amazingly, the lake was calm now. There was no wind, so there were no waves for which it was famous. Nor did she notice a single boat. Fishermen had long come back from the morning fishing and it was still much time before the evening trip.

She had missed this sight. It was true that the lake seemed to her an endless sea once, but after all, she was just a child the last time she saw it. Now she had knowledge of the area it occupied and even how deep it was. During the lessons, when they talked about maps, she looked at this area especially carefully. She had one of the maps with her. Just in case she had to travel and she didn't have it at hand, she learned it by heart. So, she knew where the largest cities were in the homeland and at what distances they lie, where the roads lead, how the mountain ranges run and where Jordan flows. The maps may not have been extremely accurate, but thanks to them one could imagine what the world looked like.

She took a deep breath, spread her hands as if to fly. She liked to do it. Laughing, she spun around.

"I'm at home!" she called out.

She looked up at the sky. It seemed to her that high above she saw a white dove circling above her.

\* \* \*

Marta noticed a small caravan moving towards their property. She went out on the road. Her heart was beating strongly. She had been waiting for so many days. At the head of the group, she noticed two riders. She put her hand to her forehead to see better, and one of them then kicked his horse. Only travelers from outside of Galilee rode horses, most often the Romans. However, it wasn't them. The person who rushed the mount was a woman.

After a moment, she stopped right in front of her and jumped to the ground.

"Marta!" she embraced her, almost lifting her. "My dear!"

Marta was stunned and happy to see her sister, but she did not expect such a warm welcome from her. So, at first, she stiffened and moved away a little. Nobody had hugged her since the times when Mary lived in the house. However, after a while, when it turned out that the guest was not going to let her go, her body felt pleasant warmth and the stiffness of her muscles began to subside.

"Marta..." Mary sniffed and snuggled into her sister's neck.

She was crying. Her tears did not drip, they flowed in wide streams. Marta's shawl and dress absorbed them. Mary was still hugging her and sobbing. Finally, also Marta's eyes moistened, the tears flowed, and then a downpour came. She had not cried for many years, and when she began, moved by the fact that she felt her little sister by her side, she could not and did not want to stop. A lot of them had accumulated. Now, finally, after years of containment, they found an outlet.

They stood embraced, hugged tightly, and swayed slightly sideways. Just like in childhood. When they finally separated from each other, took a step back and saw their red faces and wet noses, they began to laugh.

"My little, my beloved..." Marta took her sister's hand. "Come on, you're home!"

Lazarus stood in the doorway

"You're an adult!" Mary exclaimed admiringly and embraced him.

"Not only adult but also married and with children!" he laughed. "This is my wife Ruth and these are our daughters. Rebecca, Judith, say hello to your aunt."

Behind him stood a short, quite stout, pretty woman. She held the hands of two little girls, who tried to hide behind her. She pulled them forward.

"Hello, Mary, I've heard a lot about you," she nodded in greeting.

"We're a family, let's hug each other!" Mary embraced her cordially, then crouched beside the girls. "Rebecca, Judith, I'm your aunt, my name is Mary."

They chuckled shyly.

"I feel that we will be friends."

She stood up, smiling radiantly at everyone who greeted her.

"Come, my dear, I will take you to our father," Marta took her hand. "He's been waiting for you eagerly."

"The others, people and luggage, are coming," she indicated to a caravan approaching the house.

"I'll take care of them," Lazarus assured her. "Go to your father."

They stopped at the door where Syro had formerly a workroom.

"I moved his bedroom here," Marta explained. "When it happened, he couldn't move. His arm and leg got paralyzed. He had big problems walking. Recently, he hardly gets up from bed anymore, he has no strength. Come on in, but remember that he gets nervous easily and tires quickly.

Marta opened the door and let her inside."

It was quite dark in the room. Thick curtains hung in the windows that once let so much sun in. A small lamp smoldered by the bed. The ill man was sleeping.

She sat on the edge of the bed. She looked at his emaciated, unshaven face. One could see even in the dark how pale he was.

He opened his eyes. "Mary?" he looked up in disbelief.

"Yes, father," she leaned forward and kissed his cheek. "I'm here..."

"How great. I've been waiting for you."

"I'm back."

"Permanently?"

She kissed him again.

"Right, I should have expected it," he looked away.

"Father, I haven't decided yet. I came, I am here. Let's enjoy the meeting," she stroked his slim hand. "I missed you so much," she added. "I missed you."

"I missed you too, but I decided not to disturb you in Egypt. If I came or buried you with letters, you could not fully and freely walk your path. You would be burdened with Israel even more than you are."

"I have Israel in my heart," she put her hand on her chest.

"Have you finished your studies?" he wanted to know everything as soon as possible. "Tell me!"

"I became a priestess of Isis," she confessed, knowing that it would not please him, but she preferred to say what was most important first.

"I thought it would go this way." She was afraid she would upset him, but he didn't seem too moved. "It is hard for a daughter and granddaughter of a priestess not to become one too. But you know, you shouldn't share this information here. They may not appreciate your achievements."

"Is that why my mother changed her name?"

"It is the place ruled by Adonai here. Supremely. There is no place for priestesses. Of any kind. Better remember it."

He didn't order. He said it with great concern.

"I have a wise, educated daughter," he laughed with effort. "What can I do? Apparently God wanted it that way."

"Apparently, father." She was glad that her arrival put him in a good mood and restored his strength, or perhaps added to it. "God wanted it that way, but it was thanks to you, father, that his will was realized."

"Help me get up!" he raised himself on a good elbow, and when he was sitting with the pillow under his back, he disposed, "My daughter has arrived! We will make a sumptuous dinner. Let's rejoice. Today I will get up, shave and dress. Lazarus! Marta!"

Mary knelt on the bed and embraced him. "Father, dear, I missed you so much," she confessed, and apparently she didn't cry out all her tears during her greeting with Marta, because they appeared again. "I love you!"

She snuggled into him, and he embraced her with his good hand.

"I love you, child."

When she finished kissing and stroking him, she opened the door wide.

"Marta, Lazarus, Ruth, children, come here!"

At her call, they appeared in the chamber almost immediately, and she announced with joy, "Father feels better. He decided to get up for dinner today!"

220

"Marta, manage what's necessary. Let them catch chickens. We will celebrate!" Syro exclaimed, trying to make his voice sound healthy and joyful.

* * *

Marta had been managing the kitchen and the whole house for years, and because she was prudent and practical, expecting Mary to arrive any day, she arranged with the shochet that when she calls for him to come kill the hens, he would also bring a previously salted shoulder of a young ox with him.

She knew it was her father's favorite dish, the preparation of which he always supervised himself. She remembered how he cared for every detail, and how after dinner, the revelers, merry with wine, danced and sang Jewish songs. She knew that he liked these memories. So, she wanted to surprise him without informing him about the main course.

Earlier, she also ordered to prepare wine. For children and women, it was diluted in a proportion of one part of wine per ten parts of water with the addition of honey and cinnamon. For men, three parts of water were added for one part of wine and cloth bags with thyme and mint were thrown into the amphoras.

* * *

Not many people ate at the tables in Galilee. To eat meals, people sat around the hearth. It was also not customary for women to eat with men. They prepared and served dishes, but sat down separately to eat them. It was different at Syro's home. Many of the old customs he had previously cultivated, changed since the time his wife appeared there, brought from abroad. But he could afford it. He was the wealthiest merchant in the area. He had the largest estate, he knew the world, and because he adhered to other most important daily principles of Halakhah; he determined himself what customs regarding the table should be followed in his own home.

When the household members and guests gathered around the table, the servants brought water bowls and linen towels. Everyone washed their hands. Then a tray of bread and a bowl of salt appeared on the table.

Throwing a handful of salt on the bread, Syro began, "Be blessed, Adonai, our God, king of the universe, who makes the earth bear bread."

The gathered lowered their heads. The dinner began.

Father broke the food and gave it to the banqueters. Marta could now gesture to the cooks to start serving dishes. A plate and a cup for wine were placed in front of everyone, and a tray with cucumbers and jugs with wine and oil appeared in the middle of the table. The aroma of garlic and young fennel filled the room. The cucumbers came from their own garden. They were picked two hours before dinner, carefully peeled, cut into eighths, sprinkled with a sauce made of chopped dill, salt, garlic and oil. They were perfect for soothing the heat of the passing day.

"Father, this is Sithathor, you must remember her. My teacher and guardian from Egypt," Mary decided that it was time to properly present her trusted guardian to the dinner participants. "I am grateful for her decision to accompany me."

Sithathor made a distinguished nod towards Syro and the other family members. She watched them carefully, especially Marta. She was exactly how she imagined her. Mary had always talked about her with admiration. So, Sithathor heard how beautiful, smart, good and resourceful she was. Later, when Syro was in Egypt, she learned that Marta was managing two properties, the one in Magdala and the other, smaller, in Bethany. Also, that she gave up getting married in order to look after her father and brother. She admired her at a distance. Now she had the opportunity to meet her, and after seeing her skillful actions, the restraint and rigor that she imposed on herself, her household members and the service, she was even more delighted with her. She thought she was similar to her. She preferred to be lonely, without a man, but independent. Professional in every word and gesture, a perfectionist, she liked her own well-organized world. It was clear to Sithathor that Marta, like her, had chosen the path fully consciously, and was very pleased with it. She would not exchange her refined, harmonious dignity for anything else.

"Sithathor is in our area for the first time." Syro was pleased with her arrival, in fact, from the moment he saw Mary by his side, he liked everything in the world. "It would be appropriate then to tell our guest something about our customs."

"I will be grateful," she appreciated his suggestion.

"I traveled a lot around the world and I know how important it is to know the customs of the place you come to, and yet Sithathor has never been here, and Mary left when she was a little girl, so she too can use a little reminder."

"Father, we are all ears." Mary guessed that Syro wanted to warn them, especially her, to be restrained and remember the strictness of local rules, and remind her of how much they differ from Egyptian ones.

"Well, as you probably know, we are God's chosen people. He gives us special protection, but, therefore, we have many obligations to him. They start already at birth. On the eighth day after his birth, a boy should be circumcised, this is a sign of joining the Jewish community. A woman who gave birth to a boy is unclean for seven days, one who gave birth to a girl, for 14. Adulthood begins for girls aged 12 and for boys 13 years old. From this point on, they must comply with Halakhah. It's our law. It regulates everything. It tells us how to pray, what and how to eat and how to treat others."

"It makes things a lot easier when the law regulates so many areas of life" Sithathor noted politely.

"Sometimes it's quite burdensome. You know that a Jewish man can't admire the beauty of women, talk to them in public, listen to them sing, can't even smell their perfumes?"

"I heard that homosexual relationships are banned."

"Homosexual? There is no such thing here. Everyone should have a wife and as many children as possible. Also, we don't talk about gender issues in public."

"Oh, I'm sorry."

"Attention, this is one of my favorite rules: it not allowed to resist your parents, embarrass them or, God forbid, call them by their names – this is unacceptable!"

"Of course," Mary smiled. "Nobody would dare to come up with such an idea."

"Everyone should pray three times a day and keep kosher. We only eat what is kosher."

224

"We have nothing but delicacies prepared for tonight, father. Of course, only kosher," Marta interjected, proud of what the cooks had prepared under her guidance.

"Your cucumbers are the best in the world," Mary praised her sister while eating another piece. "Just yummy, yum. Although I have to tell you that I learned from my Greek friends how to make similar things, but with thick sour milk. Excellent for hot weather."

"I know these. We also make it sometimes, but today we could not serve it, because according to kashrut, you cannot combine meat and dairy dishes, and we are going to eat meat in a moment."

"Interesting," Sithathor remarked politely again.

A proper upbringing dictated that when in a new place, one should listen carefully, smile, praise the culture of the place and the kitchen of the hostess. From time to time, but not too intrusively, one should also ask questions that the hosts could answer with pleasure.

"Milk and milk products, as the food derived from the mother, symbolize life," explained Syro.

"Meat symbolizes death. That is why Adonai forbade us to eat these products together. They are separated, as well as life and death, but both come from God, so they are good and needed."

As he spoke, the servants took the already empty cucumber tray. "Serve us the chickens," Syro ordered. Almost immediately, a large tray with meat and vegetables appeared on the table. Syro's eyes lit up.

"Marta, you know how to please me!" he cried, looking at the center of the tray.

An ox shoulder, stewed with aromatic vegetables, lay proudly among the pieces of chicken, arranged on the edges of the tray. It was Syro's favorite delicacy. Fennel tubers, whole onions, and salsify roots surrounded it. The whole dish was sprinkled with chopped coriander, pepper, and drizzled with wine vinegar.

Syro got up. He approached the tray and, despite his limitations resulting from the disease, he portioned the meat and distributed it to the revelers. His eyes were laughing.

"Daughter, you gave me a really nice surprise. After such delicacies I will be even healthier."

"Let it be so, father!" Marta was clearly pleased with the praise.

Everyone was delighted with the appearance, aroma, and soon also the taste of the dishes. There was silence because the revelers got busy eating. The excellent meat melted in the mouth, vegetables, which absorbed the sauce, also tasted delicious. Marta looked with joy at her beaming father and the content revelers, and he looked at her with pride.

Only these two knew that in order to obtain such a dish, you had to make a lot of effort in the kitchen. Marta remembered how often her father shouted at the cooks that they should make a shoulder with vegetables, not a shoulder soup. She was glad that her dish turned out excellent.

It was a double joy because she was also preparing a surprise for the next day.

Similarly to her father many times before, Marta added chicken's feet to the cauldron with meat and herbs over the hearth. They were not served on the table, however. The glue from the chicken feet intensified the taste of the sauce, and her father claimed that this dish increased body flexibility. However, the addition of chicken's feet to the cauldron in fact caused that meat leftovers from the feast, left overnight, stuck together in the bowls. If the dishes were previously greased, it was enough to turn them upside down the next day, knock them out onto a board or a plate, and a delicious dish was ready. When the jelly was covered with a sauce made from chopped young fennel, garlic, wine vinegar and olive oil, it was excellent on a hot day.

\* \* \*

Dinner was coming to an end. Fruits were brought in: melons, grapes and sycamore figs. When the cookies were served, the smell of cinnamon spread. Syro's favorite delicacy also appeared on the table: locusts baked on a stone in honey, salt and pepper. Their sweet-salty-spicy taste attracted even children.

When the crunching resounded, Mary got up from the table.

"And now it's time for presents. Can I, father?"

"Of course, gifts" he laughed, happy.

Finally, he had all his relatives with him, he felt better and ate an excellent dinner. Mary's arrival gave him strength and almost put him on his feet. He still had a problem with his hand, but he did manage to cut the meat, even though the day before he could not move either the upper or lower limb. He no longer felt the pain, bothering him so much before. True, Lazarus assisted him to the table, but he did not need any help with eating from Mary, who, as an honorable guest, sat on his right and was ready to support him at any time.

"I remember that you brought us gifts from every journey when we were kids," Lazarus sighed. "You've always remembered about us."

"Yes, Mary and I have always had the most beautiful fabrics for our outfits in Magdala," Marta added.

"Well, but you always wore gray and black anyway," Syro remarked almost reproachfully.

"I can see our father is indeed better because he is starting to tease me," she reciprocated a bit waspishly, but the atmosphere was so nice and she was so happy that her parent felt better, that she immediately caught herself and added gently, "As we all know, there are worlds where women in gray are safer."

Mary noticed that the conversation was entering a slippery slope. She didn't want to let that happen. At least not during the first celebratory dinner. She remembered as if through fog, that Marta was not submissive to her father as a child, and that she clearly and firmly communicated her opinions already then. Now Marta was a mature woman, her father was an elderly, sick man, and their relations did not change much. They teased each other, ran into small clashes, but they liked each other very much, they respected each other, and, most importantly, they loved each other.

"Now I'm back from a trip," she walked over to the chests she had ordered to put in the dining room against the wall, "and I have gifts. For everyone! Who wants gifts?"

Her joy infected the girls. They moved toward her, and when their grandfather nodded, letting them speak, they started jumping.

"Me, me!" they called one over the other and, when not stopped by their mother, they ran to Mary.

"Here's something for Rebecca," Mary took out from the chest an elongated, decorative sack, made of soft red fabric, and handed it to the girl. "And this is for you," she handed a wooden, beautifully decorated box to the older girl. They both sat on the floor and began to unpack the gifts.

After a while, Rebecca took a little man out of the elongated sack. Parts of his wooden body were connected by strings. You could move his head, arms, legs and even his torso.

"Is it a girl or a boy?" the small girl asked resolutely.

"It depends what name he gets," Mary explained, kneeling beside her. "Have a look, maybe there's something else in the sack?"

Rebecca reached deeper and took out a few pieces of small clothes. When she realized that they were the dresses for the wooden doll, she clapped her hands and jumped up in joy. She grabbed the gift and ran to her mother.

"Look what I got! Little wooden girl," she put the sack and the doll on her lap.

"A wonderful gift," said Ruth. "Say thank you to your aunt!"

The little girl ran to Mary and threw her arms around her neck.

"It is amazing what people can come up with," Syro shook his head in disbelief. "I've traveled a lot, but I've never seen such a cleverly constructed creature."

"Maybe you didn't pay attention to the dolls?" Lazarus excused his father.

The older girl looked at her sister's gift, and when the delight over the doll died down, she politely stated, "It's my turn now." After checking if everyone's attention was on her, she unpacked the box.

Judith looked similar to Lazarus. Like him, she was thin and had a long, rather serious face. She didn't talk much, but when she spoke, it was obvious that she was an intelligent girl who watched the world with a keen interest.

"What is this?" she was puzzled. She took small figurines in her little fingers to look at them closely.

"It's senet," Syro said. "Your aunts' favorite game. Mine too."

"Isn't it too early for her to play that?" Ruth worried.

"It's never too early for senet," Mary patted Judith on the head. "How old are you?"

"Almost six."

"Your aunt Mary won against me in senet when she was younger than you are now," Marta came closer to Judith and crouched down.

"Because in her kindness, Marta let me win," Mary laughed.

"Not at all!"

"But, aunt, we can make a deal that you let me win too, okay?" suggested the little one.

"Yes, you are right," Syro admitted. "Judging by what and how she says, she should quickly master the rules of the game. Maybe I'll teach her?"

The time had come for other gifts. Syro received a pitcher of an excellent drink from Aida and Karim. Lazarus got a scroll with Plato's writings, his wife a small box with fragrant body oils, and Marta a wonderful red shawl made of thin silk, and a few pieces of beautiful fabrics.

"Well, I heard you prefer gray dresses, but maybe it's time to change something?" Mary excused herself while handing presents to her sister. "Here, too, the world must open to women at some point."

"I wouldn't count on it too soon" Marta said sarcastically. "Centuries will pass, and we will still hide behind gray fabrics."

"Stop complaining already!" Father hit the table with his fist. "One independent woman in the house is enough."

"Marta, I'm back," Mary comforted her, kissing her father on the cheek. "Now we will bring women's rule here!" she laughed out loud.

"May you not have to learn that these are the matters not to be joked about here…"

Marta knew that only her younger sister could tease her father in this way. She also knew that Syro knew the world. He was everywhere and saw everything, and after all, he once chose a woman from Egypt, where colorful dresses are not only welcome, but they are commonly seen every day. He was the one who sent his little daughter to study at the "place of corruption," as the country on the Nile was called in Galilee, and he did it fully consciously.

"Okay," Mary summed up, "so Rebecca will dress her doll in colorful clothes, and we will start learning to play senet tomorrow, yes, Judith?"

"Why tomorrow?" The girl was surprised. "We can do it today! Grandpa promised."

"My blood!" Syro was happy. "We'll start today, you're right. Grandpa promised, so he will teach you."

"Can he teach me too, once he is at this?" Ruth pleaded.

"Lazarus didn't do it?" Syro was surprised. "What do you do in the evenings then?"

"I assure my father that we have a good time," Lazarus did not spare his father a rebuttal.

"Our world is ending," Syro concluded. "As soon as I got sick, the children talk back to me, my daughters and granddaughters play senet, even my daughter-in-law wants to learn. Furthermore, they want to wear some colorful inventions from a depraved world instead of gray, decent dresses!"

Everyone knew he was joking and lamenting, but he didn't really complain. He was happy and proud of his family. Finally, after a few months he spent in bed, the pain eased enough that he could stand up, sit, eat and even cut meat at dinner. He promised himself that if these were to be the last moments that God had given him in this world, he wanted to spend them with those he loved the most, and that if they hadn't felt it strong enough before, it was time for them to learn his feeling."

"And now something else," Mary called, asking for attention by raising her finger. "I want to introduce someone else to you."

Sithathor, who, unnoticed by anybody, left the company for a moment, stood next to her with a sizable basket.

"What do you got there, auntie?" Judith ran to her, and Rebecca followed her immediately.

"Attention, attention!" Mary grasped the lid of the basket, and when everyone was looking in her direction, she raised it.

Leo stuck his head out of the basket and looked around the room curiously.

"A little tiger!" Judith was delighted. Rebecca began to squeal with joy and jump.

"This is Leo, my cat" Mary explained. "I've had him for a long time. He's quite old already, but he's very lively, which you will certainly see many times."

Leo came out of the basket and studied the surroundings curiously. He had a collar with precious stones on his neck.

"You could probably buy half a village for the bauble on his neck," said Syro.

"It's a gift from Aida and Karim.

"And here the corrupt world of Egypt has arrived at our humble doorsteps," Syro laughed and picked up the goblet with wine.

"Cats are our friends," Sithathor said. "It has been like that for centuries. In Egypt, we love them, we consider them the holy messengers of the goddess Bastet. They live with us. They are members of our families. When they die, the owner shaves his eyebrows as a sign of mourning, and the animal's body is mummified."

"That's sacrilege," Marta was indignant.

"Let's call it an eccentricity of the minikin world," Syro softened what she said.

"A cat always knows our mood," Sithathor continued, undeterred. "He can find places that hurt, and lying on them, and often even massaging them, removes the inconvenience of our bodies. Besides, he is Bastet's eyes – the goddess looks at our world through them."

"Do you really believe that?" Marta did not give up.

"We really do, and we have for centuries. As you know, Egypt was built on magic," she joked, but no one laughed except Mary.

Syro took a sip of his wine and sank in his thoughts. He remembered Aset and the time when she stepped into this house to change his world forever. He remembered the cat who was with her then. Bastet disappeared when her owner left. One day she left the house and no one ever saw her again. Later he found out by accident that she was taken in by Joanna, the wife of Chuza, the steward of Herod Antipas.

Marta looked at her father closely. She imagined that Mary's cat might have brought back the memory of the animal belonging to his Egyptian wife. She watched his father's eyes glaze.

"Maybe you want to go to bed now?" she asked quietly.

2

Since the time half of Syro's body became paralyzed, the doctor visited him every few days. He studied and watched the changes taking place. He was worried. Things were not going in the right direction. The patient did not try to recover – he gave in to the divine judgment and waited passively for what would happen next. He didn't want to eat, he wasn't going to move unnecessarily. The medic encouraged him to exercise the paralyzed part of the body and make the associated effort, but he did not feel like it. Of the treatments that the doctor recommended, he only agreed to compresses made of heated bags filled with salt from the Dead Sea.

The situation changed after Mary's arrival. The patient regained a will to live, began to demand nutritious meals, got up from bed, leaning on his cane, walked around the house and garden. As promised, he taught his granddaughter to play senet and even to read. However, he did not have enough patience for this, and Judith, although very intelligent, did not match Mary from her childhood, so he abandoned this occupation. He even started exercising. He did gymnastics with Lazarus's help and allowed the doctor to massage sore places.

"I can see that the patient has decided to come back to life." The medic was happy to see Syro making a clear progress.

Mary talked to him in the garden. According to the Halakhah, a girl who was more than three years old, could not be alone with a man in a locked room. The same rule also applied to boys. Only the age was different – they could not be in a room with a person of the opposite sex since the time they turned nine years old. Mary knew this law, however, she invited the doctor to the garden not because of it, but because she did not want Syro to be present at their talk.

"Medic, what is wrong with my father?"

"God willing, he will live."

"Can you be more specific?"

He looked at her carefully. He decided that her directness and disrespect she had just shown him, was due to her foreign upbringing, so he did not comment on her rude words.

"Your father's body was out of balance. The blood began to flow faster in one half than in the other," he explained as simply as he could, trying to make her, as a woman, understand his words well.

He was convinced that she was thinking slowly, she did not understand what was being said to her, and if he gave her something too complicated, it would confuse her, and he wanted to avoid it. He knew how proud Syro was of her. He claimed that she was so smart that he managed to teach her how to read when she was five years old. The doctor pretended to believe it, because why should he hurt the feelings of his richest patient? He'd heard so much about her since his illness started, that he thought he knew her like his own daughter, whom he never had, by the way. He did have a son though, so he was very proud."

Now this famous Mary was standing before him. She was beautiful, which he noticed with pleasure. However, seeing her, he was even more convinced that since she had already received a gift from God in the form of beauty, she could not be wise as well. Such phenomena rarely go hand in hand, as he thought.

"As far as I know, a drooping corner of the mouth, a stiff neck, aching eyes, photophobia and paralysis of one side of the body mean that blood flooded his head, right?"

He looked at her in surprise.

"Yes."

"So it's good that he survived at all?"

"God was with him."

"It may happen again, right?"

"Why such knowledge in such a young person?"

"I studied a little." She remembered her father forbidding her to mention Philae and the priestesses to anyone. "I heard from various women. I like to listen to wiser people," she pointed at him and bowed her head.

He preferred to find her answer satisfactory, though it flashed through his mind that this girl was hiding something and that she had probably more knowledge than the little fragment she had just revealed.

"What herbs did you suggest for the blood treatment?" she asked innocently, blinking like a girl who wants to captivate an interlocutor.

He wasn't fooled, however. That was too much! "Blood treatment?" he was indignant. How can a young woman know such terms?

"Lady, with all due respect to you and those from whom you gathered your knowledge: I know what I do. My grandfather and father were medics and probably my son will be one, too. We don't reveal the secrets of our art."

"I just wanted to hear what herbs you use," she excused herself, wishing she had asked him the question. She didn't realize it would have such an effect on him.

"If I told everyone what medicine I use, I would soon have nothing to live on, because everyone would be able to heal themselves," he decided that it would be safest to close the issue with a joke.

He liked her. She was pretty and clever – a rare combination. She was the daughter of the wealthiest man in Magdala. He rubbed his hands at the thought appearing in his head.

She laughed. She decided that it was better to end the conversation before asking another, in her opinion, an innocent question, as a result of which the medic would see her as his competition.

She was so tempted to share with him the knowledge she had obtained from Charmion, to show him her trunk filled with medicines. To talk to him and find out his opinion. He was a wise man, after all, she was certain of that. Yet, at first, he treated her like a beautiful girl, and then, when it turned out that besides her appearance she had also something to say, he felt threatened.

* * *

"My father told me you knew about illnesses, lady," Samuel looked at her almost in the same way Marcus once did.

She knew that look. She saw it in many men. In Alexandria, in public places where she always showed up with her grandmother or Sithathor, they also looked at her this way. On the ship by which she sailed to Galilee, intense gazes accompanied her at every turn.

If it wasn't for the presence of the Greek, hired by her grandparents and guarding her, and Sithathor, who didn't leave her even for a moment, who knows if the things would stop with just glances. Sometimes she felt that they were sticking to her, that they were dragging her soul into some abyss. Sometimes they were pleasant, they carried admiration, but they all had something in common. Each time she felt like a tasty morsel they looked at with appetite, and which made their mouth water at the very thought of what it might taste like. At first, they embarrassed her, later she got used to them, and finally she stopped reacting to them at all.

Samuel looked at her with eyes full of curiosity and delight. They were not blue like Marcus's, but they shone and attracted with equal strength. Tall, slim, swarthy, he had black thick hair and long, delicate fingers. His robe was impeccably clean.

"I know" is an overstatement," she decided to investigate who she was dealing with. "I heard a bit, I saw a bit. And now, above all, I'm worried about my father. I try to support him in his illness, so I would like to know as much as possible about it. Your father, sir, has been a medic for generations, he has great knowledge. You too, probably. Have you accompanied him in practice for a long time?"

"Since forever." He was flattered that she was interested. Like most people, he liked to talk about himself.

"Have you received an education somewhere or do you draw from a rich family treasury?"

"I draw from the treasury?" He laughed. "It's exactly how you said, I draw from the treasury. You speak well. Your language is so..." he was looking for the right word "...refined."

"Thank you."

She didn't want to explain that she had been learning it by reading the Torah in the evenings. She knew it was restricted for men only. She decided that maybe it wouldn't make him happy. Besides, even though she felt a kindred soul in him, they did not know each other long enough for her to reveal such secrets to him."

"I heard you came back from the world. Where have you been if I may ask?"

"As you know, I'm the daughter of a merchant."

"There's not a wealthier one in Magdala."

"Maybe so. For me it meant that I traveled a bit in the footsteps of my father."

"It sounds mysterious."

"I think everyone here knows my mother was from Egypt?"

"So they say."

"Exactly. So, I spent the last years right there at my grandparents' house. That was my mother's last will."

"You soaked in that world," he said. "You look and speak differently from the women from here."

"But I assure you that I feel local."

"That's good."

"Because?"

"Because..." he hesitated if he could say what he intended at their first meeting "...because my father thinks you would be a good wife for a medic."

"Your father is looking for a wife?" She pretended not to understand what he was talking about.

"Well, maybe I didn't make it clear enough: my father thinks you would be an excellent wife for," he emphasized the word he was going to say by lifting his finger, "a future doctor."

"Oh I see!" she laughed. "You know your father saw me only once in his life?"

"But he likes you very much.

"I guess so do you?" she crossed her arms flirtatiously.

She was a priestess of Isis, she knew how to enchant the interlocutors.

"I admit you are intriguing. And as I said, quite different from the women around."

"I understand that due to my father's illness, and the fact that I am different from the women you know, you will be a frequent visitor here?"

"If only you allow me."

He was stunned by her directness. He had never seen such an attitude in any woman.

"I will be glad to have you as a guest. Of course, if it is in accordance with local customs, which I have not yet fully learned."

\* \* \*

She was thinking about Marcus. She missed him. "How beautiful a longing can be when you have someone to long for," she sighed. She wondered where he was and what he was doing. Whom he met, what was filling his days. Why didn't he give a sign of life? It had been almost four months since she learned that she had to go to Galilee as soon as possible, and he was still silent. He had to know what was happening to her because she sent him a long letter before the expedition. He wasn't in the port of Alexandria when she left, and she had been counting on it so much. She was worried that something happened to him. Maybe he was sick in bed, or got injured in a battle, and she didn't know it? Maybe something terrible happened in his life, and she didn't support him?

When she was falling asleep in her father's former bedroom, which she occupied upon arrival in Magdala, she thought about her beloved. Is it possible that he would forget about her? Did the oaths of eternal love they made to each other, mean nothing? Were his words that she was the woman of his life, and he would never love any other, not true? She knew it was not so. She loved him and he loved her. She felt with all her heart that what had united them was real. So, what happened that made him silent?

At the same time, the words of the old woman from the inn still crept in and came back to her mind like an echo: "Your first wife will die," "You are the chosen one," "You have wings." The other ones, warning him not to love a woman who... She chased them away, but they kept coming back persistently.

* * *

"Where do you keep the fabrics I brought you?" Mary entered her sister's chamber.

Not much has changed there since they lived together as girls. If you put her baby bed back in, everything would look like it used to be. "Sithathor can sew very well. She could make new dresses for you," she sat next to her.

Marta was checking the calculation of home expenses. She made lines, combined them into tens and these into hundreds. She added, subtracted, multiplied. When she heard Mary, she put the stylus down.

"I put them away. They are here," she went to the trunk standing by the wall.

"I'll help you open it," Mary held the heavy lid.

The chest was hiding real treasures.

"Wow! You have all kinds of treasure here!"

"Things pile up over the years..."

Mary knelt, began to extract the contents and lay it on the floor. There was a lot of it: scarves, fabrics, dresses, jewelry, and even exquisitely decorated sandals, purses and boxes and bottles of bizarre shapes.

"Where is it from?"

"Our father brought presents from his travels. And since your mother's treasures are also here, the chest is full of precious things."

"You don't use it at all!" Mary was not only surprised but almost outraged. "What are you waiting for?"

"Where could I use it? Where should I go in dresses made of the best fabrics? When to wear necklaces, bracelets and earrings? Or golden sandals? Well, tell me? When I go to the market with a maid, or when I tend to the garden? Or maybe when I meet women in Magdala? Or maybe when I massage my father's paralyzed leg?"

"Yes," Mary interrupted her.

"Yes, what?"

"Yes. You have to put on beautiful dresses for each of these occasions!"

"Stop making jokes. It is cruel!"

"They are for you, not you for them. Don't wait for better, more suitable opportunities. They may never come. Take advantage of what you have. Put on the beautiful clothes, golden sandals, wear jewelry. Why not?"

"Because it is different from where you grew up. You don't understand this reality. It's harsh. And gray. Just like me."

She sat on the floor next to her sister.

"A distant, beautiful world is closed in this trunk. Your mother belonged to it. You are from there too."

Mary embraced her.

"Your mother was like a noble, colorful butterfly. Do you know she was the first person to say "my beloved" to me? You are the second one. Mine never addressed me that way, and I am like her. You are very much like Eucharia."

"Do you know her real name was Aset?"

"I know. I promised her I would never reveal her name to anyone. She asked me not to. Father and her knew how she would be treated if people knew her background. Here people are ruthless. You're lucky you lived in Egypt."

"Marta, I am a priestess of Isis," she brushed the hair back from her neck and pointed to the place where she had the tattooed mark. "I want you to know that."

"Your mother had the same mark and in the same place, so she almost always wore her hair loose. She was so beautiful and good. She loved the whole world, you know? And the world loved her. She had peace and strength in her as if she were sure she was on the right path. That's how I remembered her. I cried a lot when she left. I felt like I was alone in the world."

"Nobody hugged you or comforted you, right, my love?" Mary understood her pain.

"I had only you. But you were so tiny. A defenseless crumble. And also all alone."

"Thank you for taking care of me. You were like a mother to me."

They swayed in one rhythm and cried.

"My beloved, brave Marta," Mary whispered in her ear. "My wonderful, wonderful little sister. My little one."

She cuddled her, wanting to reward her for the lonely childhood, the maturity forced by the circumstances, her father's severity and lack of interest. She wanted to thank her for the love she gave her, the care, attention and heart. For the fact that she devoted her own childhood for taking care of her and taking over the role of a mother. And she was only 10 years old.

"Can I interrupt?" Sithathor asked timidly, opening the door slightly. "I knocked, but you probably didn't hear me."

Mary reached out to her.

"Oh, we just like to cry," she joked through her tears. "You can join us, you are welcome!"

Marta rose from the floor and adjusted her dress.

"We checked the contents of the chest and the childhood memories came back," she excused herself.

"I understand," Sithathor reassured her. "I'm a woman too. I can imagine, Marta, how hard it was for you when you took on so many household chores as a girl. I admire you."

"Stop it!" she protested. "I'm not used to it. Nobody has told me more nice and touching words in the last 15 years than you in recent days. I feel embarrassed."

"You can handle it!" Mary kissed her.

"I see you found a lot of treasures in your trunk!" Sithathor reached for one of the dresses on the floor.

"It's quite a pile."

"You have to start using it. And as soon as possible!" Sithathor looked through the things on the floor. "I can even see a men's tunic from byssus! Wow! A real wealth."

"Is that byssus?" Mary asked. "I saw similar at a reception in Cleopatra's palace. Dignitaries wore them. Those who know this stuff, know how much they are worth."

"You have been to Cleopatra's palace?" Marta's eyes were quite dry already.

"Yes, it happened a couple of times. But let me tell you, the trails of the queen are long gone."

"I can guess how much new stuff you have experienced in these years."

"We'll have a lot of time for stories."

"I have your word! And I'm glad you know what byssus is. Because, as you can see, we have it, but to be honest, I wouldn't suspect it is as valuable as you say. Just a simple men's long tunic, only extremely pleasant to the touch. It is obvious that this is not a simple canvas. Probably that's why it lies in this chest among other valuables," she explained to herself."

"The byssus is the most precious cloth in the world," Sithathor explained. "It is made from threads produced by sea mussels."

"Something that lives in the sea produces threads? Incredible!"

"Yes. This fabric can survive eternity."

"Let's give it to father as soon as possible," Mary decided.

"Your father undoubtedly knows what this cloth is and how much it is worth," Sithathor told them. "I'm sorry to say that, but maybe he prepared it for his last journey? Offer it to him particularly gently. He is in serious condition, you never know how he can react to such a gift."

"I'll do it" Mary decided. "I'll bring it to him right away."

She took the dress in her hand, "What if he doesn't want it? He knows about its existence; he would wear it if he wanted to. He is the one who once bought it," Marta wondered.

"If he doesn't want it, then I feel that when the time comes, there will be someone who will be equally worthy," Mary hugged the fabric to her heart.

Then something strange happened. She screamed. She felt a shock. It was so strong that she slumped to the floor. Falling, she pressed the dress to her chest. She closed her eyes, and a worrisome, heavy, despairing thought crossed her head. It concerned the coming death. It was so painful that she felt a stab in her heart. It announced something violent and powerful that would shake the earth.

She froze. She knew it was a vision. This was how the priestesses described the moment when it appeared. She experienced it so clearly for the first time. She understood that what had happened to her before and what she hopefully called visions, did not remind them at all. Those could only be premonitions. Now she felt a huge buzzing in her head, then a flash, and immediately after it, more images, as if illuminated by lightning. She saw a man in a long byssus tunic. His hands were raised. His face was lit with such brightness that she could not see its features. She only saw the figure. He was reaching out to heaven...as if he were asking for something? As if he were giving in to something? At the same time, he triumphed. She felt great anxiety associated with this vision. She was trembling. She stopped breathing.

When she opened her eyes and her breath came back, she had no doubt that she saw something that was about to happen in the near future. In fact, she sensed rather than saw it, because it was more like the anxiety of her heart than a specific image. She understood that the one she had seen would play a significant role in her life. She did not know who he was, she did not suspect what would connect him with her, but her heart already sensed it. She was crying.

\* \* \*

Rabbi Yitzhak rarely paid visits. Those who wanted to seek his advice or asked for his blessing most often came to the synagogue, and in an emergency - to his home. However, he did not hesitate to make an exception for ill Syro. The merchant constantly supported the synagogue and the community, made generous sacrifices whenever he could, studied the Torah together with others, and celebrated holidays and festivities in accordance with the principles of Halakhah. He was a good Jew. Rabbi Yitzhak liked to talk to him. Syro knew the world and people, he had been in many places, he had seen a lot in his life. He could have moved to some other place long ago, more dignified and richer, where, perhaps, it would be easier for him to live. But he chose Magdala. He used to say that he came to this world here, and he wants to leave it here. Rabbi appreciated what Syro did for the commune.

When he became ill, Yitzhak immediately visited him. It saddened him that such a respectable man was already preparing to go to the other side. He would prefer to have him around for a long time; he worked well with him. *"The Lord works in mysterious ways,"* he thought. "What is meant to be, will be."

When the news that his daughter had returned home and that it had put Syro on his feet spread around Magdala, the rabbi decided to visit him again. He wanted to see the one who was said to look and act like a foreigner, attract men's eyes, dress shamelessly, have a cat wearing a golden collar, and who came to her father with a huge caravan, riding a horse at its head and bringing such great gifts that they grew in the stories to almost the size of the gifts that the Queen of Sheba once gave to Solomon.

Yitzhak went to Syro's house in the company of his son David. The boy was already 20 years old. He was smart. He read books and studied with the scribes of Jerusalem. He knew the

Pentateuch almost by heart. He could listen carefully, but also discuss. He was thoughtful, diligent, and followed the divine words carefully. Yitzhak believed that with the help of the Most High, his son would someday become a rabbi like him. David knew Syro, Lazarus and Marta, and on a couple of occasions, he even had a dispute with Lazarus about the wisdom of the Book. However, the age difference, the frequent illnesses of Lazarus, and later his marriage and moving to Bethany, to his father's estate, meant that their acquaintance did not develop into a friendship. Yitzhak regretted this a little because he thought that children of the wise and wealthy should be in touch with each other. Because as they would someday replace their parents in this world, it would be good for them to form bonds at youth to be useful in later life. Being wise and wealthy is a gift from God, the rabbi believed. If you already have this gift, you also have obligations to God and the community, to those who are in a worse and tougher situation. While being together, and feeling the support of other strong and generously gifted people, you can do much more for the good of the world than by acting alone.

"Rabbi, you know Marta and Lazarus well. And you've already met Ruth and her daughters," Syro greeted him in the garden. "And this is my youngest, Mary."

As was the local custom, she bowed her head modestly and waited for her father to tell her to come over. She intended to follow the rigid Jewish principles to please him, and not to hurt the rest of the family.

"Mary, welcome to our land," Rabbi nodded at her.

She looked at her father like a well-behaved daughter, waiting for his consent. When he confirmed, gladly appreciating her efforts, she slowly approached the rabbi, still without looking up.

Yitzhak looked at her approvingly. She was pretty like the world was. He was not surprised that she attracted men's eyes and raised anxiety among women. But wasn't it God's intention to give such a beautiful creature to the world? Undoubtedly, this young woman was a wonderful gift of the Supreme to her father, family and their whole community. Maybe she wasn't perfectly properly dressed, her colorful dress and scarlet shawl had to be a challenge for local women, but what does the outfit matter? Out of everything we have, it is the easiest thing to change.

"Mary, child, you're at home. God bless you," he raised his hand and she bowed even lower, accepting the blessing. "Be a joy to your sick father and all of us."

She bowed again and returned without a word to a place behind her father, where she had stood before.

"And this is David, my son, the pride and comfort of my old heart," he gestured at the tall young man standing a few steps behind him.

"Please, have a seat," Syro, leaning on his cane, showed places to the guests.

After the rabbi sat down, the other men did the same. The women were standing, as was customary, ready to leave.

"You can go now," Syro turned his head in their direction, but his eyes thanked mostly Mary.

He appreciated her effort. He knew that she was so restrained mostly because of her respect and love for him.

After a short but nice conversation, the rabbi was saying goodbye to Syro:

"I'm glad that I found you in better health and that I could meet your daughter. Let her be a comfort for you. Someone like her certainly gives joy to her father's heart. It's good that she came back to us. I'm leaving now, but God just inspired me that I should talk to her and give her some tips. What do you think?"

"I would be grateful, rabbi, if you would like to treat her like your own child."

"You're right, Syro, after all, all the children are ours," the old man stroked his long beard.

"Your Mary is quite pretty. I am thinking, you know, just to myself, that if God allowed, maybe your daughter and my son...?"

He looked meaningfully at David.

"Who among us knows the Lord's intentions?" Syro immediately understood what was going on, he did not intend to ruin the rabbi's dreams, but he also did not see his son as his son-in-law.

He was hoping for someone in a much higher position. He promised himself that as soon as he would get better, he would go to Jerusalem on this matter, for he already had several ideas about the direction of these things. He knew that his daughter was at the age when the queue of candidates was to be expected, and as at the same time she was beautiful and had a significant dowry, he imagined what a tempting catch she would be.

"I spoke to your father, child," the rabbi began after she bowed again, summoned by Syro. "You haven't been here for many years. You grew up outside the home in a different culture and customs. Because of the friendship and respect I have for your father, and because you belong to our municipality, I have advice for you. A father's advice. If I had a daughter, I would talk to her with the same care as with you now."

She stood in front of him, head bowed, and listened to his words as commanded by tradition. Next to her sat her father, brother and the Rabbi's son. She wondered what she would hear.

"A parrot is a beautiful animal. Colorful, eye-catching... People look at her with pleasure. They love her. Some people are worried about her appearance, because, you will admit that she is quite unusual. But this is how the Lord created it. People are wondering: "What is the parrot for? This is not a useful bird." And if someone has her at home for some reason, they keep her in her cage or cut her wings so that she doesn't fly away.

She guessed what he was getting at, but she wasn't outraged. She was amused by his argument. She knew the ending, but she listened to his words to the end with her head lowered humbly.

"Other birds, the gray ones, fly freely without restrictions. They make nests, have babies, sing and fly at will for the Lord's glory. They do not attract anyone with the color of their feathers, they are happy and safe. Nobody thinks about cutting their wings or locking them in a cage. Our women are like these gray birds. Modest, almost invisible, not conspicuous. We have our rules here, and obey God's law. We are God-fearing and modest, and colorful clothes disturb us. Mary, you came from a country where life is different than here. Out of respect for your father, whom you love, and the family you have here, adapt to us. Don't mess with our women's heads. Be one of us. Put on a gray dress, like your sister Marta. And replace the scarlet shawl with a more subdued one."

\* \* \*

"I don't think I will fill at home in this place," Sithathor decided. "It's not my world, lady. I am here with you so that you would not feel lonely. I am glad that I could support you during the first months of your stay in the family home, but I want to return to Egypt now. I feel like I wither here, I'm a stranger. I don't want to change my habits and customs. I do not intend to convert to Judaism, I want to be able to worship the Goddess freely and wear colorful dresses."

"Have you heard the rabbi?" Mary guessed.

"I admire you for listening humbly to what he had to say."

"He said it out of kindness" Mary assured her. "At first I was indignant at what I heard, later amused, but it finally realized where I really am. Neither the rabbi nor anyone in my family is guilty for living here."

"Mary, you can always come back home, to Egypt, at any time." Sithathor knelt in front of her and put her head in her lap. "Dear child, you know I watched you grow up. I was with you when you became a woman. I watched your development. I cried when you became a priestess. You are wise and sensitive and Egypt is your world. You'll be really free there. Rabbi is right, they'll cut your wings here or put you in a cage. Get out of here as soon as possible. Run away. This country is not friendly for women like you. You are unique!"

"I'll be here while my father is alive. It's my duty to him. And whatever happens, I won't change my mind. When he leaves, and I want him to be with us as long as possible, then I will think what to do next." She gave Sithathor a hand, helping him to her feet. "I understand your decision. It's a difficult place for women like us. I am grateful that you are with me, that you help me and that I really have support in you. You know what?"

"Yes?"

"I think you are the only person in this house who understands me fully."

"They all support you."

"Yes, but only you really know what life I lived before and who I am."

"Leo knows that too," Sithathor laughed.

"Right. How could I forget about him?"

\* \* \*

"Mary, Mary!" Marta's scream was heard early in the morning. It was coming from their father's chamber.

At dawn, Marta came to him with breakfast, as she did every morning. She found him dead. According to the medic who arrived quickly, death occurred at night and was immediate.

The deceased's children closed his eyes and mouth and laid the last kiss on his forehead. Windows and mirrors throughout

255

the house were covered with dark cloths. The body was washed and anointed with fragrant oils, and the smell of myrrh and aloe vera spread throughout the house. It was wrapped in a funeral sheet filled with aromatic herbs, the face was covered with a scented cloth. The law dictated that he would be buried as soon as possible, preferably on the same day.

Syro's funeral was held according to the eternal principles. After a short vigil at the corpse, the body was placed on a funeral stretcher, which was carried by friends and relatives of the deceased. Women always walked first in a mourning procession. After all, they were the daughters of Eve, because of whom people were banished from paradise, and death appeared in the world. Marta and Mary, and with them, Ruth and her daughters, walked solemnly after the stretcher, weeping, in mourning black robes. They were followed by women from the city, among them the weeping women, rented and well-paid. They wailed and, as was customary, tore their clothes, uniting in pain with the family and friends of the deceased. The male part of the conduct was led by Lazarus. As the customs dictated, he had his head and cheeks carefully shaved as a sign of mourning. Musicians followed the men.

After laying Syro's body into a rock cave and closing it with a large flat stone, Lazarus invited mourners home to treat them with lechem oni, or a bread of the crying, and wine diluted with water.

"Nothing holds you here now." Sithathor stood in Mary's chamber.

Syro's death and funeral delayed her trip.

"Will you come home with me?"

Mary was sitting by the window, in a dark dress and with her head covered. She had hardly left her chamber since her father's funeral.

"Sithathor, I feel my home is here too."

"Of course, my dear, it is."

"I want to stay here a bit more. I do not know how long. But now I am not able to think about travel or Egypt. I feel bad, I feel depressed. I was hoping that my father would recover. He felt so well already."

"Where he is now, there is no pain. He is happy."

"I don't know where he was taken. And whether Sheol is a land of happiness. According to Jews, the souls are waiting for the coming of the Messiah there. It is only when the Messiah appears on earth that the closed gates of paradise will part, so that he will be able to take them there."

"I don't know their religion. But thinking about what you said now, I would like to know why the gates of paradise were closed.

"Because Adam and Eve committed a serious sin. They ate the fruit of the Forbidden Tree. As a punishment, God banished them from there and ordered them to live in hard work, toil and pain."

"Is this a tree of life like ours? With all the past and future written on it?"

"Something like that."

"Well, regardless of the reason, I understand that after death their souls are waiting in Sheol for the coming of the Messiah?"

"Exactly. The Jews are waiting for the coming of the Messiah, thanks to whom they will be able to renew the covenant with God and the gates of paradise will be opened for them again."

"Well, I know that. In short, everyone alive and dead are waiting for the chosen one to come, right?"

"Yes."

"Great. I hope he won't make them wait too long" she joked. "Seriously, I am convinced that your father is really well where he is now."

"May it be so, my dear," Mary appreciated Sithathor's words, but she also understood how much effort it was for her to function in Magdala. "I know you wanted to leave earlier already, but the ceremony held you back. Thank you for staying with me."

"I can't imagine leaving you in this situation. Forgive me for leaving you now, but I really miss Egypt."

"Go and may the Goddess guide you." Mary stood up and bowed to Isis three times, touching her forehead, lips and heart.

Sithathor did the same, then hugged her tightly. "Mary, don't reveal your sign to anyone. I am begging you very much. Do not show the ring, do not bow to the Goddess when you are among them. She is in your heart, she will not be angry that you are praying to her in silence. This is the only chance for you to function peacefully. And when the right time comes, come back to Egypt. Your place is there."

### 3.

A month had passed since Syro's death. Lazarus and his family decided to return to Bethany. Their house was there - they began to live in it right after the wedding. The small property had belonged to the family for a long time, but apart from Syro, anyone else from the family was rarely there. The house was managed from a distance by Marta, who came there about once a month and stayed for several days. Many years earlier, when Lazarus got married, their father decided that it would be better if the young couple lived there. His son would be able to work independently, and Ruth would prove herself as the housewife.

During their father's illness and after his death, Lazarus and Ruth and their daughters stayed in Magdala. However, when the first period of mourning was over, they decided to go back home together, and Mary went with them.

Bethany was close to Jerusalem. The city gates were five miles away. There were not many houses, but all were built of stone and looked solid. Most of them had presses for olive oil and grapes, some also had ritual bathhouses. The houses usually had an internal courtyard, surrounded on one side by the owner's home, and on the other by servants' flats and utility rooms.

Mary hardly remembered Bethany at all. Lazarus convinced her that as a child she had visited it twice, but it was only when they got there that she really realized she must have been there

259

earlier. She recognized the house; the wine press, carved in the rocky ground and connected through the juice draining channels to the lower reservoir, also seemed familiar to her. She even thought she remembered the huge clay jugs closed with clay plugs. There was always a small hole left in them, through which the smells of the forming wine came out.

"Oh, there's a garden, trees and benches are still in the same place!" She cried with joy at some point.

"This you can't remember" Lazarus laughed. "When you were little, those trees were not here yet. I also ordered a bench to be placed here. Quite recently."

However, it seemed to her that she knew the garden. That she had seen it somewhere. That she embraced these trees and had been sitting in their shadow before. Furthermore, she remembered someone else's presence there. Someone she loved very much. Who could it be? Or maybe she had once dreamed about this place? And this someone? Or maybe what she felt about the garden was not about memories, but about the future? She asked herself a lot of questions that she couldn't answer. Regardless of where she saw these trees or this garden, she was sure she knew them.

Ruth and the girls collected fruit and prepared them for drying. They were sitting in the cool air of the main chamber of the house.

"Sometimes, when I'm sick, a man I know visits me," said Lazarus. "Basically a friend. Good one. He sits here with me and we talk. He is smart. He knows politics and looks prudently at the future. As if he knew everything that could happen. I value him very much."

"It is good you have someone like that."

"He is outside of the political disputes. He gives the impression of looking from above on what is happening around as if he were above it all. He knows a lot about Pharisees and discusses their views. He does not agree with many Sadducees' views."

"Maybe he's the Essene from Qumran?"

"Sister, you have been out of the country for so long and you know such things?"

"I was interested in what was going on here. I'm from here after all."

"But you're a woman!"

"Come on…"

"I'm sorry," he excused himself. "I keep forgetting."

"I am like everyone else, except that I was given the opportunity to learn."

"Mary, women generally have weaker minds and are unable to comprehend politics."

"Lazarus, you are my brother and you say such absurdities! If the boys didn't have the opportunity to read the Torah, participate in debates and talk about politics, do you think they would know anything? Give women the opportunity to learn and you will see what will happen."

"The world will end?" he joked, knowing full well that Mary was right.

"Yes, indeed, a world of some kind will end. The one where some can learn and others cannot, where some have rights while the voice of others is not taken into account even in court."

"They put silly stuff in your mind in this Egypt, sister."

"Lazarus, a woman here can't even talk to a man!"

"I'll tell you something: my friend thinks that men and women are made of the same clay. When he visits me, he talks to Ruth and even to the girls. You'd be surprised how open he is in this regard. He has peace, harmony and warmth about himself. When he is here, I recover."

"Is he a medic?"

"No."

"A priest?"

"No."

"Who is he then?"

"He says he's waiting for a sign. A signal from above. And that he will then start to fulfill his mission."

"He is a mysterious man."

"Unusual."

"I'm glad you have such a friend."

"I hope you'll meet him someday."

"If he has such a positive influence on my beloved brother, there is no other way. Our paths will surely cross one day." She picked up a white pen lying on the chest of drawers, standing by the long wall.

"It's from him. He left it for me when he was here last time, " she brushed her lips with the pen and felt trembling internal anxiety and expectation. "Search for signs" the words of priestess Agnes appeared in her head, "They will direct you to the right path."

"What was that?" she wondered. It was the second time in the recent period that she felt something strange. A heart flutter, some indefinite fear? Longing? A forecast of something that was to come? She felt that her state was related to the man her brother was talking about.

"What's his name?"

"Jesus."

\* \* \*

Mary stayed with Lazarus for almost a month.

When she returned to Magdala, Marta went there. She had not been to Bethany throughout her father's illness, so she wanted to go there and see what the estate looked like after her long absence. She also intended to look at how Lazarus was dealing with the bills. Although her brother had long been an adult and had a wife, with whom they ran a house in Bethany, she still helped them, supported them not only with advice but often with money, because Lazarus was not the most resourceful of men.

In Marta's absence, an unexpected guest came to Magdala.

Mary was in the garden when she heard the sound of approaching horses. A moment later, five Roman soldiers stopped in front of the gate.

"Lucius?" The rider in front, hid beautiful images she recognized a companion of the happy expeditions in Alexandria, one of Marcus's closest friends.

Hardly believing her eyes, she ran to him.

"Is it really you?" She happily grabbed the bridle of his horse.

He jumped to the ground. They embraced each other and hugged like old friends.

"They are my subordinates" he introduced the other men, saying their names. "We are stationed in Nazareth, but now, as you can see, we're on a patrol. My other soldiers are touring around the lake. I decided to visit Magdala."

"You must all be thirsty," she guessed. "I invite you in!"

Lucius's subordinates were hosted in the garden, and he followed Mary home.

"How come you became a soldier?" she asked as they sat down and drinks and snacks appeared on the low tables.

"My father gave me an ultimatum: I'm getting married or I'm starting a career in the army?

"You really preferred the army?"

"If you saw who he wanted to marry me with..." He shook in disgust. "I assure you that in my place, you would choose an army, too."

She thought he might not be telling her the whole truth, but she did not care, it was so good to talk to him! She felt as if the old days had returned, and she was again sitting in the reception room in her grandparents' estate on the Nile, or in one of Alexandria's wealthy homes. She was a lady. Beautifully dressed, laughing, distinguished. She could talk freely about almost all topics, she didn't have to keep her head down and pretend she had no face. She could look the interlocutor in the eye and enjoy his interest, discreet and not obtrusive, but not concealed either. Thanks to Lucius, she was in her world again for a moment. She was breathing deeply. She played with words, teased wittily, she was not afraid to demonstrate her femininity.

They remembered past times, Alexandria, night expeditions in disguise, trips to temples, games, races and everything that they enjoyed until recently.

"I've lived here for only a few months, and sometimes I have the feeling that this never happened" she confessed. "As if that world existed only in my imagination."

"Are you all alone here?"

"Sithathor, my guardian, was here, I don't know if you remember her, but she wasn't awed by Galilee. She left almost immediately after my father's death. I am grateful to her for supporting me for so long."

"She left, you stayed. How are you doing?"

"I have the cat" she joked, but it sounded so sad that when she realized that, she could barely hold back her tears.

"If it's so bad, why are you still here?"

"That's a good question." She took a date in her fingers. "I do not know. I feel like I'm waiting for something. I feel suspense as if something important was about to happen and that's why I should be here."

"A premonition, yes?"

"Something like that."

She was surprised that she had not thought about it before. There was anxiety in her, a tense anticipation, but of what? She didn't know. She was sure she should be on guard right here, in Galilee.

"I like it here at your place. You have a beautiful house, I, wouldn't expect something like it here. It is great to talk to you and would like to stay longer, but duty calls. I've always liked you very much, but, well... you preferred Marcus."

"Right... Marcus. Do you know how he is doing?"

"To tell you the truth, I came here partly because of him."

"Oh yes?"

"I have a letter for you. He knows you're here, and as he has a friend who has been an officer in Galilee for almost a month, he decided to use me as a messenger. This has come recently." He took out a small roll. "It's a mail from Rome."

"From Rome?"

"He's there now. He probably explained everything to you in the letter." He stood up, "I must go now. Thanks again for the warm welcome."

"Will you visit me again?" she asked, thinking only of what the letter might contain now.

266

He seemed to be waiting for this question.

"With pleasure. In a few days?"

"'Sure!"

"Won't this be a problem for you? The local customs are quite strict."

"Well, at worst, no local boy will want me for his wife," she walked him to the gate.

She waited for him to get on the horse and leave with his people, greeting her in Roman style. She waved goodbye, and when they disappeared, she ran into her room. Her cheeks were burning and her hands were trembling. It read:

*Mary,*
*I love you and I will always love you. I think about you constantly. You are the woman of my life and I swear at everything that is important and sacred to me, that it will be so until the end of my days.*
*When I learned that you had to leave because of your Father's illness, I immediately set off to say goodbye to you. Although we promised each other that we would see each other only after a year, I decided that the situation required me to visit you immediately. However, when I reached a Philae, you were already with your Grandparents in Alexandria and you were sailing away. Imagine how I suffered not being able to see you.*
*I decided to tell my granduncle how I feel about you and what my intentions are towards you. His reaction made me very sad. He told me to return to Rome immediately and not to show him my face until I wise up. I write you exactly how it was, I will not hide anything so that you know the situation.*

*When I arrived in Rome, my parents sent me to Gaul almost immediately. They said that it would do me good if I got to know nuisances of life, I would learn what real men do, and my body would experience hardships. I made a long journey as a messenger of the emperor. I reached the edge of the Empire. I was where the lands of cold winters begin. I saw snow and ice-covered rivers in the Brits' lands belonging to Rome. I reached my destination, handed over imperial orders and returned home in one piece.*

*I've been in Rome for two days now. I learned that Lucius became an officer and was delegated to Jerusalem. It's quite near Magdala, where you should be now. I use imperial mail to pass this letter to you. I hope my friend will give it to you as soon as possible. He had a crush on you, watch out for him!*

*I think about you – about us – constantly. I love you. I'm waiting for you. As soon as my words reach you, please reply. You are the love of my life.*

*Forever Yours*

*Marcus*

So, he was thinking of her! He loved her, missed her, dreamed of her! He is safe and sound. He traveled and that's why he didn't write for so long. Oh, her wonderful Marcus! How was he supposed to send a message from the frosty end of the world? He could not. He was wonderful! She was only worried that his family did not seem to approve of his idea of getting involved with her. However, with his letter with love confession in her hands, she didn't want to think about it.

Lying on the bed, she kissed the scroll that he had in his hands so recently.

As promised, Lucius visited her soon. The day before, like a well-mannered young man, he sent a messenger asking what time he could visit the next day. He came with two young officers.

She was prepared. Already in the evening she took a long bath and ordered the maid to anoint her body with oils. She took them out of one of her trunks and mixed them in the proportions recommended by the priestesses. The house smelled of nard and fresh flowers. Since her father's death, she had never anointed her body during her mourning. Now that more than ninety days had passed since the tragedy, according to the Halakhah she could already do it. She asked the young maid Ethel for help. She protested, refused, wondering loudly whether it was improper, said she would not do it, but at Mary's firm request she finally gave in and, supported by her instructions, for the first time in her life did something that could be called a massage. She did not like what she was doing, she did not want to look at Mary's naked body, she thought that she was committing a sin, but she did what the lady told her to do. She promised to herself, however, that she would talk about the debauchery that was going on in this house with someone God-fearing.

For the meeting with the Roman guests, Mary took her Egyptian clothes out from the trunk and wondered for long time which one to choose. She was still in mourning, so it could not be anything provocative. So she chose a dress that was, according to her, modest, and simple, covering shoulders and elbows, long to the ground, only with slight slits on the sides. It was of deep green color. She decided that such outfit would be the most suitable for the meeting with Lucius and his friends. She expected that even if Rabbi Yitzhak saw her in it, he would consider it modest and, as he used to say, ordinary enough.

She almost gave up on jewelry altogether. She only wore silver earrings in the shape of large wheels. They had no stones or other decorations. It suited her condition and mood.

"How great to meet a lady in this wild country," one of the men accompanying Lucius bowed.

His name was Philip.

"Lucius did not exaggerate anything in his stories about you," a young man named Aurelius bowed his head respectfully.

They had a good time talking, laughing and eating. It turned out that Egypt is so strongly associated with Rome that they easily found many mutual friends. They liked each other; they felt good with each other. Young, educated men far from the wealthy homes of their parents and a girl lost in the reality still alien to her. She relaxed with them. During the meeting, she forgot about mourning, loneliness, sadness and the fact that she should not laugh out loud, stay in a closed room with men or wear dresses other than gray or black.

Ethel, indignant, watched what was happening at home in the absence of noble and God-fearing Marta. She brought more dishes and set them on low tables, topped wine for the guests, but she looked so discontented and outraged that, at some point, Lucius asked her.

"And what are you so dissatisfied with, miss?"

He didn't speak her language, so she didn't even understand that he was addressing her.

"Ethel, the guest asks what is the reason to your dissatisfaction."

The servant stopped, put her hands on her hips and stated bluntly, "I'm sure God wouldn't like what's going on here."

4.

The situation in Israel was like a pot of soup boiling under an airtight lid. The fire was large, the dish bubbled with increasing force, and as the steam could not find an outlet, the lid bounced more and more, moved by the rapid evaporation. So that the soup doesn't boil over, someone put a heavy stone on the lid. The boiling became so intense that the pressure could make the pot burst. It was the moment when the vessel would burst with internal force if the fire was not reduced or the lid was not removed.

The prosecutor who was acting as the governor of the Empire in Judea was hated by Jews. His greatest misdeeds included placing Roman pictures in Jerusalem, which was considered a sin against God, robbing the treasures of the Temple and using them to build an aqueduct, and above all, bringing in groups of invaders. So he could not be liked. The continuing rise of taxes, and most importantly, the attempts to influence the change of the Jewish religion, added fuel to the fire. What Rome managed to do peacefully in other conquered territories, had no chance of success among the people of Israel.

With their unwavering faith in the one, invisible and almighty God, Jews did not allow the possibility of worshiping other deities at the same time. Knowing the prophecies of the olden ages, they waited for the coming of the Messiah who would free them from the dominance of despots and restore the glory of the Temple.

People were waiting for a revolution and the arrival of the new. The political situation was tense. The country was boiling. The Romans and those who sided with them were not among the favorites of the inhabitants of Galilee, and Mary not only entertained Roman officers in Magdala, but often went on several days-long trips with them.

\* \* \*

One day, when she was staying with Lazarus in Bethany, she decided to return to Magdala together with Lucius, Philip and Aurelius, who were just returning north with orders from Jerusalem, and knowing that she was with her brother and intending to go home, they decided to take her with them. She gladly accepted their offer. She liked them. She was sure that the trip in their company would be pleasant, and because they traveled on horseback, also quickly. They decided to get to Jordan and ride north along the river. They were just passing by a place where a small stream flowed into Jordan, the only one that never dried up.

"Do you know that according to legends, this is where the prophet Elijah was once hiding? Let's stop," Mary reined her horse. "Something is going on there!"

"You amaze me with your knowledge," Aurelius listened eagerly to everything she had to say.

He was fascinated by the history of the people of Israel, and even though she was raised and taught in Egypt, Mary was for him a source of knowledge about the land in which he found herself. "Elijah was a prophet and many of his predictions came true" he boasted that he also knew a lot. Jews believe that Elijah will appear on earth again and this will herald the coming of the Messiah. Old books say that the new Elijah will be killed in a shameful way.

"Some see Elijah in John the Baptist," Lucius added.

"If this is him, then I would not wish him that the prophecy in the old books would come true," Aurelius laughed.

"Everything is possible in this country," said Philip.

"Essenes, Pharisees, Sadducees, Zealots and all of them are crazy." Philip did not try to understand the distinctions among Israeli, or their political interdependencies.

"Some recognize the Temple, others do not, some live in celibacy, others have wives, some obey rituals and laws, others are far away from them. Everyone is arguing, quarreling and fighting with each other, and in addition they try to use us in their games."

"And we, the brave soldiers who represent Emperor Tiberius, do not want bloodshed, because it is not in our interest at all," Lucius summed up, winking an eye at the others.

He liked to emphasize that as Romans, they were mediators in these lands.

All three laughed.

"Right," still croaking, Aurelius supported Lucius. "We are to take care of peace and order. And to make sure that the taxes flow into the treasury of Rome and that our people receive the free grain on time."

"We neither want nor have to fight them." Philip, who disliked the local reality most of all three of them, said seriously now. "They fight to finish each other."

"You are right, soldier." Lucius was in a good mood. "We, as the good ones, make sure that no uprising breaks out. So we are, in fact, peaceful mediators. We care about maintaining a fragile balance. We are soldiers of order and we can be proud of ourselves."

Aurelius listened to what his colleagues were saying, he laughed with them, but at the same time he was closely watching what was happening in the distance, in the place pointed out by Mary.

"It's John the Baptist, I think," he adjusted himself on the horseback. "The one they say is the Messiah. You see?" He pointed at the man submerged in water, "that one over there!"

"They are all messiahs here," Philip did not intend to stop joking. "There are several of them for each cubit of the ground."

"It's a serious matter, just look what's going on there. They treat him almost like a god." Lucius was also watching closely at what was happening in the distance.

"I told you that some people call him the Messiah," said Aurelius.

"What does it mean exactly?" Inquired Philip.

"That he is the chosen one who announces the arrival of the new paradise in which everyone will be happy. There will be no hunger, no exploitation, no disease, no calamities, you know, these kinds of things."

"Beautiful," Philip mocked. "No wonder they listen to him so eagerly. If I were as poor as them, I would also be pleased to hear that things will get better for me soon."

"I was preparing a report for Rome. I have accurate information about him."

"So what's up with our Messiah?

"They tell stories about him like from the ancient myths. You know, born from almost a virgin and such."

"What exactly?"

"Well, listen then: he was born in Judah. His father was the priest Zacharias, and his mother was Elizabeth."

"She was a virgin?"

"Almost."

"'Almost a virgin' is only possible in this crazy country."

"I'm joking of course. They didn't have children. And they were both of age when people are rather not expecting children anymore."

"Oh, don't exaggerate, the history knows virile old men."

"But in the case of women, pregnancy in old age is not as common."

"Jews have seen such cases," Mary interjected. "Isaac's mother Sarah was ninety years old. Her husband Abraham was a hundred years old when he begot him."

"Impossible, people don't live that long."

"They do," Mary said. "Sarah died at the age of one hundred and twenty-seven, and Abraham lived to one hundred and seventy-five."

"Really?"

"So they say," Aurelius nodded, but he didn't quite believe these legends himself.

"Well, what about this Elizabeth?" Inquired Philip.

"The angel announced to her husband, Zachariah, that Elizabeth would give birth to the Messiah," Aurelius continued.

"Did she believe it?"

"How could she not believe, if soon after the angel's visit it turned out she was pregnant?"

"And how did her husband take it?"

"Generally speaking, he was apparently skeptical."

"He didn't sleep with his wife?"

"They say that so many years after their wedding, these matters belong rather to the sphere of myths and stories from ancient history."

"Well, so he didn't believe that his wife had been visited by an angel, even though that angel had said to him himself that he would come?"

"Although he was a priest, he probably doubted. Especially that the wife stated that it was not the angel who was the perpetrator, but God. The angel only announced her the good news. And you know what? Their God punished Zachariah for his lack of faith by taking away his voice."

"Knowing his severity, it's good that he spared his life."

"Yes, Adonai is like our Jupiter when he throws thunders."

"And what happened next?"

"Next, John was born, called the Baptist by people. His parents were old, but they managed to live long enough to raise him, and only then they died. John wanted to become a priest, like his father, it seems that he was close to the Essenes for some time, but in the end he chose the life and meditation in the desert. There, probably after a long fast, when he began to have visions because of hunger, God told him to cleanse people by baptizing them in Jordan, call for conversion and proclaim the coming of the Son of God. That's how John became a prophet."

No one commented on his words. They rode closer.

"Looks like he hasn't shaved since his stay in the desert?"

The Prophet stood knee-deep in water, and a long queue stretched out before him. Everyone wanted purification, washing away their sins, and conversion. Focused, they left themselves at his disposition, and he forgave them, washed them from their sins, and blessed them on God's behalf.

"The world will not cease to amaze me," Lucius concluded.

"I like this guy," Philip laughed out loud. "He baptizes everybody who wants, does not reject anyone. Everyone has an open path to paradise."

"I guess it's more complicated than we think. At least politically." Lucius had always liked to go deeper into the topic.

He knew a lot about the fractions and groups fighting in these lands. Before he came to Jerusalem, he had read the reports and studies delivered to Rome by the scouts and emissaries of the empire.

"He takes followers and supporters, and thus money, away from the old priests, the scholars who consider themselves the only ones authorized to interpret the Torah," he explained. "Priests hate him and others like him. If these divisions deepen, a revolution, or at least an uprising could break out. Then we too will be in a difficult situation."

Mary listened attentively while staring at one point. A man stood on the hill. She couldn't see what he looked like from a distance, but something about him attracted her. She strained her eyes. He was looking at the sky. At one point, he slowly spread his arms sideways. He turned his open hands toward the sky. She couldn't see his face, but imagined his eyes were closed. He stood still and she stared at him.

Suddenly she looked up. A white dove flapped its wings in the sky, as if suspended directly above him.

"Goddess, what do you want to tell me?" Mary whispered.

She felt a shiver and goosebumps. Her body trembled.

"Everything all right?" Lucius worried, noticing what was happening to her.

"See that bird over there?" She pointed out.

"I see it. It's a white dove. She flaps her wings in the air."

So she did not have hallucinations, the bird was really there.

"And can you see this man? She gestured again.

"Yes. The skinny guy in a tunic of shiny fabric?"

"It's not the fabric that shines, it's the glow around him. This man is someone extraordinary."

Lucius lightly struck the sides of the horse with his heels. He thought that they had been standing in the sun for too long because Mary had hallucinations.

"I think it's time to continue our journey."

At his sign, everyone kicked their horses.

"Yes, let's go," she followed them.

However, the picture of the man indicated by the dove kept bothering her. She stopped the mount and looked at the hill where she had last seen him. He wasn't there anymore. He was just entering the river.

She attracted him with her eyes. He turned around. Their eyes met. She felt the promise of something unknown, distant and attractive. She shivered.

The man approached John the Baptist and bowed his head to him.

"Mary, are you coming? Lucius called.

5.

"We'll go to Magdala," Marta suggested one day.

In principle, it was not a suggestion, but the decision of the older sister, and as such, it was not subject to discussion.

"You will dress appropriately and we will walk around the city," she encouraged. "Let them see you. They must see for themselves that you are no different from them."

"Am I?" Mary doubted that this was a good idea.

"Why? You feel you are better?" Marta didn't like the tone of her voice. "Because you're prettier? Because you know more? You have colorful outfits made of delicate cloths? Isn't that hubris talking through you?"

"No, I'm just saying I'm different."

"Different doesn't mean better!" Marta stood in front of her as if to fight.

"Different doesn't mean worse!" Mary stood in the same way. "And since I am here, I always feel that I am treated like a necessary evil. You indulge me, take care of me as of a child, believing that I will finally wash the traces of Egyptian depravity off myself." "You are still so young," Marta was not going to fight her. "But I don't want you to confuse tolerating certain issues by me with blindness. I see perfectly clearly what is going on. You don't want to adapt, you want the world to adapt to you."

Mary fell silent, lowered her head, then stretched out her hands to her.

"Maybe you're partly right. Maybe you are even more right than I would like to admit. I may indeed be presumptuous, but I always mean well."

And when Marta smiled forgivingly, she added:

"Come on, let's hug, we're sisters after all. We should not argue. We have only each other."

\* \* \*

They went to the city the following day.

Marta personally chose a dress for her sister. It was gray, covering the whole body, showing only face, hands and feet. She also chose a black scarf for her to cover her head.

"Let me put on the one from my grandmother Aida. The scarlet color will comfort me.

"The time of initial mourning has passed, but good daughters should mourn their father and emphasize this with their dress for at least a year," Marta explained. "This is the custom. This is what Halakhah says."

"Mourning is carried in the heart."

"Of course, but even in your progressive Egypt, if I am correct, it lasts ninety days."

"Ninety days have long passed."

"We are not in Egypt, but in Israel."

"Let me have the scarlet one, it's a gift from my grandmother."

"Fine, have it your way," Marta hugged her sister.

They walked and bowed to the people they passed. They stopped by some women for a longer or shorter conversation. Marta introduced Mary, even though everyone knew exactly who she was walking with.

"Remember that you do not speak to the elders first, and when a man speaks to you, you do not look him in the eye," Marta instructed her. "Be nice, smile and don't talk too much. Understand?"

They reached the well, which was a meeting place for women. All of them took their water from there. It was the place for socializing. They exchanged information there, consulted each other, there they talked about what was happening in the city and in the world.

"This is my sister. You might have already heard about her?" Marta said to the oldest woman.

"Marta, you're a decent person. Just like us. Even though you don't have and never had a husband or children, but you are god-fearing. You sacrificed yourself to your father and brother, it's commendable. This is what a woman should be like," she heard.

"But your sister is not like that," added another.

"How do you know? Look at her. Doesn't she look just like us?"

"People say various things about her."

"Not the best things," another said.

"What, for example?"

"That she hosts Romans," said one.

"That she wears dresses like a queen and behaves as if she were one herself," another added.

Complaints followed one after the other.

"She has no shame, she talks with men, reads books, speaks in other languages and does it specifically so that her servants would not understand her, she is plotting with the Romans, receives letters from far away all the time, who knows what is in them..."

"She's confusing boys, she looks them in the eye and laughs loudly."

"She brought a mirror with her and looks at it for hours, so she probably deals with magic. And what kind of color her scarf is?"

"On top of that, she has a cat that she treats like a human. He has a collar worth ten donkeys or more."

"She prays to foreign gods."

"She anoints her body with precious oils, like those condemned women from the house of pleasure. And this scarlet shawl? Who wears such things?"

Mary was standing with her head down, as Marta had commanded her. She intended to humbly listen to the complaints, but they became more and more painful and turned more and more into an attack.

"This is Mary, my sister. She is standing right here before you now," Marta interrupted them, making her voice calm, even though anger was building up inside her. "Is she like you say she is? You judge her without knowing her, without exchanging even one sentence with her? It is a sin! God is looking at you from up there!" She raised her finger, pointing to the sky.

Her voice was still subdued, but it betrayed her agitation.

"Who are you to judge her?" She called, taking her sister's hand. "Do you think that if she is a little different, then she is worse than you? Is this hubris speaking through you?"

She told them the same words she had used while talking to Mary the previous day. When she realized this, she bowed her head to the eldest woman, nodded at a few of them, pulled her sister's hand, and they headed back home.

\* \* \*

"You adapt or you die. These are the rules of the world," she raised her voice after they reached home. "Time to wake up. You are no longer in Egypt. Here the norms are really strict. Even the scarf must be gray. You saw the women here. They judge without knowing. They criticize even though they haven't exchange a word with you. They condemn because they heard something from someone."

"It's human. It is like this everywhere. Galilee is no different in this respect from any other place. We are all the same. We like to judge and criticize things without knowing them. It is more difficult here because the world is quite hermetic and closed because you have been stripped of something very valuable. Maybe that's also why you are so critical of other women."

"Maybe you're right. But after all, not knowing any other world, we feel good in the one we have. Each of us has somehow found her place in it and if someone wants to destroy the old order, we will resist."

Mary admired her sister. She was so smart, and yet she was not educated in any temple.

"Where do you get such great wisdom of life from, Marta?

"I've always spent a lot of time thinking. As you know, father was rarely home, and there were many books in his chamber. I read them all. With no exception."

"Without anyone's help?"

"With God's help!"

"You are very independent. You've created your own world."

"I feel good in it."

"You're a bit like Lilith. A little bit. Mainly on the issue of independence."

"Lilith?"

"You don't know about her, because there is no trace of her in our father's chamber. However, our oldest books mention her. Someday I'll tell you about her."

"You said "our"? Really?" Marta was intrigued not by the fact that she could find out something about a woman she had never heard of, but because Mary, probably for the first time since returning, used the word "our" to refer to the place where she was born! And this happened after this terrible meeting at the well. After all, she could feel offended, say that she is fed up, that she is leaving, that it is not her world at all, meanwhile she says "our" and wants to tell her about Lilith. An amazing girl with a very complicated soul. "Who is she really?" She wondered.

"I said 'our' because I'm from here after all. I was born here. Here is my home, but at the same time I feel that Egypt is also my home. As you know, I am a priestess of Isis, though I also worship God. I do not see this as a discord, there is no disharmony in it. My mother chose the place for my birth consciously. She knew what she was doing. It was meant for us, and my adult paths also brought me to Galilee. I will tell you about Lilith and I will also tell others, because the local women need me more than those in Egypt. There are no priestesses here, the Goddess was chased away from here. Lilith hadn't lived here for long. Maybe we need to invite her again or at least tell about her to those who have been robbed of her?"

"Do you want a revolution here?"

"I gave gifted senet to my niece."

"Yes."

"You nod, because you can play it yourself and you enjoy it. You've been secretly reading books for years. But admit it, quite honestly, when you saw what was in the box, it seemed to me that you probably didn't want me to teach Lazarus's daughter to play. Why?!"

"You're wrong. I would like them to know how to think. But you are right. Maybe I didn't want them to be too wise, because I know what pain is associated with it. Let people fantasize and they will suffer. Teach them to read and they will find out new worlds and possibilities. It is easier for those who did not know the knowledge and did not taste the pleasure of thinking. What do they need senet for? It helps you develop. When a person does not think, it is easier to live."

"Are you bitter?" She realized in surprise.

"Perhaps precisely because a long time ago a priestess of Isis, your mother, taught me how to play senet. She opened my eyes. I realized how little I could do."

"Everyone creates the world closest to him at their level. It depends on each of us what it is like."

"Oh, my love, I remember you always wanted to be a bird."

"And I am, Marta, I am."

\* \* \*

"I know the fate of those who bring bad news," Lucius came alone and without warning.

He was hot. It was obvious that he did not spare the horse.

"Let's sit down," he said. "I thought I should give you this information. We are friends, I want to be with you also in the times that are difficult for you."

"What happened?" Mary's heart was beating so strongly that it seemed to her that everyone could hear it.

Since the first visits of Roman soldiers "unfortunate ones, according to Marta "Mary had never been alone with any of them. She promised this to her sister and kept her word so far. So now, as soon as Lucius jumped off his horse, Mary sent for her sister, who immediately abandoned her chores in the pantry and joined them.

So Mary, Marta and Lucius sat in the chamber, in a place where guests were always welcomed.

"Speak, I'm ready," Mary sat upright, with a studied lady-like smile on her face.

She looked just like her grandmother Aida receiving guests while knowing that they brought information she would rather not hear. She guessed it was about Marcus. Lucius's behavior did not imply that something final happened to his friend. He certainly lived and was healthy. Otherwise Lucius would not act this way. All in all, she probably expected what she would hear in a moment, she had felt for some time that something she might not like was happening. However, she was calm, at least on the surface.

"Mary, I have news from Rome. Mail has arrived."

"Go ahead," she encouraged him, trying to keep strong herself.

Marta sat down next to her and took her hand. She knew the story of her sister's relationship with Marcus.

"In short, Marcus is after the wedding," Lucius blurted out. "He got married, pressed by his family," he excused his friend.

He was watching Mary, because he had not said everything yet. She looked calm. The only signal showing how much she was moved by what she heard, was that she unwittingly, but slowly, turned the ring on her left finger, as if it would help her stay calm.

"You want to say something else, don't you?" She smiled sadly.

"You'd better find out right away. Sooner or later it will reach you anyway."

"Tell me."

"The girl he married is pregnant. That's why he had to do it. It's a matter of honor."

"Poor thing," Mary remembered the words of an old woman from the pub.

"Poor?"

"You don't remember? Your first wife will die."

"Right! The terrible old woman from Alexandria who pretended to be a priestess. Of course I remember," he understood what she meant.

"Exactly," Mary looked away.

"You don't really think that this prophecy will come true?"

"I hope not. I don't wish anything bad to anyone."

\* \* \*

Lucius's words were soon confirmed by her grandmother's letter.

*Mary, my beloved, do you know how much I miss you? The house is empty without you, my heart is crying. I would follow you to hug you. Believe me, I would get on a ship and sail to the wild country where you are. However, I can't do it. I regret this very much. I am stuck in bed. A physical distress happened to me, because of which I rely on the help of Sithathor and the servants.*

*It was like this: one morning a messenger arrived with a letter from your grandfather. He rarely writes. And if he happens to do it, it means something important has happened. So it was also this time. Karim, as you know, often goes to Alexandria. Business is keeping him there. Stephany takes good care of him and the house, so I have peace of mind. Recently, Karim is there even more often than before, but the situation requires his presence. You probably remember that he has a lot of contacts in*

*Rome. He knows everyone who means something in those circles. Your friend Marcus's granduncle holds all the strings in his hands and everything about trading with Rome depends on him. Due to the fact that Marcus liked you so much, we had some problems. But I don't want to bother you with them, especially since your grandfather managed to deal with it. Now, after many efforts and actions that were to alleviate the rather inflamed situation, everything has returned to normal.*

*Surely you remember your departure from Alexandria, when you were in a hurry to meet your father? Of course you remember. I knew you expected to meet Marcus at the harbor. We already know why he wasn't there. When you sent him the message that your father was sick, he left for Philae immediately. We missed each other. When he reached our estate, you were already on the ship.*

*I know from well-informed sources that Marcus confessed to his granduncle how he felt about you. Unfortunately, he did not receive the reaction he would dream of. Moreover, he was sent to Rome, and from there, at the order of the emperor himself, he went somewhere to the North to provide some important documents to the troops stationed there. When he came back... Well, honey, I wonder how to say this to you? It can be painful for you, but I think things always go the way the Goddess wants, and that what is going to happen, will happen, whether we want it or not. Remember, you once told me about a prophecy Marcus heard from an old woman. That his wife will not enjoy a long life. I admit that when you told me that, I was constantly praying to Isis and offering her generous sacrifices so that you would not become his wife. Maybe it's cruel, maybe ruthless, maybe when you read it you will hate me, but believe me, you are the most important person in the world for me. I love you very much, I want you to be happy, to make your dreams come true, to follow the path of the mission and accomplish your life calling. Marcus is an extremely nice young man, but I didn't think he was destined for you. A girl with the signs you have cannot just be married to a Roman. Even the most handsome one.*

*So, sweetheart, the news is that Marcus, by necessity, married a girl from the Julius family. She was pregnant. These things happen. They were apparently meant to be together.*

*Anyway, when I read the letter from your grandfather, I got a little upset, I stood carelessly and fell down so unfortunately that I broke my leg. Something also happened to my hip. In the end, I don't move at all, I am lying in bed and everyone pampers me with treats. If it goes on like this, I will become a huge, fat matron. Of course I'm kidding, I will never let that happen. I want my wise and beautiful granddaughter to be proud not only of her grandmother's mind but also her appearance.*

*My love, I will recover soon. And then I'll come to you or maybe by that time you will come back home? In the meantime, remember your path. Don't stray from it. Listen to your voice. It will always tell you what is right and which way you should go. Trust yourself. And remember that the Goddess's power is with you.*

*Loving you the most in the world*

*Your grandmother Aida*

*P.S. I entrusted the management of the property to Sithathor, she is doing very well. Your little Dobrawa is growing and developing every day. She speaks quite fluently already, also in Greek. She mentions you often.*

Mary put the letter down on the trunk. She lit on a red lamp, set it in the center of the room, and knelt down. She made the triple sign of the Goddess, bowed her head, touching the floor with her forehead, and prayed quietly.

She asked Isis for health for her grandma, for strength and fast healing of her fractures. She also asked for a blessing for herself, so that she could follow the path given to her by the Goddess with confidence and courage.

Ethel was looking at her through the half-open door. She was terrified.

### 6.

Leo didn't like it when the house was full of guests. It always caused confusion in which he didn't feel good. He liked to hide in some secluded corner then, but it was not always possible. Sometimes the guests wanted to admire his sophisticated cat's manners, his intelligent mouth and the stone-studded collar. Mary then took him in her arms to show him to them.

For some time now, guests visited the house quite often. Mary decided that neither the place nor time should limit her. She thought she wasn't doing anything that was reprehensible according to her. She just wanted to live by the customs she was used to. Of course, this was not entirely possible, but she thought it was worth trying.

So even though she knew that this was not well received in Magdala, she invited Lucius and his colleagues to dinners, which often went on long into the night. They were happy to accept her invitations, feeling that thanks to Mary, they functioned in the world of civilization in which they grew up, or at least in its substitute. Everyone was young, healthy, beautiful and at their prime. They liked each other's company. They talked about everything. They were direct, enthusiastic, they had open minds. They were soon joined by Samuel, the son of the medic from Magdala, and David, the son of the Rabbi. At first quite restrained and keeping to themselves, both quickly fit into the company. Also, apparently, they did not have opportunities for creative exchange of thoughts, heated disputes or discussions in their everyday life. And because they came from different worlds, there were a lot of topics that threw off sparks.

At one point, they were joined by Berenice, the daughter of the commander of the Roman army in the northern part of the lands of the people of Israel. Sometimes one or two friends came to Magdala with her. The group was growing.

"I will tell you how I see it," Aurelius wanted to show off his familiarity with the subject, but also to confront his knowledge directly with those concerned. "Well, in my opinion, and Roman reports also talk about it, there are several groups in Galilee. The three most important are: Pharisees, Sadducees and Essenes."

"You don't have to be a Roman officer to know that," joked David, who didn't belong to any of the groups mentioned by Aurelius, but he had his sympathies.

However, as a son of a medic and a future doctor, he thought he should not disclose them. After all, he cared for the health of people with different views and all of them paid him the same. So, he tried to maintain restraint in revealing his political sympathies in his everyday life. Just in case.

"Don't interrupt him," Samuel rebuked him. "Maybe it's worth listening how the invaders see us."

"First of all, we are not invaders."

"O really?" Berenice laughed.

Her father commanded the Roman army, and, as he claimed, it was a peace mission, but she had no doubt what role Rome played in the local world. And she didn't like it at all. She talked about this with her father many times, and he blamed the views of his only child on the young age, lack of experience and youthful rebellion. He was convinced that when she would get married, her view of the world would change.

"We came here at the invitation of Herod, to help him maintain peace," Lucius decided that since he was of the highest rank, it was his duty to care for the good name of the army and Rome.

"It's really touching," Berenice laughed. "The Roman army has been answering invitations of various local rulers for centuries and goes to their countries to support them in maintaining peace. Are you really so naive to believe it?" She stood up and started walking around the chamber.

She went to the jug with wine and poured some into her goblet.

"Long live the peaceful Roman army!" She raised it up.

"Berenice now presents us with the typical behavior of a jaded child of a wealthy and important parent." Philip stood next to her and also refilled his cup. "She does not lack anything, has no worries, thanks to her father's position, but also, let's say it boldly, to her beauty, charm and intelligence, and she has a wide range of admirers. She lives the way she wants, she does everything she wants. In her free time she is upset that her father is an occupier and that she belongs to a privileged group. Your health, Berenice! I am your devoted admirer."

"Philip, I hate you! Hold it!" She handed him the cup, laughing loudly, and when her hands were free, she punched him in the chest first, and when he looked at her with admiring eyes, she kissed him on both cheeks. "I am glad that you are here. I am glad that you all are here because I think the boredom would drive me crazy."

"Well, we already know Berenice's position," concluded Lucius. "Maybe we could come back to he topic and hear what Aurelius has to say in these matters?"

"Sure, let him talk, I'd love to find out too." Berenice sat down in her seat, straightened her back, put her knees together and smiled like a lady, showing that she was ready to listen to the lecture.

"So, as I said, the three main groups are Pharisees, Sadducees, and Essenes." Aurelius knew that breaks like the one a moment before, could occur often.

It didn't bother him at all. He liked this atmosphere. Hot discussions, sometimes interrupted by fun events, were his element.

"The Pharisees have the most supporters, simple and poor people love them," he said with conviction. "The Sadducees have most aristocrats and rich people among their followers. The Essenes live around Qumran. They are also scribes, radical zealots, Sycarians and herodians. There are also supporters of John the Baptist, who calls everyone for conversion. Remember, the unshaven one that we saw when he was baptizing people in Jordan."

"Lots of groups," said Philip. "I've always said it was hard to understand it all."

"I have mentioned only the most important ones," Aurelius explained. "And for formality's sake, let me add that most pious Jews do not identify with any of them. They simply believe in Adonai and try to stick to his rules."

"What do you think differs between these groups?" asked David, who heard for the first time the situation in his country presented so clearly.

"The main difference between the Pharisees and Sadducees is that the former believe that God gave Moses not only the Torah, but also the oral tradition, passed down from generation to generation*. The Pharisees believe that after death, a man will rise again in his own body, that he has an immortal soul which will go to either hell or heaven, depending on his merits. They recognize that God directs everything that happens to people and the world, and they also recognize the existence of angels. The Sadducees, however, proclaim that God does not intervene in what is happening on earth or in man's personal life, or does it very rarely. Good and evil, prosperity and unhappiness depend, for the most part, on the will of man and everyone chooses for himself which path to follow. At the same time, they reject the immortality of souls and do not believe in the resurrection. They recognize only the Pentateuch in the Bible, they completely reject oral tradition."

"And the Essenes?" inquired Philip. "Tell me, let me have these matters sorted out in my head once and for all."

---

* M. Rosik, "In the footsteps of the Pharisees and Sadducees", http://www.mariuszrosik.pl/?p=3670 [access: 28.05.2017].

"They are the most restrained and bound by rigors of all. First, they avoid contact with the Temple, and thus with Pharisees and Sadducees, they live in small villages far from the others, and most interestingly, they say that all their goods belong to the general public. They have no wives, strictly adhere to the rules of ritual purity, and everything that concerns Halakhah. In their villages around Qumran, they rewrite holy books and store them in caves, which they consider almost holy."

"So that leaves only Zealots, and we will have the most important groups covered. Don't talk about the others, because I am already confused enough with what you said."

"Zealots fight with us. And not only with us. They are also against those whom they consider to be collaborators, that is, basically all other groups. They believe that whoever is faithful and obedient to Rome, betrays God. They believe that by fighting, they will speed up the coming of the Messiah, who will free their nation from Roman slavery. In short, they are fanatics."

"Well, so we know now what's going on," Berenice, like the others, listened to his words with focus. "Now please explain who is at war with whom, apart from the Zealots who fight everyone, and why are Roman peacekeepers needed here?"

"Zealots are ready to give their lives for freedom and independence, but they and all the others fight mainly among themselves," Aurelius had the answer ready, because he gave it to Rome several times before. "And what do they want? Influence, money, and obedience among people."

"Just like everywhere else then?"

"More or less."

"And we make sure they don't kill each other?" Berenice continued.

"Probably not quite that, but indeed, as Lucius says, we are a kind of conciliation force.

"Ensuring at the same time that grain and taxes feed the treasury of Rome regularly and in large quantities," Samuel could not help himself.

"The accuracy of your observations, Samuel, is admirable," Berenice laughed. "I already thought that none of you oppressed by Rome would speak. Bravo, bravo!"

"Rome treats us as a source of raw materials," Samuel continued, encouraged by her words. "It's no secret to anyone. The supreme authority is held by the Roman prefect, Pontius Pilate, and although appearances of autonomy are maintained, even though Herod Antipas has great power, everyone knows what it is really like. Rome decides on the majority of the most important issues. We are under occupation. All in all, I'm not surprised that the Zealots want a revolution, but I personally think that this is not the way."

"I would like to remind you again," Lucius tried to guard the objective truth "We are only guarding the order and the collection of taxes here."

"Let Samuel finish," Berenice protested. "What do you think is the right way?"

"We should work, learn and get rich, at the same time reaching an agreement with each other, because we are in serious conflicts. And people like this are easy to rule. A truce is needed, someone who will unite us. At the moment, I don't see such a force."

"Maybe it will appear," Mary said.

"What do you mean?" Berenice jumped in her chair.

She had not discussed with people her age for a long time. Meeting in this group gave her great pleasure.

"Nothing specific, I have a vague feeling, I see in the distance something that is a brightness and it is coming, emerging slowly. This is our future."

"Hmmm... you talk enigmatically as if you had visions. Fortunately, optimistic ones, which means we can be hopeful. We are waiting for the forthcoming brightness because it will change something." Berenice took another sip of wine.

"I think that's exactly what will happen."

Mary's presentiment was not strong. As she said, it was just a veiled announcement of something that was approaching. She couldn't look deeper yet, she wasn't focusing on the message that came to her. She didn't need to see it more clearly. She was a priestess but did not concentrate on her mission. Besides, she hardly remembered about it at all. The words from her initiation that she was the Guardian of the Gate of Light, that she was to follow a bright path, were still somewhere in her head, but they were only like an echo from a distant time and place.

Now here in Magdala, in her family home, she has become the one who receives guests, initiates discussions and directs conversations, like her grandmother Aida once did. She was blossoming in their group, she was its undisputed star, and she liked it. Although she missed Egypt very much, thanks to her friends, she felt good as a world lady at her home in Magdala.

She created a place that was an enclave of peace, pleasure, high-level discussion, and, despite the frequent difference of views, of the mutual affection of all who took part in this substitute for a worldly life on Lake Kinnereth.

Marta, initially very averse to what was happening, carefully watched and listened to the meetings. She hardly said a word. It wasn't something that Rabbi Yitzhak would have praised after all. At the same time, however, she also knew well that he certainly could not clearly condemn it. Besides, Mary was almost a foreigner and, after all, a co-owner of Magdala, which put her in some areas almost on a par with men. And she was an adult. Although she did not have a husband, she was in a completely different situation than all other women in this city. So Marta not only participated in the meetings, but she even liked them, especially since they were joined by the daughter of the Romans commander, whose unit was temporarily stationed in Nazareth. Berenice behaved like Mary. She was casual, laughing, loved discussions, games and was a young, educated, well-groomed woman.

Marta had never met anyone like this before. Until now, she thought her sister was unique in her behavior. She reminded her very much of Eucharia, whom Marta still remembered with the greatest affection, despite the passage of time. Sithathor, the third Egyptian known to Marta, who came along with Mary from Philae, was more like Marta in her restraint and severity. And here, with Berenice joining the group, it turned out that there are other women in the world who behave and dress almost like her sister. Marta breathed a sigh of relief.

\* \* \*

"I heard that you were once in the house of pleasure in Alexandria, dressed as servants?" Berenice asked one evening. Marta was already tired and went to bed, and David and Samuel decided that it was time to say goodbye, and went to their homes on foot.

Only five of them remained: Mary, Lucius, Philip, Aurelius and Berenice. Everyone was supposed to spend the night at Mary's. In fact, they were also going to go to bed, they were quite sleepy. They drank a lot of wine, they had fun. It was almost midnight when Berenice, laughing and still not done with having fun, remembered what Lucius had once told her.

"I asked you not to tell anyone about it, didn't I?" Lucius laughed.

"The whole world knows it," Berenice objected. "And you would be surprised how many have already followed you! Visiting such a place has always tempted me too."

"What stops you?" Aurelius was always willing to take on new challenges.

And because he liked Berenice very much, he was ready to fulfill her wish.

"Mary, do you have any suitable clothes?" Philip was also interested.

"Will we go with the novices?" Lucius left the decision to Mary. "They don't know the world at all. I don't know if they will be able to behave properly," he joked, glancing at Aurelius and Philip, of whom he knew well that they had visited Magdala's house of pleasure many times.

"This is not the most suitable place for a young lady," Mary looked at Berenice meaningfully. "Your father wouldn't be happy if he found out you were there."

"So? He just shouldn't find out, it's as easy as that!" Berenice stood up. "Mary, you won't let me go alone with the guys, will you?"

"Eh, dear, if you knew how harsh the local customs are!"

"I just want to get to know them at least a bit."

"Then this is not a good place to start. Do you know that Moses banned Israeli women to prostitute? You won't meet them at the house of pleasure. There are mainly foreigners there. If we find a local woman, it means that she has fallen so low that lower than that there is only the eternal abyss of damnation."

"It sounds inviting. Let's go there, Mary, come on please! Come with us!" She embraced her friend's waist.

"Of course I won't let you go there alone."

"What do you mean alone? We are going," Philip stood next to Berenice. "We'll defend you to the last drop of blood if the need arises!"

"I hope it won't be necessary," Mary said dryly.

"And I'd like it," Berenice chuckled. "Why not? It would be something to remember."

\* \* \*

An older, obese woman looked them up and down and let them in.

"Youth came to look or to use?"

They looked at each other.

"To look, I guess." Lucius assumed the role of the head of the group.

"But who knows," Berenice laughed.

"In any case, you pay in advance for the entry." The woman reached out "And then... who knows."

"As you can see, paying is the most important thing here," Mary explained to Berenice, while Lucius talked to the owner about the price.

"The girls here make their own money. Not everyone has wealthy parents who support him," the woman snapped after hearing Mary's words, while counting the coins she received.

"That's how it is in this world," Lucius was not going to start a discussion with her, after all they were here just for fun.

They entered a dark room. Mary immediately remembered Alexandria, Marcus and the little, scared Dobrawa. She saw that Berenice was intrigued. She understood her. When she came into the house of pleasure in Alexandria, she had similar feeling. She was moved. She didn't like what she saw, but something made her look at it. Berenice reacted the same way as she had once.

"Show me your medication room," Mary asked the owner, not wanting to watch what she once had.

"That's some strange whim, miss," the owner laughed hard, shaking the folds of her belly, visible under her dress, and led her to a small room deep inside the building. "You can look all you want, miss, but don't touch anything! Can I leave you alone? You won't take anything, will you?"

* * *

When they returned to the property in the morning, Lucius stopped them for a moment before going to bed.

"Nobody can know that we were there, remember that. You will probably leave from here soon, and I'm not sure what will happen to me, but I am a man anyway, so visiting such places by me is not outrageous. However, Mary lives here. If the local women find out she was there, I'd rather not be in her place."

"I would say selfishly that I would prefer my father not to find out where his only child spends her time," Berenice added.

Ethel stood behind the door to the kitchen. She was listening. She did not understand almost anything, but from the tone of their voices and their outfits they were still wearing, she concluded that they had returned from some highly suspicious night trip. Otherwise why would they be wearing servant's clothes? She decided to find out where they had gone, because she sensed that it was certainly not a place that the Most High would encourage to visit.

"Tfu!" She spat indignantly, knowing that nobody could see her. "How can I live in a house where God's laws are traded in?"

* * *

With time, young people became so close that they decided to go on a further trip. They wanted to see the fortress in Masada, considered to be the greatest in this region of the world, and see if the Dead Sea really is so salty that it is possible to lie on its waters. Aurelius was attracted by the technical solutions that the building was famous for.

Masada was the most powerful, never-conquered fortress. It was built on the edge of the stony desert by the Dead Sea. It was very difficult to access, because it was built at the very top of the only plateau in the area, and surrounded by very steep slopes from every side.

King Herod, father of Herod Antipas, liked this place and expanded it considerably. There's a reason they called him the Great. He left behind such wonderful and modern buildings, that despite the fact that a lot of time had passed since his death, they were still viewed with admiration, and his knowledge of construction craftsmanship was widely discussed in the world.

Neither Mary nor her Roman friends, who served in the army in the northern part of the Jewish territories, nor even Samuel and David, who often visited Jerusalem which was really close to the Dead Sea, had ever been there. So when Lucius proposed a trip to the south, during which they would stop, among others, in Masada, they accepted the idea happily.

They took servants, the necessary equipment, and set off. They planned their way so that the journey would take as little time as possible.

They did not travel through Jerusalem, but through Jericho, the oldest city in the world, according to the stories. It was said that centuries ago, when Joshua "the successor of Moses "came to the Promised Land with the people, he conquered this city that had never been conquered, because he listened carefully to God's orders. The walls of Jericho were tall and strong. They could not be crossed and no one could destroy them.

However, as everybody knows, who has God's support and obeys his orders, may really do a lot. So it was also this time.

God commanded Joshua to walk evenly at the head of the army around the walls, every day, early in the morning. The priests were to lead the Ark of the Covenant, which accompanied the Israelites on their way from Egypt to the Promised Land, and play shofars[*] loudly. It happened as the Lord commanded. For six days the Israelites circled the walls of Jericho, and the instruments resounded loudly. They were supported by the Ark of the Covenant, in which God's power lived. On the seventh day, following Adonai's order, they circled Jericho seven times, playing trumpets all the time and still marching evenly, and when they stopped, they gave a powerful war cry. Then something unusual happened: the huge walls of Jericho shook and fell. The Israelites took the city. Since then, it had always belonged to them.

So they were looking now at the areas Joshua had conquered centuries earlier. The high mountains of the Judean Desert surrounded them. The bare beige and burgundy peaks were cut by deep canyons. As far as the eye could see, there was no vegetation here. From time to time, a small dried ball of desert rose appeared, pushed by the wind.

\* \* \*

"Samuel, David, you know a lot about your ancestors, you cultivate traditions," she began, when they sat at the sea on thick mats, laid out for them by the servants, during a break in the journey, "you boast of the wisdom of Solomon."

"He was the most intelligent king on earth," said David.

---

[*] Curved trumpets made from sheep horns, allowing for a very loud sound

"Do you know what connected him with the Queen of Sheba?"

"She gave him so much gold that it's hard to believe even today," Samuel laughed. "A nice woman. I would like to meet such a queen."

"I'd love to hear about her," Lucius was serious.

"I like that kind of stories too," Aurelius encouraged her. "I know many of them. Of course, I have also heard of Queen of Sheba of course, but I suppose I don't know the same side of her as you do. Am I right?"

They valued her education and knowledge. They have seen on several occasions that she was much better educated than them, although she tried very hard not to make them feel that way. And as she was also unnervingly beautiful, she intrigued them so much that they were drawn to her as if they were under the influence of some magic.

Berenice also liked to listen to her. Besides, most girls and women in her surroundings, no matter how old they were, most often behaved as if it was obvious to them that Mary knew better, had wider knowledge and much more experience.

"Sure, tell us," said Samuel.

"Talk." Like Samuel, David knew the story of Makeda, but he was very curious what version of it Mary would tell them.

"Her name was Makeda," she began. "She loved wisdom above all else in life. It was said about her that there was no queen in the world more beautiful, richer or smarter than her. Her country was famous for its huge dam, which irrigated orchards and gardens, for the trade "the main routes leading to countries inhabited by yellow people were there. Sheba provided the world with the highest quality nard and myrrh. In Makeda's time, her country lay on both sides of the Red Sea, it was mighty and rich. The queen ruled it wisely."

They listened attentively.

"From an early age, apart from wisdom and beauty, she also had a special gift," she suspended her voice. "She experienced revelations."

Everyone, including Samuel and David, looked up at the same time, and looked at her with interest.

"Yes, Makeda was haunted by visions. She saw what was happening in distant places, or what was about to happen in the future. She knew her path from an early age. She went to meet King Solomon with the largest caravan the world had seen, because that was what her inner voice told her to do. She wanted to meet the ruler and draw from the treasury of his knowledge. She thought that wisdom was more valuable than all the silver and gold of the world. As you probably know, Solomon was also famous for having over seven hundred wives and three hundred concubines. Each of them was beautiful and ready to fulfill any of his whims. So how could Makeda make him interested in her? And I need to add that besides the fact that she wanted to draw on his knowledge, she also dreamed of a trade treaty that would guarantee Sheba's participation in the ventures and profits that the king planned."

Aurelius smiled to himself. He was a fan of history. As he explored knowledge of these areas, he heard about the treaties that the Queen of Sheba signed with Solomon a thousand years ago, thanks to her beauty and intelligence. He did not think, however, that Mary also had such knowledge, because where could she have it from? He knew that she had studied in the temple of Isis. He heard that the women educated there had extraordinary knowledge and skills, but he did not realize they knew history, especially of such distant times and places.

"She appeared before him in a veil covering her face, made him guess her riddles, and put him to tests, and finally he fell in love with her so much that he offered her a marriage. As you know, Solomon is the author of the most beautiful songs about love, as they say. And do you know that he wrote it inspired by his affection to Makeda? And that if it wasn't for the Queen of Sheba, there wouldn't be a Song of Songs? Their love was powerful, it stood the test of time. They parted so that everyone could rule their kingdom, but they always remained perfect partners for each other. He was the only man of her life. She loved him with beautiful, pure love."

"She should have stayed with him," Berenice sighed.

"He asked for her hand, but she preferred to be the independent queen in Sheba. She loved her country and had a sense of duty, so she had to come back. In addition, it turned out she was pregnant."

"Oh!" One of the girls cried out.

"Right," Mary laughed. "The matter was complicated by the principle that a woman could only sit on the throne of Sheba if she was a virgin. And Makeda, after visiting Solomon, was not one anymore."

"And?" asked the same woman who just screamed. "What did she do?"

"There were priestesses of the Lady of the Moon around her. It was this goddess who looked after Makeda and her country. They had long known what path was written for their mentee, because they knew her visions, and they had similar ones anyway. As you know, priestesses can look behind the veil of time. They can look into the past and the future. So it was clear to them that the child was to be born by and due to the will of the Goddess. After all, nothing happens on earth without divine will. The queen gave birth to a beautiful boy and returned with this extraordinary divine gift to her country. She brought numerous gifts with her, she returned triumphantly. The boy, who had been called the "son of the Goddess" from the beginning, was thus greeted with joy, and the queen, since she was still a virgin, or at least the priestesses claimed so, sat on the throne of Sheba and ruled until she gave power to her heir."

"Beautiful story!" Berenice was delighted.

"It's not the end, is it?" Aurelius was sure it would be continued.

"When she was pregnant, she had special visions. God spoke to her three times and passed his warnings for people. He ordered the king to write down and disseminate them so that they would become an appeal to the world. Solomon did it, he immortalized the words of his beloved very accurately. The prophecies were terrible. They talked about what awaits mankind if it does not follow the divine commandments. They also talked about something that would change the course of the world: the coming of the Messiah."

"I think those times have come now," Aurelius was pleased. "After all, here in Galilee, you hear about messiahs at every corner."

"Do you remember John the Baptist? They call him that too."

"He is a harmless madman! Remember, we saw him by the Jordan as he baptized people claiming to wash away their sins."

Mary shuddered at the memory of the figure of a man she saw then, and a dove hovering over his head.

"In any case, many signs indicate that the world is really going to change a lot."

"What will this change be?" Aurelius wondered.

"Who knows? But it has been talked about loudly for a long time, in all temples. What will happen, will stop time."

"And then what?" Berenice got scared.

"And then it will start again. Just like that. It'll pause for a moment and then start again from the beginning," Mary explained.

"It's the optimistic vision," said Lucius. "As the wise men say, a lot depends on the point of view."

\* \* \*

They followed the path to the top, which people called the Serpent. The access to the Masada fortress was possible only from this side. The other slopes were so steep that nobody in their right mind would try to get up the mountain that way.

The fortress was almost two hundred years old, but it became a modern place and the pride of the people of Israel only since the time of Herod the Great. It was him who expanded it and made everyone who visited it once remain impressed for the rest of his life by its charm, functionality, glamor and momentum with which it was built.

Now Masada was a border watchtower. The soldiers caring for the interests of the emperor of Rome, but also of his great supporter, Herod Antipas, stationed there.

From the time of Herod the Great, Masada had had every luxury, at least in the part intended for the ruler and his guests, and it was there that the travelers were to stay. As the fortress was abandoned by dignitaries, Berenice managed to ask her father to use his influence and connections so that they could use the chambers for special guests.

Already on the spot, Lucius, who had great social skills, arranged that they could see the most important parts of the palace for a reasonable fee. They only failed to get to the king's chambers. None of the servants dared to open them for them. Herod Antipas ruled hard. Nobody wanted to mess with him, and letting anyone into his apartments could be severely punished.

They wished they could see the most famous chamber in this part of the world. They knew that it was built on the edge of the cliff and belonged to the most guarded parts of the North Palace. Only Herod Antipas and those whom he personally invited were allowed to enter there. This place was said to have floors that were heated or cooled, depending on needs, and lined with the most beautiful mosaics in the world, as well as walls decorated with paintings of unusual colors "the paints were imported from the most distant parts of the world "and enriched with precious stones and ores. Roman-style sofas were lined with swan down mattresses, silk-covered cushions and poufs served as footrests, while the tables were made of pure gold and mother of pearl.

The ruler, who loved baths, had the world's most beautiful pool, whose one side was a fragment of a cliff. It had a wonderful view of the surrounding mountains and the Dead Sea. It was said that Herod the Great loved to rest on the edge of the abyss, drinking the finest wines in the pool in the company of the most beautiful women who walked the earth.

"I don't know if you know, but we're over one thousand three hundred feet above the Sea," Aurelius boasted of knowing the terrain.

"I can imagine how hard it was to erect it all," Berenice looked around.

They were on the top. The Serpent Path led them to a narrow gate. They were let through by a guard who had been warned about their arrival. Only previously announced guests could enter the fortress.

"Look!" Aurelius pointed at the buildings in turn. "The West Palace is the largest, over there. The small buildings in front of us are the blocks of the officials, and a synagogue should be behind them. On the far left, at the very end, as you can see, is the South Fortress, and here, closest to us, on the right, is, as you can see, a watchtower. Next are the tanks for collecting rainwater, and behind them, a bit further, grain is grown. The soil has been brought from fertile fields. To the right, where they will probably lead us soon, we will see massive storage buildings and baths. They were the pride of Herod the Great. The baths have very modern water heating or cooling systems, and so much food was stored in the warehouses that if the place had to be defended, it would be enough for the whole crew and their families for a hundred years or more. Well, at least that's what they say."

Aurelius, Lucius, David and Samuel laughed.

"And what daredevils would like to conquer this fortress?" David put his hands on his hips. "The only path that leads to the top is so steep that I must admit that I feel really tired after climbing it, and I am not a weakling."

"You are right, the road seems to have taken its toll on everyone. Maybe to relax a bit, we will first use the famous baths of Herod?" Berenice dreamed of taking a bath, despite no showing any signs of fatigue at all.

They followed the soldier who showed them the way. Only Mary did not move. Nobody noticed that she felt dizzy.

She leaned against the wall. She closed her eyes.

As if in a dream, she saw terrible scenes. Desperate, distraught, crying men were killing their wives and children. They pierced their hearts so that death would be as painless and quick as possible. They were Zealots defending the fortress against the Romans, who built a high siege tower, and additionally set it on an embankment, and this way they managed to break the wall. The defenders knew they stood no chance. When it became clear that their further resistance was pointless, they chose suicide instead of slavery.

She knew she had a vision, and this event could happen in the future. She also heard the words: "Let's not die as slaves of our enemies, but let's part with life as free people, together with our children and wives"[*]. Immediately afterwards, she saw the defenders burn everything that could become the prey of the

---

[*] J. Flavius wrote about this in the *Jewish War*; they are said to be the words of defenders' leader Eleazar ben Jair.

Romans, leaving only granaries filled with food, as a sign that their act was not caused by hunger. When the men killed their families, they drew ten of them whose task was to kill the others. When these men completed their mission, one of them pierced the hearts of his companions, and finally his own.

Mary saw hundreds of bodies laid evenly side by side. She knew there were nine hundred and sixty of them[**].

"Mary?" Lucius touched her shoulder. "Are you OK?"

She opened her eyes. She knew that she had a vision, and that something terrible could happen in this place someday.

But she was also sure that there was no need to tell her friend about it.

\* \* \*

"You are the priestess of Isis, aren't you? So you are no stranger to the pleasures of the body."

Lucius's eyes were getting bigger. He gazed lustily at her body submerged in water. She was in a dress, but the wet cloth stuck to her skin so she looked as if she was naked.

"I am not..." she murmured.

It was her feisty female confidence in her that spoke. She narrowed her eyes and felt the wildness of the goddess Bastet in herself. She flexed her body. She spread her arms from side to side, stretching.

---

[**] Today, Israeli soldiers take a military oath in Masada. It contains the words: *Masada will never be conquered again.*

"You are right: you have to take advantage of the moments that the gods give us. Life is so beautiful and at the same time so short," she laughed.

Strong wine circulated in her blood, of which they drank a lot. It was seasoned with herbs that relaxed the body. As servants assured, the same as those used by Herod the Great. They made his guests and himself always have a great time. Unbeknownst to the others, Berenice asked the slaves to season the wine with a double portions of these herbs. They drank it first for dinner, which they ate with appetite, and then again when they went to the thermal baths, already in great moods and holding each other up.

Three bathhouses were waiting for them. Thanks to a clever design, water and floors in each of them had different temperature. The pools were heated by external furnaces, while underneath the floors there were poles with cool or warm water flowing around them.

The modern technical solutions impressed them as much as the beauty of the interior in which they found themselves. Colorful mosaics, walls decorated with paintings, fresh flowers, the smell of fragrant oils and aromatic, thick wine, with which their goblets were topped continuously, made them relax quickly, and tiredness was replaced by laughter, jokes and playfulness.

The air temperature, the music coming from somewhere behind the walls, the men's admiring eyes, laughter of Berenice and her friends, and finally the touch of Lucius's hand, who was stroking her neck, made Mary want to have fun too. She wanted to forget the vision that greeted her as soon as she crossed the gate of the fortress, finally throw away her sorrows, the longing for the unknown, her thoughts of loneliness and dilemmas of heart and soul, and to indulge in fun. Without restraints or thinking of the possible consequences, without caring for conventions and customs. She felt that she could do anything and that she should do whatever she wanted. Because why not? They were in a safe place far away from the rest of the world, and everyone knew each other. They felt good together, liked and respected each other.

She decided that she would give voice to her femininity, desires, needs and longing. She will no longer restrain and hold herself back. She wanted to have fun. She is a priestess after all, she can do everything. She should be concerned with not only raising the spirit to a higher level "after all, the body also has its rights and it demands that she takes care of or lets others do it. And then... come what may. Let the world end tomorrow. She felt that in Herod's terms, only here and now was important.

"Mary, they are so handsome, I like them very much," Berenice called, splashing her with water.

Berenice did not care about the fact that "they" were next to them and could hear her every word. Just the opposite "she seemed to find it extremely amusing and be an additional incentive to provoke and show off.

"Which of them do you like?" Mary loved what Berenice was doing, but she thought it would be good to find out her preferences when it comes to men, so that they wouldn't accidentally get in each other's way in their play.

"Each one of them!" She called, sitting on the edge. "Look at them, they're all lookers, aren't they? Ha ha!" She laughed and sprayed her with water droplets again. "Let's play! Since the world is falling, there is nothing to wait for. Maybe we can go wild before it ends? Hahaha!"

Her short tunic, completely wet, emphasized her shapes. She knew she was beautiful. She saw it in the eyes of men, all of whom would be ready to give their life for her right now at her beck and call.

"I'm really delighted with each of them. Look how wonderful they are!"She reached out her finger and pointed in turn. "Philip, Aurelius, Samuel and Lucius! Even the future rabbi David! Ah, those guys, sweet like honey!"

"You are greedy!" Mary laughed, not knowing herself anymore. "Leave at least one for each of us."

"All right," Berenice agreed kindly. "Girls, say whom do you want."

The men laughed, they liked this game more and more. Only David sat on the side. Only his feet were immersed. Perhaps he had not drank enough wine, because what was happening did not please him at all.

One of the girls was not happy with what she saw either, so she left the pool.

"I'm leaving you, these are not games for me," she announced.

"You haven't drunk enough wine!" Philip, who apparently liked her most of all the girls, judged with disappointment.

"Let her go, I stay," said another girl, extending her hand to him. "I'll take care of you."

"Well, in that case, you're right, let her go." He moved toward her, took her outstretched hand, and kissed it.

"I going to crush out, too." David took his legs out of the water. "Samuel, are you staying?"

"Yes, I will sit here for a bit. Maybe, as a medical practitioner in the making, I will be useful on the spot?"

"I hope there will be no need..." David was disappointed with his answer. He believed that what was beginning to happen, was disliked but not only himself as a future rabbi, not only by the girl who had just left the room, but also by Samuel. They both came from Magdala and both believed in similar moral principles that were far from the promiscuity found so acceptable by the Romans, and, as he noticed with disgust, also by Mary.

"What if someone fainted? The water is really warm," Samuel tried to justify himself, tempted by what was beginning to happen around. "I will stay, I can be useful here."

"Go now, bores," Berenice urged the people out. "Hi, you there!" She shouted to the servant waiting at the door. "Bring some more wine! Can't you see that our goblets are empty?"

Then things went as they were set to happen.

Mary didn't notice when and how Lucius got so close to her that she felt his breath on her neck. She was shivering when he kissed her for the first time. And later, not knowing how and why, she was kissing him. Immersed in water, she put her legs around his hips. She melted into him, and later, when she was feeling good, screaming with pleasure, she dug her nails into his back and her teeth into his neck. He was pleased. He laughed and kissed her without restraint. It seemed to her, although she wasn't completely sure, that Lucius was replaced by Philip, then Aurelius, and later she did not know at all what

319

was going on and where she was. She felt she was swimming around. Out of the corner of her eye, she noticed that Berenice was lying on the warm floor nearby. She was laughing. Lucius ate fruit arranged on her naked body and licked the thick wine mixed with herbs and honey from her skin.

She liked what was happening, even though she wasn't sure if what she was experiencing was not just a figment of her imagination. She felt good. She felt relaxed. Finally, her body was fully relaxed.

She waved to the goddess Bastet, who was sitting by one of the columns and watching them with the mysterious smile of the kitty.

"Mary, you should become my priestess," she said in a singing voice. "It's not too late yet, my dear. Get on the ship, return to Egypt, my temples are waiting for you. You are beautiful and smart. You would be an excellent priestess of love."

\* \* \*

The sun had set for a long time, and a large bright moon took its place. A gentle wind was blowing from the sea.

After the play in the thermal baths, those who took part in it, slept through the day. Mary didn't wake up until sunset. When she realized what had happened the previous night, she wanted it to be just one of her visions. She couldn't remember at all how she had reached the chamber intended for her, and when she found that Lucius was lying next to her in the bed, she quickly put on her dress and went outside.

She went for a long walk. There was a wall at the edges of the massive hill top they were on. There was a perfect view of the whole area from there. Passing by the soldiers, she came to a place where there was no one. She sat on a stone. Below, the sapphire blue of the Dead Sea was framed by the yellow-gold stones of the desert.

"Mary, we've known each other for a long time... "Lucius said.

She turned around, surprised. He stood behind her.

After she left the room, he opened his eyes, and when he realized that he was alone, he went looking for her. He found her quickly.

He waited a long time for the right moment. He had promised himself a long time ago that he would talk to her, and after what had happened at night, he decided that he had not only the full right to it, but it was his duty.

Evenings were already cold at this time of year, so he covered her back with the coat he brought with him. She thanked him.

"Do you remember the old woman's words?"

"What old woman, Lucius?"

She stared at the rock sculpture in the distance, which seemed to her to be a stone figure called Loth's Wife, illuminated by the moon. She was glad he hadn't mentioned what happened at night. They both acted as if it did not happen.

"The one in the pub in Alexandria, you know, this fortune teller."

"Oh, this one. Yes, sure. I also sometimes think about what she told us then."

"Right. I remember perfectly well what she told Marcus. I thought about it many times. She warned him."

"You think so?"

"Her words were like a song. *Don't fall in love with a girl who reads. Don't fall in love with a girl who gets lost in music. Don't fall in love with a girl who...*"

"Lucius, what do you want to tell me?" She didn't take her eyes off Loth's Wife.

"Mary, you are just such a woman. One who reads, writes, dances, sings, gets emotional, one who thinks. The old lady was talking about you."

"You think so?"

"I knew it already then, she was talking about you. Do you know why? He took her hand to make her take eyes away from the opposite hills and look at him. Because I loved you then already. I was delighted with you since I first saw you. I knew that only you matter and that I will do anything for you. But you were with Marcus then. You didn't see anyone else besides him. When he left, and later when he got married, I thought I might have a chance..."

She looked at him in surprise but did not say anything.

"Why did I come here? Do you really think I dreamed of a career as an imperial soldier in Galilee? Really? I am here only for you. I was just waiting for the right moment to tell you this."

She knelt before him. She stroked his cheek.

"Thank you, Lucius."

"Thank you, Lucius? That's all? After what I told you and the last night? Will we pretend that nothing happened? Is that what you want?"

"For now, yes."

"You still love Marcus despite what he did to you?"

"No. I said goodbye to him already. I was with Marcus, because I didn't understand my path. I couldn't recognize it. I loved him very much, but now I know that then, in Alexandria, after the old woman's words, I sensed that we would never be together. I wanted to be with him, believe me, but something told me that we were not meant for each other."

"And I? I am here for you. I love you. Say one word and I will marry you. Tomorrow. Even today. And I will live with you wherever you want. We can stay here if it is your will, we can live in Egypt or go to Rome. My family will welcome you with open hands. I talked about you with my mother and father. And you know what? I have always known that, but after what happened yesterday, I am absolutely sure that you are the woman of my life."

"Maybe after yesterday, Aurelius, Philip and I am not sure who else, because believe me, I really don't know what happened there, maybe they could say the same?" She was cruel to him and herself. "You know that some herbs were added to the wine. What was happening got out of control for all of us. It will be better for each of us if we forget about it."

"I don't regret anything. I love you and I want to marry you. You are wonderful, and you didn't let Aurelius or Philip as much as touch you. I am saying it so that you know."

She didn't know if the last sentence was intended to calm her down, or if it was true. She preferred not to ask.

She was silent. She felt that he really loved her. Everything he had just said and what he had done in recent months testified to this.

"Lucius, my dear," she cried with emotion.

Since the time of Marcus, she had forgotten that someone could love her. She closed herself to feelings. She didn't notice them. She, who once read human emotions and intentions so easily, thought that what connected her with Lucius, even after the last crazy night, was above all a friendship. How could she be so wrong? Here she hears that he came for her to the province, for her he lived in a military camp, and took care of her. And in addition, he told his parents about her. "Oh Goddess, how could I be so blind? How could I close myself to the world so much that I didn't notice the love he was offering me?"

"Lucius, know that I value what you said very much. You are especially close to me. I am very touched. I didn't suspect in my wildest dreams that it was as you say. Your feeling is an honor for me. You are a great man."

"But?

"But I don't know my path. I'm at a crossroads. I don't know where the gods will lead me. I cannot and do not want to make decisions now. The time for them has not yet come. You honor me with a feeling. This is the greatest gift that can be offered to another person. I love you too, but my love is not enough to make a decision about living together. I don't know what will happen next and I say it with all my heart: maybe I need time? I don't know, forgive me."

7.

That day Mary went to the city for no particular reason. Something was attracting her there. She put on a simple dress, threw a scarf over her head, and left. There were many people gathered near the synagogue, in the square. She wondered what they were doing there. It was quiet. They did not shout, as is often the case on such occasions. They listened, staring at one person.

She stopped and put her hand to her forehead to shield her eyes from the sun, and at the same time to better see. She looked at it for so long that at some point she thought that what she saw was a dream. That she wasn't standing on the street by one of Magdala's stone houses at all, but that it was just her imagination. She would wake up in a moment, and the image she had before her eyes would disappear.

He was standing on the platform, among the people. He was surrounded by several men who formed a kind of cordon around him. He was talking. She could not hear him, he was far away, but she could clearly see the bright, twinkling golden aura surrounding him, the kind that accompanies only the chosen ones.

He looked almost like a statue. He gestured moderately. People stared at him in speechless admiration.

She closed her eyes. A breeze blew. She felt a soft flash in her head, like a brush of light. She saw the figure of a man standing on a hill at Lake Kinnereth and a dove above his head. A moment later, the memory of the softness of the byssus appeared in her fingertips and she remembered the outfit that was waiting for a stranger in the chest. Another flash made her realize that the one who was now standing in Magdala and talking to the people, was the one Lazarus had told her about, and whose presence she had sensed once in the garden at Bethany. He was also the one she saw on the hill above the lake.

Yes, it was him. The one whose name was Jesus.

She looked, focused. She prayed.

And later, when he set off with his companions to continue his journey, and the people began to leave, she gratefully paid tribute to the Goddess, so that no one would notice. She looked nostalgically at the man walking away and returned home.

* * *

Marta had been visiting Lazarus for several days. During her absence from Magdala, David visited Mary.

"I know what I'm saying is unusual," he began timidly. "But you are not an ordinary woman."

They were sitting in the garden. When David visited her, he was particularly careful with Halakhah, knowing that her sister was not at home. As the son of a rabbi and, as he trusted, the future rabbi, he lived according to the principles and law of Moses. So he could not and did not want to be alone with a woman in a locked room. It was different when they were in a larger group. At such times, even though it was a bit at odds with his habits and values, he talked to her like the others, freely and openly. It was these meetings, in which her Roman friends participated, and what he noticed during them, that prompted him to act.

326

Well, it seemed to him that Lucius had turned his feelings towards the one he liked, too. He also had reasons to believe that Samuel, the medic's son, was serious about Mary.

So, trying not to remember what he saw in the Masada thermal baths, or maybe just because of what he saw there, and to avoid anyone beat him to that, he decided to talk to her. A general talk first, to find out her attitude towards him, and later, if everything would go his way, his father would talk to her brother about it. Although Lazarus lived in Bethany, he was the only man in the family, so it was with him that such matters should be discussed.

"I know you grew up somewhere else, but I don't mind," he said. "We've gotten to know each other a bit and it is not a problem for me that you are extremely open-minded for our standards, and educated, too. This is even interesting and can help in the future. You know the history, geography, you read the works of the masters. You seem to have even learned the basics of medical treatment. To be honest, I admire you for that, you are the only woman I know who knows so much. Besides, I really like you."

"I value you too, and I'm glad we gave each other friendship," she answered neutrally, with a smile encouraging him to continue speaking.

"As you know, I'm a son of a rabbi. My father is a Pharisee. Although I'm not as conservative as he is, sometimes my sympathies turn to the Sadducees, and sometimes I have other, completely independent thoughts. I suppress them. I know that being a scholar is a great obligation. You have to fight mental temptations, try not to succumb to false and misleading voices.

I'm following in my father's footsteps and, as you know, I'm studying so that I could take his place one day."

"You are very consistent in what you do. This is admirable."

"I'm glad to hear that. Especially from you, an extraordinary woman in my opinion. Thank you. As you probably know, I'm already at the age when a man must look for a wife."

"Really?" She was kindly surprised, which was supposed to be another encouragement for him to continue.

"Yes. Have you already decided what you are going to do next?"

"I'm still at a crossroads."

"Will you stay here or come back to Egypt?" He asked the question and was immediately scared by his directness.

"It is giving me sleepless nights. I understand that you ask as a friend. So I'll answer you like a friend. I would like to come back to my grandparents' house, I still miss them a lot, but at the same time, something keeps me here. On the one hand I still feel strange in Magdala, and on the other, I feel as if I had been given some powerful commitments to the people and places here. I have a hard time living with it. I am not able to make a decision yet, but I believe that the solution will come."

"God will show it to you."

"I'm counting on it."

"Mary, you need male support and protection. Maybe if you had someone, your life here would be better? A man who would be a refuge for you, could finally make you feel completely at home here."

"Do you mean someone specific?" She asked, absolutely sure of his intentions.

"No," he lied awkwardly. "Although in principle, I admit, yes. After all, as a future rabbi, I can't avoid the truth. Yes, I mean someone specific."

"David, I don't think we should talk about it, according to Halakhah?" She decided that she would no longer pretend that she did not understand.

"Mary, if I feel your favor, I will ask my father to talk to your brother."

"Don't ask him."

"How come?"

"It is an honor for me that you would like to take care of me, but I am not ready to make a decision yet. To tell you the truth, I don't know what to do in my life, let alone who should my husband be. Please, support me, I need it very much. I am happy that you are near and that I can always count on your sympathy and kindness, but I am asking you for patience."

"I will pray that God shows you the way."

"I will be grateful to you for prayers in my intention," she took his hand. "Thank you for being here."

Near them stood Ethel, holding a tray with drinks. She was supposed to put it on the table in front of them, but when she saw what was happening, she stopped. Looking at Mary and David's intertwined hands of, she cried out as loudly as she could, so that not only they, but also all the servants could hear her:

"What I see in this house cries vengeance to heaven!" She returned to the kitchen with the tray, without giving them the drinks. Mary followed her.

"What's going on, Ethel? What is your behavior supposed to mean?"

"I'm sick of it! I am leaving the place where God's commandments are traded in! This is worse than Sodom and Gomorrah! You were holding hands, I saw it! You are a shameless sinner!"

"What are you saying, your tongue hurts me..." Mary was calm.

"My tongue tells what the eyes have seen and the ears have heard."

"You don't always have to believe them, because maybe they don't have the full picture?"

"I saw and heard!"

"Don't accuse or condemn if you don't know the case."

"I know it."

"The testimony of your senses is not enough to accuse anyone! Human tongue may be the most dangerous tool in the world. It can hurt and even kill. Use it wisely. Don't hurt others with gossip and false accusations. Keep it in check. Tame the thoughts that want to give bad shape to the words. Sometimes it's better to say nothing than to say one word too much. Words are silver but silence is golden."

"You will be condemned!"

"See with your heart, it can see more than your eyes. And do not tell false testimony against your neighbor!"

Ethel would not listen any further. She pushed Mary and ran out of the house.

\* \* \*

She rushed into the city. At the well, she spat out what had been gathering in her for months. Women listened to her eagerly.

"Sodom and Gomorrah are nothing next to it!" She cried, and more and more people were gathering around. "She receives men, talks to them, they eat together, speak foreign languages so that nobody could understand them. Demons live in this house, she keeps them in the trunks, which she brought with her from the barbarians. She has devilish herbs and poisoned stones in them. She also holds dresses there that lure men, she has jewelry that the world has never seen. A demon which follows and destroys us, looks at the world through the eyes of her cat. Where this cat stands, flowers wither. And she knows no shame! She seduced David. I saw it! Terrible things are happening in this house! Women together with men, night meetings, inappropriate laughs, the Romans! Have you seen her shawl? It is crimson. It's the color of the invader's soldiers, the color of shame! Pah!"

The groups of women shook their heads over what was happening in their neighborhood while swatting away the flies, which had recently become extremely bothersome. Some were murmuring menacingly, and there were also some who were shouting something. They all listened to Ethel with interest and growing indignation. It had been whispered in the city for a long time about what was going on in Syro's house since he passed.

\* \* \*

While the situation at the well was becoming increasingly tense, and Ethel spewed more and more accusations, a messenger on horseback reached Mary. He brought a letter.

As soon as he left, she unrolled it.

*Dear beloved Mary!*
*I don't know how to convey this tragic message to you, but I'm aware that it is me who should do it.*
*Our wonderful Mrs. Aida, a woman of a big heart, your wonderful grandmother, has passed away.*
*It happened completely unexpectedly.*
*As you know, she had an accident some time ago. She wrote to you about it. She broke her leg and hit her hip, but everything was getting better. The medic claimed that the bone was healing well and the hip, even though it was still bothering her, was also in better shape. It annoyed her that she had to lie down. You know, as always, she was very active. She was getting up more and more recently. The medic said that she should not do this, but she did not listen to him.*
*One morning she got up from bed without anyone's help. She told me later that she had slipped. She fell over and, unfortunately, her thigh fractured again. The bone cracked in the same place as before. I ran to her as soon as I heard a scream. The medic also appeared as soon as possible. She was treated, we gave her painkillers because she was suffering a lot. I also called Charmion from the temple, because the matter seemed serious to me. The priestess was very worried. She said breaking in the same place again would not bode well. She*

*looked at the little boards that the medic had applied, added her best ointments, those made of herbs, at which the priestesses perform rituals three times a day, she prayed for Aida's recovery, and promised to come the next day.*

*I called for both the medic and Charmion again at night. Your wonderful grandmother had a very high temperature, she was delirious and screamed. They gave her medicine. The fever subsided for a moment, but quickly returned even higher. Charmion, the medic and I were with her all the time. She did not regain consciousness. Charmion said that when the body is weakened, bad forces often invade the site that has been broken again, and they cannot be chased away by any means.*

*Aida left us early in the morning.*

*I sent a message to your grandfather. He must be on his way. He was with Stephanie in Alexandria. He has stayed there almost all the time since you left. Know that Your Grandma did not blame him for that. She told me many times that so many years after their wedding, she is glad that she can live in friendship with him. And in the end, she herself chose Stephanie, and suggested her to him personally. She always said about her that she was not only a beautiful girl, but also a good one. I am writing to you so that you do not worry that Karim will be left not taken care of. As you surely know, Stephanie has always been extremely attentive to him.*

*My dear, beloved Mary, I am and will be at the estate. I have been managing it since my return from Galilee, and I seem to be good at it. I hope that despite the tragic changes I will stay here and wait for you. Your grandmother has always said that it is not only hers but also your house and that you will inherit it after her passing. I don't know if you know it, but she made a document long ago in which she gave the property to you. So you are its owner.*

*Forgive me for writing this now. I imagine how great a shock the death of our great Aida is for you, because I too still can't pull myself together, but I would like to ask you what your plans regarding the estate are. As I wrote, you are its owner now. You can of course sell it, if it is your wish, but I hope that it will not be so, and you will soon return to us, to our great joy. In the meantime, I offer myself as the one who can manage your assets. I am able to manage it so that it will continue to bring profits from the gardens and orchards as it has till now. Please, think about it, beloved Mary. I am waiting for your decisions. Can we expect your return in the near future?*

*Of course, I took care of mummification and everything related to the funeral with the greatest care.*

*Dear Mary, I send you my kisses, I am praying for strength and health for you in these difficult times.*

*Yours forever, devoted to your*

*Sithathor*

Mary read to the end, dropped the letter and fainted. When she opened her eyes, David was kneeling over her. He was trying to revive her, and talking to her tenderly.

"What happened? "She asked, coming back to her senses.

"You were lying here when I came," he explained. "I came back because I thought I should support you in your confusion. You should know that Magdala is the place for you. Your home is here, and not anywhere else. I came to tell you, but I found you fainted."

She remembered the content of the letter.

"I learned that my grandmother died."

"I am very sorry for you."

Suddenly, their quiet conversation was interrupted by a scream.

"I curse you, Mary, and this whole house!" they heard.

It was Ethel, who, having left the women at the well, came for the rest of her belongings. She stood in the garden, watching what was happening. She could not know about the letter, or that Mary had fainted and David was saving her. As many times before, she reacted to what her eyes saw.

"This woman is possessed!" Ethel's scream turned into a lament. "She seduces any man who stands in her path. God, can you see that?!" She raised her head and hands to the sky. "She even bewitched the son of your servant, Rabbi Yitzhak. Impossible! Sodom and Gomorrah!"

She called out, threatened them with a fist, turned around and ran towards the city, forgetting her bundle.

"Ethel, it's not what you think, listen!" David called after her.

She didn't even stop for a moment. She ran as fast as her feet took her. Finally, she felt obliged to do something about the public sins that she witnessed.

"Nothing good will come of it..." David knew the local customs well. "I should run after her before she screams her ridiculous version to the whole city."

"I have such a bad reputation in Magdala that nothing can make it worse anymore," she reassured him, standing up and dusting her dress off.

"May you be right. However, if you feel better, even though you have received such devastating news, let me go to the city. I feel that I will be needed there. It is better that people hear not only from Ethel what has happened here. I'll explain it to my father first. I prefer him to learn from me. And you better not leave the house. Close the gate and don't open it to anyone. I recommend it to you as a friend."

\* \* \*

Ethel ran out of breath. When she stood at the well, she shouted out, crying:

"People! I saw it. I saw it a moment ago. With my own eyes. As I am standing here before you. She seduced David! She is possessed by demons. We have to save ourselves! She will bring destruction to our city and all of us! Let's do something before it's too late! I saw it, I saw it! I swear. Come there with me! We must act before God punishes us all!"

"You're right. Away with her!" One of the women called out.

"She is a stranger, let her come back to her place!" Another shouted.

Subsequent voices merged into one shout, encouraging to take the matter into their own hands.

"Let her practice her spells where she came from!"

"We don't want her here!"

They walked toward Mary's house, threatening with their fists and waving with whatever they had in their hands. Women and men, who joined the group unnoticed, became one erratic force that no one had control of. They yelled as they walked.

"She brings a curse on us!"

"Slut!"

"Sinner!"

"Possessed!"

Mary heard screams. People were already outside her house.

She regretted not listening to David and not closing the door, but it was too late. They ran into the garden and then home. Speeding up, they turned over the furniture, they did not care about the small objects placed against the walls.

She stood to face them. They stopped, surprised, but only for a moment.

"What do you want?" She folded her arms.

"Sinner!" Ethel shouted, and then more insults came.

Everything happened quickly. They surrounded her, began to spit and kick. Someone grabbed her hair, someone slapped her face, someone jerked at her clothes.

They dragged Mary outside the house and threw her to the ground. She got up.

"What have I done to you?"

"Get out! We don't want you here!"

"Whore!"

They were shouting one over another. Someone picked up a stone and threw it. After the first one, more stones followed.

People spat at her, kicked her and threw whatever they found at her.

Leo suddenly appeared. He stood in front of his mistress and started making cat screams with all his might to scare off the attackers.

"Egyptian witch!"

"She has a cat in her service!"

"It's a demon!"

"A devilish force!"

Stones fell also towards Leo. One of them hit him on the head. Blood spurted and the animal fell over. His body was trembling.

Mary took him in her arms and shielded him.

"My love..." she whispered.

Goddess Bastet looked at the hateful crowd. "There is no place for you here, my little one" she whispered in his ear and patted him with her divine hand to relieve his suffering. "I will take you to Egypt. You'll always be good there."

His eyes fogged, he licked Mary's hand goodbye and after a while, he was dead. And the crowd, instead of calming down, began an even stronger attack as soon as it smelled blood. Mary tried to get up, hugging the dead cat.

"Barbarians!" She called out.

More stones flew.

"Go away!" she heard.

"Witch!"

She saw someone take her Egyptian stuff out of the house, and another set it on fire, but she was completely indifferent to it. She got up with the rest of her strength and got out of the gate of the estate.

Curses chased her and more stones reached her.

She was fleeing.

When she turned around for a moment, she saw Ethel standing at the gate. She was threatening her with a fist.

\* \* \*

"When I entered the garden, she was unconscious." David explained to his father. "A letter from Egypt lay next to it. I looked at it. It seems that her grandmother died and Mary inherited the property on the Nile. I revived her."

"If I inherited wealth, I would probably faint too," Yitzhak nodded with understanding.

"She was very close to her grandmother. She spent almost all her life so far with her. She fainted when she found out she was dead."

"The Lord works in mysterious ways. Good that you woke her up. You should take care of her, who knows maybe Adonai will join your paths?"

"Exactly, father."

"So you say that our Mary has inherited a fortune? She has been the most attractive virgin in Magdala so far, even though her father left only half the estate to her. Now her value has increased even more. It's good you helped her. People should be helped."

339

"Father, Ethel came when I was reviving her. You know how she is."

"God-fearing?"

"Maybe even too much."

"There is never "too much" when it comes to godliness."

"She began to shout about Sodom and Gomorrah, and divine offense. She called Mary the worst names and rushed into town."

"Oh, not good," the turn of events worried the rabbi. "Nothing good will come of it."

"That's why I come to you, father. Something needs to be done to calm her down. She is ready to stir up the whole city against this poor girl."

"The Lord works in mysterious ways. Whatever is to be, will be."

"I'll go to the square, see what's going on. A big crowd has gathered there. You can hear them screaming even here."

"Let them shout, they will get tired of it quickly. You have to let them get wild. People have to express their emotions. From time to time, a little row does good for the community."

"Is this what God's books teach us?"

"Yes, they teach us that too. There is a lot of wisdom for every occasion. You are young, you have a hot head. After you live a little longer, and study the Scriptures, you'll know that getting involved in human disputes is never right, especially when the strongest emotions are involved."

"But a tragedy can happen there, father."

"You'd better keep silent and watch from a safe distance. Not getting involved on either side is also a sign of wisdom."

"But here there is no doubt. Mary is slandered wrongly."

"I see you like this girl."

"Father, you just praised me for helping her."

"There is no point fighting the crowd. The crowd must be allowed to let their emotions leave them. If Mary understands what they shout about her, it'll do her some good. She is stubborn. It is worth dulling her ferocity - she will be a better wife then."

"What do you advise then?"

"Do not leave home, wait for developments. Anyway, can you hear? The screams died down. People dispersed."

Seeing his son's displeased face, he added:

"All right, I'll talk to Ethel."

\* \* \*

When she woke up, she saw the sky covered with stars. She was lying in the bushes. She didn't know how she got to this place and where she was. She hurt all over and her body was covered in wounds. She was unable to move. She was thirsty.

"Lady, save me," she whispered and lost consciousness.

When she opened her eyes again, it was slowly dawning. She looked around. She was by the lake, but she didn't know where. Certainly not very close to home, because she did not recognize the area.

She remembered the events of the previous day. The letter from Sithathor, her despair at the news of her grandmother's death, then David's face bent over her, Ethel shouting curses and all the horrors that followed.

Her whole body ached. She touched her bruised face. Then she heard voices, they were getting closer. They belonged to men. They were drunk. They were probably coming back from a pub. She cringed and lay motionless.

"Hey, look, I think the lake gave us a gift," one of them croaked.

They came closer. Mary curled up even more. She couldn't run away. She had no strength to crawl "pain and fear paralyzed her. She couldn't even chase away the flies that sat on her aching body.

"If the lake gives us something, it means that it is a gift for us." One of them leaned over to examine her. "A bit roughed up, but will do."

"She's lying and asking for pleasure," said another.

"If she asks, we won't refuse..." Another stood before her. "I can be first."

There were seven of them. They stank of the stench of long unwashed bodies. Their jagged and carious gums and lips stank with old alcohol. Two were holding her hands. She tried to break away, but she knew that she had no chance. She lacked the strength to defend herself, so she stopped struggling. She was lying as if dead. And she was dead. She wasn't there. Her soul flied away to the heights and dissolved into space.

And they raped her, one after the other, and it did not matter to them whether she was breathing or feeling anything, or whether she was alive at all.

When they finished, they stood up, each spat contemptuously in her direction and went away.

She did not know how long she was unconscious and how many times she fell into darkness. When she opened her eyes, she saw a wineskin with water and a piece of matzah. Some good soul left them for her, seeing her condition and misfortune. She summoned all her strength. She reached for the wineskin and tried to open it for a long time. Her injured fingers refused to obey her. When at last, with the greatest effort, she succeeded, she fainted again. When she regained consciousness, she remembered the skin. Fortunately, it was next to her, and the water did not spill out. She drank greedily. Then she broke a piece of matzah and put it in her mouth. She was chewing slowly.

The mangled body had no strength left for despair. Her thighs were covered with dried sperm mixed with her blood. Her temples throbbed, her skin burned, her beaten places hurt, she was bruised and injured. But she did not think about it.

She remembered the words of Charmion from the temple: "A kite is the Isis's bird. When her young are in danger, their mother sends them a signal to pretend to be dead. They do it well enough that the predator leaves them alone." She decided to hide better in case the rapists returned. In a superhuman effort, she began to crawl towards the bushes. She prayed all the time, asking Isis for support.

"Lady, save me, please, or have mercy and take me to yourself. I have no more strength.

343

She thought that eternity had passed before she finally reached a safe place, crawling. In fact, she moved only about a dozen cubits away and fell into darkness again."

When she opened her eyes, she was able to drink some water. Miraculously, the skin bottle was strapped to her waist and she unconsciously dragged it behind her while crawling. This time she did not lose consciousness as before, but for the first time since she got at the lake, she simply fell asleep.

While she was sleeping, rapists stood over her again. They were back.

"See? She's waiting for us."

"It was so good that she decided not to move from place."

"Well, she's lived to see us!"

"Hey, pretty girl, we're here!"

However, none of them even touched her. They didn't have a chance.

A figure dressed in black appeared before them. They were not able to recognize its gender under the scrolls of the cloth. It looked like a big, strong man. It took out a large knife from behind the belt.

Mary was asleep. In the dream she saw the bright figure of a man. He was standing on the hill, arms outstretched. He called for her. She wanted to go to him, but she couldn't, her legs were too heavy. She tried to fly, but she had no wings. She wanted to rise without them, she knew that she could, but something limited her, some weight she couldn't bear, something she couldn't deal with, something that didn't let her rise to the light. She tried to break through the invisible ceiling that hung just above her head, limiting her. She was struggling, trying, but it seemed she had no chance. And just when she wanted to give up, a familiar flash appeared that allowed her to see things clearly. She understood what the problem was. "Get rid of the burden of the body and your spirit will become free." She remembered the words of Priestess Agnes and saw her figure, colorful dress and multi-colored scarf waving in the wind.

And later Isis came to her. She had the face of High Priestess. She touched her and a miracle happened: after a while Mary floated in the same space and glow in which the illuminated man appeared a moment before. The goddess shielded her from what might have happened.

When she woke up, she was in a cave. Nefer knelt beside her.

"No, you're not dreaming. It's really me," she said gently. "Goddess sent me. She always cares for her priestesses."

She put a small bottle by her lips.

"Drink it," she asked. "It will help you. You will fall asleep and I will be here with you. You're safe now."

"Nefer, you have become a brave hemet?"

"That was the will of the Goddess." Nefer made a triple gesture.

"Great that you are here. Thank you."

"The High Priestess saw that something bad was happening to you. She was worried that you would leave this world before you could fulfill your mission. There are so many evil forces against you. They wanted to prevent you from completing your mission. They are present among people more than ever now, they do not want something that would reopen the Gates of Light to happen. They are muddling, plotting, disturbing. They're sipping venom into hearts. Swarms of black flies are their sign. You probably saw them many times. The priestess ordered me to support you and tell you to remember that what doesn't kill you, will give you strength and for sure will change you irreversibly. Don't give up, you're the chosen one. Go." She bowed her head.

## 8.

After returning from Bethany, Marta found the house in such a state as if a hurricane had passed through it.

The terrified servants did not touch anything until her return, fearing that if they would clean up and remove the damage, she would not realize how great the wickedness had taken place there.

When she returned, David immediately appeared, brought by his remorse.

"I've been looking for her everywhere for five days," he assured her. "I even hired people to help. She dropped off the face of the earth."

"David, the servants say you were here a moment before it happened. Tell me what you know!"

Marta didn't care that she was alone with him in a locked room. It didn't seem to bother him either. The situation was unusual. Marta was shaking with emotions and her jaw was clenched, she was in a fight mode and prepared for a battle. Neither he nor any of the maids had ever seen her like this.

"Tell me what happened, now!" She ordered and pushed him into the chair.

He told her everything to the last detail. He didn't even forget that he had looked into the letter from Sithathor. He knew that it was certainly important, and it rightly seemed to him that after what had happened at home, it could have disappeared somewhere, maybe even irretrievably.

"My poor little Mary..." Marta wrung her hands. "Where can she be now?"

"I really looked for her everywhere," he assured her. "The trails led to the lake, but at one point they stopped."

"I'm about to go in search!" She stood up. "And you do something to make people feel the harm they did to her. You owe it to her!"

"I'll try."

"No: "I'll try", you have to do it! God is looking at you, remember!"

* * *

Marta searched carefully every place where she thought her sister could be hiding. First she went to the lake. Exactly to the place where they once found her with her father, when she wandered alone from home as a little girl. She wasn't there. She searched the thicket and bushes by the lake. She looked into every hollow in the rocks of the hills, but found no sign anywhere. She noticed a lot of blood in one place. It was splashed over stones.

"Someone had to fight here, and with great force" she thought. Then, quite unexpectedly, a figure appeared in front of her inner eyes, in her head, dressed in black and with a big knife in its hand. She thought she also saw seven men, repulsive and at the same time scared. "What is that?" She was surprised. She had never experienced anything like it before. After a moment, she saw a bloody scene: the black figure cut off a man part of each of them, and it acted so quickly, that even those to whom she was doing it at the moment, had trouble understanding what was going on.

Terrified, Marta fell to her knees. But this was not the end of the vision. Here the woman in black, because Marta already sensed that the fighting figure was a female avenger, pushed the bleeding pieces of what had recently been a part of their bodies, into each man's mouth.

Marta lay down on the stones and began to sob. Her crying turned into a wail, then a loud howl. She already knew what had happened to her sister in this place, as well as what punishment had befallen the rapists.

She also knew that she should return home, because Mary is now safe and in the best care. And that she would get her sister back soon.

\* \* \*

That same night something woke her up. It seemed to her that she was called by the woman avenger from her vision. She ran to Mary's chamber. Her sister was lying in bed, carefully covered. There were numerous signs of beating, wounds, bruises and scratches on her face and hands, but she was sleeping peacefully.

Beside her lay a purse filled with vials and bags of herbs. There was the same mark on the bag as Mary had on her neck.

From that moment Marta didn't let anyone into her chamber. She took care of her sister herself. She looked after her, fed her, washed and cleaned the room. She didn't want anyone else to see her condition.

* * *

Marta looked at Lucius' pleading eyes.

"She's been through a lot lately."

"This is why I am here."

"I don't know if she'll want to see you. She doesn't leave the room since it happened."

"Let me in. You know I'm her friend."

"It's also because of you that she is in this state."

"I'll get her out of here. This place is bad for her. We will leave to Egypt or Rome. I will marry her. You know I love her."

She led him to Mary's chamber, told him to wait outside the door, and went inside herself.

"Lucius is here," she announced.

"I don't want to see anyone."

"He's a friend."

"I know."

"Shall I let him in?"

"It's better for him to not see me like this."

Lucius was standing at the door just as Marta had told him, and because they were ajar, he heard every word. He knocked and entered without waiting for an answer.

349

"I found out what happened and decided to take a break in the army." He stood beside her bed.

It was dark in the room. Mary was laying in the middle of the bed, curled up. When he came in, she cringed even more.

"I don't want you to look at me," she sobbed.

"I won't if you don't want it. But I promised myself I will not leave you until you recover. You are not safe here, you need protection. I will ask your sister to give me a place to put my mat on. I will protect you from this wild mob."

"Stay if you need it."

"You need it," he snarled.

"If you think so, stay. But I don't want you to come here and look at me. Please respect that."

"You can be sure that I will not do anything against your will."

"Thank you, you are very noble."

"I love you."

Lucius stayed in Syro's former chamber. He waited patiently for Mary to invite him, but she still did not leave the room. Marta claimed that her wounds were almost healed, but her soul was so mangled that she still needed a lot of time to recover. So much time that nobody was able to assess how much. And Lucius didn't want to wait that long.

Before leaving, he knocked on her door again. She didn't answer. He opened it and entered.

She was lying on the bed with her eyes open. She stared at the ceiling. She looked almost as beautiful as before, but her eyes were completely empty. He came close. She didn't move.

"Mary?"

No reaction. Marta was telling the truth, things weren't good with her. Things were even worse than on the day he came to protect her.

He was worried about her condition, but he was proud of one thing: since he lived in this house, no one from Magdala dared to cross the gates of the estate.

The inhabitants of the town acted as if nothing had happened. They didn't talk about it among themselves, and even at home, when no one could hear their conversations, they also carefully avoided it. After the lynching they had made, the bad air that had long accumulated in them, was released. Even the flies, so many of which had been recently flying around the well, somehow dispersed around the town and returned to the houses where they normally lived. It happened just as Rabbi Yitzhak had predicted: the sources of the negative emotions of the group, which must occasionally find an outlet somewhere, were exhausted, and the bloodlust got satisfied.

Lucius leaned over Mary. Looking at Mary's face, which resembled a mask from up close and did not express any emotions, he said, hoping that something would get through to her:

"I'm leaving, but I'll be waiting for you. Always. In Jerusalem, Alexandria, Rome, wherever I am. All you have to do is let me know and I'll come for you. I love you. Also now, when I don't know where your spirit is wandering. And I'll never stop. A woman like you is for life. If I have to, I will wait, even if it takes forever. I am yours. And I will always be."

* * *

She was woken up by nausea. She did not have time to get out from the bed, when the insides tugged her so hard that she leaned and vomited on the floor.

She had no strength to stand up. Every particle of her body protested against what was happening. Her head was exploding, her skin burned, and her hair was coming out in a handfuls. The bed was full of them. Some she tore out herself in her sleep, other fell out. She looked at her stomach. It had bloody scratch marks. There was also dried blood under her fingernails, and bloody marks on the sheet.

Nightmares tormented her at night. She saw the terrible, distorted faces of men above her, smelled their hideous, repulsive stench. They were on her again, tore her apart, pushed her, murdered her body and soul. And again, just like then, she bit, scratched, kicked, tried to brake free, howled with terror, humiliation and pain.

She woke up later. Wet, hot, terrified and shaky. Hugged by Marta.

"My baby, my love, it's okay," she said, stroking her head.

"Marta, I can't take it, I can't take it anymore, I'm going crazy!" She complained. "I have no more strength. I'm sick."

"You'll get better. Everything evil will pass, you will forget, it will be fine."

* * *

But it wasn't. She felt worse and worse. One day she realized that she was pregnant. That the bandits who had attacked her, had planted a seed in her, and that it was so terrible for her that she couldn't live with it. She had no strength to think, but she felt with her whole heart that she was so devastated and mutilated that she could not bear another misfortune "the fruit of what happened to her.

She felt disgusted with herself. She couldn't look at her body, injured and scratched, and in addition, filled with what the rapists had left behind. She fell into despair and howled in an inhuman voice. She was pulling her hair out. She tugged at her temples first, wanting to hurt herself and punish her body for what had happened. Later, when it did not help, she grabbed them by a handful and jerked them until they came out of the head with patches of skin. When the resulting wounds began to heal, she ripped off the scabs and scratched because she didn't want them to seal. Thanks to petechia and blood, she felt the of her body despair even stronger.

To punish it even more, to remember how miserable and weak it was, she was inflicting more wounds on herself. She cut the skin on the inside of her thighs with a sharp shell. She watched the red drops running down her legs... and continued cutting. The wounds were getting deeper and longer. She didn't let them scar. Blood dripped from the wounds and then pus appeared. As soon as they dried up a bit, she cut them again and, crying, watched them, despairing over her pain, smallness and powerlessness.

As soon as Marta noticed what was happening, she decided not to let her out of her sight. She sat next to her and tried to stroke her and hug her. Mostly unsuccessfully. There were nights when she was so tired that she fell asleep exhausted and nothing could wake her up. Finally, when she had no strength left, she decided that her a trusted servant, who swore she would not tell anyone what she would see or witness, would spend every other night with Mary. She kept the secret.

* * *

One night Mary regained enough consciousness to reflect on what had happened. She came to her senses. She looked at things as she did in times when she had no tragic experiences yet.

She realized with full strength that she had been raped, she was pregnant, and she had to do something about it. She also knew that she couldn't tell anyone about it, because they would stone her. No one could find out, not even Marta. Even if her sister might suspect something, she had no right to burden her with such terrible information. It sufficed that she suffered alone. She was obliged to protect her sister.

The maid who guarded her at night, left the room for a moment.

Mary was wondering frantically what to do. She knew that one of the chests she had brought from Egypt contained herbs "also the ones that could help in such situation. They gave hope to women who were pregnant but did not want to be. She took advantage of the situation that she was alone. She managed to lift the heavy lid, although with some difficulty. However, to her horror, the chest was empty.

She sat on the floor and sighed helplessly. She wanted to cry. "Girls from Magdala don't cry," she remembered her father's words. He said them when he left her with her grandparents in Egypt, and she felt tears gathering. "And what do they do when they want to cry?" she asked then. "They look at the stars."

So she came to the window and looked at the sky. It was dotted with bright spots. They shone as if nothing happened. Constant, cold, uncompassionate, as if they did not know what misfortunes she had experienced. She stood there and watched in amazement that no matter what was happening to her and what tragedies affected her, they still shone in the same way, they did not fall, thunders did not strike, and the sky did not fall on the villains' heads.

Then she remembered that when the crowd pulled her out of the house, Ethel most likely indicated the chest to the women and probably said that there were poisons and potions there, which Mary added to cakes and drinks in order to lure men. She remembered how she had said it to David as a joke once, and Ethel had witnessed it. And because with her little mind she took everything literally, she probably thought it was true.

She also remembered that when they dragged her out of the house, she saw out of the corner of her eye how the women who had apparently emptied the contents of the trunk, had burned everything they found in it.

So she was deprived of her herbs and bottles with mixtures. She thought that there was no rescue for her. "This is the end. I can not live like that. I was dePhilaed, disgraced and my dignity was taken away. And in addition, I carry in myself a tragic reminder of the crime."

However, she was a priestess, one of those famous for never giving up, even in the situations that seemed to have no way out. She cried many times in her life, even though she was from Magdala, she despaired because she did not know what to do, but she was always looking for a solution. She didn't give up "it wasn't her style. This is how it was also this time.

When her guardian returned, she pretended to be sleeping peacefully. She breathed evenly and didn't move. The servant lay down on the mat next to her bed and fell asleep.

Then Mary silently put on a black, long, loose dress, wrapped her head in a dark shawl and slipped out of the house. It was late evening. The town was almost asleep, but life was just waking up in the district she headed for.

She sneaked along the side streets, keeping close to the walls.

"Let me in, I need herbs. "She tucked a coin into the hand of the girl who was standing by the back door of the house.

She remembered this place "she visited it quite recently with friends. They were here only for a moment, but long enough to compare it with the one they saw in Alexandria. She asked then where they kept the medicines. She remembered that she had given the coin to the owner, who personally led her to a room similar to the one she had seen in the house of pleasure in Egypt.

She was going to this place now. The owner looked at her closely. After a moment, she was surprised to recognize her as the woman who had paid her to see medicines quite recently. It was when lady-like girls in the company of handsome young men visited her for the first time in the history of her business. She knew then that she would remember this strange visit for a long time.

"What do you need?"

"Help me."

"Come," She nodded, guessing what was going on.

Because what could be needed by a girl, until recently beautiful, wise and liberated, rich and open to the world, but not in the best shape now, to put it in mild terms, and to put it simply, in a rather deplorable state? Something that planted its consequences must have happened to her.

They entered a tiny room that Mary knew from her previous visit.

"You'll drink it in the morning," The woman handed her a bottle filled with green liquid. "And this in the evening. All the way to the bottom. Then wait patiently. It will be over within three days. It will hurt. You will bleed, you may even lose consciousness, but everything you do not want, will come out of you."

Mary opened a purse for her. The woman took three denarii from her. It was a lot, equal to three days salary of a winery employee. Normally she would take one at most, but she knew that her guest could afford it. So why not take advantage of the opportunity? Mary was in such a shape that she paid no attention to it.

"Someone better be with you," the woman added. "After all is over, drink a lot of water. And if anything happens, come, we will help you."

Mary returned home in the same way, unnoticed by anyone. She tiptoed through her chamber. Her guardian was still asleep. Or was she just pretending? In any case, the woman's body didn't move.

Mary lay down and fell asleep immediately. She slept for the first time since the rape, without waking up, without the use of anesthetic herbs, until the morning.

"It looks like you slept better today?" Marta set breakfast for her.

"Yes, I was calmer."

"For a moment it seemed as if someone was walking around the house at night. Did you hear it?"

"I just woke up."

"I'm glad you're better, honey."

The maid on guard by her bed bowed without a word and left the room. Mary thought that this woman knew about her night trip, but that she should not worry, because she would never tell anyone, even Marta.

And Marta, smiling for the first time in many days, watched with pleasure as her sister devoured two eggs, a piece of matzah and drank a glass of milk. She was glad because it was the first meal in a few days that the convalescent ate almost with appetite.

"I think I'll get some more sleep..." Mary put her head on the pillow.

"Sleep. This is the best medicine," Marta took the board on which she brought breakfast, and left the room on her tiptoes.

As soon as the door closed, Mary reached for the bottle. She shook it, opened it and drank the contents. There was no more than ten sips. The liquid was so unpleasant to taste that she had to try very hard not to vomit.

"Yours is the blood, Isis, yours is the power, Isis, yours is the magic," she whispered. "Look after me, Lady."

She made the triple sign of the Goddess and fell asleep.

She woke up when the sun was high in the sky. She felt no pain or nausea. She was looking at the ceiling.

"What if the potion doesn't work?" She wondered. She wanted a release from the terrible poison that poisoned her body and soul. Marta could not find out about anything that she was carrying a reminder of the rape, or that she had taken a measure to remove it. Her sister had suffered enough because of her. This wonderful Marta, God-fearing, well-organized, hard-working, meticulous, professional, and at the same time with such a great, good, tender and sensitive heart! She saved her, stuck her neck out for her, protected her with her own body, and finally she looked after her like the best doctor. She couldn't tell her what had happened, even if she really wanted to, because with each passing moment she was more and more convinced that she had a duty to protect her family from the frightening news.

"And here is broth for my beloved sister," she heard.

Marta brought a soup in a clay bowl and set it on a wide board in front of her.

"Eat, it'll do you good. A sleep and nutritious dishes always put you on your feet the fastest."

She ate everything, to the satisfaction of her sister, and smiled gratefully.

"I think I will sleep again," she covered herself from head to foot.

She wanted to disappear.

"Sleep sweetheart, sleep."

When she woke up again it was dark. There was no one in her chamber.

She opened the second bottle with the green liquid and drank up again. It was as unpleasant as the first one.

Lying, she made the triple sign of the Goddess, asked her for protection and fell asleep again.

In the morning she woke up with a fever. She was wet with sweat. Her stomach ached. Marta was with her and cooled her head with wet cold towels.

At noon the pain was so great that she had to try hard not to scream. Hundreds of knives cut her stomach, and then she felt something inside her break. She started bleeding. At first, small dark brown threads slowly flowed out. Later, when she was writhing in pain and biting the pillow so as not to scream, she felt some connections tear inside her. She rose a little to look at what was oozing from her. She put her hands on her stomach, trying to soothe the terrible pain. Then she felt a gush of something. A blood clot appeared on the sheet. Surprised, she reached between her thighs and touched it with her fingers. It was dark brown, gelatinous and warm.

Marta, who had previously kneeled by her bed, praying, jumped to her feet. She looked terrified, but was calm.

"Breathe, my love. Everything will be all right," she assured her sister, holding her hands.

The terrible pain that Mary had felt since morning had subsided. She felt some relief and raised her elbow to look what was going on between her thighs. She didn't make it because she got sick. Her body released the remains of the poison accumulated in her stomach. Along with it came bile and saliva with a very sour smell. Her body ached, she was shivering alternately with sweating, but she guessed the worst was over.

Marta knew that she had to wait with the change of the dirty shirt and bedding until Mary would rest a bit. So she wrapped her in fresh sheets, covering what was stained with blood and vomit. She opened the windows wide "she could do it now. She was almost certain that Mary would not scream anymore, so they would not risk outsiders hearing her.

Despite the windows open, the chamber was still stuffy, and the smell of blood mixed with the stench of vomit. However, Marta knew that this was not the most important thing - what mattered was that the crisis was over and the worst was behind them. She felt so. She really wanted to ease her sister's suffering.

She cooled her sweaty forehead. She sat beside her and stroked her hands, waiting for the fever to drop even more. Only later, when she decided that things were going in the right direction, did she bustle silently, tidying up the battlefield. She did not comment on the presence of a large, gelatinized blood clot. She rolled up the dirty sheet and replaced the mattress, sure that she had to burn the dirt, and in such a way that none of the servants could see it. Later, she dressed Mary in a clean shirt. She could do it already. Her sister was recovering with every moment, and when she made sure that she was breathing almost calmly now, because her fever was down, she settled down next to her and fell asleep. Calmly - just like her.

### 9.

A dozen or so days after this event, Mary's body was healthy, but her spirit was still restless.

And the demons crept in her head again.

They had the hideous faces of her rapists and laughed mockingly. They circled and mocked her, seeping curses into her ears, panting over her face with a terrible odor, cut her body, pushed inside her through all the openings and burned her with venom from within.

She was chasing them away, but in vain. Demons hid somewhere for a moment, got quiet, and when she began to breathe calmly, they reappeared, croaked sneeringly, mocking her helplessness and powerlessness.

Sometimes they were big and looked like huge storm clouds - then she cringed in fear because there was no escape from them. Sometimes they would shrink to the size of a mouse and crawl over her bare feet, or sit down somewhere in the corner and watch events or provoke them.

"See, everyone already knows," they hissed in her ear like an infernal chorus.

And thanks to them, she saw Ethel as she ran to Rabbi Yitzhak and told him about Mary's terrible sins. That she had added magic potions to men's wine in order to possess them, that she was a witch, that she had a full box of poisons and planned to kill the inhabitants of Magdala. She also prays to Isis, and yet everybody knows that she is a demon, she wears a ring with her signs and performs secret gestures that make her immortal, anoints her body, and the mixtures she uses for this is the work of the Evil himself. In addition, she has colorful dresses and scarves that contain venom, and everyone who touches them will stay infatuated by her pernicious charm.

She also heard Ethel tell the rabbi about her trip to the house of pleasures. The maid testified that Marcus, Lucius, and even Samuel and David had succumbed to her demonic charm, that she had seduced them without their awareness. That she has wings which she hides in boxes and puts on at night to fly over the area and drink blood of newborn children. That her second, secret name is Lilith. In barbaric Egypt, where she was trained to minister to demons, everyone has a second secret name. Yes, Mary is the rebellious Lilith and she was punished for that by God because she killed what she carried in her own body, drinking the secret mixture she bought from the same sinners as herself. Because she did not comply with the law, did not bow her neck and did not want to be like the women around her. "She is Lilith!" Ethel screamed in her head, and Rabbi Yitzhak stood and nodded, moved by what he heard.

Mary also saw Ethel saying the same thing she told the rabbi to the women at the well.

"You have to stop it, she's a sinner. She seduces our men, depraves women. She makes Sodom and Gomorrah here and wants to teach our daughters this damned senet game!"

The women in the square were shaking brooms, ladles, pestles, hooks and sickles. The men had forks, cleavers and hammers in their hands. Incited by Ethel, they headed for the property they already knew.

The demons showed the crowd the way and kept it excited. They laughed at Mary, showing her the Rabbi, busy with his own affairs. And he pretended not to hear what was happening in the city, reading holy scrolls in the synagogue. His son assisted him in studying the Scriptures.

"Nobody will help you, nobody!" the demons mocked her.

Later she saw Marcus. He was holding his pregnant wife by the hand. He stroked her bloated stomach and waved to Mary.

"I will always love you!" He cried out. "You are the woman of my life, but you read, write, know how to count and know the lengths of rivers. You know the names of queens from the past. I can't be with someone like that."

She also saw Lucius. He rode a horse in the gear of a Roman officer, his helmet glistening in the sun. He was proud of himself. He had no flaws or weaknesses "he became a walking ideal.

"You will always be in my heart. I'm waiting for you. And I'll always be waiting." He showed her a place on a horse in front of himself.

She knew that she could jump in there at any moment, that he would lock her in his strong arms and that she would always be safe with him, like in girly stories. But she did not care about the fairy tale. She wanted a life in its truest form.

The demons giggled.

"Lucius is not suitable for you? You wouldn't be independent with him? Your antics would finally end?"

Men and women were getting closer to her home. This time she closed the gate and bolted the door, then locked herself in her chamber and curled up in a corner. She was prepared for what would happen. She put on the most beautiful dress she brought from Egypt, an expensive necklace, long gold earrings and leather sandals decorated with the same ore, which she wore only during the most important holidays. She attached a purse filled with coins to her belt, and a small water bottle. She also armed herself with the knife that every priestess always carried with herself. She covered her head with a crimson scarf from her grandmother. She wrapped herself tightly with it. After a while she heard the banging on the gate, and soon afterwards, a loud crack of the broken wood. The gates were shattered and the crowd burst in. People were speeding up the stairs, trampling everything they encountered along the way. They dragged sleeping Marta from her bed, pulling on their hair.

"Pray," they shouted at her. "Your sister is a demon! We'll chase her out of here. We don't want her here!"

"Leave her alone, barbarians!" Marta tried to defend the entry to her sister's chamber.

They pushed and nudged her, and when she fell again, they tied her up and gagged her mouth. She fought, trying to break free, but in vain.

The demons opened the door, which Mary had bolted from the inside, for the executioners. The crowd went at her, screaming. She couldn't recognize who was who, she just covered her head with her hands to protect herself against the blows inflicted on her. They pulled her out of the house. Same as before. They spat, pushed, threw stones and told her to leave the town.

She escaped, not waiting for more blows. She ran with all her might. She was running away without looking back. She knew that if she did, God would turn her into stone just as he had once done to Loth's wife.

## 10

She collapsed into darkness.

She was not there. She disappeared. Ceased to exist. She fell into an endless abyss devoid of walls, floors or ceilings. There were no buildings, roads, plants or anything from the world she knew. Great nonexistence. Nothingness. It was not a home of good or evil or anything that she could name. And she didn't exist either. She was there, not feeling whether she was or not. Did she die? She didn't even know that.

And then blackness opened. She felt the stench of fear and despair. She heard dramatic, painful callings, excruciating cries, almost inhuman screams. A fire that burned everything appeared in the blackness. A fire that digested existence. One from which there is no escape. Its tongues were almost reaching her, and then she noticed that she had wings. She unfurled them. She wanted to fly away, escape from this terrible place. To soar, return to the world she knew and try to start all over again. To stand up, raise her head, live, feel the fullness of existence. But her wings were weak and broken, destroyed in the fights. Only few feathers remained on them.

Somewhere very high she saw light. She missed it desperately. It was the brightness that is given to everyone when they are born. She held out her hands to it.

"A change is a secret," she heard the High Priestess. "At first you don't know how to treat it, but love lets you see it as an opportunity. When we lose something, something new is born. Without the love you have within you, you would not be able to discover for yourself what is coming. Allow yourself a metamorphosis, develop a taste for a secret. Don't be afraid of it. Get into it. Let it become your world. A change is a boon of love.

Everyone's life consists of experiences. There are physical and spiritual rapes, betrayals, abandonments, body wounds, insults, humiliation, and violence. Turn the tragedy into something useful. Your body is just a shell, it's like a dress you put on while you're here. Take care of it properly and it will serve you well. Turn the dramas that happen to you along the way into strength, and, armed with power, support those who are not yet able to cope alone.

Give yourself the right to an anger about the pain someone has caused you. By forgiving the evil, you don't erase it, but you help yourself. The constantly incited anger is like impurities. The longer we accumulate them, the more odor they emit. Force yourself to go beyond what closes you off from the world and what hurts you. Ask the Goddess for strength, and when it comes to you, accept it with gratitude. Strengthen your heart, stand up and be a powerful guardian of a female power."

When the High Priestess disappeared, Mary heard another voice, also familiar.

"You will heal yourself when you enter the path leading to brightness." Priestess Agnes emerged from nothingness, in a colorful dress as usual. "Open your eyes and look. Let your healing, the highest gift of love you can give to yourself, be a reinvention of yourself for you. When you reach the inner voice and connect with the Goddess, you will know the fullness of being. You will then feel the indescribable joy of such fusion. And by getting to know yourself, you will also feel God's presence in other people and in the whole world."

Mary raised her hands to the sun.

"Help me!" She called out.

However, the fire had already reached her wings. They ignited immediately. She threw herself on the ground, screamed and rolled around to extinguish it, but it was too late. It took over her whole body. She was writhing in pain. Her arms and legs were on fire, her torso shrunk. She stopped feeling. And then she turned into a snake. An eternal one. The one from which the world hatched. She performed the last pre-death dance, full of despair. She knew it was over. The fire consumed her.

She disappeared.

The world ended.

* * *

And then she was reborn.

She was lying in the middle of the circle. She was completely naked. Curled up like a newborn baby. Scared. Before her, in her and around "everything was unknown. She wanted to scream, but what filled her mouth and throat, prevented letting out any sound.

She saw female figures. There were twelve of them. She knew that they came from various parts of the world, each representing the highest level of initiation. They achieved brightness. Women such as them were called Priestesses of Light. Nothing was a secret to them. They were one with everything that surrounded them. They were the world. They were the Goddess.

They stood over her, arms outstretched, blessing and giving her their power.

"The ones that were before us, are here now," the priestess with her face painted red and with colorful feathers in her hair said in a rough-sounding language. "It is done. Here the feminine line has united, we are all here."

The night sky flashed with brightness. Its gates opened. A strong light appeared high, directly above Mary's head. Its stream flowed down and surrounded her with care, creating a soft cocoon around her.

"The Guardian of the Gate of Light, wake up!" They called together, each in her own language.

She understood all the words they said. She knew they were talking to her, that they were calling her, but she couldn't answer, she couldn't even move. She was still suspended, outside of time and space. She was afraid to open her eyes, look around, get up. The cocoon enveloped her and gave her a sense of security. She felt good in it. She didn't want to leave it.

"We look after the balance of the universe," a woman with slanted eyes announced in her language. "We cannot allow the harmony to be disturbed."

She leaned down and drew a circle on the ground, divided it with a sign of a snake, and put a dot in each part. The halves were mirror images of each other and formed the yin and yang symbol.

"There is divinity within us." The priestess dressed in wolf skins took a step forward. "And in every living being." She raised her head and howled like a wolf.

Somewhere in the distance, a herd answered her.

"The body is a temple for the spirit," said the Greek woman, gesturing gracefully. "Let's treat it as sacred. May the energy of love always prevail in it. It will repay us with what we give to it."

"Manasa Devi gives you a gift." The one who held snakes in her hands, bowed. "Here is a peacock feather. It is a sign of the benefit of poison and the ability to take it without harming the body. Manasa Devi teaches how to transform it into good karma. Anger, lust, spells, jealousy and everything else that does not serve us, they are all a poison. Not only does the peacock not die from it, but by accepting it, it strengthens its dignity and beauty, using the poison to obtain the unique color of its feathers. Each of us can do it too."

"A woman has the power to materialize everything she wants. The condition is that she does so in a sincere intention and in communication with power." A barefoot priestess in a wreath made of apple branches spun around her axis, took a flower from her hair and laid it next to Mary.

"Each of us is a tree of life." An old woman in a simple blue dress was holding a persea*. "We should know what the fruits of our tree are. What do we feed those we love? What do we give to those close to us? What fruit does the world that surrounds us taste, thanks to us?"

"There is power within us!" Cried the tall, beautiful woman, black as ebony, covered only by a loincloth and shell ornaments jangling on her neck. "We can beat anyone if we need to. Magic

---

* A type of fig, considered by many to be the paradise forbidden fruit, which Eve tempted Adam with; the symbol of Isis.

is on our side. We hold it in our hands and we will not give its power to anyone."

After her, more priestesses spoke up, and Mary became stronger with each subsequent word they uttered.

"The life-giving energy circulates between heaven and earth," sang the one who looked like a half-translucent angel. "A woman, as a temple, can accumulate this energy. Female energy is pure light. It affects everything that concerns living entities. If it is suppressed, locked or confined, we will not control the calamities, the world will be plagued by wars, conflagration and death."

"A woman knows the secret of birth, participates in the miracle of life. Her heart and womb are roses. They have the power to summon the light. Wherever the goddess is, there is smell of her flowers. The white, life-giving female energy smells the same. Our task is to cultivate it." A priestess with wide hips and huge breasts, with an armful of plants on her hands, laid a rose at the Mary's feet.

"Here is the sign of power that I am passing from Lilith." A mature woman in a headscarf knelt down and placed a chain with a star symbol in front of Mary. "Now the grandmother of the people of Israel is in hiding, but when the time comes, she will come down on earth again and will cleanse her name. Here is a sign of the always connected and inseparable masculinity and femininity. I hand it over to the Guardian of the Gate of Light." She laid it next to Mary.

"Tjet and Djet*, like the star of David, yin and yang, triquetra and other symbols unifying the sexes, they are the

---

* The Egyptian symbols of masculinity and femininity, the

372

power," said the High Priestess. "Separately, they also have great power, but if they occur together, they form a force that nothing and nobody can overcome."

Mary was still lying in the luminous cocoon, but she was slowly starting to open her eyes.

The priestesses held hands. They raised their folded hands up.

"Guardian of the Gate of Light, wake up!" They called out as loudly as at the beginning of the meeting.

Invisible walls trembled. The ground on which they stood began to crack. The sky flashed.

"Guardian of the Gate of the Light, wake up!" They called for the third time.

Then the cocoon disappeared, and she began to straighten her body, slowly, as if after a very long sleep. When she felt power in every part of it, she stood up, raised her hands, and from her throat resounded a cry so powerful, that the world shook in its foundations.

She was naked and strong in the middle of the star space. There was nothing around her and there was everything. She heard heavenly music.

Then her grandmother Aida emerged from nothingness. A young beautiful woman walked by her side. Mary knew that this was her mother. Behind them walked other women who had lived before her.

equivalent of Chinese yin and yang.

"Be strong. Never give up. You are here, enjoy it. Life is the greatest treasure we can receive."

They surrounded her, cuddled, stroked, patted, kissed her, and when they decided that she was already standing firmly on her feet, they began to disappear one by one, smiling at her tenderly. The smell of roses was left hanging in the air.

She was alone.

"I was born again!" She called so loudly that the universe heard her voice. "I am a priestess, the Guardian of the Gate of Light!"

# CHAPTER III

# THE APOSTLE

### 1.

She fell on her face and embraced his feet. They were covered in desert dust, and the sandals were so dusty that their original color could not be seen. He had been walking from afar. He had just entered the city.

He raised his hand. The men accompanying him stopped and surrounded her. They looked at her, curious about the Master's reaction.

Some of them knew who she was. Mary, lady at Magdala, sister of Marta and Lazarus. Educated in Egyptian temples, a worldly woman, independent, confident, trusting her wisdom, convinced that she can do anything. Intriguing, controversial, depraved. Wealthy, rebellious and free. And on top of this, beautiful. Until recently.

For several months it had been said that evil spirits had possessed her. That she is crazy, unstable, mad. She was seen in the desert and on the waterfronts, in the sketchy districts of the city, wandering aimlessly, alternately crying and laughing. She wailed softly and sobbed like a child or screamed, scratching, kicking and insulting everyone who tried to approach her.

Raped, beaten, spat on, despised. A low-life. An outcast. Possessed woman.

She howled like a badly injured animal. She alternately sprinkled sand on her head, screamed without restraint, tugged at her hair, scratched her face, ripped the remains of her dress. Saliva mixed with foam ran from her mouth. Her bloodshot eyes showed panic, fear, suffering and confusion, but also desperation mixed with resignation and powerlessness.

Her silk dress, once magnificent, was now frayed and stuck to the emaciated body. Mary Magdalene was sore and bruised. Old and fresh wounds covered her skin. Long hair, once so carefully cared for, had not seen a comb or oils for a long time. Matted, tousled and dirty, it completed the picture of a downfall.

The crowd was getting bigger. Those who had thrown stones at her and spat at her until recently, were now looking at the Master.

The fame of a miracle worker, healer and teacher had followed him for a long time. Some proclaimed him the Messiah or even the Son of God. Students and onlookers wondered how the one who claimed love to be the most important commandment, would treat the one that should have been stoned long ago.

And she had no strength. She couldn't keep going any longer. She was running away like a fatally wounded dove. With her wings broken, feathers torn out and her beak beaten. Hunched at his feet, she wanted to run away from cruelty, injustice, lack of understanding and the fate that had long seemed inevitable to her. She was on the edge. Injured to the limits of human endurance, she wanted to die.

At the same time, she had to make the last effort. She owed it to herself. Herself, her grandmother, High Priestess, father, mother, sister, brother, the past and the ideals, to which she remained faithful until recently. The priestesses who had taught her a lot, but did not say how cruel the world can be, how it rejects those who are different and condemns those who do not comply with the rules. "Adapt or die "should be the principle they teach the young at temples", she thought.

And she wanted to look in the eyes of the one who was not afraid to live his own way. Just as before, at Lake Gennesaret, when their eyes met for the first time, when she saw in them the vastness of space and freedom that she missed. Now she wanted him to look at her again, touch her, cleanse or reject her, condemning her to non-existence. He was her last chance for a new life or a death, finally ending her suffering.

Jesus bent down. He reached out to her. She knelt. He put both hands on her head. He kept them like that for a while.

"Stand up! You are healthy," he announced.

She rose and looked him straight in the eye. There was not a trace of insanity on her face anymore.

"I found the beloved of my soul, I held on to him and I will not let go..."

## 2.

After Jesus calmed her spirit, she opened her eyes. She saw men around she hadn't noticed before, because she was staring at him. She had been heading towards him for a long time, and it was him who she should meet. He was to help her finally cleanse herself of the demons of the past.

She didn't remember how she arrived in the city, she didn't know how she got to the square. As she walked, she only thought that for her cleansing and leaving the abyss to be complete, she had to find the man above whom the dove spread its wings.

When it was done and she opened her eyes, she saw the world as she had known it before. She saw people, animals, plants, houses, but now everything also existed in a different dimension, it was covered by an aura she had not noticed before. It was an element of a powerful, eternal whole. It was a small seed in time and space. She sensed it.

As a reunified part of this world, she understood more than ever. Her heart was open. The touch, smell, the ability to look, hear and feel "her senses gave her pleasure she had never experienced before. She was born again. She was here and now. She could feel the body in every little speck of it, and her renewed spirit found a wonderful home in it. Now she could appreciate it. She was alive. She understood that this was the greatest gift she had ever received and knew how great a challenge and commitment it was for her.

When she saw the world again, when it appeared to her in dimensions of existence that she did not understand before, she opened her arms to fly. Like she used to do when she was a little girl. She didn't care that Jesus's companions were looking at her, that she was standing in a crowd of people who had recently driven her out of her own house. She spread her arms, feeling slowly and with sensual pleasure how her invisible wings straighten. She tilted her head back, felt the wind, which brought the scent of roses. She smiled at the world. Now she was fully herself "Mary of Magdala. The same as before, but now really strong, confident of her power, and at the same time, humble.

\* \* \*

When Marta found out that her sister had appeared at the square in Magdala, and that Jesus had driven demons out of her, she ran there immediately.

She met Mary on the road when she was walking home.

"My love!" She hurried toward her. She was running fast, joy carrying her. However, after a while, she slowed down. Something told her to stop.

Her sister was changed. There was a shine coming from her and she was surrounded by a bright glow. She wasn't walking, but floating. Her feet barely touched the ground.

"Great god!" She cried out, stunned.

Mary raised her hand in greeting.

"I'm back!"

Yes, it was her sister, the one she loved so much. So what that she changed so much?

They run into each other's arms.

"My baby," Marta whispered.

The woman around whom she had just seen the extraordinary glow, was the same girl she had hugged in her arms so recently. The one she missed for many years when she left for Egypt, who returned as a worldly lady. The one who suffered so much evil and whose body and soul suffered so much that to defend herself, she escaped in insanity, rushed blindly and ran away no one knew where from the demons chasing her. And who finally came back from the infernal abyss. Stronger than ever, liberated, free. With the wings that lifted her off the ground.

Once Mary was moved easily, but this time it was Marta who was in tears. They both swayed, nestled in each other, just as they did in childhood. And they felt good.

"Cry, cry, my love," Mary whispered. "Female tears have healing powers."

\* \* \*

She had been kneeling in front of the silver round mirror and staring intensely at it since morning. She felt the stars on her hands and feet pulsate more and more strongly. They had been burning since Jesus put his hands on her head. As if something had unlocked, as if a wall that separated her from what was intended for her cracked and collapsed. She was on the side she had been striving for all the time. Was he the gate through which her path led? Did he have to touch her to make her fulfill her destination? Was the fact that she became a Priestess of Light who comprehends everything and connects with the whole world through love that reaches the primal energies of life, finally achieved through the contact with him? Was he her missing element?

She was floating. She could leave the body and connect with the universe, feel its rhythm, hear divine words addressed directly to her. Yes! She was knowing and seeing, she knew the past and the future, she united with those who lived before her.

Finally, what she had been waiting for, also happened: staring at the mirror, she heard the words of the High Priestess.

They reached her as if through a fog, from afar, but she perceived them clearly.

"Leave the past and go in search of the truth. Treat everyone encountered along the way as a teacher. Let what is happening to you, whether good or bad, be a valuable lesson to you. Forgive yourself and others for mistakes. Look at yourself and the world. Serve the truth!"

She knew she had made contact. Communication channels that she had once heard about in the temple, opened up for her for good. Those she dreamed of being available to her as a girl. They were the world's oldest ways of communication between those priestesses who reached the highest level of enlightenment.

"The past is behind me. Yes, I deliberately leave it behind. Former weaknesses have become my strength," she whispered.

"You released your white energy. Use the power of a rose and a potion of tears," said the High Priestess. "The end of time is coming. You have a mission to fulfill. Go, the Goddess will lead you."

The High Priestess made a triple sign of a blessing and disappeared.

Mary opened her eyes. She was sitting on the floor in her chamber in Magdala. A silver round mirror lay in front of her, and the room smelled of roses. Her tears dripped onto the smooth surface of the mirror. They flowed to form a picture. She looked at it. It was the same sign that appeared on her ring and on her neck, the one by which priestesses all over the world recognize each other.

\* \* \*

The torn clothes in which Mary appeared in Magdala were burned.

Marta also took care of her sister's body. She helped her personally with the bath, combed her hair and oiled her skin, polished her nails, massaged her damaged feet. And when her outside returned to its former condition, she decided that they would leave for Bethany.

"We will visit Lazarus," she announced. "He was so worried about you that he got sick. Ruth wrote that our brother is too weak to get out of bed. For a month when you were away, he fought with black wings again. We will go there. It will do good not only to us, but also to people in Magdala. We'll be back when the mood calms down. Now people in town talk about nothing else but how Jesus banished demons from you and healed you. Those who threw stones at you and cursed you, unfortunately, still think that they were right, because in doing so, they fought not with you, but with demons. Rabbi Yitzhak did nothing to make them aware of how much harm they had done to you. They blame only you for what happened. At the same time, they feel relieved that you are already healed, the demons have disappeared and, according to them, everything has returned to normal, so they do not have to feel guilty. They will now want to see you as the proof that miracles exist. I will not allow it. We have had enough pain."

\* \* \*

Before they left, Samuel and David arrived to visit them. Each one separately. Mary received them in the garden. She did not want to expose Marta, them or herself to caustic remarks that she did not observe Halakhah. Although she still did not see anything inappropriate in the fact that two people of different sexes stay together and talk in a closed space, she decided that she would never again cause trouble to anyone consciously.

"I'm glad you are back," Samuel began uncertainly. He did not know how she would receive him and how to talk to her, and he felt obliged to visit her. After all, she was the girl with whom he had traveled, played, talked and had a good time until recently. When she got sick, he didn't know how to behave. He agreed with the diagnosis made by his father, who believed that she was affected not by the disease of the body but of the soul, judging by her symptoms, which were widely talked about in Magdala, even though he himself did not see the patient. And that in such cases a rabbi would be more helpful than a medic.

When he learned that Jesus chased evil spirits away from her, he decided that it would be decent of him if he confirmed his friendship. So he was now sitting across from her and watching her curiously.

She was still beautiful. Maybe even more beautiful than before. She was the same Mary he had once admired so much that he was thinking about marriage, but now he felt and saw how much she had changed. She was still distinguished, she smiled beautifully, but completely differently than before. She was lit by an inner light, much stronger than he had seen in her before. When he looked at her, he wouldn't dare think for a moment that she might want to be his wife. Her every move and sentence made him realize how much out of this world a creature she was.

"Maybe you'd like my father to see you?" He offered, confused, unsure what to talk to her about.

"I appreciate your concern, Samuel, but I won't need the help of a medic. I am healthy."

"Thanks be to the Lord!" He bowed his head and stood up.

"Mary, I should leave now. I have many responsibilities. As you know, I help my father.

He was abashed and tense."

"Of course," she did not want to prolong this moment, apparently difficult for him.

"Be healthy and may God lead you, wherever you are."

"May it be so." She gave him her hand for goodbye.

Although he had seen this gesture at her home before, he was still not used to it. The women in his environment did not do this, but he took her small long fingers in his hand, just as Lucius and his Roman colleagues did. He bowed his head. And as he was standing before her, he felt with all his might that Mary was a woman for whom everyone should show respect.

She made the sign of the Goddess over him.

\* \* \*

"They say Jesus drove out the demons oppressing you..." David greeted her with an unspoken question.

"It is true."

She also received David in the garden, like Samuel.

"This man is a miracle worker," he was honestly impressed.

"They say he's the Messiah."

"I admire what he does, but the Pharisees are not happy with him."

"Because they are afraid of him."

"They say he's a disturber."

"Do you think so too?"

"Father says..."

She interrupted before he finished.

"What do you think?"

"I don't know."

She fell silent and closed her eyes. She sat upright. She put her hands in the hollow of the joined thighs, one on top of the other, forming a basket. She breathed deeply. He was sure he shouldn't speak. He felt that something was happening that he could not experience or even understand, although he had been studying the Torah for years.

"You will become a rabbi, David, son of Yitzhak," she said without opening her eyes. "You will condemn Jesus like other scribes. Later you will open your eyes, but it will be too late, because time will stop and start again. The new era will come."

"Mary... Are you having a vision?" He wanted to make sure when she opened her eyes.

Until now, he had only read or heard about it. Personally, he did not know anyone who really had the gift of seeing the future.

"David, don't feel guilty that you didn't save me from what happened," she didn't answer his question, but he knew he was right all the same.

"That was my path. Thank you for what you did not do, and for what your father did not do. You didn't defend me. It is also thanks to you that I am on the right path today. You have become my teachers. I am really grateful to you."

She reached out and he, like Samuel before, bowed so deeply that he almost touched her hand with his lips. He did not do this, however. He didn't dare. He knew he did not deserve such an honor.

\* \* \*

It was dawning. She woke up when the moon was high. She tried to get to sleep again, but she was only tossing from side to side, so she got out of bed. Her legs led her to the roof. She took the old senet out of the cabinet and set up the pawns. She sat down and studied the board.

The wind blew. It brought a familiar fragrance. Grandmother Aida used such oils.

She realized that since her death, she hadn't had the time to mourn her appropriately, to say goodbye and miss her. She focused so much on her suffering that she forgot about the woman closest to her. And yet, she realized that now, her misfortunes, the biggest ones, began when she found out about her death. "How is it possible that she gave me no sign when she was dying? "She wondered. "Or maybe she was talking to me, but I was so occupied with my own affairs that I didn't hear her? I was only focused on myself."

She remembered David's visit, the letter she had received from Sithathor a moment earlier, the fainting and everything that happened next.

Now, sitting on the terrace in Magdala, when the sun began to rise, and the wind blew the smell she knew so well, she began to cry. She wrapped herself tighter in a warm shawl and remembered the tenderness with which her grandmother embraced her when she covered her with the duvet before bedtime, when she was little, sang songs and kissed her cheek. She missed her touch and voice, her kindness, patience and understanding.

Then she remembered her father. His feigned dryness, under which there was a good soul and a big heart. She remembered when she stretched his cheeks, and he did "brrrr" at her request. She realized how he must have missed her mother all his life. How he missed her. And, above all, how much he loved her. He had no more women after her. She imagined how much he craved warmness, love, tenderness and touch.

She understood that when she climbed on his knees one day, making him teach her how to read, she brought him back to reality and led him to accept the world without Aset. She missed his arguments about Adonai, how he delicately drew her attention to the fact that the mentality of the Jews was different from the Egyptian one, and asked her to be careful. She also thought with gratitude about the fact that he took her to her grandparents and allowed her to study in the temple "after all, he could easily find a reason not to.

She loved him so much, and she had little opportunity of being close to him in her life. There were so many things she wanted to tell him but they ran out of time.

Later she saw Marcus. She understood that he had gone his own path and that they would never be together, because it was not meant for them from the beginning. Once, when talking to Lucius, she said that she probably did not love Marcus as much as she had imagined. But that wasn't true. She just wanted to console herself that way. She loved him like no one else in the world. She gave all of herself to him, body and soul. She believed that they were made for each other, and when she learned that he was with another, her heart broke into small pieces. She was lying then, telling herself that it was just an adventure. She was lying to herself because she wanted to save herself. To put a mask of indifference on her face, and arm her heart with insensitivity so as not to die of pain and despair.

It used to be this way. Now that some time had passed and she had gone through so much, she understood Marcus. Somewhere under his skin he was afraid of being with her. He encountered difficulties and opposition from his family. He did not want to overcome them, despite the fact that he spoke and probably thought that he wanted to. He loved her, but he did not intend to fight his parents and grandparents, but above all, his spirit was not able to resist forces stronger than him. They both were not born to be together. Simply. Now she understood this and humbly bowed her head before the wisdom of the Source.

Finally, she also thought about Grandpa Karim and the fact that he was with Stephanie. It seemed obvious to Sithathor that Mary knew this. And she had no idea. She wondered how it was possible that she had never noticed it. How could something like this escape her? She considered her grandparents a model marriage. The information Sithathor had given her in the letter was like a heavy blow to the head. But now, after a while, Mary understood the reasons for her grandma's leniency and acceptance of this situation. She very much wanted him to be happy, and as his love for her, despite closeness to Stephanie, did not diminish even a bit, she accepted what was happening. Because she loved. Boundlessly.

Mary understood the world better now. She didn't judge, she was just a part of it. She could hear the thoughts and know the feelings of others "including those who were no longer alive.

She was wrapped in a pleasant fabric. She was swaying sideways. So many misfortunes fell on her in such a short time, but she was sure of it now, what people had done to her was also largely a consequence of her behavior. A behavior that, according to the inhabitants of Magdala, was indecent, offensive to God and tradition, that is everything that was sacred to them. She understood that now. She did not like their lifestyle once, their parochialism, closing to the world. She hated that they did not live like her family and friends in Egypt. In her heart, she despised women who had never met any priestess and had almost no knowledge of the world so dear to her. She acted as if she challenged them. And she suffered the consequences. She remembered the words of the Great Priestess: "We learn something every day. What doesn't kill you, will give you strength, and for sure will change you irreversibly."

She had changed, that was for sure. She was more humble now, and stronger than ever.

"I will enter the tomorrow, strengthened by yesterday's weaknesses," she thought, cocking her chin proudly.

Then she saw her mother's shadow. She had not visited her for so long. She was beautiful. She resembled herself from the time she used to visit Mary in her childhood. Now, as she did before on the same terrace, she came up to Mary and sat down opposite her. She nostalgically touched the senet figures. Mary read peace and contentment from her face. The Egyptian silently informed her that now everything would be all right, then she smiled tenderly at her daughter.

Mary looked at her for a long time, then extended her hand toward her. The warmth of her mother's soul slowly filled her. When it reached her heart, Aset looked at her proudly and dissolved into the air.

Mary got up and turned her face to the sun, then spread her arms wide as if to fly.

A new day was starting.

\* \* \*

Ruth greeted them at the door of the house. The girls stood next to her. Seeing their aunts arriving, they began to jump happily.

"I can play senet now!" Judith boasted, before they could get out of the cart.

"Me too, me too!" Rebecca echoed her.

They seemed to have grown since the last time she saw them, but they were still just little girls. Mary and Marta leaned so that their faces were at the level of their nieces' eyesight. Ruth joined them and they hugged each other, shouting other one another.

They were joyful, they were happy about the arrival of their aunts, but also because for some time Lazarus had felt better.

"Looks like you are connected somehow. He always gets sick if something bad is happening to you," Marta noticed as they greeted him.

"I have been Mary's protector since childhood," he laughed. "I defended her when the black wings attacked her, so now that she was in bad shape, I was fighting them too.

He believed that this was the case, but Marta and Ruth took his words as a joke. And as he smiled mischievously when he talked about black wings, they were almost certain that what he was saying was just playing with words."

"I will gladly give you all my strength also now." He took his sister's hand. "I know you need it badly."

"My love..." Mary kissed his forehead. "You've protected me since childhood. Thank you. But now think only about yourself. I am strong and I will remain so."

"You know better how to use power well."

She had long been certain that her brother supported her with energy and that when she was in danger, he felt it and shielded her from black wings, because that was how he imagined the evil he defended her against. She described it to him this way in her childhood when she was attacked for the first time, and he still saw it like this. When he was grown up, when he sensed that something was threatening her and he fought to protect her from a distance, without moving from place. It exhausted him very much.

Now he was still weak after the last long struggles, but the strength was returning.

When they arrived, he sat on the bed, emaciated and pale, but pleased. He was glad to have his sisters next to him. Mary hoped it would get better every day, although something in his eyes worried her a lot. She didn't like his words that he would give her his power. She believed that what was said could become a reality. She protested.

"Now I will support you. Time for you to draw strength from me."

"Mary, as a child, when you were attacked by wings, remember? Everyone said I saved you. But we both know you saved me. If it wasn't for your power, I wouldn't survive their attack."

"We're connected by blood ties. This is a powerful commitment that works both ways. And so it will be until the end of our days."

\* \* \*

Lazarus called him a Master or a Teacher, like his disciples. He liked when he visited. Conversations with him were the greatest pleasure he knew. Words flowed like music, soothed and warmed his weak body. After each visit he felt his strength was growing.

Now he was waiting for the guests outside the gate. He bowed low to those arriving. Jesus embraced him cordially and, when invited inside, he crossed the high threshold, but did not take even two steps.

Mary was standing in the middle of the house, just behind the gate. Jesus stopped. They looked into each other's eyes.

And something amazing happened. Everything around them disappeared. The time stopped. There were only them.

Smell of roses appeared, the air stilled, and tears flowed down her cheeks. He opened his arms and embraced her.

"I've been going to you for so long..." She snuggled into him.

"It's good that you are here now, Mary," his voice soothed her expectation, stroked her longing and was a promise.

Lazarus, Marta and Ruth looked at them in surprise. Mary and Jesus had met only once before and it was in unusual circumstances, so it was quite unusual that they greeted each other in such a way. However, on the other hand, they knew that it was thanks to him that Mary was alive and with them. He banished the demons of the past from her and restored her to the world.

At the same time, they couldn't help noticing that these two were connected by some magical thread, something fleeting, timeless, which defies human judgment. They looked as if they had known each other for centuries, as if they were soul mates and their bond had been established beyond them and had always existed.

Jesus wiped her tears and she kissed his cheek.

"Rabbuni*, thank you."

"Mary..."

Roses smelled again.

She led him to the garden.

---

* From Hebrew: rabbi means a teacher, rabbuni is a diminutive, similar to: "beloved teacher".

Students followed him. They did not know what was happening behind the gate, they did not see the scene of Mary welcoming Jesus, but they waited patiently for Andrew following Master to let them know that they could come in.

There were twelve of them. Andrew, Simon Peter, James, John, Bartholomew, Thomas, Matthew, Simon the Canaanite, James, Thaddeus and Judas.

When they settled in the garden, Mary was able to take a closer look at them for the first time. Earlier, when Jesus chased demons from her head, she was in a different space and too stunned by what was happening to pay attention to the people and the world that surrounded her. Now she was in Lazarus's friendly home, with his wife and daughters, with Marta, and above all, she herself was changed.

She looked at these men: simple, unsophisticated, shy in her presence, a little clumsy in their movements. Each of them nodded in a greeting. They settled down to rest after the trip. Marta, Ruth, her little daughters and maids were busy preparing the meal. Mary stood next to Lazarus, who quietly, so as not to disturb the resting men, explained to her who was who.

Some of them were previously disciples of John the Baptist, and after he was gone, they joined Jesus. She had heard from Lazarus before that they were simple people, and now their appearance and behavior confirmed this. Lazarus said that, like almost all other boys in this area, they also finished their studies at synagogues and were able to read the Torah, and as many as seven of them were studying in Capernaum. And it was said that there was no better school in Galilee than this one. However, it was definitely not the type of people Mary could meet in one of the mansions or palaces during intellectual discussions or fun games in Egypt.

"This is Andrew." Lazarus pointed out to her a rather gloomy, well-built man "he is the brother of Simon Peter and a sort of manager of this group. When Jesus chose him, he was thirty-three years old. He is the oldest of them, probably also the most responsible and best organized. They say that almost nothing happens without his knowledge and consent. In addition to his brother, he has three sisters and, since he is not married yet, he lives with Simon Peter. They are both fishermen. Just like James and John, those over there." He pointed to two brothers. "The four of them are fishing together. They are partners."

"Simon Peter doesn't look to be tired of the long journey..." Mary watched as the man with big muscles and thick beard talked vividly about something, gesturing strongly.

"You mean he talks so much? He is like that. He likes to talk, sometimes faster than he thinks," he laughed softly. "But I value him. He has healthy views."

"He looks like a serious man."

"He's good and honest. And three years younger than Andrew, so fortunately he listens to him sometimes. Otherwise, his straightforwardness would probably have hung him. He is married, has three children, lives in Bethsaida. As I told you, he also does fishing."

"One day Jesus will say that he is a rock. And that he would build his church on him."

"You think so?"

"I know that," she smiled and stroked his hand tenderly. "And that young man, see, over there, is he also a student?" She was surprised.

"This is John. You're right, he's the youngest in the group. He is James's brother, I told you. The four of them work on a boat."

"He's still a kid, he doesn't even have facial hair..." She smiled affectionately.

"He is intelligent and extremely sensitive. You will like him."

"I like him already."

They both laughed. John looked indeed like someone everybody loves. Because of his age, he was not very tall and still frail, shorter and thinner than Mary. His face with delicate features was surrounded by fairly light medium-length hair, not very thick. His dreamy eyes were always laughing.

"Jesus has many disciples, but these twelve here are closest to him. There are also women among those who follow him, he teaches them, do you know that?"

"You mentioned it before. And I am honestly surprised that it is possible. I wonder how they function among so many men and how much they are condemned by those who see them."

"In the right time, maybe you will meet the teacher's mother. She is an amazing woman, you'll see how quiet and modest she is. But it is not only her who is with him. There is also, for example, Susan, the daughter of a rabbi from Jerusalem, or Joanna, the wife of Chuza. She is a real lady, I think you would like her. In a sense, she is similar to you.

Sophisticated, independent, educated. She always knows what she is saying. In fact, even though the students might somehow tolerate their wives in the company, they do not like them speaking in public, but they really value Joanna's words. In addition, she is rich and supports them generously with her purse. Jesus forbade taking money for healing, but people feel obliged to thank him somehow. She also does this, transferring the funds to Judas, who holds the group's finances. In addition, what can I say, her presence gives them splendor. After all, she is a lady from the royal court, the wife of the steward. She is not just anybody. This is not a wife of a fisherman, carpenter or shepherd. She is a great lady, and yet she follows the Master, listens to his words and in addition, belongs to the ones closest to him."

"I heard it and I still can't believe it. I imagine what must have happened in the life of the great lord Chuza, the governor of Herod, to let his wife wander after someone like that. I guess neither he nor Herod belong to the devotees of Jesus..."

"That's an understatement! Remember, I once told you what the situation is like. Everyone has been talking about the coming of the Messiah for some time. Every now and then one of them appears, and there are many madmen among them. Well, but after all, John the Baptist was not crazy. They were afraid of him and that's probably why they got rid of him."

"I heard the story of how he died, it was terrible. I still don't understand how this could happen."

"Ask Joanna when you meet her, she will tell you exactly. She was an eyewitness to it. I think this is also why her eyes opened and she saw the corruption of the place she lived in."

"The old prophecies are being fulfilled. Seers have long preached them. Many say that time is getting complete now."

"The Prophet Isaiah said that when the true Messiah would come, the blind would regain their sight, the deaf their hearing, the mute their speech, and the sick their health[*]. This is what has happened since Jesus got among us."

"There were many more prophecies. Did you know that the queen of Sheba, Makeda, also talked about the coming of the divine Savior?"

"What else did they teach you in Egypt, sister?" Although he valued her tremendously, he was still wondering how broad her knowledge was.

"I have heard a lot about various topics." She kissed him.

"I'm really proud to have such a sister."

"And I'm glad I have a protector in you. You are a good and wise man."

"If I were also healthy, I would not be sitting at home, but rather follow the Teacher."

"Well, this way you are lucky, because he comes to you," she supported him with a tactful joke, because she understood how much it bothered him to be weak.

"His every word is like a priceless balm to me. Really. It seems to me that I've waited all my life to hear them. "The kingdom is inside you, and it is outside of you. When you know yourselves, then you will be known, and you will know that you are the sons of the living Father. But if you do not know

_____
[*] Is 35.

yourselves, then you are in poverty, and you are poverty."* Say, isn't that beautiful?"

"As the Romans say: *nosce teipsum*, which the Greeks translate into *gnothi seauton*, and we: get to know yourself."

"Right, it sounds good in Greek and Latin too, but God is lacking there."

"God is everywhere, my love. Also in Greece and Rome." She kissed him again and left.

He thought "how many times already in his life?" that he had an absolutely unique sister. He watched her approach Jesus. Leaning against a tree, he was looking far away. He was resting. She nodded at him and he showed her the place next to himself. She sat at his feet.

He was beautiful. Tall, handsome, harmoniously built. He had strong arms, slim fingers and an eye-catching face. Balance and peace was the first thing noticed by everyone who looked at him.

Mary looked at him enchanted, too. She didn't seem to see the world beyond him.

"God is everywhere. In every little element of everything that lives, and he is sent by him and is him," she thought, looking in the same direction he was looking at. She knew that he had all the knowledge, that he had reached the highest possible level of consciousness. He knows what the Light is, because he is the Light, he builds the world on love, because he comes from it, is it and goes toward it.

---

* Gospel of Thomas, 3.

They looked into distance without saying anything, their thoughts floating beyond time and space.

Then Marta came up to them. She worked in the kitchen with other women, preparing a meal.

"Lord, do you not care that Mary left me alone to serve everybody?" She asked, pretending to be slightly offended, but with a hint of joy in her voice, pleased that she had such wonderful guests, including the one who saved her sister. "Tell her to help me."

He also smiled.

"Marta, you are worried and upset about many things, but only one thing is needed. Mary has chosen what is better, and it will not be taken away from her[*]."

"If you don't have to, don't use energy for things you don't like. Today's feelings create your future world," Mary added. "You don't like service, so leave it. Sit here with us, meditate, look, listen."

"You don't even know how happy I am that you are back to your old yourself again," Marta kissed her forehead.

In fact, it didn't bother her at all that she runs, tries her best, prepares food and serves guests. Ruth and the maids were helping her after all. True, she would gladly sit in the garden, ponder, listen to the words of the Master, but above all she was grateful to him that he brought her sister back to life. And Mary, as far as she was concerned, could do nothing, look at the sky, read scrolls or make her notes all days long. The most important thing for her was that she was already healthy. She

---

[*] Luke 10: 38–40.

also knew that no one would take care of her guests better than she did, so why wouldn't she? She liked order and kitchen. Serving such outstanding guests and their satisfaction gave her pleasure.

"I've never felt more myself in my life than now," Mary answered Marta, but she was staring at the Master. "Yes. I'm happy. I feel good."

"I'll join you in a minute," Marta said. "And I will listen, listen, listen..."

\* \* \*

Mary quickly found a common language with Matthew, Luke, Bartholomew, and above all with John. Already on the first evening in the garden in Bethany, they willingly listened to her, discussed with her, appreciated her experience, education and her view of the world. Proud Simon Peter, inaccessible Judas, sitting on the side, or James, instructing others, rejected her. First of all, they were surprised that she was with them. They blamed her for engaging the Teacher, for taking him away from them, and blamed him for giving her too much attention. From the very beginning they tolerated her presence only for the sake of the Master.

When they saw her eyes staring at him with absolute love, they were certain that the Teacher gained a new, faithful student, who would follow him like they did. They were not happy about it, but what could they do? His opinion was the most important. Besides, the others treated her kindly. Although she was a woman, she was not the first one among them. They had to learn how to deal with this situation, so unusual and embarrassing until recently.

When the sky darkened and the stars appeared, John sat next to Mary, who was sitting alone and thinking.

How young he was! And at the same time beautiful and delicate. She was looking at his face, on which there was indeed not even a trace of a stubble, even up close. His beaming eyes said how much he was involved in what was happening around him, and totally devoted to Jesus and what he brought into his life.

"Saying 'yes' to the Lord is the courage to accept life as it is, with all its fragility and smallness, and often with all its contradictions and lack of sense." He poked in the hearth with a stick and stared at the sparks that flew up to the sky.

He spoke to Mary, but she understood that he was speaking first and foremost to himself to sort the things in his mind he often thought about.

"Living according to the rules he proclaims means accepting our homeland, our families, our friends as they are, together with their weaknesses and pettiness. It also means: accept anything that is not perfect, pure or filtered, but still worth loving all the same. Is someone not worthy of love because he is disabled or somehow different? Is someone who is a foreigner, a sick person, or a prisoner not worthy of love? Jesus embraced the leper, the blind man and the paralytic, he embraced the Pharisee and the sinner. The world does not belong only to the strong, beautiful, healthy and rich[*]."

---

[*] A statement based on a speech by Pope Francis in 2019 during the World Youth Day in Panama.

"John, I think the same way. Thank you for saying that. We don't know each other well yet, but from the first moment I saw you I have known I like you."

"I like you too, Mary. Welcome to our team."

\* \* \*

Most students fell asleep, laying down on blankets spread at home and in the garden.

Not Mary, however. She left her room and went to the end of the garden. She stood under a tree, and as she stared at the moon, the Master appeared beside her.

"Behold, God has become a man, so that man could become God," she said quietly and thoughtfully.

For the first time she realized so strongly that she was living in a time when God appeared in the body of a man, and she was a witness to it. Really! She was standing right next to him, at his fingertips.

"There is one God," she said. "Alpha and omega, the beginning and the end, the Absolute embracing everything and being everything. It is the beginning and the end, it is everything everywhere. Those whom we consider to be gods, to whom we pray, are his sons and daughters. God gives us the emanations that we are able to comprehend. Earlier, before you appeared in the world, his children were never human. They have always been gods. In Egypt, we had Amon, Aton, Osiris, Hathor, Isis, in other parts of the world the power over souls was exercised by local gods, but none of them was human, none walked the earth among us. You were the first to be sent as a human being, so that you would experience life just like us, and so that we might follow the path of love while getting to know

403

you. You show the new path to everyone. To those you chose yourself and those who sought you, just like I did my whole life, and finally found you. We will follow the only right path, indicated by you. We have a signpost. I would like to speak about the divine love like you do, in a clear and simple language. I want to speak primarily to women, show them that divinity is a great power of a bright light that is within them. I want to speak clearly, understandably and simply."

He stared into her eyes. And she never looked down.

"You have been generously endowed," he smiled in the same way as he did when she greeted him at the gate in Lazarus's house. "There's light in you, of which you speak so beautifully. You got it from Him, and He guides you. Let it be fulfilled. Talk to people, preach the Gospel. Come with me. Let's go together."

He touched her for the first time when he chased demons from her. It was a purifying touch "a divine seal placed on her heart. Then the brightness fully prevailed over the depths of evil. Later they embraced each other at the gate for a greeting, it was like a revival of an old relationship that had lasted since the beginning of the world. A confirmation of a unity and coexistence.

Now he reached his hand out to her again.

She gave him hers. He held it firmly. She was sure he would never let her go again. She felt safe, she arrived at her destination.

Then the earth shook and the sun burst in her head. Its rays spread at the speed of light, reaching every particle of her body's microcosm. His warmth poured into her and she felt she was floating above the ground. She soared, carried by their joint power. Among the stars, their souls were entwined and became one. They completed each other.

"I've waited a long time for you," her soul said. "I was walking to you along bumpy paths. It was a long way. I was hungry for the beauty of life, I drew from it in handfuls, I got to know its charms and misery. I learned and opened my eyes wide, wondering at the complexity and at the same time, simplicity, with which the world is composed. I loved and I lost. I fell and didn't have enough strength to get up. I was in the darkest depths of perdition. I had visions, my mind opened to connect with the universe. I became the Guardian of the Gate of Light. It was my path to you. I followed it to finally meet you.

I saw you by the lake, when the dove spread its wings over you, when John the Baptist paid you homage. When I first heard your name here, at the home of my brother Lazarus, I knew that once we would meet, we would never part. I heard voices and saw signs that led me to you. And here you are."

3.

Since Jesus and his disciples left his home, Lazarus was getting weaker. One could see how the soul was leaving him with each passing day.

"Take back the strength you offered me. You need it," Mary asked him when there was nobody else in his bedroom. "I give it back to you every day, but it bounces like rays from a mirror. It won't come back to you unless you want to receive it."

"Mary, you are the chosen one," he was leaning on a headrest. "We both know that. I am proud that I could protect you when you were growing up. It really is an honor. I also know that you will have a difficult path in the near future, you will need a lot of strength, that's why I gave it to you. In a good cause. One worth giving your life to. I did it consciously, believe me. Not only for you, but also for him. Because he will need you now. I do not know what will happen and which path he will lead you, but it will not be an easy path. So be with him, support him. He is clarity. Just like you. And one more thing: promise me you will make sure that those, who are not awaken yet, will not convince you in the future, that the truth you see is a hallucination. We both know and every enlightened, sensitive person knows, that there are things in heaven and earth that even philosophers with the most powerful heads not only do not think about, but they have not even dreamed of."

Mary closed her eyes and looked at the days to come. Her visions were bloody, full of pain, suffering, and so terrible that she lost her will to know the future. But she managed to shake them off and made a promise to her brother:

"I promise you. Whatever I see and anything unusual I will witness, I will give faith to my eyes and my heart. And may it happen."

* * *

There was crying in Bethany. Lazarus passed away. People came from Jerusalem, Magdala and other cities to be with Marta, Mary and Ruth after they lost the only man in their family.

"Death is not the end, nor is it a sentence, but a birth to a new life. It is a light at dusk," Mary comforted the women after they said goodbye to Lazarus and were sitting in a dark house in the evening, the night after burial. "Life does not flow, it does not go out. The living do not die[*]."

\* \* \*

When Marta learned that Jesus was approaching Bethany, Lazarus's body had been laid in his grave for four days already.

She went out to meet the Master. Mary stayed at home "she was too weak.

"Lord, if you were here, my brother would not have died," Marta greeted Jesus, sobbing softly. "But I know that God will give you everything you ask him for, even now."

"Your brother will rise from the dead," he replied with conviction.

"I know that he will rise from the dead on the last day," she did not allow herself to accept what she heard.

"I am the resurrection and the life. Whoever believes in me, will live, even if he dies. Everyone who lives and believes in me will never die."

She stared at him, arms folded on her chest. She didn't know what to think about what she heard.

"Do you believe?" He demanded a confirmation.

The students stared at her face. They knew his power to influence people. He looked at them, spoke and they trusted him completely. So it was also this time. Marta no longer hesitated, her doubts disappeared. She nodded.

---

[*] Ps. 17.15.

"Yes Lord! I strongly believe that you are the Messiah, God's son, who was to come into the world."

She fell to his feet, and when he blessed her, she ran home to tell his words to her sister.

Mary regained strength in an instant. She ran to greet him on the road. Like Marta before, she fell at his feet. People from all directions, who had earlier come to mourn Lazarus and comfort his beloved women, came along with her. Now they wanted to see the one who preached amazing words about love, healed people, did miracles, they were curious about what could happen.

"Lord, if you were here, my brother would not have died," Mary burst into tears, still embracing his feet. "He loved you so much."

"Where did you lay his body?" He gave her his hand, helping her to her feet.

He hugged her. The gathered people held their breath. Hardly anyone dared to exhibit such familiarity in a public place, but he was the Master, Rabbi, Teacher, he healed, received special gifts from God. He could get away with much more than any of them, they thought he had the right to it.

When they led him to the cavern, closed off with a large rock, as was customary, Jesus stood and wept.

"He must have loved him, indeed," the crowd whispered.

"He loved him as much as people say."

"Could he who opened the eyes of the blind, make him not die?" They wondered.

"Remove the stone," Jesus commanded.

"Lord, there is a stench already. He's been there for four days," Marta cried.

"Did I not tell you that if you believe, you will see the God's glory?"

So the stone was removed. Then Jesus raised his eyes to the sky and said:

"Father, thank you for having heard me. I knew you always hear me.

People stared at him and waited for what would happen. Mary and Marta were kneeling."

"Lazarus, come outside!" Jesus cried out in a loud voice.

The assembly froze, but nothing happened. Finally, after a while, in the silence that ensued, they heard sounds coming from the cave. And then, slowly, as if he had just woken up, Lazarus came out from there in a wobbly step.

Nobody moved to help him. Some took a step back. They couldn't believe their eyes. The women fell on their faces and covered their heads with their hands in fear. Only Mary got up and looked with admiration at her brother who had been brought back to life, then at the Master who had just performed another extraordinary miracle. She loved them both. Boundlessly.

The resurrected Lazarus stood in front of the grotto. The clothes and strips of linen in which he was wrapped after his death, prevented him from moving.

"Take off the clothes and let him go," Jesus ordered[*].

------

[*] J 11, 11–44.

## 4.

Jesus visited Capernaum most often. People said it was his city. It was there that he called Simon Peter, Andrew, James and John as his first and most faithful apostles. He lived there, taught in the synagogue, healed Simon Peter's mother-in-law, a leper, a paralytic, brought the rabbi's daughter back to life, and drove the evil spirit out of a possessed man. Also there, to the students' outrage, he invited to the table Matthew Levi, hated by almost everyone because of his profession of a customs officer. It was there that he walked on the waters of the lake.

And there, because where else, he gave one of his most beautiful sermons.

"Blessed are you, the poor, for God's Kingdom belongs to you. Blessed are you who are starving now, for you will be satiated. Blessed are you who are crying now, because you will laugh[**]."

Around them, the leaves of the shadow-casting trees rustled, and the waters of the lake below whispered, admiring his words.

The apostles and disciples were sitting at Jesus' feet, and the people who arrived from all over the area, a little below them. Mary of Magdala found a place a little further, surrounded by a circle of women. As always, she listened intently to every word of the Rabbi. Each of them fell deep into her heart. She knew they were a sign of the times to come.

Whenever people learned that the Teacher and students were coming, they went to the place where he was staying. So it

[**] In: Mt 5, 3-6.

was also this time. They lined up in long queues, waiting for healing, asking for blessing, or just sitting somewhere in the shade, waiting for a sermon. And the Master taught. He had a melodious, warm, loud and crystal clear voice. His words went straight to the heart. They appealed to the imagination, encouraged, warned, and spread beautiful visions. There was silence when he spoke.

It was unusual for people that there were also women among his students. No rabbi had ever taught women. Jesus was the first. They wondered why he did it. After all, a pious Jew thanked God every day for not having formed him as a pagan, a slave or a woman. Women were not created to be taught, they did not read the Torah, they could not even be witnesses in court. They could not fully participate in services or say the prayers of Shem. Even in homes, which were their kingdoms and where they served at the table, they could not sit with the men. And with Jesus they became his disciples, they followed him, and he talked to them as if they were equal to him. It was incomprehensible to outsiders, but the students got used to it. Not everyone was happy, but who would dare to resist Jesus' will?

Mary liked to look at the faces of the listeners. One could see focus on them, often a delight mixed with anxiety that for the first time in their lives, they heard words that gave new meaning to their existence. Some of the things Jesus repeated so often that the listeners knew them by heart: "You will love your God with all your heart, with all your soul and with all your mind. You will love your neighbor as yourself," he said. And they wondered if these words meant that if someone hurt them, they should love him, despite pain and regret. "Inconceivable", they thought. Mary understood their anxiety.

411

Because it was difficult for someone brought up in the system with unforgivable crimes to comprehend that one could even try to think differently.

* * *

At that time, she was more and more often called Mary Magdalene or Mary of Magdala. Some, especially women, called her an apostle. More and more people gathered around her. She was said to be able to heal by touch, she also had herbs and ointments that bring relief. It was said that she was wise and strong, that she could speak so many languages that wherever someone asking for advice came from, she would receive it from her in the language in which she addressed her.

She never mentioned that she was a priestess. She did not say who she had studied with. She did not talk about thousands of years of gathering the experiences and writing down knowledge by her predecessors, she did not mention the names of priests, priestesses, scholars, poets and masters from the old days. She knew that her listeners did not need it. She used the language of the heart that each of them understood perfectly. They were, after all, a feminine community. One that had been started somewhere, sometime centuries ago. Each of them felt it.

Almost no one knew that high on the back of the neck, where the hairline begins, Mary had a sign of a timeless love. It was irrelevant, however, because each of them "even without knowing it "had the same one in her heart. Since forever. They just had to reach it, dust it, smooth it, polish it, show it to themselves and the world, and carry it with pride.

She taught them gently, patiently, touching each one and passing her warmth to her. It did not decrease. Quite the opposite: there was more and more of it in herself with each subsequent touch.

"You can strengthen what is good in the world," she said, walking between them. "You have such power. You are a miracle and a flower. Our hearts and womb are a divine tool.

They were looking at her and her words sounded like a revelation to them. No one had addressed them so directly before, talking about how much they could do and how strong they were. Nobody said that they were like flowers, that they can influence the future of the world with their breath, that they carry the energy of love."

She taught them how to breathe, how to let white light pass through them, so that it would become the energy of a sincere feeling.

"Look at me now," she made a smooth gesture forth and back with her hand, repeated it, and then again and again.

"Do you know what this sign is?"

Even those who guessed what it meant, preferred to be silent so as not to embarrass those who might not recognize it.

"It's a sign of infinity. That's how Divinity is written. It lasts forever, so there was no moment where it began and there will not be one where it ends," she explained to them just as Priestess Agnes in the Philae Temple once did. "Make this move like I do. Do you feel the pleasure you get?"

Women repeated her gestures, laughing and commenting.

"Sit down comfortably. So that nothing would distract you. Take the best position for yourself. Breathe. Close your eyes," she looked at them, and when she noticed that they all sank into themselves, she continued. "Imagine that your heart and womb are roses. Each of them is different, they have different colors, petals of different thicknesses, their leaves shine in many shades, even their spikes are not the same. They differ like us, but they are all flowers."

They breathed as she asked.

"Don't open your eyes. Now think of the sign of eternal Divinity that I showed you. You know and like it. It belongs to you. Make it now in your hearts. Let what is bad and bothers you, stay behind you, throw it out, leave it behind your back. The infinity gesture will help you. Make it in your souls so that the heart is the central point, where the infinity lines intersect. That's where your rose is. There is an element of Divinity there.

She saw them sway slightly, following the movements they made in their minds. Many of them looked as if they left their body for a moment."

"And now that your hearts are already filled with clarity, know that you can radiate this energy outside and give it to the world. Don't open your eyes yet. It is not the end. We keep working. We will do the same with the other rose. It is where we have a womb. Do you see it, feel it? It is there and it is waiting for your infinity sign. Make it. Let the bright breath become the energy that the world is waiting for. Give it to others, but do it with caution. It is said that the energy of love grows when we give it. But let's remember that the world is not just the energy of love. There are powers that try to destroy it, and the forces in our mortal, weak and fragile bodies are limited. Our spirit and bright energy are eternal and will last forever, but the bodies are just jugs, shells, cloth, dresses. Just as we once got them, coming here, the time will come that we

414

will leave them. Let's take care of them as best we can. Let us care that they are the best refuge for the divine spark. Our bodies are the temple for the soul."

Her words were listened to by young girls and their even younger sisters, just beginning life, as well as mothers, grandmothers and even elderly women, who were almost saying goodbye to the world. Among them were women who were educated and came from wealthy homes, wives and daughters looking for their own path, inspiration or guide, there were also those who lived their daily lives alongside their husbands, fathers, brothers and grandparents, not standing out from the crowd. There were poor ones, who only had as much as their bundles held. They all listened to her equally eagerly.

\* \* \*

One day, when she was discussing harmony and balance, and many women were sitting around her, another one approached the group. She acted as if she wasn't sure she would not be chased away.

"Welcome," Mary encouraged her to sit close enough to hear her words well.

Still insecure, she came closer and sat down.

"To sum up what I said," Mary continued, making sure that the newcomer took a seat among the others "Focus on your life. This is good for others and for you. You have a certain amount of energy, spend it on developing your love and positive actions. Any evil thought damages your body, while a bright one gives it health. So throw away what is bad, what gives you no joy, control the evil powers that want to dominate you. You can do it. You will succeed, you are strong! Don't gossip, don't plot, don't be jealous, don't tell untruth about your fellow men. You can be with others without competing and comparing. Do your affairs, find your own space and your own way. Follow it, make it beautiful. Be a woman that you will be proud of and let the ones you admire be your inspiration."

Mary looked at the people around her. They thought about what they heard.

Then the one who arrived last, spoke.

"I want to say something," she spoke shyly, but loud enough that they all paid attention to her.

"Will we let her?" Mary looked around questioningly.

"Let her stand up and introduce herself first," one of the others called out. "I want to see her."

The newly arrived got up and adjusted her dress.

"My name is Ethel. I come from Magdala," she lowered her head as if confessing her guilt.

"Ethel? Was it not the name of the woman because of whom our Magdalene suffered?"

"Yes, it's me," she admitted, shrinking within herself.

"What are you saying? Speak up because we can't hear you here!" came from somewhere afar.

"It's me. I am this Ethel. It's me!" The girl raised her head and looked around boldly. "It is because of me that Mary suffered."

"And you dare come here? What are you doing here? Have you no shame?!" Outraged voices attacked her.

Mary stopped them with a hand gesture. They fell silent, although not immediately.

"Let her finish," she said.

"I acted badly. I was stupid and reckless. I didn't think I was hurtful, on the contrary, I thought I was doing the right thing. I didn't understand what was happening. I thought Mary was sinning against God. I didn't know she wasn't doing anything wrong. I hated her, but believe me, at the same time something inside me made me want to be like her. I envied her: she was so free, wise and good for everyone. She laughed, danced, sang, and stupid me thought it was bad. Oh, how much I wanted to be like her! But I didn't have the strength to do it. I was afraid, I preferred to make sure nobody around me would sin. I saw people's mistakes everywhere "even where there was none. I condemned her for everything. I did not like any of her actions. I understood my mistake by listening to Jesus. His sermons on love opened my eyes. I know that I hurt not only Mary but also myself. I watched her instead of taking care of my own business. I saw a speck in her eye, not seeing the beam in my own. I understood my mistakes and now I've come to apologize for them. What am I saying? I have done so much harm that I come not to ask, but to beg for forgiveness!"

There was silence during her long speech. When they found out who she was, the women wanted to drive her away, but when the Mistress calmed them down, they listened. After the speech ended, they waited for Mary to react.

Ethel was standing, ready to humbly accept any sentence.

"There is time to understand your mistakes, as for everything in life. You were young, angry, rebellious, not quite aware of the damage you can do to others and to yourself. It was similar with me, I also sinned. Just like you and each of us. In Magdala I was proud and conceited, I lacked humility and understanding for others. I thought I was better and smarter because I learned more, I saw more and I knew the world. But I only had my little truth and did not want to acknowledge that others not only do not have to share it, but also they are not inferior when they don't, either. Who among us does not err and does not sin? Everyone has strengths and weaknesses. We make mistakes so that we could understand more. To meet others, but above all ourselves. Our soul needs difficult experiences in the pursuit of perfection. Each of us falls. It's human. The trick is to get up, admit the mistakes, forgive yourself and others. This was your way. So was mine too. Each of us has their path, usually quite bumpy. Now you have found yourself. I'm glad you're here."

"Have you forgiven me?" Ethel still didn't move. "But you have suffered so much because of me!"

"Thank you for that. It was a lesson for me." Mary reached out to her.

And Ethel, lifting up her dress a little, so as not to bump into anyone, squeezed through the sitting women until she reached the Mistress.

"So I can stay then?" She stood in front of Mary.

"Stay," she embraced her.

"And your headscarf, your beautiful headscarf..." Ethel couldn't finish her sentence, because she was swallowing her tears, but wiped them off, stood straight and finished strongly, looking Mary in the eyes: "Scarlet is not the color of shame, as I once thought. It's the color of strength. A great royal strength. It's your color!"

## 5.

During the time of Herod the Great, Jerusalem became a modern city. Eight gates led to it: Garden Gate, Damascus, Old, Essene, Water, Fountains, Sheep and Fish Gates. The city was divided into districts. To get to the Herod's Palace, which was the residence of the Roman governors, one had to go through the Essene Gate on one side, or through the gate under the Hippicus Tower on the other. Next to it was the palace of the high priest Caiaphas, and behind it was the beautiful district of the rich. This part was called the Upper City. The Maccabees' palace and a theater also stood there. Further spread the district of the poor, called the "Lower City". The merchants and artisans districts, grand market and the market settlement were located in the lower part of the city.

Under Herod, the Temple was so expanded that it occupied almost one-sixth of Jerusalem. A little further, but still close to the Temple, at the Fountain gate, a hippodrome and the most modern horse racing track in the world were built. At the same time as the hippodrome, the theater and royal palace, the fortress Antonia was also established. Herod named it in honor of Marcus Antonius. It was described as a city within a city. Roman troops were stationed there since the beginning of its existence, and felt at home there. According to Roman soldiers, this was the center of Jerusalem, but the vast majority of residents did not share their views. For them, the Temple of Solomon was the most important building. It was there where every pious Jew should make a pilgrimage, preferably with his family, at least once a year, and everyone did it, most often during the Passover.

Outside the city, behind the walls of the Temple, was the Mount of Olives, and on the other side of the metropolis there was Golgotha, almost devoid of vegetation, called the Place of the Skull.

At that time, more than sixty thousand people lived in Jerusalem, two times more than before his reign. There were so many of them that the water supply from the Gihon Spring was not enough, therefore Herod ordered the construction of dozens of new tanks, in which the reserves were stored. His son, Herod Antipas, inherited from his father a modern, well organized, and still growing city with a highly developed irrigation system.

* * *

Mary rarely visited Jerusalem, but she sometimes went there on her way to Lazarus and Ruth in Bethany, or when she returned from them.

She was in town now. She stood in the crowd on the Damascus Road and watched the Roman soldiers passing by. She noticed Lucius. He was riding a horse at the head of a small unit. He was heading towards the Antonia Fortress. He had no chance of seeing her the horse's hooves raised so much dust and sand that, from the perspective of men on horseback, people standing on either side of the road looked as if they were standing behind the fog. But she noticed him right away. She was happy. As soon as the dust settled, she sent Ethel to the fortress with  a message saying that she was in town. Lucius answered immediately. He proposed a meeting.

The Roman garrison in Jerusalem had usually five hundred soldiers. Officers who were stationed in other regions sometimes came there to collect or pass the orders. And that was the purpose of Lucius's visit to the city.

In addition to soldiers' quarters and baths, common rooms, warehouses, dining rooms, stables and other rooms needed by the army, the fortress also had luxury apartments for officers and guests. Lucius occupied one of them, not very big but comfortable, during his stay in Jerusalem. He shared it with Aurelius and Philip. However, his companions did not intend to disturb him during the meeting with Mary. He was alone.

When he got the letter from her, he hoped that she came to tell him something he had waited for a long time, that the disease and what she had gone through had changed her mind about their future. But from the first moment he saw her, he knew he was wrong. He looked at her in surprise. The woman who came to him, did not resemble the object of his sighs, nor the Mary tormented by her experiences. She looked and acted differently.

She had a long black dress, made of a quality fabric, but simple and almost without decorations, a scarlet shawl on her shoulders, and beautiful leather sandals, which caught his attention because it contrasted with the rest, but was a remnant of the former Mary.

"You changed your outfit, but you are beautiful as always," he greeted her cheerfully, eyeing her from head to toe. "I can also see that you still have a sentiment for expensive shoes."

She was still a lady, but without a trace of the defiance or provocation that once attracted him so much. She became even more refined, and at the same time, calm and confident. There was no sign of self-exaltation, and yet it was felt in every move she made that her self-esteem was strong. He was also struck by the impression that she was functioning in some other dimension. In addition, she had an unusual smile. She was like the priestesses he sometimes saw in temples: quiet, happy and harmonious. Her every gesture was unforced, her words carried the truth. She was a complete woman, he thought of her.

"I walk a lot now, so good sandals are important, and if they are also beautiful... Why not? "She laughed softly, sitting down in the place he showed her.

"Tell me! How are you?" Captivated by the new Mary, he wanted to know as much as possible.

"Do you remember the condition I was in when you last saw me?"

"I'm sorry I left you."

"I am glad you did. You were with me in the hardest time. Thank you for that. Thanks to you, Magdala knew I had a defender, nobody dared to bother me."

"What barbarians," he was indignant at the memory of what had happened then.

"Not 'barbarians'. They defended order in their territory. It's good they didn't stone me. They could do it after all. I probably owe this only to my father's position, to Marta, and to God's protection."

He nodded as if he understood her, but it wasn't so. He had his opinion on the customs of the country in which he temporarily had to live.

"Tell me what happened when I left. I have heard various things."

"Well, because various things happened. The most important thing is that I managed to handle what happened to me."

"I admire you. You are very strong."

"If someone comes to you with a gift and you don't accept it, then who does this gift belong to?" She asked, seemingly unrelated to the subject.

"To the donor," surprised by the question, he answered only after a moment of reflection.

"The same applies to envy, anger and insults. If they are not accepted, they remain the property of those who carry them in themselves. When I understood that, I was sure that the problem is not only on one side. I made peace with what happened. Magdala is still working through these issues in its collective sense of right and wrong. It will take them a while. Or maybe they won't handle it during the lifetime of this generation? I do not know."

"You left there for good?"

"I ran away first. Demons were after me."

"Demons?"

"Specifically, they are the demons of the past. Remember, it was a particularly difficult time for me then. My father passed away, I got information about my grandmother's death. I learned that for a long time my beloved grandfather had another woman besides my grandmother, my guardian, with whom he was very close, and my grandmother accepted it all

423

her life. What's more, she suggested the girl to him. As you know, not long before that, the man whom I loved and to whom I was fully committed, betrayed me and our feelings. Among all this, there were also you with your wonderful, forgiving love. There was also David who wanted me to be his wife, but he couldn't even take a single step without his father's knowledge and consent. There was also Samuel, remember, you liked him, whose favors I rejected, wounding his heart. There was Marta, my wonderful sister, who tried to help me with all her heart, my mostly silent brother Lazarus, and this terrible town, so cruel to me. They destroyed a lot, they even killed my cat, the last living thread connecting me with Egypt. I was at the bottom of despair. Now I understand them. I stood out so much, I did not respect their customs, I stood against all the values important to them. They had to react. And I think it was a gentle reaction anyway."

"Gentle, you say?" He interjected when she was quiet for a moment.

"Then, when they banished me from the house, I was raped. I was pregnant. I felt hatred for my torturers. If I could and had strength then, they wouldn't have saved their lives. I know they have already paid for what they have done."

"How can you be so sure?"

"The Goddess's hand punished them. She is strict but just."

When he heard about the rape, he clenched his fists and promised himself that he would get the bandits. However, when she said they had been punished, he breathed a sigh of relief.

"Do you remember the house of pleasure in Magdala? I went there to get the medicines for abortion. I got them. I discarded the fruit of rape from myself."

He listened, shocked by her honesty. He remembered how bad she felt, after all he spent some time in Magdala when she was sick, but he could not imagine it was that tragic.

"And then I went crazy."

"You went crazy?"

"Yes. I got attacked by the demons I mentioned to you. The main ones had the faces of rapists, and the others looked like those who threw stones at me. I was convinced that they attacked me again, that they were at my house, destroying everything they destroy everything they encounter along the way, tug at my hair, spit at me, insult and kick Marta. It seemed to me they drag me out of the house and throw stones at me, and swarms of flies are still circling around me. Everything was so real! I ran away and hid in the desert. I went through hell there. I descended to the darkest depths. I suffered, yelled in pain and despair, I died and I was born again many times. I don't know how I survived it. Later I learned that I spent over a month there. Marta and Lazarus were looking for me everywhere. Unsuccessfully. I think I literally and figuratively fell underground. I don't know where I was. It's a black hole in my history. My own hell. I've been where there is nothing more below. I saw terrible things. I don't know by what miracle I was able to return later to Magdala, and in addition, on the day he was there."

"He?"

"You heard about him. I'm with him now."

"Who's that?"

"It's Jesus."

"This Jesus? You are with this Jesus?"

"Yes, Lucius."

He paused. He didn't know what to say. His beloved had gone through a nightmare of which he had known so little before, and now she was with one of the country's most wanted men. It seemed that she did not realize that she had recovered from one oppression, but unknowingly got herself into another one. She probably didn't know how much the authorities were afraid of Jesus. He was salt to their eyes, painful, troublesome and dangerous. Once harmless and treated with disdain, after a series of supposed miracles he performed, he was now a threat to public order. He was said to be a stirrer and to incite people. The wealthy Pharisees considered him the worst enemy and did everything to get rid of him.

And she just told him she was with him. "With him? In what sense?" He wondered and did not dare to ask. He appreciated that she had talked so honestly to him. He was sure that every word she said was true. She did not color anything, did not hide anything - she spoke directly, just as she felt. Her whole truth.

"Do you know why I told you all this?"

"I am grateful to you that you trusted me so much."

"Do you know why?"

"Honestly, no."

"Because you loved me with all of yourself, selflessly. You gave yourself to me out of pure love. We were good together.

426

You did not hesitate to talk about me with your family, you stood by me in the most difficult moments. You loved me so much that you didn't care about yourself, about honor, or what people would say. True love is above all this. And that's the feeling you gave me. I am very grateful to you and believe me that I can appreciate it."

He didn't understand. She was here with him, she told him about her most intimate experiences, she was happy with his love and devotion, and at the same time she announced that she was with another man. It was complicated for him, but since he met her, he realized that understanding a woman was like understanding the whole world. He knew that there was no point in trying.

"I love you, Lucius," she confessed. "And it always will be so. You have a permanent place in my heart. You gave me a lot of good. Thank you."

"You love me and yet you are with Jesus "despite his efforts, he could not stop himself. "How does that make sense? If you say you love me, then be with me. I think that's what it should look like?"

"I love that you are in the world and that we have been joined by such a special feeling. I love and admire everything in you. And I am with you. With my whole heart. But I won't walk my life with you. My path is different."

"And what about my path? Have you thought about it? Am I supposed to wait forever for you?"

She closed her eyes. She smiled at what she saw.

"Berenice is looking for you. Go to her. You two will be happy."

"Berenice?" He was surprised. "How do you know?"

"I saw it a moment ago."

He believed her. She was talking with such confidence and conviction that yes, he was certain that just a moment before, when she closed her eyes, she saw him and Berenice together. He was convinced that the one who was his beloved Mary, for whom he would sacrifice and do everything, really belonged to another reality. She had seen, what ordinary mortals had no chance to experience even in the most unbelievable dreams.

He wondered how this amazing gift awoke in her, when did it happen? He thought that it must have been when she was in places she called "the abyss." It was there that she changed. She had always been different, she knew and saw more, but, perhaps, only the descent into the abyss freed her powers that had been in her for a long time, most likely even from birth.

"Mary, in that case follow the path that you say is yours. Be careful though. These are turbulent times, and the man you are associated with is considered by many to be the number one public enemy. Remember what happened to John the Baptist."

"Lucius, whatever is to be, will be."

"Remember, if you are in danger, I'm here. Always for you."

"Go to Berenice," she took his hand. "Please promise me that. You will be good with her," she assured him. "And you two get out of here as soon as possible."

He had doubts, but when she touched him, he was sure that Berenice was destined for him and promised himself that he would meet her the same day.

"Soon the time will be complete, prophecies will come true. There will be an end that will become a beginning," she added mysteriously, kissed his cheek, wrapped herself in her crimson scarf and left.

He stood still for a moment and wondered what he had just witnessed.

"She is the priestess of Isis and will always be, she is a lady because she was born one. But now, after everything she had experienced, she has become something more," he thought. "Who is she and where is she going?" He couldn't find the answer to that question.

### 6.

Joanna's husband, Chuza, managed the estates of the tetrarch Herod Antipas. When she became his wife, she was very young, and Chuza was not that important and rich yet. They both came from wealthy families. Her husband's grandparents came to Galilee from Petra. They brought with them a small fortune, which their son tripled, and the grandson multiplied in such a way that he was soon considered the one with the strongest head for business in the entire region.

When they met, Joanna was beautiful and spoiled. She could read, write, count and knew three languages well. She lived with her parents in Jerusalem. Her father was one of the most respected merchants, and her mother took care of the household. God blessed them with three daughters. The others had had husbands for a long time and as the youngest, Joanna was still with her parents, who were in no hurry to see her go, and as she did not like any of the young suitors either, she remained marriageable.

For her father, Chuza was not an ideal son-in-law. Not only his family had roots in Petra, and therefore did not belong to any of the families of David, but also his father and he were famous for doing business at the court of Herod the Great. He was known not only for magnificent buildings and close contacts with Rome, but also for the fact that "as it was said "he disliked conservative Jews so much that he ordered that the city gates be erected in place of the old cemetery, so that they would not want to enter the Tiberias he had built. And as everybody knows, the foot of any pious Jew who respects old values, will never stand on a grave.

But when it turned out, to the surprise of almost everyone including Chuza himself, that Joanna was interested in him, things happened quickly. Engagement took place, then the wedding, and Joanna moved to live in her husband's house on Lake Gennesaret, near Tiberias.

Soon she gave birth to a son and shortly after, to a daughter. At that time, Chuza became the steward of Antipas. So they lived in the royal palace and Joanna became a lady of the court.

Mary knew well who Joanna was. The information about the women who accompanied Jesus was passed from mouth to mouth. They aroused surprise, sometimes admiration, and most often mischief. It was not customary for non-family women to accompany men on a journey, to stay with them or even talk to them. Yes, the apostles were accompanied by their wives, but even they willingly stayed at home during their husbands' wanderings.

Joanna not only was not a wife of any of them, but she belonged to a completely different class. For Jesus and his disciples, she was a real challenge. She came from the royal palace. Her manners, sophistication, quality of her costumes, and manner of speaking amazed them, despite the fact that she tried very hard to behave in such a way as not to intimidate them.

When they met for the first time, Joanna looked expertly at Mary's ring.

"It's beautiful. What does this symbol mean?"

"It is a sign of perfection, inseparable bond, eternal triplet. It is the love that creates the world, the unity of everything that lives, including man as part of the eternal Divinity."

"Is that God's sign?"

"He who is everything."

"I've seen this symbol before," Joanna leaned toward Mary. "Isn't this what the priestesses of Isis wear?"

"Lady, you have great knowledge," Mary bowed her head.

"And a great respect for priestesses' actions," she bowed in return.

"I'm glad to have the honor to meet you, lady. I heard about you a long time ago already."

"I heard of you too, of course," she laughed. "I have wondered many times what the one with privileged access to the Master looks like. The one with which, they say, he shares his most important thoughts and secrets."

"Oh, they say so?"

"Exactly," Joanna's smile was trustworthy.

"So it's a bit like we had known each other before," Mary felt a special bond with Joanna.

She could read hearts like an open book. She sensed the intentions, mood and the color of the aura surrounding people.

In Joanna's aura, Mary noticed a strong red turning into intense orange. The scarlet was bright and energetic, it indicated vitality, joy of life and strength, and the strong orange spoke of enthusiasm, joy and openness to the world.

"Did you know that my husband knew your father?"

"Really?"

"They had business ties. Syro was an honest man. I first heard about you a long time ago. You were just born, and I just recently married Chuza and moved to the lakeside house.

Mary looked at Joanna carefully. She wondered how old she could be. She counted in her mind and concluded that she had to be thirty-five, maybe even forty. Was it possible? She looked so young. Or maybe she just got married early?"

"You are a beautiful woman."

"One can't deny your beauty either, Mary," she called her by her name, as was the custom for women of powerful families to address young girls.

"Thank you," she bowed like a schoolgirl, because for a moment she felt as if she was among the friends of her grandmother Aida, looking at her friendly, and expertly assessing her appearance and behavior.

Like her grandmother's acquaintances, Joanna knew a lot about women.

"So we have a priestess of Isis among us," she said. "Furthermore, the one of whom it is said that whoever as much as touches her with his finger, will be severely punished. For example, like the seven rapists."

"What?"

"You really don't know what I'm talking about?"

A shiver went through Mary. She learned to live with the past, and even made it her shield, but now, after Joanna's words, she saw again for a short moment the hideous faces of her torturers.

"It is said in the palaces that you were raped, and Isis punished those who did this to you, by depriving them of their man's parts and pushing them down their throats," she explained.

"I haven't heard of that. Maybe nobody dared tell me that? Or maybe I don't visit palaces often enough?" She laughed to ward off the difficult memories, but it wasn't easy.

She remembered Nefer and her words that the Goddess always protects her priestesses. And she understood everything now. As if on the senet board, the figures went in the right places. She understood how Nefer punished her rapists.

"This is not the first time I have been moved by Isis' sense of justice."

"I see you really didn't know," Joanna could read people. "Believe me, what I said is not fantasy. I know the case. I personally saw these men. One of them miraculously reached my husband to tell him what happened to them, and demanding punishment for the perpetrator."

"Really? I have not been very sociable recently, I do not know what was happening around."

"Chuza does not deal with such matters, but in Antipas's absence, he sometimes takes over some of his duties. In this case, not only did he not order to prosecute the perpetrator, because you tell me, who would he have to look for, Goddess Isis? Furthermore: he had the perpetrators of rape flogged for their lies about the goddess from a friendly country. As you know, he is a devotee of Rome, but also of Egypt, it is a Roman province after all, and Isis is worshiped there. Anyway, I'm sorry, I don't have to explain to you where your goddess is worshiped," she laughed. "Of course, I supported my husband with all my heart. He is a wise man."

"Wise man, but he lets you spend time with the troublemaker and his group?"

"Mary, I owe my life to this troublemaker, as you call him, teasingly, I understand. And certainly my health. Do you know how and why I got here? Do you know why I follow the Master?"

"Because you love him?"

"Yes, of course. Primarily. I adore him as a man. He is beautiful, gentle, attentive, forgiving and harsh if necessary, and at the same time, you must admit, completely out of this world. He is wonderful, we are tied by a union of our souls."

Mary felt a twinge of jealousy. She was surprised. She thought she was free of it. That, in line with the advice of the priestesses she had once learned, she knew how to be with a man on a friendly foot, without coquetting him, without thinking of carnality, without emotional tendencies, and therefore without jealousy. She was sure that was exactly how she could love Jesus. However, after Joanna's words, she realized that she was wrong. He was her spiritual brother, that's for sure, but maybe he still attracted her as a man more than she thought?

No, she didn't want it. She wanted a pure relationship, exclusively on a spiritual level.

"Have you been with him for a long time?" She asked carefully.

"He healed me six months ago. I've been following him since then."

"What did you suffer from?"

"I was dying slowly."

"Each of us dies slowly…"

"But I was dying slowly faster," she said and got amused by her own sense of humor.

"What was wrong with you?" Mary did not laugh because she understood Joanna's pain.

"I gave birth to two children. Today they are already big, we are looking for a husband for our daughter. I have always been healthy, but at some point something changed in my belly and I started to bleed excessively. On moon days I felt pain, my womb was on fire, I swelled. Something grew inside me, then it broke and a dark brown goo flowed out of me for many days. It got so bad that I was bleeding for half a month. There would be a momentary break and later it all would start all over again. I was so weak that I stopped getting up from bed. The royal medic gave me infusions, made compresses of strange ingredients, my husband made sacrifices, nothing helped. It lasted for several years. At first I was just thinner, and later I looked like a shadow. I was saying goodbye to my life when I heard about Jesus. Something told me to try. Since he had done so many miracles, healed so many, maybe there was also hope for me, I thought."

Mary forgot the little needle of jealousy that stung her a moment earlier. She listened to Joanna's story. She saw her in bed, weak, exhausted, without strength. She saw her worried husband and crying children.

"And what happened?"

"They took me to him in a litter. I walked toward him by myself, but, believe me, I could barely stand upright. My servants were supporting me. When I knelt in front of him and bowed my head, he did not ask what was wrong with me. He put his hands on my head. I felt heat filling me. I fainted. When I opened my eyes, he gave me his hand. I won't forget his smile for the rest of my life. "You're healthy," he said. "Go." I got up. I was healthy."

"The bleeding has not happened again?"

"Not once. Strength returned, as if he had poured a potion of life into me."

"The God's drink."

"Olympic nectar."

"Amrita."

"The Divine light."

They smiled to each other. They came from the same worlds. Both were educated, well read, knew literature, they were intelligent. They could name the same concept with many different words, and in addition, taken from different cultures. Each of them read a lot and had been among educated people, and many times participated in discussions which simple people considered as talking about nothing and sticking heads in the clouds.

"You've been with them for half a year already, how do they treat you?"

"I'm in a fairly privileged position," Joanna was honest. "First, of course I am not with them permanently, I come from time to time, to be in his splendor, listen to the words and watch him speak. I like it and draw strength from it. And secondly, I support them with Chuza's money, so they rather need me. Simon Peter, of course, is reserved toward me, but you must have noticed his approach to women. He is a simple fisherman. Andrew at least can refrain from commenting, but he has also made it clear to me what he thinks about my presence among them. Before I met Jesus and his companions, I did not think that women were still treated like that anywhere. In the palace, no one would afford the taunts I sometimes hear here."

"They are ordinary men, but they have good hearts. And they love him."

Instead of commenting, Joanna asked:

"And you? How did you end up here? An educated priestess of Isis, brought up in Egypt, intelligent, independent, wealthy? Is it true that you own half of your father's property?"

"That was his will."

"When you were born, I learned the story of your mother. It touched me a lot. For love, she left a beautiful world and came here..."

"Apparently this is the path along which Isis, or maybe Adonai, led her? Maybe they both did it?"

"Gods, even those strange Egyptian ones, think far ahead, they plan for years. Maybe your mother came to give you birth here? Maybe you have an important mission ahead of you?"

"God works in mysterious ways."

"Your mother had a cat. Do you know that she came to live in my house?"

"Really? I heard about her from my sister. She told me that when my mother died, one day the cat moved out and nobody in the area saw her anymore."

"She came to me."

"How come?"

"Magdala is not far from Tiberias, as you know. One of the servants let her into the house, seeing the collar around her neck. Thanks to this collar, I later found out where she came from. I wanted to give her to your father, but he said that since she chose me, she should stay with me. Bastet lived with us until the end of her days. One day she fell asleep at my feet and never woke up again."

"In my childhood I saw her spirit in our home, or so I thought. The world is really amazing. So many years have passed and I found out just now what happened to my mother's cat."

"Everything is intertwined. Ghosts reside among the living, including these of animals. The world is combined into one unity."

"You speak like the priestess of Isis."

"I am an Adonai's follower, which doesn't mean I don't know what's going on in the world and how women live somewhere else. For example in Egypt. Do you sometimes think about going back?"

"I often think about it, but now I am here. I'm fine here. I feel this is my place. For now, anyway."

Joanna adjusted her dress. She dressed modestly and moderately to meet Jesus. She was used to court luxury, splendor and anything that wealth could bring, but for traveling in Galilee, she chose outfits that were primarily comfortable and warm. The nights could be cool, and they often happened to sleep under the stars. She was always accompanied by her maids, but in order not to stand out too much, she took only two with her, so she also had little costumes or everything else she needed during the trip, because who would take care of them and make sure that the mules transport them in good condition from place to place?

"Well, tell me finally how you got here, because I keep talking mainly about myself."

"It's amazing that the steward's wife is among these people. Everyone would like to hear your story, not just me. I'll tell you about myself in a moment. Just tell me, please, what does your husband and royal court think about it? How did the tetrarch Antipas and his wife react to the fact that you spend time with such simple people, in addition led by an obsessed madman, as they say?"

"My husband is good and understanding. He thinks that my health and life are worth all the money. He really loves me. Do you know how happy he was when I was healed? He filled the purse of Judas Iscariot, who cares for Jesus' finances. And Herod Antipas and his wife? They consider my trips as whims. Of course they are curious about Jesus. Especially Herod. I told him about the Master. About his wisdom, views and the miracles he did. He said many times that he would like to meet him, but remembering the fate of John the Baptist, I would prefer not to let it happen. It is enough for my husband and me that Herod did not forbid being in his company. Because he could do it. At first, my friends were surprised that I was following the Teacher, but since they saw how much my condition had improved, they stopped commenting. I am healthy, moreover, and maybe above all, I am the wife of Chuza after all."

Mary nodded with understanding.

"You know how it is: if a poor man does something unusual, they say he is crazy. If a rich man did the same, he would be called extravagant or eccentric. I have my husband's permission for what I do, so I can do what I like. Besides, Mary, like you, I have my own fortune. Separate from my husband's. It is not as impressive as yours, because I have also heard, I do not know if it is true, that apart from some part of Magdala and Bethany, you also have an estate in Egypt, but if something happened and, for example, Chuza stopped loving me, I would not starve," she laughed.

How well Mary understood her! She knew how important a financial independence was. She blessed her mother and grandmother for taking care of this for her. In her youth, wealth was not important to her, material matters always seemed secondary to her. But when she discovered how huge work Marta and Sithathor were doing, how much effort her father, grandparents and great grandparents had to put in to gather what they had and how great comfort it gave her, she realized how grateful she was. Financial security gives you independence. Without it, even if we are not slaves, we always belong to someone. Only when we have our own resources, even the most modest, can we feel independent.

She had such security, without any merit of her own. She was simply born into a wealthy family. Knowing that not every woman was in such a privileged position, she realized that maybe she had the responsibility to make others aware and help them, as part of her life's mission of being a priestess?

"I've been here since the time he healed me," she began her story. "But I've always been walking toward him. As you say, I was born here for some reason. Maybe precisely to meet him? You're right, I was educated by priestesses. I am one of them." She brushed the hair away from her neck "Look. Do you see this sign? It's the same as on my ring. In the past, priestesses had it high on their forehead. Now showing the sign is dangerous, especially here. I show it to you because I am sure I can."

"You can," she touched Mary's neck with her fingertip.

"Go ahead, it won't burn you, she encouraged.

441

"One can never be sure with you, priestesses," she patted her hand and laughed. "I still have the punishment that your rapists have faced in my head."

"I can't say I have no hatred for them," Mary was calm. "But I don't live in the past either. What happened, is behind me. I am done with it."

"Keep it up, you're a smart girl."

"I learned from the best."

"Will you tell me about it? I would love to know what it looks like there."

"Maybe someday, why not? But first things first..."

\* \* \*

"What is matter? Will it last forever?*"

The teacher replied:

"Everything that is born, everything that is created, all the elements of nature are intertwined and united. Everything that is complex will decay. Everything returns to its roots, matter returns to the first origins of matter."

"It's difficult to understand..." Simon Peter often expressed aloud what others only thought.

"You have eyes and you can't see, you have ears and you can't hear?" Jesus was patient, although he noticed how

---

\* After: Gospel according to Mary Magdalene. Only a small fragment from the Coptic translation survived (V century AD); the Greek original is from the 3rd century and is written on papyrus.

Ewa Kassala

difficult it was for them to understand his words. "Open your minds and hearts."

"What is the sin of the world?" continued Simon Peter.

"There is no sin," Jesus did not hesitate. "You make sin exist when you act according to the customs of your corrupt nature. The sin exists in it. That is why this Good came down among you. It interacts with the elements of your nature so as to reconnect it with its roots." He looked into their faces and when he finally saw understanding in them, he continued. "That's why you get sick and die. It is the result of your actions. What you do takes you away from the roots of nature. Attachment to matter arouses passion against nature, and so the whole body is tormented. That is why I tell you: stay in harmony! And if you lose your balance, get inspiration from the appearances of your true nature."

"Lord, what you are saying is clear, thank you for these words," Joanna said.

"Let those who have ears, listen," Jesus smiled at her and looked around again. From the faces of the apostles he recognized that they were thinking about what he said. "May peace be with you. Let my peace rise and be fulfilled in you! Be vigilant and do not let anyone deceive you by saying, "Here he is" or "He is there" because it is in you that the Son of Man lives. Go to him, for those who seek, will find him. Preach the Gospel of the Kingdom."

They looked at him closely, and he continued speaking, while looking into their faces.

"For the pure, everything is pure, but for the tainted and infidels there is nothing pure, their spirit and conscience are dePhilaed. It is not what enters a man that makes him unclean, but what comes out of the mouth and has its source in the heart - for this is where evil thoughts, murders, adultery, fornication, theft, false testimonies, and curses come from. This is what makes a man unclean*."

"Lord, I am writing your words down," Mary looked up from her notes. "I want them to reach everywhere and be preached forever. When I'm done, I'll take them to the grotto in Qumran, to the Essenes. They will last for centuries there."

"I am the light that is above all. I am Fullness. The fullness came out of me. The fullness reached me. Split a tree, I am there. Pick up the stone and you will find me there*," Jesus finished, got up and left.

No one dared follow him. They knew he needed to be alone. They understood that he was regenerating his strength and talking to God, and they had time to think about his teachings.

Students also dispersed to do their chores. Mary could finally talk to the Teacher's Mother.

Mary the mother saw her for the first time. She arrived together with her sister and as soon as she greeted everyone, while her son was speaking, she fell asleep in the shadows, tired by the journey. Now she woke up and looked after the preparations for the evening meal. It was prepared by Andrew's wife, Joanna's maids and Ethel, who, after Mary forgave her the past, became her maid again.

---

* In: Mt 15.10-20.

* Gospel of Thomas, 77.

"Lady, it is an honor for me to meet the Master's mother personally, you are an extraordinary woman," she said, and bowed low.

"Child, we're all equal to God. He does not know gender, race or origin, he does not care what one possesses, after all, he who is able to cry with the crying and laugh with the laughing is really rich. The most important thing is what we have in our hearts, isn't it?"

She was a walking goodness, she was filled with love. Mary felt it from the first moment.

She had wondered for a long time what the one who once carried him inside, who hugged him after his birth, fed him, wiped his tears, watched him take his first steps, was like.

And here she was looking at this short, tiny woman. If it wasn't for the wrinkles around her eyes, she would look like a young girl. She was slim and slender, she moved gracefully, and at the same time accumulated immeasurable amount of peace in herself. Stately and calm, she belonged to women who appreciate staying behind or to the side, who like shadow, those who do not want to sit in the front row and perform in public. She didn't like to attract attention. Her outfit also testified to this. She had a gray dress, a black scarf, she did not wear jewelry on her neck or wrists, calves, fingers or ears. Her most beautiful decoration, one that attracted the eye, was her smile. An honest, unforced smile, also present in the eyes and seemingly, her whole body. It expressed love for everyone and everything around.

Mary felt respect for her above all, and then admiration and attachment.

"You are curious about me, I know," the Teacher's mother patted her hand. "You're a good girl, you are smart. You have brightness in yourself, one can see it right away. I'm glad you're with him. Someone like you is a real support for him. You love him immensely, don't you?"

"Yes, lady."

"Other women love him too, and so do his students. But I see that your love is different. You love him above the time."

Jesus' mother looked at Mary's hands. She opened her palms and stared at the lines. She noticed the star.

"Who are you, girl?"

"I am the one who loves him above the time, you are right, lady. I come from afar, I have come a long way. Now I am here and thanks to your son I know that the true love, as well as what is born of it, that is the happiness and peace, are possible on earth, in our mortal life."

"Yes, child, love is the most important thing," she nodded quietly. "Nothing matters more. Mother's love, love for a husband, parents, siblings, friends, fellow men, and the world."

"He is love. He emanates it. He is filled with it. All of him. Has it always been like that?"

"He was like that before he was born."

"How is that?"

"He comes from God."

"I heard him say it many times."

"That's how it is. Who can know this better than the mother?"

"How did it happen? Will you tell me please?"

"Only a few people know my story."

"Will I be able to join the group of this few?"

"Yes, child, I trust you. As I said, you carry light in you."

The women prepared the evening food, the men talked in small groups, some repaired sandals strained by their travel, and they sat away from them. They found a place under the tree from where they saw everyone and others could see them, but no one could hear them.

"I was a young girl. I didn't know life yet," she began. "One night, just before the morning, I was awakened by a strange glow. When I woke up, I saw a luminous figure. I was terrified. Nothing like that has ever happened to me before. I fell on my face and didn't move. It was an angel. Beautiful, bright and good. He told me that the Holy Spirit would give me a child. Believe me, at the time I was neither happy nor terrified that I was endowed in such a special way, I simply accepted his words with humility, and respected the God's will. I couldn't do otherwise. How could I rebel or even argue with the will of the Most High? You understand, don't you?"

Without waiting for a reaction, she continued.

"Since then, only unusual things have happened in my life. Soon I went to my relative Elizabeth, who married the priest Zacharias. Both of them have been dead for a long time. When I visited them, they were many years after their wedding and they already accepted that they could not have children. However, I knew that their son would soon be born and that it would happen, as in my case, through the Holy Spirit. She accepted it with real joy. She also said that I was blessed among

447

women and that my name would be worshiped for centuries. I have never been hungry for kind words, I was raised in modesty, but I admit that it worked just like the information that the angel had given me before. Believe it or not, I really felt like the chosen one, and at the same time I realized how much responsibility I had."

"Because being chosen is first and foremost a responsibility," Mary interrupted as quietly as if she were talking only to herself.

"You know it very well, you're chosen too."

"I try to live up to it and give in to what is to happen. I believe in God's infallibility."

"Zacharias however, although he was a priest, did not really believe in the miracle that happened to his wife. God punished him for that by making him lose his voice. Fortunately, only temporarily. After nine months, John the Baptist was born, and Zachariah regained his voice."

Mary looked towards Jesus. He was looking at her too. He watched the two most important women in his life talk.

"Joseph, the most forgiving man in the world, was to become my husband. We were already engaged. When I shared with him the news that the angel announced to me, he was outraged and wanted to send me away. He didn't believe my words. I couldn't understand why. As I told you, I was very young. At that time, I didn't know what pregnancy meant for a girl without a husband. Around me such situations did not happen at all, I have not heard of anything similar. I was convinced that the child appears in the family when God wants it. And in fact, that's the truth. Nothing happens without his will. However, Joseph did not think like me. He believed that in addition to God's will, some activities are needed to conceive a child. I was quite naive. How many years have passed since then? Thirty-two, almost thirty-three years, and a pregnant girl without a husband still means stoning. At that time I was completely unaware of this. I was confident and convinced that everything would be all right. And that's how it happened. God was watching over me. He sent Joseph a dream that made him not only not dismiss me, but become the best father for Jesus. He has not been with us for a long time already, and I still love him very much. He took care of us and looked after us as beautifully as he could."

Jesus talked with the disciples. He discussed something vividly with Peter and Andrew. This did not stop him, however, from glancing from time to time towards the talking women. Not only did he know they were talking about him, but he heard every word they said.

"When the time of the labor approached, a census was announced. Caesar August wanted to know exactly what taxes he should expect from our area. We had no choice, despite the approaching delivery, we went to Bethlehem. Joseph was from there, and everyone had to appear at their place of origin. We were riding a donkey. I mean, I was sitting on it, and Joseph was leading it. The road was not long, but extremely bothersome for me. However, I don't remember the trip as being bad. When we got there, it turned out that, due to the census, all the taverns and places where we could stay were overcrowded. We could no longer look for a place, I had no more strength and the child demanded to be born. I gave birth in a cave in Bethlehem, in the only place we managed to find quickly. Believe me, it was a beautiful experience. I held a small crumb in my arms, hugged him to my chest and loved him the most in the world. I didn't think before that such love and happiness are possible. It is a bond given by God, indestructible and existing unconditionally."

She looked at her son. He smiled at her.

"The shepherds bowed to the little one as to a king. I was exhausted by the travel and the childbirth, but I remember everything well."

"It was a special time for you, lady."

"Not just for me. Someone eagerly awaited came to world. I was the one who carried him and then gave birth. Do you know what it means for a simple, modest girl to learn that she is the mother of the chosen one? I wondered many times why me. How have I deserved such a distinction? Such an honor could happen to a queen, princess, maybe a prophet or a priestess, this I would understand. But me? A simple girl? It is only in retrospect that I see how much I trusted God at the time. Without this, without my boundless innocence, which I sometimes think to might even be a naivety, it would not be possible."

"Your faith, lady, let the Messiah come into the world. He chose you. You will be worshiped for centuries, they will sing songs about you and pray to you. Those around you do not quite feel it yet. But it is so in life that sometimes we meet outstanding, extraordinary, chosen people in our path, and we often do not understand how great an honor it is for us to be next to them."

"It's one of human weaknesses. We prefer to put ourselves in the center of attention. We believe that no one nor anything in the world is more important than us. We rarely pay attention to others."

"You sacrificed everything to him. You gave yourself to him fully."

"He is worth everything. I don't count. I exist only so that he could have come into the world. It is the greatest honor and privilege that the Most High chose me for this."

"Lady, you'll always be a symbol. Centuries from now, people will not think about your dilemmas, everyday problems, fears and worries. They will pray to you for support."

"Mary, dear child, what are you talking about? Only him counts. No one else."

"Everyone who is with him, will always be with him. People in the future, while thinking and speaking about him, will also look at those who accompanied him. Each of us has a role to play. We are written in divine plans. Prophecies must be fulfilled, also thanks to our actions. But it will be Jesus who will open the Gates of Light."

"Gates of Light, you say? When he appeared, strange things happened. In addition to the shepherds, three wise men came to our humble cave. They said that a star was guiding them, that his arrival had been foretold for centuries, that the world had been waiting for him and here he finally was. They wanted to bow and worship him. They made royal gifts," they gave him myrrh, incense and gold. Even though I had known who he was, the greeting convinced me even more."

"What happened next?"

"According to the Halakhah, I could not touch anything holy after the delivery. To restore my purity, Joseph and I made a sacrifice in the temple. We couldn't afford a lamb, so we gave God a couple of turtledoves[*]."

Mary glanced at Jesus and imagined what he looked like when he was born. She was moved. She thought that she would gladly hug him then and smell his delicate, baby skin.

"He was growing healthy and getting stronger. When he was a little older, he helped Joseph and learned craftsmanship. He was capable, hardworking and very thorough, and in addition, extraordinarily clever. He amazed everyone. I give you my word that I don't know when he learned to read and write. Like other boys, he obviously went to Bet ha-Sefer, the House of the Book, but he read the Torah from a young age, understood it, and even explained to others as if he were born with this knowledge.

Mary remembered her beginnings. She saw her father holding her on his lap and heard herself repeat the letters of the alphabet after him. She remembered his pride when it turned out how easily his daughter learned. The smell of home returned, longing for her father and Magdala.

Now she was looking at this good woman, the Teacher's Mother, who, as a girl, submitted to the will of God because she did not even think that she could protest. She gave all of herself in his power, without questions or doubts, trustingly. She felt respect for the unearthly power. Were it not for her submission and conviction that this was the right thing, how would the fate of the world go? God chose the best person for a mother for His son on earth.

---

[*] Lev. 12.6–8.

"When he was twelve, we went to the Passover festival in Jerusalem. As you know, every Jewish man has a duty to visit this place and make animal sacrifices to God there at least once a year. As always at that time, there were a lot of people there. We were about to come back when it turned out that Jesus was not with us. We were looking for him everywhere. I didn't have a bad feeling about it, but I wasn't quite calm. Finally, after three days, we found him in the Temple. You know how wonderful this place is, it impresses everyone."

"They say that one who has not seen it, will not understand the concept of "a magnificent building."

"And they are right. My eyes never saw anything greater, and Jesus was right there. He sat among the teachers, listened to them and asked questions. They were amazed at the sharpness of his mind and the answers he gave to the questions they asked him. "Son, why did you do this to us? Your father and I were looking for you with a heartache," I said, happy to see him at last. Do you know what he replied? "Why were you looking for me? Didn't you know that I should be in what belongs to my Father? "

"Right, it's his house."

"I didn't fully understand that then."

"He was definitely a great child. I love his past and I love him now. If I would ever have a husband, it should be him."

The Teacher's Mother smiled gently.

"It will be whatever is to happen. But remember that he does not belong to you or me, but at the same time he is a part of each of us. He belongs to us all "she explained. "And it will always be like that, because he is not from here. I have known it from the very beginning."

"None of us is from here "Mary nodded. Every word spoken by the Master's Mother was valuable to her. Although she knew well what the next sentences would sound like, she still wanted them to sound fully. She wanted to talk about her love with someone who, like her, loved him boundlessly and unconditionally. "Yes, none of us are from here "she repeated the words that had just been said. "We come here for a moment only. We get a body like a garment, which we take off at some point because it has been worn out. But he is more from there than any of us. I have never met anyone with such great power. I know that the byssus garment was intended for him: special, precious, unique. He is marked, chosen, extraordinary."

"Mary, you also wear such a robe. You are one of us, your spirit has great power. You know that, right?"

Mary smiled and looked down modestly.

The Teacher's mother continued.

"Yes, you are one of us. Your strength is indestructible and will last for centuries. Use it."

"I love him the most in the world. I want him with all my heart. Every particle of my body and soul seeks to connect with him. I would like to be his wife, have children with him and watch them grow together with him, as we grow older. I would like him to experience what is given to most people."

"It will be according to God's will. Men his age usually have a bunch of children already. Apparently, the Lord had marked a different path for him."

"It will be what it's supposed to be, I know. I am mature and my life paths are winding enough for me to understand that I really know almost nothing, even though I have learned so much and experienced a lot. I feel that I have a long way to go, full of suffering and sacrifice, but also fascinating and beautiful. I want to follow it. Since I was lucky to be here, I received the gift of life, I will enjoy it to the fullest and the best I can. I will follow the path given to me. I will do everything to bring love and leave the most beautiful trace behind me. I will walk like each of us. I will fall and rise, yes "this is also life. I will love and lose, cry with despair and laugh with happiness, I will be helpless, but also the strongest in the world. I can handle it. I will walk with my head up, with gratitude and love for the whole world. Whatever awaits me in the future, near and far, whatever happens and however my fate unfolds, nothing will change my love for him. Wherever he goes, I will follow him. I will always be with him. My role is to be with him. In my head, from time to time, I hear words from the past that I am to be the Guardian of the Gate of Light, that this is my duty and destiny, and yet he is the Light.

The Teacher's Mother listened intently."

"What will be, will be, baby," she sighed.

"I sense what will happen, Mother. My heart is crying just thinking about it."

\* \* \*

"Herod Antipas is a man who is quite... How to say it... "Joanna searched for the right word, but did not find it. "As you know, he is the tetrarch of Galilee and Perea, or simply a king. His father, Herod, was a really powerful man, people called him the Great during his lifetime already for good reason. He built many roads and erected beautiful buildings, including the fortress in Masada. Do you know it?"

"I was there, it's really impressive."

She sighed at the memory of what had happened there, but Joanna thought she expressed her admiration for Herod's flourish this way.

"Indeed. Antipas would like to match his father, but it is not easy."

"The sons of great parents never have it easy."

"Well, it definitely wasn't easy for Antipas."

What could she say about the most important man in Galilee, for whom her husband worked? She had walked the world too long, most of it in the royal court, to tell things about anyone that she could not repeat in public. She had adhered to this principle for a long time and it always paid for her. She was reserved now, although she was convinced that she could trust Mary fully "out of habit, but also for fear that her words would be heard by the wrong ears.

"After all, John the Baptist was killed on his order," Mary understood her caution, and as she wanted to finally hear the story of what happened at the court first-hand, she asked the question directly. "Were you there then?"

"I was, unfortunately," Joanna knew that she would not avoid going back to the events that had kept her awake for many nights, and still caused tears. "Herod Antipas received Galilee and Perea for management after his father's death. He can issue the death penalty in the territory of these lands, and his authority does not cover only Roman citizens. There is the fortress of Macherus* in Perea, which Antipas made his residence."

"It was there that John the Baptist was beheaded."

"Exactly. As I said, I was there then. However, a lot happened before it got to this crime, because that's how we should call this event. I'll tell you about it. Antipas's first wife's name was Phasaelis. She was the daughter of Aretes, who ruled in the Nabatean kingdom, with the capital in Petra. This marriage guaranteed Antipas a quiet border in Perea, because Aretes and his state is, or rather was, a buffer for desert nomads. And now the story really begins, so listen."

"I am listening."

"Well, Antipas often traveled to Rome. During one of his trips he met Herodias. He fell in love with her at the first sight and, as they say, she also fell in love with him. Wonderful, right? A thunderbolt from clear blue sky! A great joy. The problem was that she was the wife of his brother Philip. Imagine, then, how great their love was, if Herodias abandoned her husband, and Antipas promised that he would send his partner away."

"To think that it could be just a beautiful story about unrequited love..."

Joanna lowered her voice to a whisper and leaned toward Mary.

"When I learned that Phasaelis was to be sent away, I didn't want to believe it. I liked her, one could know what to expect from her. Of course, she took what had happened as a grave

---

* Today it is the Jordan territory.

insult and she fled to her father even before Antipas could return home. He came with Herodias, who brought her daughter, Salome."

Joanna's throat went dry, she reached for the wineskin with water and took a few sips.

"At that time John the Baptist appeared there. He preached about the coming Kingdom of God, and when the king returned with his new wife, he said many times, publicly and very emphatically, what he thought about her. It reached her quickly, and believe me, Philae she is not a gentle and nice woman."

"I heard something about it."

"At her prompting, the tetrarch ordered to imprison John the Baptist in the dungeons of Macherus. We were sure that he only wanted to scare him, because why would he kill someone so harmless? However, that's not what happened. Even though I was sick, I remember a lot from that day "everything happened on Herod's birthday. Lots of guests, a great party, wonderful dresses. The first such a great social event since the return of the ruler from Rome. Herod wanted to show himself properly, and so did Herodias, too. The party was organized with a flourish, providing lots of attractions. As I said, I didn't feel well at the time, but I had to appear there, Chuza couldn't come without his wife. Maybe it's better for me that I don't remember everything exactly. Of course, I remember Salome's performance, so famous already. And I remember it well! It was the most mesmerizing dance I've ever seen. She writhed like a snake, bent her body in such a way that although I have seen a lot, believe me, I would not think it could be possible. She had her eyes fixed on her stepfather all the time. She used magic, I'm sure. Anyway, they say that she learned dance and magic from priestesses. And you know best that you priestesses can do everything!"

Mary wanted to deny it, but Joanna didn't even look at her, because her thoughts were at the time and place she was talking about.

"It is true what people say: Herod insisted that she dance, promising that he would fulfill her wish, no matter what she asks, even if she wished for half of the kingdom. When she finished, nobody could shake off the impression for a long time. This dance captured the senses, especially of the men, in such a way, that those who saw it would not ever be able to free themselves from this memory again."

"I wonder what temple she was studying at."

"I do not know. But what happened next... Mary, I can't describe..." Before her eyes appeared a picture so clear that she covered her face with her hands and began to cry. "As you know, because there is no one who would not know about it, Salome, prompted by her mother, demanded that the head of John the Baptist be brought to her on a tray."

"Oh my God!"

"And Herod fulfilled her wish!" She covered her mouth to stop the words that were about to get out. "He murdered the prophet! Because of her, because of Herodias and Salome. Both are bad, one is worse than the other!"

"Who do you have to be to do something like that?"

"Herodias behaved like a demon, just like her daughter. Both have a terrible, black abyss inside them. I heard servants saying that they cover the whole body at night with the blood of freshly born kids, especially the face, and that flies, probably attracted by the smell of blood, need to be constantly kept away from their chambers."

"Are they under the rule of evil powers?"

"I don't know in whose power they are, but certainly not God's. They got rid of John the Baptist because they were afraid of what he was saying. And it wasn't because he had called Herodias a sinner many times. Salome acted as if she wasn't thinking about her offended mother at all. As if she were ordered to do so by some force that could not stand the Prophet and that he had so many followers, and that he preached the coming of the Messiah."

"Evil exists, you need to counteract it, take care of the brightness. Love is only there."

"That head on the tray..." Joanna covered her face again. "... it was a turning point for me. I fainted then. Chuza took me home. He explained to the king that I didn't feel well. Anyway, everyone knew that I had been sick for a long time. I had the right excuse to leave this terrible place, with its promiscuity, indulging the wildest and most ridiculous whims, this only seemingly better world in which I have lived for so long. I got back home. You know the rest, I met Jesus and he healed me. Not just from the bleedings. He also opened my eyes. I will be forever grateful to him."

\* \* \*

*My dearest in the world, wonderful Mary,*
*I am writing to you to give you information about the property*
*and what is happening with us.*

*I look for a letter from you every day. I haven't received any information for several months. I'm worried. The last messages I received from Magdala were from Marta. She wrote that you had been sick but that everything was slowly returning to normal. She also informed me that you were moving to Bethany for some time. Later she fell silent.*

*I hope everything is fine with you and your family. I am concerned about the news that come to us from Jerusalem. There seems to be some upheaval brewing in Israel, is that right?*

*Mary, everything is in perfect order in the property. We care for the garden and the orchards. Everything is growing beautifully. Sales of products are also at a satisfactory level. When you come back, I hope you will be satisfied with my actions and their financial effects.*

*Your grandfather Karim is healthy. He sees us rarely, but watches over everything from afar. Stephanie is still by his side and is running a house in Alexandria.*

*Your little Dobrawa is already quite a big girl, smart and brave. I teach her how to write and read. She's doing well. We often talk about you. I promise her that when you come she will be able to show off her skills. Of course, I also taught her how to play senet.*

*Mary, everything is as it was in the temple on the island, to our joy. Despite external storms, the Romans treat us with due respect. The goddess watches over us all and her whole home, but the priestesses say that a difficult time is coming and that we should all prepare for it. As you know, they are always right.*

*For now, we do not feel a threat, everything flows in the old rhythm. We wake up, pray, work, go to rest. And so every day. All this in peace and focus. Thank gods, disasters bypass us. For years the Nile floods regularly, feeding our fields. So we live and enjoy what we have.*

*We miss you very much. It is your home. It is waiting for you just like all of us.*

*Beloved, may the Goddess look after you, may the God of Israel also protect you. Wherever you go now, whatever direction your life paths take you, remember that you are strong and wise, that you can handle everything, because the inner voice guides you.*

*Mary, most beloved in the world, I miss you very much, I would like to be able to one day greet you at the gate of your property, kiss you warmly and know that you are home again.*

*Devoted to you forever,*

*Sithathor*

## 7.

Six days before the Passover, Jesus came to Bethany, where Lazarus lived, whom he raised from the dead*.

A feast was arranged for him. Marta served, Lazarus was one of those sitting at the table, and Mary took a pound of the highest quality, precious nard oil and anointed Jesus' feet and wiped them with her hair.

The house filled with the smell of the plant.

"Why wasn't this oil sold for three hundred denarii and the money given to the poor?" Asked Judas. "A farmer earns all year as much as it is worth. And only if he is hard-working. Don't you think it's wasteful?"

He was taking care with the group's money. He tried to manage it so that they would never be short of it.

Everyone's eyes fell on Jesus.

"Leave her!" He reacted strongly. "She kept it to anoint me for the day of my funeral. "You will always have the poor, but you will not always have me."

Then Marta entered, carrying a festive outfit in her hands.

"Rabbi," she knelt in front of him "We've been holding this for you for a long time," she handed him the folded tunic.

"Do I see well that this is byssus?" Judas recognized the precious fabric.

"We have kept it especially for you, Rabbuni. It will be right for you for the Passover festival in Jerusalem," added Mary.

---

* After: Jn 12, 1-8, Mt 26, 6-13 and Mk 14, 3-9.

Earlier, they soaked the dress with aloe and myrrh. This way, in addition to being soft and shimmering beautifully, it had a scent that was associated with the holiday.

Judas, rebuked by Jesus, did not comment on the gift, but in his head he counted how many denarii the outfit that the women had just handed over to the Master was worth.

\* \* \*

"Do you know what diksha is?" Judas stood in front of Mary and looked her in the eyes.

"I do not know this word."

"Is there really something you don't know?"

"It's nice of you to say that, thank you," she didn't want to hear the malice in his voice.

"Priests in the distant lands of the East use it. Diksha is when man makes himself available to God as a tool and God accepts this sacrifice. The most interesting thing is that man doesn't know how he will be used. And yet it can be different ways."

"What are you getting at?"

"I wonder how much Jesus was born the chosen one, and how much he devoted himself to God in a diksha manner."

"I wonder how this term applies to you, Judas. To what extent God has chosen you to do what is written for you. And to what extent you have devoted yourself to God."

"I gave myself to him fully. I obey him, listen to his voice and fulfill his will, so that the fate would be completed."

"Poor Judas," Mary kissed his cheek. "I feel sorry for you. And thank you for being so devoted to the Teacher."

While they were talking, Joanna came up to them.

"Are you talking about money?"

"As you know, I had the honor of managing the group's finances. And I will say immodestly that I think I am doing quite well. Also thanks to your help and the generosity of others."

""You received free, give free", Jesus said," Mary admonished him. "Stick to it, Judas! Don't charge money for healing."

"I don't do that."

"I would like to believe you!" Joanna laughed. "Just like in the fact that the purses you keep are not leaky."

"Are you accusing me of something?" He got upset.

"I feel like you like money more than you should."

"I assure you I'm honest."

"Poor Judas..." Mary kissed his cheek again. "...poor you."

She turned and walked away. Only Jesus noticed the tear that flowed down her cheek.

\* \* \*

He and his students were sitting in a place which people began to call the Mount of Beatitudes, since the time he gave a memorable sermon here. Here, he recently multiplied five loaves of bread and two fish so that he fed five thousands people, which of course was immediately announced a miracle.

He liked this place, he was fond of it. During the day, and often at night, at full moon, when the moon was not covered by the clouds, the whole area was visible: the waters of Lake Gennesaret, Capernaum, Kinnereth, Magdala, and even Bethsaida. Sometimes it was also possible to recognize the distant lights of Tiberias at night.

"The strength that is within you comes from me. It has been given to you for the whole world, because you are the ones who will save the whole world. I told you from the very beginning that you are not of this world. I'm not from it either. Rejoice and be glad, and add joy to joy, for the time is completed so that I may wear my robe, which was meant for me from the beginning until the time of fulfillment. Rejoice and be happy, for you are blessed before all people on earth, because you are the ones who will save the whole world. Let anyone who has ears to hear, listen!" Jesus ended the long discussion with his disciples that continued long into the night, and rose to leave the fire.

It was basically a lecture, not a discussion. He was talking and they were listening. He repeatedly explained the more complicated matters to them, but also patiently answered questions and clarified difficult issues.

Mary hardly spoke at all. She had been silent since one day Peter said to Jesus:

"Lord, this woman is unbearable for us because she deprives us of the opportunity to say something since she speaks so often."

In fact, Mary had no problems understanding what Jesus was saying, but after all she was educated, she knew books, languages, and had read and appreciated poetry, philosophy, drama and comedy for years. The priestesses prepared her well for her role in life. When Peter criticized her, she decided to quiet down. She realized that the students were not as prepared as she was, and they might have difficulty understanding the Master's words.

What Jesus talked about, was not easy. It required not only focus and absolute concentration, but also complete opening of hearts and minds, making an effort to get to the bottom of it. He told them the most important truths. He spoke about eternal love, transcendence, other dimensions, about Paradise and Hell, about the essence of humanity, heavenly spheres, mysteries revealed to the world, soul, prophets, primeval causes of the universe, Treasury of Light. He used simpler words because he knew those would be the only ones they would be able to comprehend. He became a human to speak the language of people.

Jesus left the fire and entered the darkness. He sat under an olive tree. He leaned his back against its trunk and looked up at the stars. Mary also left the circle. Everyone was so lost in considering the Teacher's words that no one noticed when she followed in his footsteps.

Almost silently, she walked over to the tree he was sitting under and sat down at his feet, without asking for permission. She rested motionless for a long time, just like him, staring at the stars.

The gentle sound of the waves on Lake Gennesaret came from below. The moon was full. It was reflected in the water.

She rose. She walked a few steps and stopped in a place that overlooked the entire area.

After a while, she heard that Jesus stood behind her. He embraced her gently but firmly. She leaned her back against him, resting her head on his torso. She felt safe.

"My Lord, command me to speak openly," she asked quietly.

"Mary, the blessed one, whom I will make perfect in all the mysteries of the High, speak openly, you, whose heart appeals to the Kingdom of Heaven more than the hearts of all your brothers[*]."

She had long wanted to tell him what he knew perfectly well. She wanted certain words to be spoken. So that, despite the fact that they both realized they had been joined by a complete and perfect feeling "because it was timeless "from the first moment they met, she, like every woman who would be in her place, wanted to name it, to specify the sentiment whose existence had always been known to both of them.

"Rabbuni, I love you the most in the world. I've been going to you all my life. I want to be with you always."

"I love you, Mary. Be with me as you have been and will be forever," he kissed her hair. "I embrace you and encompass you whole. I feel every part of you, I touch your soul, which is as beautiful as yourself."

His warmth permeated her. She felt that it was pouring into her and filling her with a divine, sunny breath. She was trembling. Tears streamed down her cheeks.

"We are one, Rabbuni. I only want you. I always have. I was born to be with you. The purpose of my every step was so that I

---

[*] After: Pistis Sophia, p. 32.

could meet you, and now I touch your light. I absorb it. I penetrate it. It creates me."

Her senses focused solely on feeling the Divinity. She was no longer just a woman, she became part of him. As if the two elements of a timeless unity, once disconnected, merged now.

"Mary, you are the fullness that embraces all blessings, that will be glorified by all generations[*]."

"I will always love you because we are one."

"Mary, your legacy will be the whole Kingdom of Light[*]."

She took his hand. He allowed it. They followed the path down to the lake in silence. The moon lit up the way. They sat on the shore, on warm stones. Waves washed their feet. They no longer used words, they didn't have to. And yet they talked. They exchanged their thoughts silently. She "a priestess, lady, apostle, and he "the Messiah, Master, Teacher, the one whom she called Rabbuni.

"I am a woman who got to love God. How should I think about you, how to desire you?"

"Love."

"You are an unattainable ideal and a fulfillment. How to love you, how to be with you?"

"Be desirous."

"How to get closer to you? How to last? How to make it possible for me to feel you always and fully?"

---

[*] Ibid, p. 54.

[*] Ibid. p.110.

"Let's be one."

## 8.

"High Priestess, is that you?"

Mary thought that maybe she had just got in touch with her mentor through the silver thread of the cosmos. Maybe she was summoned by her, and now she had a vision so real that she thought what she saw was a reality?

"Yes, Mary, it's me," a woman in a long black cape and a hood pulled deeply on her forehead, showed her face. "You're not dreaming."

Mary moved closer to her. They were in one of the narrow streets of Jerusalem. It seemed that the High Priestess was waiting for her.

"Lady, forgive me for asking, but what are you doing here?"

She took her hand, opened the nearest door and pulled her inside.

"We can talk safely here." She lit a small lamp. "This is the apartment of one of our priestesses. We use it when needed."

They sat on wooden stools.

"I came to Jerusalem, like so many others, because I couldn't miss what they had foretold for a long time," she began. "This year's Passover will be a very important time for the whole world. I saw priestesses from all the continents. They blend in with the crowd - each of us can do it perfectly - no one will notice us, but we recognize each other. There are also priests and magicians here, including those who were brought to him by the star when he was born. We came from all

470

directions to be witnesses. Signs have been appearing for a long time, the predictions clearly showed the time and place. We are waiting. The city is full of people, tension is in the air. Everyone can feel it, but none of us can interfere with what will happen here. These are divine matters of the highest importance, because they relate to the cosmic balance. Time is going to stop soon. Yes, it'll stand still," she confirmed, seeing her face. "But you know that. It will be a borderline moment. The old age will end and a new one will begin. People say of something like this as "the end of the world." It will happen right here in this city.

"Yes, I can feel it too. Do you know when exactly this will happen?"

"Do you remember my vision at your initiation? Later I had several more. But, to tell you the truth, I know as much as you do. Maybe even less..." She thought for a moment. "Yes, definitely less, because you are in the center of the events. I enter the same cosmic spaces in which you also appear, but I do it from afar and I just look at it. We both know that the most important will happen any day, and then you will fulfill your mission."

"Great Priestess, I'm on the right path, I know that. I have felt it in my heart, mind and guts for a long time. I have disturbing premonitions and visions, including very bloody and terrible ones, however, believe me, I will accomplish my mission, although I still do not know what it will be."

"You're already fulfilling it. The truth is in you. Listen to the voice, it will lead you. The moment I saw you when you were a little girl, it became clear to me that you are special. All the signs and visions confirmed it. What you do now and where you are, is another proof that you have been chosen."

471

"Now I am a student and probably a bit of a partner of Rabbi."

"He has divine power. He is currently the most powerful in the world."

"He marked me with his seal. He put his hand on me. I am a bride and I love the love itself. I am a priestess in the service of love."

"It's just like you say. After all, you have become the Guardian of the Gate of Light and will always remain one. Through the ages. This is not your only mission, but certainly the most important one."

"Yes, the Guardian of the Gate of Light. I can still hear these words in my head."

"You don't remember your initiation?"

"After what I have recently gone through, the years in the temple of Isis seem a dream to me."

"Because you were in a different space, like all of us. For you, it was the first out-of-body experience of its kind. Remember exactly what you saw then. Only you know your mission exactly. Although we were all together in the holiest place of our temple then, and connected in the power of the Source, neither of us knows what was happening in the hearts of the others. Not even me. The goddess revealed your purpose only to you. Only you can remember it. No one has insight into your secrets unless you choose to reveal them to somebody. Close your eyes. Return to that moment."

Since the time she left the abyss, Mary had been able to move her thoughts quickly in the time and space of the universe. And so it also happened now.

She saw herself kneeling before the holy fire burning on the tripod. Other girls were praying next to it, forming a circle. She heard the words of the hymn said by them. She saw a bright glow hovering above them, turning into a luminous braid, traveling through the expanses of the sky.

She remembered everything. Again, as back then in the temple, she heard the voice of the Goddess clearly. She found the words, their meanings, and the explanation of what had been bothering her since she had fallen into the abyss of perdition. She remembered what was waiting patiently asleep in the space of time, and what was often trying unsuccessfully to break through to her mind with short signals. What demanded a revival in her heart, just saw the light of day. It stretched and unfurled wide its bright wings.

Now she not only heard the voice again, telling who she was, but finally understood what it meant for her.

She was the Guardian of the Gate of Light. She gained the full power.

\* \* \*

Berenice was standing in front of her.

She looked just as beautiful as when they used to meet at Lake Gennesaret. Just like then, she was laughing, ruddy and happy with her life. She was in Jerusalem to accompany her father, who was stationed there with soldiers before the approaching Passover. His troops were brought to the city from the north, because the security measures had to be strengthened, as usual on such occasions.

"Mary, I found out you're in town and I came to thank you."

"Nice to see you, Berenice."

Mary lived with Joanna at her sister. They stayed there for the holiday. The city was so full of people that if they wanted to rent something in the center, close to the Temple, they would have no chance of finding a place. And it wasn't appropriate anyway to stay somewhere else, while having a family in the city. Joanna's parents lived in Jerusalem, each of her two sisters had a large house in the city's most affluent district, and they were both ready and happy to host Joanna and her increasingly famous friend.

Mary pointed to the chair and sat down on the other chair opposite her.

"I will be returning to Rome soon," Berenice said happily. "Lucius too. We'll get married there. My father agreed, and Lucius's parents are favorable as well."

"Congratulations with all my heart. You belong together."

"Lucius told me it was you who encouraged him to take this step. Thank you."

"You'll be happy, you can be sure about it."

"Do you know I've always liked him? But I didn't dare to approach him because I thought he loved you. Even after Masada and what happened there, he was staring at you with such an admiration that I dreamed that any man would ever look at me like that. And ideally, that man would be him."

"You really are made for each other. Take care of your happiness. You have wisdom and joy, as well as goodness, sensitivity and curiosity of the world. Lucius is enchanted by you. And you by him, so everything is as it should be, right?"

"Mary, do you know that you give light to other people? You've always had something extraordinary about you that I wouldn't even try to name. It was fleeting and so unearthly. As if you weren't from here. And now, forgive me for saying this, since the time of your difficult experience, you are of course still the same Mary, but also as if, really, believe me, that's how I feel... You are like... a goddess!"

"Berenice, my dear, what are you saying?"

"We have their statues in Rome. There are various goddesses. All of them beautiful, spiritual, haughty, noble, they fight for their own, they are independent and wise. Minerva, Venus, Juno, Diana... they know what they want, they never give up. They are equal to the gods, they argue with them, discuss, seduce them, get angry, take care of their own, do not give up, achieve their goals. You are just like them. I admire you. Here in this country, women need you. They don't know they can be like that, and you show it to them. You open the way for them, show them the door through which they can enter and walk towards the light as if you were its guardian. Right, I know... What I say sounds like a Lucretius poem or something, but I really feel it this way. As if you were making a bright light shine on us through a large gate somewhere up there. Mary, I love you! Really. You are a wonderful woman! Can I hug you?"

\* \* \*

A day later, Lucius visited her.

"I know Berenice has already thanked you," he began. "I want to do it, too. Without what you told me, I would not notice that I let my happiness go by."

"Lucius, she was meant for you. You will live happily ever after."

"If a priestess says so..." He saddened.

"What do you want to tell me?"

"I got news from Rome."

"From Marcus?"

"He wasn't the one who wrote to me, but the letter is about him."

"Is it fulfilled?"

"You know it already?"

"I loved him very much. Such a bond can never be broken completely. Especially if you don't want to. And I don't want to "I still love him. When he is touched by a tragedy or in danger, I know it."

He shook his head in disbelief.

"How could she know about Marcus's wife's death?" he wondered.

"I'll never understand how you all do it."

"We?"

"The priestesses. I will remember the old lady from Alexandria for the rest of my life. She said she was a priestess once."

"A woman who once became a priestess, will always be one "she recited the old formula.

"All the more so," he concluded.

Until now, matters of priestesses interested him when they concerned himself or someone close to him. This time, however, it would be different. He wanted to know more.

"Tell me... How did she know Marcus's wife would die? She couldn't even suspect who would that be."

"Why not?"

"Right. Actually, why not?" He laughed. "But seriously: tell me how come you know?

"Some of us can enter a state through which the past, the future, other worlds and eternal space can be seen."

"So what does that mean? In your opinion, the future is predetermined, recorded somewhere..." He waved his hand "... and nothing can be changed in it?"

"Not at all! Each of us can do everything. What is written there..." She pointed to the same place as he did a moment before "...there, is your potential, direction, possibility, but whether what can be seen there will come true, is a complex matter. We can change the world, shape it so that it is good for us. We can cause wars or build peace, by using our own energy."

"And more specifically?"

"You still don't understand?"

"I'd rather you clarify."

She thought about it.

"If I had married Marcus..."

"You would be already dead today," he blurted out.

"Possible and probable. But not necessary."

"Now I don't understand anything anymore..."

"Long ago, when we were together, it seemed as if everything had conspired against us. His parents were against, my grandparents saw no prospects for us, the old woman presented us with a terrible future. Only the priestesses in the temple were calm. They often looked into the future and did not see us there together."

"So what?"

"So if I had felt with all my heart that we were meant for each other, I would have done everything not to let us part. Had he been convinced that we were made for each other, he would have overcome every obstacle. We would both feel it inside that we want and must follow a common path, and if it were to be this way, that's what would be. However, as you know, things went differently."

"I loved you with all my life. I was sure of my feeling."

"Yes I know. It was beautiful. And I loved you and I love you, Lucius. However, this is a different kind of love. We can be next to each other without being together. We are friends. Love and friendship are related feelings, but not the same. Sometimes we get lost in them and we can't recognize them properly. You love me like a friend. I am grateful to you for that."

"And Berenice and me? Do you really know how it will work out for us?"

"If you don't spoil it, you'll really live happily ever after," she laughed, patting his hand reassuringly.

He stood up.

"Time to say goodbye," he explained. "I have to go, there is a lot of commotion in the city. There is tension in the air. The tiniest spark can cause an explosion. We are on the highest alert."

"A lot will happen during this Passover."

"I would prefer it to be calm. I am sailing with Berenice to Rome during the holiday. Will you stay here for long?"

"We will see," she answered evasively, and got up as well. "It's good that you're leaving, it won't be quiet here. You will definitely feel better in Rome."

"Will we see each other again?"

"I think so."

"Think so? As a priestess, you should know that for sure," he kissed her cheek.

"There is such a probability," she joked sadly.

He stopped.

"If you could potentially know something about which I should be informed as an order officer in Jerusalem, could I count on you telling me about it?"

"Lucius, this Passover festival will be really special."

"We guess this, unfortunately. Not only Jesus is in the city. We have received many signals that other suspicious individuals have arrived, from almost all around the world.

They don't reveal themselves, but we know about their presence. As long as they do not bother us, we do nothing about it, but we are aware that something extraordinary is going to happen, and we are a bit afraid of it."

"It will be what will be. Judas has already got his silver pieces."

He decided that the conversation was taking too long, and Mary was beginning to speak in riddles that he couldn't decipher. Or maybe, simply absorbed by the return to Rome awaiting him, he didn't want to know what they meant?

He kissed her again, bowed, and left.

\* \* \*

In the scheme of the events, Mary had not thought about her former friend for so long that when she stood before her, Mary barely recognized her. She looked different than in times when they were close. When she finally realized whom she was looking at, she wondered first of all what her old friend was doing here.

"Zoe?"

A woman in a long, wide coat, her hair covered with a wide dark headscarf, nodded and pulled her hand. Through a narrow gate, they entered a courtyard of a household.

They were in the middle of the city. Like every year, the feast of Passover brought crowds of pilgrims to Jerusalem. As they walked, each in their own direction, they squeezed through the narrow streets, they bought drinks, fruit, pies and whatever could quickly satisfy hunger and thirst at small stalls, placed against the walls of the houses. They carried bundles, and the richer moved in litters, rode on donkeys or carts pulled by mules.

"Zoe, is that really you?" She repeated as they sat on the bench.

She stood in a corner of an improvised diner, which functioned in this place only during Passover.

Nobody paid any attention to them. Both were dressed in gray, and their heads were covered with wide scarves. They looked like most women around them. They asked the girl who stood before them, ready to take the order, for something to drink.

"I am accompanying the High Priestess," Zoe whispered into her friend's ear.

Their heads almost touched. They didn't want anyone to hear them.

Mary took her hands in hers and closed her eyes. A moment later she knew everything.

"I assist her," Zoe confessed, not knowing that Mary had already seen what she wanted.

"After I was ordained, I decided that I wanted to stay in the temple. My mother, who is Greek, as you may remember, returned to her family home after she decided I was an adult. My father never gave a sign of life since the time he mysteriously went missing, and we have not sought him. I did not want to go with her to Greece, but when I was left alone in the great villa on the Nile, I felt lonely and I decided quite quickly to return to Philae. Soon I became an adjutant of the High Priestess."

"Great!"

"I don't have visions, I can't travel in time, I'm not a material for a medic or hemet. At least for now. But I'm good at organization. Thus the High Priestess decided that I would help her at work. That's why I'm here, it's a secret mission of course, you understand. I can tell this to you, as not only one of us, but as the Guardian of the Gate of Light."

"I understand," Mary was so pleased to see Zoe, sit next to her, hold her hands and talk to her, that she listened with joy to all she said, even though she knew everything about her from the moment when she listened to her soul while holding her hands. Her senses, highly sensitive to danger recently, told her that they were safe and that they could talk in peace.

Zoe was honest, open and good. She did not use protective barriers that would not allow Mary or anyone else to look into her soul. "I have to tell her that she should learn to create a firewall. Not everyone who can look into other people's hearts has good intentions. I'll do it, but later. Now let's enjoy each other," she decided.

"Nefer is here with us," Zoe whispered even more softly "but I don't know where. I suspect that even the High Priestess does not know this. Nefer replaced Awenger, you know that? Awenger is now primarily training girls."

"I'm so glad to see you, my love," Mary's eyes, usually sad these days, laughed.

The time was extremely difficult for her, she knew what awaited her in the coming days, and the presence of Zoe and the awareness that Nefer was somewhere nearby, gave her comfort.

"Mary, they say these days will be dangerous. You are close to the one who is a threat, according to many. Have you thought about protecting yourself?"

"Dear, just like you, I am also fulfilling my mission here. In the sense you are thinking, I am safe."

Zoe felt calmer.

"The priestesses say this world is about to end. Is it true?"

"The end usually means the beginning of something else."

"The priestesses say that the Goddess's power will become dormant."

"But it will last. It will be quieter, but it won't disappear. It is not possible. As you know, she is eternal."

"The priestesses say that the Goddess will go to a long sleep, and you, as the Keeper of the Gate of Light, will watch so that she would survive."

"There are other Priestesses of Light. I am not alone."

"But you're the Guardian of the Gate. And you will be the one to open the door to the world for it again when the time comes."

"You know a lot, Zoe."

"I told you who I am assisting."

"It would be good if you closed the door to your thoughts for those not authorized "Mary decided to warn her."

"I remember about this. You don't think I'm stupid?"

"Not at all. But remember that there are powers that can read easily in the heads and hearts of others, and they are not always good. Your knowledge is very valuable, also because you accompany the High Priestess."

"Oh, look what I have here," Zoe parted the cleavage of her dress. "She personally hung it around my neck."

She stroked the amulet through the fabric. It rested between her breasts in a small leather poach. "Thanks to it, no unauthorized person will enter my soul. I am protected. Only Priestesses of Light can read me, I am open only for them. So you, Mary, probably know everything about me. I don't have to tell you anything."

"Zoe, you are my friend, I love listening to you."

Zoe kissed Mary in her mind.

"When here everything is over, will you return to Egypt?"

"I do not know."

"How come? You know everything!" She called out perhaps a little too loudly, because a few people looked in their direction, so they covered their heads tighter with the headscarves, and curled up in order not to attract attention.

Mary felt like in the days of Philae, when Zoe was often convinced that she should know everything and expected that she would work miracles, or at least she would know a way out of a hopeless situation.

"When you finish your mission here, come back to us. The gates of the temple are always open for you. You have to spend time somewhere, while waiting for the Goddess to decide that she wants to wake up."

"Isis will retreat for a while to manifest itself primarily in women's hearts. The world is developing like a spiral.

484

Sometimes the Goddess is the stronger one and sometimes it is God. It's like the sun and the moon: one is shining while the other is not, and yet they are not mutually exclusive, they coexist. Now the male's elements are winning, and this is how it should be, this is the way of history. The time of a strong God is coming. He is already here. He first appeared briefly in Egypt in the form of Aton, then came as Adonai. What is happening, will consolidate the new order of things. No one will take the crown from the goddess, because it's impossible, but it won't be the best time for her. However, she will come back someday, strong and powerful."

"And you will help her in this."

"That's my task."

* * *

Mary Magdalene opened her eyes.

It was dawning. She stood in the window. She looked at the rising sun. Another day was waking up.

She thought about who she was and who she could be for the women who surrounded her, and for those who would seek support in her in the future. The words appeared by themselves in her head and arranged into clear sentences.

"No matter where and when they think of me, I'll show them their power. Whether they are with someone or alone, whether they love now, or remember love, have already said goodbye to it, or are still waiting for it, I will tell them that they are powerful, strong, wise and beautiful. That they are a completeness also in wandering and falling, and when they are looking for a way and cannot find it, but what is important, they keep walking and do not give up. I will remind them that they have strength. And they always had. Or I'll wake it up in them. I will help them reject what limits them and enslaves them, I will be with them in the most difficult moments. In weakness, pain, loss, powerlessness and in the greatest life dramas. I will accompany them in their way as a quiet, supportive friend, as one of them, just like them. I will share my power. When we share it with others, we become stronger. Thanks to women's circles, we become the queens of our lives. Everyone of us. I will reach out my hand to you when you are in need. Please accept it. And when someone next to you ever needs your hand, give it to him. Be yourself. Be the woman you want to be. Use, create, give, always remembering that you are here only once. Do what you think is right, good and proper. Follow your mind and heart. Be smart and good. The Light that is within you will lead you. Trust your inner voice. Go with dignity, with your head raised high, and when you stop, wipe the travel dust off your dress and look into people's eyes. And into the sun. Smile to yourself and the world. Carry and give love. It is the most important, it calls us to life, we exist thanks to it, and at the end of the road here, we come back to it. Whether we like it or not "we are all love.

\* \* \*

Mary did not sleep that night. She could not. She didn't even lie down. Throughout the day, until the evening, she felt such a huge anxiety that her body was trembling. She had chills, she was cold and hot alternately, she was dizzy.

"No, I'm fine," she reassured Joanna and her sister. "I will rest, lie down and I will be better."

She tried not to let her know what was happening to her. She knew that she would need their strength and help in the coming days, and that she would receive it from them. But for now she still wanted to spare them the anxiety.

After supper she quickly went to her chamber. She sat on the bed. She couldn't stop her tears, but they didn't flow down her cheeks "she felt them in her throat and in her heart. Her soul cried. It wailed in pain and despair. It knew what would happen soon.

She lit a lamp, fell to her knees and began to pray.

The inevitable was approaching. A breakthrough was coming "the end of the old and the beginning of a new time.

She wanted and had to be with him. Now. She was the Guardian of the Gate of Light after all. She should accompany him when he would cross it. She couldn't run, she was too far. She wouldn't make it. So she closed her eyes, focused her thoughts, imagined that she spread her wings and soared like a bird.

After a moment she was there. She saw the apostles. They were sitting around Rabbi and eating supper.

He was focused and as if absent. His body radiated an unusual glow. The brightness was even stronger than the one she had seen around him a long time ago on the Jordan, when John the Baptist baptized him.

The students were silent, staring at the Master. And he was saying[*]. "This is my commandment, that you love one another as I have loved you. There is no greater love than that when someone gives his life for his friends. You are my friends, if you do what I command you. You did not choose me, but I chose

---

[*] In: J 15-16.

you and that the Father would give you everything, whatever you ask Him in my name. Now I go to the one who sent me, and none of you asks me, "Where are you going?" But because I told you this, sadness filled your hearts. However, I am telling you the truth: my departure is useful for you. Because if I don't leave, the Comforter will not come to you. And if I leave, I will send Him to you. Here comes the hour, and it has already come, that you will scatter everyone in their own way, and leave me alone. But I am not alone because the Father is with me. I have conquered the world.

The students listened stunned. They felt that an extraordinary moment was coming, that prophecies would soon be fulfilled and they would witness it.

Mary's soul watched them quietly.

It has always been obvious to her that there is one God - an Absolute embracing and encompassing everything. He is the beginning and the end, he is everything and everywhere. Those whom people consider to be gods, to whom they pray, are the sons and daughters sent by him, the emanations of divine power. God gives people exactly the emanations they need. Until now, the sons and daughters of the Absolute were gods or heroes, but never humans. However, the time has come and God sent his son to earth, who is a man almost like everyone else. And it is him who is to make the revolution. To show people the new way. It will be a path of love.

She loved him, admired him, absorbed his every word, was delighted with him, felt a part of him. She knew that he was teaching and showing how to live, that he wanted to end the barbaric sacrifice and that he would give rise to a new civilization. He is the Master, Teacher, Son of God and her beloved Rabbuni. However, he must leave before the prophecies can come true, he will give away what is most precious to him: his life. He will sacrifice himself. That is why he became a human.

He can perform any miracle, heal, walk on water, make a storm calm down or revive the dead, but he will allow to be humiliated, beaten and cruelly executed. He will not do anything to prevent this, or to stop the suffering that will happen to him. He will let the inevitable happen. He doesn't have to do it, but he wants to. He will do it in the name of love for a man - so that the covenant with God could be renewed, so that he might go down to sheol and overcome all the evil of this world, so that the souls waiting there could go to Paradise. So that the time of love of a neighbor, of divine goodness and bright light could begin. Time for a new chance for people.

She looked at him with love. She watched the students, still sitting stunned.

Then Jesus said, looking up to heaven:

"Father, the hour has come. Surround me with the glory that I had from you before the world came into being. I'm not in the world anymore, but they are. I'm coming to you. As long as I was with them, I saved them on Your behalf, and made sure that none of them would die, except for the son of perdition. They are not from the world, just as I am not from the world either. Sanctify them in truth. Your word is truth. As You sent me into the world, so I sent them into the world. And for them I sacrifice myself so that they too may be sanctified in truth. I am asking not only for them, but also for those who, thanks to their word, will believe in me; so that everyone would be one, like You, Father in me, and I in You."

The soul who already knew what was going to happen soon, returned to Mary. Her body shook with a shiver so strong that she fainted.

\* \* \*

John ran over as fast as he could. It was dawn when he knocked on the house door. A sleepy servant opened it. He had seen John before, and as his mistress, her sister Joanna, other household members and Mary from Magdala treated him as a trusted friend, he knew that he could and should let him in. Especially because John seemed extraordinarily agitated.

Mary's fainting after the vision did not last long. She got up just before John knocked on the door of the villa. The servant did not have to run to her room, for she appeared in the hall as soon as the apostle entered the house. She immediately ordered to wake Joanna up.

"Let's sit down and you tell us everything," she asked while her friend joined them, in her night coat, surprised, but without any questions.

Mary reached for a pitcher, filled a cup with water and handed it to John.

"Speak," she asked.

"At supper*, when the Evil had already persuaded Judas' heart to give him away, knowing that God had given him everything and he was coming to Him soon, Jesus got up from the supper and put his clothes down. He took a sheet and wrapped it around his waist. Then he poured water into a bowl and began washing the students' feet and wiping with the sheet.

---

* After: J 13.

He came to Peter, who said, "Lord, you want to wash my feet?" The master replied, "You don't understand what I do now, but you will understand it later."

"What did Peter answer?" Joanna asked.

"He was embarrassed. *No, you'll never wash my feet,* he protested. *If I don't do this, you will not participate in me,* the Master explained to him. It was clear that Peter still did not understand what the Teacher meant, but he was ready to fully submit to his will, because he said: *Lord, not only my feet, but also my hands and head.* Jesus explained: *The bathed one only needs to wash his feet, because he is all clean. And you are clean, but not all of you.*"

"How come?" Joanna was surprised.

"He knew then who would give him away, so he said: *You are not all clean.*

"Judas gave him away?" Joanna jumped up from her chair. "What are you talking about?!"

"Let him finish."

Mary tried to be calm, but under the mask of self-control, she hid a despair. She had long understood the inevitability of what had just happened and what was to come soon. She was trembling with sadness and pain. Her heart was crying, though no tear came out of her eyes. She was calm and ready for what was to come.

"And when he washed their legs, put on his robes and took his place at the table again, he said: *Do you understand what I have done? You call me a Teacher and a Lord, and you say well because I am them. So if I, the Lord and the Teacher, have washed your feet, then you should also wash each other's feet. For I have set an example for you to do as I have done to you. Truly, I say to you, a servant is not greater than his master, or a messenger than he who sent him. You will be blessed when you act according to this.* He suspended his voice. *Now it is necessary for the Scripture to be fulfilled. I am telling you already now, before it happens, so that when it happens you may believe that I am.*

Mary listened carefully to every word. They were a message - a clear and understandable one. Like her, Rabbi knew exactly what awaited him, he decided on this path himself. She wondered how much his students understood.

When telling his story, John had tears in his eyes.

"*Truly I tell you, one of you will betray me*, he said. I asked him who it would be. He replied. *The one for whom I dip a piece of bread and to whom I will give it.* And so he did. He handed the soaked bread to Judas, saying: *What you want to do, do sooner.* Judas ate and went out into the night, huddled, sore and shaken."

"The Lord said: *The Scripture must be fulfilled,*" Mary repeated John's words. "Such was the divine plan. Poor Judas was its tool. Yes, you are right, Rabbi knew what awaited him. And he went this path."

"Mary, what are you saying?" Joanna worried, seeing that her friend's spirit was less and less present. "Tell me what you know, please."

"Scripture is being fulfilled, time will stop soon."

Joanna looked at her, worried.

"Dear, you know so much. What awaits us? Speak!"

"It's inevitable. If what we hear about it and what comes soon would not happen, the gates of paradise would not open for us. The Messiah is among us, thanks to him, the waiting souls will come out in sheol and ascend to the Lord, and God will make a new covenant with people."

"You speak in riddles. Do you know what will happen?"

"I had visions, I saw it. Let's wait. We can do nothing, we are only witnesses, let us appreciate and accept this honor with dignity."

"What happened next?" Joanna decided to turn to John, believing that, perhaps, if she would learn what happened later, she would also be able to better understand Mary's words.

"When Judas left, the Master talked to us, but still not everything was clear. *Children, I have only been a short time with you. You will look for me, but where I am going, you cannot go.*"

"He said goodbye to you," Mary explained sadly. "He's leaving to God.

John did not comment on her words."

"He said also: *I give you a new commandment, that you may love one another as I have loved you. That you would love each other in the same way. This is how everyone will know that you are my disciples, when you love each other.*"

"A beautiful message," Mary sighed.

"Yes. And clear. Everyone understood these words. When he finished, Peter asked a question that neither of us dared to ask. *Lord, where are you going? Where I'm going, you can't follow me now, but you'll go later.* Peter was surprised and said: *Lord, why can't I come with you now? I will give my life for you!* Jesus answered as if he knew the future well: *Truly, I am telling you, before the rooster crows, you will disown me three times.* Peter was embarrassed and asked no more questions. We all felt the sublimity of the moment. We already understood that the Master was saying goodbye to us. Believe me, it was difficult to stand there and listen to his words. He comforted and guided us. He gave us strength, but what he said was not easy. *Let your heart not be troubled. Do you believe in god? Believe in me too! There are many apartments in my Father's house. I'd tell you if it wasn't so. I'm going to prepare a place for you. I will come again and take you to me, so that you could be where I am. You know the way where I'm going.*"

"I wish I was with him..." Joanna cried.

"I am with him all the time, and thanks to my intermediation you are there, and so is every woman," Mary assured Joanna, taking her hand.

From that moment she held it constantly.

"Later, Thomas asked. *Lord, we don't know where you are going. So how can we know the way? I am the way and the truth and the life,* answered Jesus. *"No one comes to the Father except through me. And then he added: Whoever believes in me, will do the works that I do, and even will do greater than these. And whatever you ask for in my name, I will fulfill it. Whoever knows my commandments and obeys them, loves me. Whoever loves me, will be loved by my Father, and I will love him too, and reveal myself to him.* He talked for a long time. We were all listening to him. He filled our hearts with love. *This is my commandment, that you love one another as I have loved you.*"

"This is the most important thing he has to convey to us," Mary's spirit was absent, but she heard what John was saying, and her lips were clearly saying words. "Loving. An order to love. This is the most important thing he brought when he came to us, which is why he emphasized and repeated these words many times."

"Some of his sentences were understandable to us, and others were worrisome. He repeated them in the hope that we would understand, but I do not know what it meant when he said: *A moment, and you won't see me again, and another moment, and you will see me.* He also said that the time had come that we would scatter. That everyone will go in a different direction and leave him alone. And he emphasized that he would not be alone, because the Father was with him. He also said, *I have conquered the world.*"

"Keep talking. I want to know how it ended," Joanna was impatient. "Probably the whole city will talk about it before the day wakes up for good."

Mary sat still, staring at the future. Her eyes were foggy.

"As I said, the Master explained his message to us for a long time. Finally, we went where we had been many times, behind the Kidron stream, to the olive garden. And there it happened!"

"What happened, will you say finally?" Joanna was on tenterhooks.

"Judas, accompanied by the Sanhedrin guards, came there with lanterns, torches and weapons. When he indicated Jesus to them, we understood the Master's earlier words. And he didn't hide. He asked, *Who are you looking for?* They replied, Jesus of Nazareth. *I am him. If you are looking for me, let everyone else*

495

*go*. The guards wanted to take him, then Peter reached for his sword, swung and cut off an ear of one of them. Then the Master ordered him: "*Put the sword in its scabbard. Should I not drink from the cup my father gave me?*"

"It is being completed," Mary whispered again.

"What are you saying, dear?"

"Time is getting complete. Everything happens according to the prophecies."

"They arrested him and led him to the high priest. I followed them secretly so that they would not see me. I still heard Peter, who also followed the Master, disown him three times when caught and asked if he was his student. Then the rooster crowed and I ran to you."

\* \* \*

When the story finished, another unexpected guest knocked on the gate. It was Lucius. He came tightly covered with a civilian coat, and he put a hood on his head.

He was no longer in an officer's clothes, because he was preparing to leave for Rome. Besides, he didn't want anyone to recognize him, because in those hot times it would only bring trouble to him and those he visited. Joanna's sister's house was always open to her and her friends, but the situation in the city was so tense that knowing what was happening, Lucius would not dare to expose anyone to any danger.

Mary came back to reality again. She got up when Lucius entered. She knew he wouldn't come without a good reason. He had recently told her what was going on in the city, and she knew that a special time had just begun. It was obvious that what would happen, would matter to the future of the whole world, that there would be a breakthrough bringing the changes that the visionaries and prophets did not hesitate to call the end of the old and the beginning of the new.

"What's going on?"

"Before I leave, I wanted to share the news with you," he began immediately after he greeted them in a hurry. "It's not good. Your Jesus has been arrested! I wanted you to know about it. Especially you, Mary."

"John just brought us the same message," Joanna said. "He was there when it happened."

"Will you sit down?" Mary suggested, noting that everyone was so confused that they were still standing around the guest.

"You're right, let's all sit down," he decided that as a soldier, he should calm down the household and himself. "Let's not go crazy."

"Lucius, you are leaving for Rome tomorrow," Mary calmed him, seeing how nervous he was. "Everything will be fine. As I told you, you and Berenice will live happily ever after, don't worry about it."

He smiled and once again in his life wondered how come she knew how he feels and what he thinks.

"We'll see," he sat down and sighed deeply. "I hope everything ends well."

"Will you say what happened?" Joanna wanted to organize their knowledge of events.

"Since you already know about the arrest, there is basically nothing more to say. They say that Judas, one of his most

497

faithful disciples, received thirty pieces of silver for indicating him. I also know that your Master was not at all surprised by what happened. Apparently, he acted as if he expected it. One of his students drew his sword to defend him, and even cut off the guard's ear. Our scouts say Jesus put his hand on his wound and healed it, but I wouldn't believe it. In difficult situations, people see all kind of things. However, it is undoubtedly true that your teacher gave in without a fight, claiming that whoever lives by the sword, dies by the sword. He also asked the guards to let his students leave. I heard that the apostles willingly accepted the opportunity given to them, and fled."

"They dispersed," John protested. "That's what the teacher told us to do."

"All right, let's call it they dispersed. You're right, young man, that sounds better. But the truth is that people in such situations are so terrified of what is happening that they are frozen in place, run away, do not admit the connection to the arrested person, disown him or defend him fiercely. It's normal, it's always been like this, ever since the world was young."

"Was he taken to the palace of the high priest?" Joanna pressed.

"Yes. First he ended up at Annas, who was once a high priest. In the meantime, the high priest Caiaphas, his son-in-law, had time to call the Sanhedrin. Seventy-one members are in it, but apparently everyone was prepared for what happened, because they appeared immediately," Lucius continued. "According to them and the local law, Jesus committed many crimes. He faces severe punishment. I think that priests will not know mercy. You must know that they want his death!"

"Death?" Joanna couldn't believe. "What do they accuse him of?" She was terrified, but concrete, because despite what she heard, or maybe because of it, a plan was immediately created in her head. She did not panic in difficult situations, but she focused, looked for solutions, and acted.

"He healed the sick on the Sabbath and claimed that he could do it despite the holiday. It was not only in this case that he gave a new interpretation of Halakhah. He did not call himself the Messiah, but he allowed to be considered as such. The worst thing is that he claimed to be a son of God, he called for a revolt, destruction of the Temple, and change of the existing law. He talked about the kingdom. And he was called a king."

"His kingdom is out of this world," John interjected.

"It's not relevant at the moment. They captured him and it is to be expected that they will not let him go easily. The Sanhedrin decided this, and its will is almost sacred here. According to them, Jesus destroyed the old system of values and rebelled against the established order. They arrested him at this strange night time so that there would not be too many supporters around him, because there could be a riot. The situation in the city is tense anyway."

"Lucius, what are your predictions?" Joanna was still thinking how to help the Master.

"We expect the Sanhedrin to unfortunately want to have the issue done with our hands. We suppose that today, tomorrow at the latest, it will ask Pontius Pilate to punish the prisoner. And he must cooperate with the high priest, in order to maintain peace and remain in the grace of Caesar."

"What punishment can we expect?"

"I think Pilate does not consider him dangerous. He will either let him go or he will do something symbolic to satisfy the bloodthirsty Sanhedrin. Simply put, he will give a scare to Jesus, thereby reassuring the high priest and his followers."

"It will not be enough for the Pharisees. Annas and Caiaphas, and all other priests have long wanted to get rid of Rabbi," Mary said quietly, looking somewhere into space.

"It can be like that. That is why I come to you. Maybe something can be done? One should try to influence Pilate's decision somehow. I'm thinking forward, because for now, we are not sure that the case will go to him."

"I met his wife once," Joanna decided to lay out the plan that was taking shape in her head. "She is a great woman. I did not talk to her for too long, but even during a short meeting sometime in Jerusalem, when I had the opportunity to visit Pilate together with Herod's court, she seemed sensitive and cordial."

"Yes, Claudia Procula is known for her gentleness," Lucius supported her.

"I'll go to her. Or not, we will go to her together, Mary, and tell honestly what brings us to her. We must save the Master! I feel that the Sanhedrin will not be gentle on him."

"The apostles have scattered, they are hiding, they do not want to be the next ones arrested. Other students are also unlikely to admit that they know him," Lucius wondered aloud about the possibilities for action. "Claudia Procula basically does not leave the palace. As far as I know, she rarely receives guests from outside."

"Maybe she will accept the wife of the governor Herod Antipas?" Joanna straightened, sure she was right.

"She should," Lucius confirmed. "If more feminine support is needed, I think Berenice will join in too. We don't leave until the afternoon. Unless I should stay?" He addressed the last sentence to Mary.

"No, Lucius, take Berenice to Rome today, just as you planned. We can handle the situation here with Joanna and John, right?"

"If we convince Claudia, Pilate will also be on our side," Joanna believed.

"Pontius loves his wife and respects her opinion," Lucius assured them again.

* * *

Claudia Procula was the granddaughter of the Emperor Augustus. When Pontius Pilate became Roman governor in Judea, she accompanied him there as his wife. She did not like the climate of Jerusalem, and she was completely put off by its customs, so she rarely took part in the festivities and was reluctant to make new friends. She hardly ever left the palace in which they resided, spending her time thinking, talking to the wives and daughters of military commanders and the few guests visiting her. She also looked after two children. She had a ten-year-old girl and a five-year old boy. She supervised their education, often participating in lessons and activities that she planned for them with great care.

Since the time she and her husband settled in Jerusalem, she had dreams. This was how the city affected her. Some of them carried such a strong message that she considered them prophetic. They were expressive, intense, convincing. When she was dreaming, she had the impression that what she saw was more real than what she experienced every day. With time, she became more and more immersed in the dreamy reality and more and more willingly escaped into it from a world that did not seem attractive to her.

\* \* \*

Although it was early morning, she welcomed them without asking unnecessary questions. As if she knew that they should meet, as if she had been waiting for them. She received them in the chamber, to which she usually only invited the family members or trusted guests.

"I met people he healed, I talked to them. I believe that he is the chosen one, you don't have to convince me of that," she greeted them.

"Lady, have you guessed why we came to you?" Joanna was surprised that the meeting did not take place in accordance with the current court customs she was used to, and which she expected in the palace of the Prosecutor of Judea.

"Of course," She indicated chairs to them. "All of Jerusalem does not talk of anything other than his arrest. I don't think that in such a situation you would visit me to talk about clothes and hairstyles?"

"Lady, thank you for your kind willingness to receive us." Despite everything, Joanna decided not to abandon the court rules, and to apply at least the part about thanking for the opportunity to meet. "We come to you as the Master's student."

"I know he was detained by the Sanhedrin's order." Claudia was in favor of simplifying matters. "I feel very sorry for you. I also heard that the high priests want him dead, that's outrageous!"

"This is a misunderstanding, lady. He is not guilty of any of the accusations they make," Joanna assured her, understanding from what she heard that Claudia Procula was on their side.

"He is a healer, he heals by touch, raises the dead, promises a kingdom to everyone, no matter who they are or where they come from," Mary added. "He teaches love. He gives it to others and tells us that we are created to love."

"I heard it," Claudia nodded with understanding, but also with regrets. "He apparently says that if you are hit, you should turn the other cheek. In our world, such ideas have little chance of success. You understand that, don't you? What rules here is strength, violence and money. The tough laws of the people of Israel cannot be replaced so easily with the love of your neighbor."

"But he preaches it, and we with him."

"Maybe someday love will rule the world..." Claudia was a realist. "... but for now it must wait in the catacombs and hide in caves. Look out the window, see what is happening in the streets. Flogging, stoning, crucifixion, terrible, inhuman punishments, very often for minor offenses. Most people around, and this is not just about this place, are bloodthirsty barbarians. This is the world we live in. And here comes a man who proclaims that we need to love. Also those who hurt us. And what? One of his students betrays him. Do you know that he received thirty pieces of silver for showing where he was? He loved him so much that he sold him at the first opportunity.

503

What does your Master expect from ordinary people, if there are traitors among those he chose, ready to give him in for money? What and how does he teach if it does not appeal to those who are closest to him?"

"Judas did it because that was his destiny," Mary whispered.

Claudia Procula raised her eyebrows in surprise.

Joanna burst into tears.

"No use crying, my dear. It is not the time yet for a world where beautiful ideas become reality. Your Jesus speaks beautifully, but he is ahead of his times about, I don't know, one hundred, two hundred, a thousand years?" despite being surprised by what Mary said, Claudia continued to present her sober look at the reality.

"But we want to live in the world he is talking about," Joanna did not give up, even though tears were running down her cheeks. "This is the place of our dreams, it is the Kingdom of God on earth."

"It is possible," Mary said, this time louder. "It's in our hearts. It is waiting to exist. And he came here to tell us about it. *I am giving you the new commandment, to love one another,* he said. This is the new world he announces."

"That's why they are so afraid of him." Claudia, led by some irresistible need, came closer to Mary.

Mary also rose. Claudia took her hand. Joanna also stood up, following the court rules. She watched them. They stood facing each other, holding hands. They stared into each other's eyes without saying anything.

Claudia felt warmth throughout her body. Something attracted her to the extraordinary woman whom she saw for the first time in her life, but she had heard a lot about her before. She knew that she was a priestess, that she can heal, knows herbs, speaks to women, proclaims that they should believe in themselves and their power, that they can and know how to shape the world. She heard that she teaches them a special kind of breathing, can connect with the past and the future, and has many other abilities that she does not want to reveal. She also heard that she had gone through hell, from which she came out, healed by the touch of Jesus. And that since then, she had been going after him, with him and in his footsteps, but she also has her own path. And that women cling to her because they find an old, forgotten strength in her. That she can wake it up in them, bring them back to life and tell them how valuable they are.

And now, as Mary took her hands, something strange happened. She felt vibrations in her heart and womb. Right afterwards, the chamber and everything around it disappeared. A light flashed in her head, and then she floated and dissolved in the brightness. At the same moment, Mary closed her eyes. She looked into the future. She saw Claudia suffering. She also saw her husband. A vision flashed through her mind, in which Claudia and Pontius experienced many miracles and saw the signs that made them become the followers of the Master. A moment later, she saw the former governor as a martyr on the cross, and then he was taken down from that cross, still alive, to be beheaded soon. And all this by the emperor's sentence. She heard the words he said before he died. He said that Jesus is the son of God and that he, Pilate, is now coming to him. Claudia, who stood next

505

to him in this vision, had her heart broken and she followed her husband.

And even though Mary's intention was to show Claudia the future, she changed her mind after she saw it. *I don't want her to know what's going to happen she shouldn't*, she thought. *Each of us chooses our own path. In the visions we only see what can happen, but it depends on us which way we will go. Claudia's future is only her call. I don't want to influence it. Let her choose her own paths."*

"Who are you, Mary from Magdala?" Claudia returned to reality.

Mary saw in her eyes that although Claudia was floating in the same celestial spaces and saw the future too, she did not remember it. So she did not know what awaited her and her husband. She still had a choice as to what to do in Jesus' case, just like every person.

"As you know, I'm a priestess. I guard the light, I testify - this is my duty and mission. The whole universe knows that it will be an extraordinary Passover holiday. Exceptional one. The time will stop as the prophecies have proclaimed for centuries. I am here to be with him in this moment."

Joanna listened and watched in silence. She knew that both women were in a different world for a while. One that is unknowable, distant, divine. And she had the honor to be a witness to this. She felt goose bumps all over her body.

"Lady, will you save him?" She asked, kneeling before Claudia.

"Stand up, Joanna." Claudia made a court gesture, to which Joanna happily reacted.

She was a normal, well-grounded woman after all. She was glad to see all three of them again in the reality she knew. Concrete, tangible, with stone floors that made knees hurt from kneeling on them.

"Your master is an extraordinary man. And, I think, he will soon stand before my husband who will decide his fate. My heart is with you. I can promise that I will do everything in my power to make the punishment he receives the lowest possible. And I advise you and everyone associated with him not to show up in public places. For him who has been declared a troublemaker and all who are with him, it is not quite safe now."

\* \* \*

As predicted by Lucius, the Sanhedrin did not intend to take responsibility for the fate of the one who was called the Messiah. Admittedly, his confession of being a son of God meant for them a blasphemy punished by death, but their sentencing of anyone during the Passover could not only cause indignation, but also serious riots. They expected therefore that Pontius Pilate would accept the responsibility, and, as the governor of Rome, he would pass a sentence satisfying for them, for he could make decisions in political matters, and the call to disobey Rome by proclaiming oneself the king and speaking of the kingdom was undoubtedly a political issue.

\* \* \*

It was early morning when Jesus was brought to the palace of Pontius Pilate. Neither the high priest nor the representatives of the Sanhedrin wanted to go inside, fearing that close contact with the pagans, especially during the

Passover, could de Philae them. So they stopped in the courtyard. A large crowd gathered there.

"We have found that this man is inciting our nation. In addition, he forbids paying taxes to Caesar, and says he is the Christ and the King*," the high priest Annas spoke loudly, so that everyone would hear him well.

"What are you accusing this man of?" Asked Pontius Pilate.

"He is a criminal. Otherwise we would not have given him to you."

"Take him and judge him according to your law."

"We can't kill anyone."

Well, everything was clear to Pontius. As he expected, the cunning high priest decided to burden him with the decision. He had no choice. He entered the palace and ordered that Jesus be brought before him. He was curious, he had heard a lot about him. He wanted to see up close the man the Sanhedrin feared so much that it demanded the death penalty for him.

"My kingdom is not part of this world. If it were, my servants would fight that I would not be surrendered to those who came for me. But my kingdom is not from here."

"So are you a king or not?"

"You say yourself that I am. I came into the world to bear witness to the truth. Everyone who advocates the truth, listens to my voice*."

---

* Lk 23, 2.

* J 18, 37.

Pilate listened to a man who just a few days ago was enthusiastically welcomed by the inhabitants when he arrived in the city. He was preceded by the fame of a healer, teacher and miracle worker. Now he was standing in front of him beaten, spat on and insulted. A man of whom the Sanhedrin was afraid "the powerful political, religious and judicial power, and in fact the most important authority for the Jews. Pontius knew that the priests began to fear him when the news of the healings he was doing reached them for the first time, and when people began to talk about the resurrection of Lazarus and many other miracles, he became their number one enemy. They thought, despite many signs and prophecies, that the Messiah could not come to earth just like that, and be the son of ordinary people like Mary of Nazareth and the carpenter Joseph.

"I see no reason to convict this man," Pontius said after a short conversation with the accused, stepping out in front of the crowd again.

"He teaches all over Judea and stirs up people. He started with Galilee and reached all the way here!" the crowd shouted.

Hearing about Galilee, Pontius decided with relief and hope to send Jesus to Herod Antipas. After all, he was his subject, and the tetrarch had the power to issue all legal decisions regarding his subjects. Luckily, Antipas was in Jerusalem during the Passover.

The Tetrarch, who had heard so much about the Teacher, was happy to receive him. He hoped that he would see one of the miracles Jesus was famous for, that he would talk to him and find out where his power came from.

He was careful, however. He still remembered John the Baptist, and how, against his will, he had to fulfill his promise given to Salome and behead him. He still felt bad about that situation. After this unfortunate, as he thought, event, he never promised anyone anything if he was not sure what the request was about.

He received Jesus willingly, especially since he remembered the enthusiastic stories of Chuza's wife, whom Jesus healed from the hopeless illness. Joanna often talked about his causative power, gentleness and skills, how beautifully he spoke to people and how strongly he touched their hearts.

However, Jesus stood with his head down, as if having accepted what was to happen to him soon. He waited. He was focused. He didn't pay any attention to Antipas. He didn't answer any of his questions. He seemed absent.

The Tetrarch was disappointed, and even worse, he felt ridiculed. However, knowing about Jesus' supernatural powers, he did not intend to punish him either, just like Pontius Pilate. It was enough for him to have his conscience weighed heavily with the death of John the Baptist, who absolutely did not deserve it in his opinion.

Laughing and mocking Jesus, he ordered his servants to dress him in a royal cloak and lead him back to Pontius Pilate. He wasn't going to have anything to do with this.

"I questioned him, but I did not find him guilty of what you accuse him," announced Pontius. "Herod Antipas has a similar opinion. This man did nothing to deserve to die. Therefore, I will punish and release him[*]."

---

[*] Luke 23: 14-16.

The crowd howled. People were disappointed. Confident that the flogging punishment would satisfy their thirst for blood, Pontius ordered the soldiers to carry out the sentence.

* * *

"Mary?"

David, the son of Rabbi Yitzhak, stopped in mid-stride. He came to Jerusalem on the occasion of the Passover, like so many others. He was walking to the Temple when he saw two women by the wall, on one of the narrow streets leading to it, who seemed to be cramped in pain and powerlessness. They did not look poor or disheveled, they certainly were not beggars or women condemned or rejected for some reason. Why did they catch his eye? Their faces were hardly visible from under the layers of fabrics and scarves, and yet they projected extraordinary dignity. They were spiritually noble "that's how he thought about them.

"Mary?" He came close enough to have no doubt that one of them is his friend from Magdala.

"Peace with you," she bowed her head. "Joanna, this is David, son of Rabbi Yitzhak, I told you about him once, remember?"

Joanna nodded, just like Mary.

"Can I help with something?" He declared, not knowing whether he should ask directly what was the reason for their overwhelming, visible despair. Their faces were as pale as if all the blood had drained from them. The pain on them was so terrible that it must have originated in the deepest recesses of the soul.

Mary didn't answer. She just swallowed and looked up at the sky. It was blue, calm, but dark clouds were coming in from afar. A light wind blew. A few strands of hair got out from under her headscarf.

"Jesus was arrested," Joanna broke the prolonged silence. "Pontius Pilate sentenced him to flogging."

"I've heard, the whole city doesn't talk about anything else," he admitted.

In such a difficult situation, he wasn't going to talk about the stories that circulated about her not only in Magdala. He didn't believe in most of them. He could not imagine that this woman, no matter what her past, would agree to live with a man without marriage, even if she loved him very much. To those who condemned Mary for joining Jesus and his disciples, he explained that she was one of many who were captivated by his teachings, and that the world was changing and maybe some women should be allowed to learn, or at least officially listen to the rabbis.

"Mary, I have heard for a long time from many sources that you were following him "he did not intend to hide that he knew about her situation, but at the same time, he tried to be gentle because of the pain that did not disappear from her face."

"Yes, you heard it right, I'm with him."

"Me too," Joanna said.

Mary straightened and raised her head.

"And I am proud of it. Very much."

"Me too," Joanna also straightened up.

It encouraged him.

512

"He is a troublemaker, a revolutionary. He wants to destroy the eternal order, he incites people, proclaims himself king of Israel," he began to list, as if he had forgotten their despair and wanted to punish them, Mary in particular, for her bold eyes and proud look. "Who needs the coup he is calling for? Don't we have enough problems with Rome?"

"What are you talking about?" Mary did not protest, she did not have the strength and did not see any sense in it, her question was gentle and sad. "You don't understand what's going on. He was sentenced to flogging, which is to be carried out today. Tell me: for what?"

"There are really many reasons. You should be glad that it ended up with just flogging."

"It is not the end." Mary lowered her head again, and the color that returned to her face for a moment, faded again. "Unfortunately."

And instead of convincing him, she took his hand. She knew it was a better way to divert his thoughts than even the best explanations. Anyway, she didn't have time for them. It was also completely unimportant to her that such gestures did not befit a woman, especially in a public place. He stiffened, but did not withdraw his hand. He felt a friendly warmth. It flowed from her fingers and filled his body before he knew what was going on.

She took another step towards him. They were separated by a breathing distance now. She was still holding his hand. She looked into his eyes. He looked as if he was hypnotized.

"David, you do not understand Jesus now, and even condemn him, because you do not know him." Unlike him, she knew what would happen in the future. "You think he's an enemy because you didn't get to know his teachings. Be sure, however, that in five years you will completely change your mind. You will treat his messages as your own and join a group of followers. You will be ashamed of having condemned him, but then it will be much too late for you to meet him personally. You will become his zealous worshiper and will teach others about him. Meanwhile, now, today, walk your path, it's yours only. Each of us can come to Him in our own way. The path can be long, bumpy, winding and uphill, but it is us who decide whether and how to follow it at all. Everyone has free will and makes their own choices, because everyone has their own path to heaven."

She released his hand. He sobered and looked around. Life was going on like every day. People did not seem to notice them, they passed them as if they were not there at all.

"Go now, David," Mary turned him gently toward the Temple. "We'll meet again, although at another time and in another place. You will be changed then."

"And you? Will you change too?" Joanna asked quietly as David walked away, uncertainly putting foot after foot as if he was waking from a sleep.

"I will be Mary Magdalene then..." she mused. "But let's not talk about the future, let's look for Teacher's Mother, we will need each other now more than ever before."

\* \* \*

He was scourged with a leather whip with small metal balls and pieces of bone attached at the ends. In this way the strokes were more painful.

514

The first hits caused bruising, the next tore the skin open, the following broke the muscles and reached the bones. At first, Jesus screamed in pain, fainted many times, was poured with water and brought to consciousness, beaten again and revived again. Finally, only his moans were heard, and when the eyes of the torturers saw rib bones, and the back became a bloody pulp, the moans ceased too, and Jesus fell unconscious[*].

The sun was rising over Jerusalem.

Mary Magdalene prayed fervently all night and asked that she could take on at least some of the terrible pain that was inflicted on her beloved. She was kneeling under the high wall of the Antonia fortress, because there, on the other side, a cruel punishment was being carried out on him. Tightly wrapped in a headscarf and curled up, she did not attract anyone's attention. She became almost invisible, and the guards left her alone, seeing that she did not disturb anyone, and thinking that she was one of the unfortunate beggars or the madmen, always abundant in the city.

She was close to the Master all the time. She heard his screams, then the moans, and finally a quiet sigh of relief when the punishment was over.

Her soul was with him all the time. It didn't leave his side. It whispered soothing words in his ear.

\* \* \*

---

[*] Based on the traces recorded on the Turin Shroud, it was calculated that Christ received about ninety double or triple hits.

In the morning Mary Magdalene got up from her knees. She looked reproachfully at the sun that had not gone out, and at the blue clouds that floated in the sky as calmly as if this terrible torment had not taken place.

*Time was supposed to stand still*, she thought. And she knew that the worst was yet to come.

She suddenly realized what responsibility she held as the Guardian of the Gate of Light. She knew that she had to relieve Jesus of the suffering that awaited him, at least a little, because they would be so terrible that no man could bear them. She promised herself that she would be strong until the very end "for him and for the times to come. Meanwhile, she did not hesitate to use one of her amazing skills: sending dreams to people and entering them, and even directing them. She decided to send a dream to Claudia Procula[*].

And that's what happened.

The wife of Pontius Pilate dreamed that she was sailing.

Suddenly a storm broke out. Claudia stood next to the captain and clearly heard him say, *God must have died. How can God die? It is impossible*, she was surprised in her dream. *Don't you remember? Your husband, Pontius Pilate, condemned him. He died on the cross.* She felt dizzy. She fell. Darkness engulfed her. And when she regained her senses again, she heard the growing voice of multilingual, million-people choirs. People from all over the world said in different languages: *Tormented and buried under Pontius Pilate...* She started screaming in pain. Her head was bursting into pieces. She

[*] Claudia Procula's dream is taken from the radio broadcast *Born to be king* by D.L. Sayers

didn't want her husband's name to be remembered for centuries as the one who killed God. "*Nooooo!*" she howled. Immediately afterwards she woke up, terrified and weeping.

When after the flogging Jesus stood before Pontius again, she ordered the maid to pass a message to her husband. She wrote it on a small piece of paper. *I implore you, have nothing to do with this Righteous, because today in a dream, thanks to the divine message, I suffered a lot because of him*.*"

"Can you imagine me refusing my wife? She had a vision. I will not sentence him. Claudia thinks he is a saint," Pontius Pilate reacted to the note.

"This is another proof that he uses magic," Caiaphas had no doubt who he was dealing with.

"He entered your wife's dreams because he knows you love her very much," added Annas. "Don't give in to Evil, it's his doing. Judge with justice. This man is calling for a revolt, riots will break out because of him. You must nip the revolt in the bud. You don't want the emperor to find out that you didn't react in time and didn't get rid of the one who calls himself King of Israel, do you?"

"Priest, do not instruct the Rome's governor!" Pontius was indignant.

"I wouldn't dare. I am only providing advice for our common good and for maintaining order in these difficult times."

---

* After: Gospel of St. Nicodemus.

"It's Passover, your great holiday. Don't you have the habit of pardoning a convict on this occasion?" The governor tried every excuse not to condemn Jesus.

He was sure that the Sanhedrin's punishment did not correspond to the offense of the accused. As an expert and participant in politics, he was perfectly aware that what was happening was the games and efforts of the Pharisees, trying to prevent Jesus from gaining popularity, and thus taking away their followers. Claudia's dream only further confirmed that his intuition in this matter was not mistaken. He was dealing with someone special. *What if he really is the Messiah?* He wondered. *He has a very strong personality, it can be seen from every gesture and word he utters. This is someone really unusual.*

He did not want to get involved in passing a sentence on him, and after Claudia's strange dream, he was already certain that he should do everything to avoid responsibility for this matter.

"Here is Barabbas, a villain and a bandit, and this is Jesus, called the Messiah!" He cried as the guards, at his command, brought and put Barabbas before the crowd, next to the convict already standing there. "Which of the two do you want me to release?"

The crowd, incited by priests, demanded:

"Barabbas!"

"Free Barabbas!"

Pontius Pilate did not hide his surprise.

"What then should I do with Jesus whom they call the Messiah?"

"Crucify him!" Many voices answered.

"What has he done wrong?" The governor kept trying.

Nobody listened to him anymore.

"Cross, cross!" People shouted.

Seeing that he would not achieve anything and that the crowd's agitation was rising, Pilate asked for water and washed his hands in front of the crowd, saying:

"I am not guilty of the blood of this Righteous one. This is your doing!"

Then the people shouted:

"His blood on us and our children!"

Reciting these words was the customary approval of the judgment.

Mary Magdalene and Joanna watched the events. They stood among the crowd, covered by scarves and sore from despair. They didn't say a word for the whole time.

\* \* \*

The Teacher's mother was alone. Crying, she prayed silently. Her forehead touched the stone floor. She covered her head with her hands, as if to shield it from something or someone. It was obvious that she was suffering unimaginably. She was preparing for what was to come.

Mary Magdalene kneeled next to her and also started praying.

\* \* \*

Golgotha was the hill of which it had been said since time immemorial that the skull of Adam, the first man, was buried there[*]. In Aramaic, the skull is *gulgalt*, hence its name. Executions were carried out there, and it was there that Jesus was supposed to walk, carrying his cross.

Dressed in a scarlet coat, with a crown of thorns on his head, beaten and humiliated, with a patibulum[*] tied to his back and supported by his right arm, surrounded by soldiers and the bloodthirsty crowd, he set off on his way. He was barely standing upright, and the wounds were so deep that the soldiers were surprised that he was alive at all. His back was one bloody wound. After the nighttime flogging, he was so exhausted and weak that as soon as a part of the cross was placed on his back, he fell down under the weight, but, prodded by the soldiers, he got up and moved ahead.

Both sides of the road he walked on were filled with people. Some shouted something, threatening him with fists, others stood still, terrified by the terrible suffering of the convict.

Jesus' robe was soaked with blood and sweat. He walked without looking up. He had no strength for it.

Suddenly, somewhere in the crowd, there was a cry of pain and a desperate wailing[*].

---

[*] It is mentioned, among others, in Origen's works; skull "*golgota* (Greek), *gulgalta* (Aramaic), *calvaria* (Latin); today there is the Basilica of the Holy Sepulcher there, erected by the mother of Emperor Constantine the Great, Saint. Helena, in AD 326.

[*] Cross beam.

"Who is that woman, moaning so miserably?" One of the soldiers asked.

"She is the Mother of the Galilean," said one of those standing nearby.

She was pale, her lips were blue and she looked miserably. She leaned against the pillar of the gate in front of her. She had no strength to take even a single step.

"It's for him." One of the soldiers put a fist before her eyes, in which he held nails, intended to nail Jesus to the cross.

She collapsed and would fall to the ground, were it not for the women who supported her.

And then she saw him. Bending under the weight, he staggered. In a crown of thorns, with a pale, wounded, bloody face, with dried blood in his beard. The torturers dragged him by the cords attached to his belt. As he passed, he slightly raised his head, wounded by thorns, and looked at Mother with eyes full of longing, seriousness and pity. At the same moment he stumbled and fell.

All she saw was her beloved, emaciated, tortured son. Executioners and soldiers disappeared from her eyes, she only saw him. She felt new strength. She ran into the road, broke through the executioners, and fell to her knees by him, wrapping her arms around him.

---

* From this point on, the description of the Way of the Cross and Jesus' death is derived from: A.K. Emmerich, *Way of the Cross according to the visions of the saintly Anna Katarzyna Emmerich,* Wrocław 2010. A movie: *The Passion* was made according to her vision.

"Son!"

"Mother!"

Seeing this excruciating scene, women and many a man wiped away tears. Even some soldiers felt a slight prick around their breasts because they thought of their mothers.

"Woman, what do you want here?" One of the soldiers walking by the side called out. "You should have raised him better, then he wouldn't get into our hands."

He cackled, proud of his joke, and pulled her away from the convict.

John, who suddenly appeared by her side, escorted her to the gate where she stood earlier. There she fell to her knees, her back to the retinue, so as not to look any longer at what was happening. Where she knelt and put her hands, knee marks and hand prints were left in the hard stone.

Mary Magdalene knelt beside her and embraced her with tenderness.

Jesus, driven by the overseers, kept walking, but he was so weak that he stumbled almost every step.

People of higher social status were just passing in groups through there on their way to the Temple.

"God, this poor man is already dying!" There were shouts of pity. "How can you torment someone so much!"

Mary Magdalene spotted Simon from Cyrene in the crowd.

He was coming back from work in the field. He wasn't forty yet, he was tall and strong. He was wearing a short, tight caftan, his thighs were wrapped in rags, sandals on his legs were strapped to his feet. He didn't cover his head "that's how she knew that he was a pagan. He was walking by the wall, glaring at the convict with disgust. He did not like what he saw, but he was not a Jew, so he did not get involved in the affairs of the locals, he had his life and avoided everything that could cause him trouble.

Mary Magdalene directed the soldier's eyes and thoughts towards him.

"Hey you!" Simon of Cyrene heard.

He raised his head and realized that, unfortunately, the tall Roman was pointing right at him.

"You, I'm talking to you!" The soldier pointed his finger so that there was no doubt anymore that he was addressing him.

He stopped.

"You will help him!"

He refused, excused himself, did not want to, but they forced him. The prisoner was so abused, bloodied and covered with mud that Simon approached him with undisguised disgust and repulsion, but he had no choice but to do what he was told. Nobody dared to argue with the soldiers of Rome. After a while he was carrying half the weight of the cross. The procession continued.

When at some point Simon accidentally touched the hand of the convict, he immediately felt a strange change. He was overwhelmed with such extraordinary emotion that he was eager to help carry the burden further, and he even felt that he was awarded. Mary Magdalene smiled sadly. She could help at least as much.

Jesus' task was easier, but his body was on the verge of exhaustion. He had an unbelievable thirst, he was sweating bloodily, he had no strength left.

Then Veronica appeared. About two hundred steps from the gate where Jesus had recently fallen, there was a beautiful house standing on the left side of the street, separated from the rest by a courtyard accessed by stairs. The villa was surrounded by a wide wall, closed with a shiny grille at the front. When the procession was passing by this building, a young woman ran out of it "it was Veronica, a wife of the Sanhedrin member. After pushing her way through to Jesus, she fell to her knees before him.

"Let me wipe your face, Lord," she whispered.

Instead of answering, Jesus took the scarf she gave him and pressed it with his hand to his bloody face, moved it over his face and gave it back to her. She kissed it, slipped it under her coat, and stood up quickly. It all took a short moment. Her bold behavior stunned the soldiers and the executioners, the mob began to push closer to see what was happening, causing the procession to be stopped for a moment.

The executioners, angry because of the break, and even more because of the act of public worship to Jesus, began to tug and beat him again. Veronica ran into the house and fainted from the strong emotions.

When the servants revived her, she took the scarf in her hands. The bloody face of the Master was pressed on it with amazing accuracy.

And he, carrying his burden, supported by Simon Cyrene and ruthlessly rushed by the torturers, went on. He just passed the Garden Gate and got outside the walls of Jerusalem. Golgotha was close, he could see it clearly. People walked before him, behind him and on his sides. The soldiers rushed and poked him, pulling the cords attached to his belt more and more, screaming for him to go faster, and mocking him mercilessly.

He was on the verge of exhaustion when he heard the great lamenting and wailing of women. He stopped "with superhuman effort he gathered the last of his strength to do that. Mary Magdalene closed her eyes and sent a bright light towards him. He straightened slightly.

"Jerusalem daughters!" He turned to them. "Do not weep for me, but for yourself and your children! Here comes the time when you will say: blessed are the infertile and those who have not given birth, and breasts that have not fed! Then you will cry: mountains, fall on us, hills, cover us! For if this is done with a green tree, what can be done with the dry one?"

They listened to him and their hearts treated his every word as a prophecy. He looked at their worried faces, wet from crying. He wanted to comfort them.

"Your crying will not be without a reward, from now on you will walk a different path of life."

They fell to their knees before him. They felt that brightness fell on them along with the words he spoke.

Mary Magdalene embraced the women with her thoughts - from that moment they were never to leave the path.

The torturers pulled the ropes again and rushed the horrible procession uphill. Lamentations, cries and wailing were heard all around.

The pained mother followed his son at a distance, supported by John on one side and Mary Magdalene on the other. None of them were crying anymore. They prayed silently.

Mary was constantly trying to comfort Jesus with her thoughts and to take off at least some of the pain from him.

Finally, the bloody procession reached the summit of Golgotha. Jesus lost the last of his strength. He gave in to everything that happened without a word of protest, his spirit was more and more absent.

The torturers began to rip off his clothes - first a coat and a belt, by which they had pulled him on the ropes, then a woolen outer robe. They also took a long, narrow scarf off his neck, and finally got to the tunic that Mother had woven from him. However, the crown of thorns was blocking them, so they tore it from among his hair, tearing the wounds on his heads again.

And behold, the trembling Son of Man stood covered with blood, bumps, bruises, dry and open wounds. He was wearing only a loincloth. His body was ragged and swollen, his back and shoulders ripped to the bone, the shreds of clothing stuck to the edges of the wounds and to the dried blood on his chest. He staggered in weakness. His torturers put him on a stone, put the crown of thorns back on him and told him to wait until they decide by playing dice, who gets which of his robes.

Later, they took his hands and dragged him to the cross. When they nailed him to it, blood splashed their hands.

By the order of Pontius Pilate, a tablet was attached to the cross on which he hung, to explain, in accordance with the

Roman law, the reason for his condemnation to death. It read in Greek, Latin and Hebrew: "Jesus Nazarene, King of the Jews"[*].

The Teacher's Mother - curled up, numb and unconscious from pain - lay nearby, her forehead to the ground and her hands covering her head. Soft moans were coming from her mouth. She cried with the tears of all mothers who despair every day, all over the world, of the helplessness that they can do nothing when their children suffer and die. Women stood around her. They understood her pain and tears perfectly. Each of them felt as if she was losing someone she loved most in the world.

Right next to them knelt Mary Magdalene. She was pale but focused. She didn't cry. There was a glow coming from her. She crossed her arms and closed her eyes. She prayed, taking over some of Jesus' pain.

Her soul soared. She could see the Gates of Light in the distance. They were powerful. They were waiting for the one who was soon to come. She smiled and tears flowed from her eyes.

After a long time, she heard him, as he cried out loudly, hanging nearby on the cross:

"It is done!"[*]

---

[*] Hebrew: היהודים מלך הנצרת ישוע ""Yeshu'a HaNatserat Melech HaYehudim"; Latin: "Iesus Nazarenus Rex Iudaeorum"; Greek: Ἰησοῦς ὁ Ναζωραῖος ὁ Βασιλεὺς τῶν Ἰουδαίων ""Iésús ho Nazóraios ho basileus tón Iúdaión".

[*] J 19, 28-30.

The curtain in the Temple was torn in two, from top to bottom, the sky above Golgotha was lit by a powerful lightning, the ground trembled and the rocks began to crack.

Jesus died.

Then the time stopped, and Mary saw how the Gates of Light slowly began to open.

\* \* \*

Joseph of Arimathea, a wealthy disciple of Jesus, received permission from Pilate to bury him. He did this in accordance with the custom of burying the dead "the body, wrapped in fragrant burying cloths, was placed in a recently carved rock grave. A large stone was rolled to close the entrance.

The Mother of the Master, Mary Magdalene and others who took part in the burial, sat for a long time in front of the closed cave.

None of the women were crying. They were waiting for what was to happen soon, which would renew the covenant with God and change the fate of the world.

## 10.

Three days have passed since the Master's death. Stunned, moving as if in a dream, she stood in front of the tomb. It was empty. She saw luminous messengers sitting inside, calm and confident that the world was heading in the right direction. They told her that Jesus was no longer here.

She went among the olive trees. The sun was shining. It was warm, the air was shaking, the smell of roses was everywhere.

"Mary!" She heard and looked at the figure emerging from the sun.

She froze.

She would recognize His voice everywhere. Yes, it really was Him! He stood before her in a bright glow, the one she knew and loved most in the world, wise, strong, beautiful and good. The same as always, still, completely changed. His body radiated an unearthly glow, his robe looked like woven from stars, and his body seemed to float above the ground.

She wanted to run up to him, embrace him, cuddle him. She was sure that if she could even brush his skin, all the pain and despair that had accompanied her over the last days would be gone forever. However, something was holding her back. She couldn't even take a step, and she wanted to so badly. She closed her eyes. She held out her hands to him.

"Don't stop me, I haven't joined my Father yet[*]," he said gently and lovingly.

---

[*] In Latin: Noli me tangere, in Greek: me mou aptou, in Aramaic: al. tiqerabbi.

She loved him and knew that it would always be so. Tears streamed down her cheeks.

"Rabbuni!"

# EPILOGUE

She was standing by the well on the big square. She was in a modest dark dress, her head was covered with a scarlet scarf. People listened carefully to what she was saying. From time to time, women sighed and wiped tears surreptitiously. They loved her. She was one of them. They felt that they were just like her "their Mary Magdalene.

"It's me, Mary of Magdala, Mary of Bethany, Mary of Egypt, possessed by seven demons, called the sinner. I am a priest, a lady and an apostle. I'm a woman. Condemned, despised, rejected, exalted, chosen, enlightened. The eternal Guardian of the Gate of Light. I am each of you. A single and common fate. A cry and a shout, happiness and joy, intuition and knowledge. I'm a woman. The wisdom of the world with its wealth, misery, goodness, suffering and relief. I am love - eternal, permanent and unchanging. I am from here and from there. I am a part and the whole, the Source and the eternal fire. I'm a woman. I go on."

# Additionally, we include in the book:

English translation from https://www.biblegateway.com/, King James Version (KJV)

From the Gospel of St. John:

Now there stood by the cross of Jesus his mother, and his mother's sister, Mary the wife of Cleophas, and Mary Magdalene. (19, 25).

Then took Mary a pound of ointment of spikenard, very costly, and anointed the feet of Jesus, and wiped his feet with her hair: and the house was filled with the odour of the ointment. (12, 3).

But Mary stood without at the sepulchre weeping: and as she wept, she stooped down, and looked into the sepulchre, and seeth two angels in white sitting, the one at the head, and the other at the feet, where the body of Jesus had lain. And they say unto her, Woman, why weepest thou? She saith unto them, because they have taken away my LORD, and I know not where they have laid him. And when she had thus said, she turned herself back, and saw Jesus standing, and knew not that it was Jesus. Jesus saith unto her, Woman, why weepest thou? Whom seekest thou? She, supposing him to be the gardener, saith unto him, Sir, if thou have borne him hence, tell me where thou hast laid him, and I will take him away. Jesus saith unto her, Mary. She turned herself, and saith unto him, Rabboni; which is to say, Master. Jesus saith unto her, Touch me not; for I am not yet ascended to my Father: but go to my brethren, and say unto them, I ascend unto my Father, and your Father; and to my God, and your God. Mary Magdalene came and told the disciples that she had seen the LORD, and that he had spoken these things unto her. (20, 11-18)

From the Gospel of St. Luke:

And the twelve were with him, and certain women, which had been healed of evil spirits and infirmities, Mary called Magdalene, out of whom went seven devils, (8, 1-2)

Now it came to pass, as they went, that he entered into a certain village: and a certain woman named Martha received him into her house. And she had a sister called Mary, which also sat at Jesus' feet, and heard his word. (10, 38-39).

From the Gospel of St. Mark:

Now when Jesus was risen early the first day of the week, he appeared first to Mary Magdalene, out of whom he had cast seven devils. And she went and told them that had been with him, as they mourned and wept. And they, when they had heard that he was alive, and had been seen of her, believed not. (16, 9-11)

Apocryphal Gospel according to St. Mary Magdalene:

English text highlighted in grey is from https://thegodabovegod.com/a-complete-translation-of-the-gospel-of-mary/

Only the Coptic translation from the 5th century Gnostic Gospel according to Mary Magdalene (Greek original from the 3rd century) has survived. Only a small piece of the papyrus remains. The initial pages 1-6 and pages 11-14 are missing.

**Page 7**

"What is matter?

"Then matter will be destroyed, or not?"

The Savior replied," all natures, all forms, all creatures exist both within and alongside each other, and they will finally be reduced down to their individual roots. For the nature of matter is reduced to those of its particular nature. He who has ears to hear, let him hear."

Peter said to him, "Having explained all things to us, tell us this, too: What is the original sin of the world?" The Savior answered, "There is no sin per se; rather, it is you yourselves who make a thing sinful when you perform the acts that partake of adulteration, which alone is properly termed 'sin.' That is why the Good came among you, to purify every nature, in order to restore it to its original state." Then he went on, saying, "This is the reason you [grow ill] and die, for *the spirit ever seeks escape from admixture with the body of death* of the one who *is not yet enlightened.* He who has ears to hear, let him hear."

**Page 8**

"Attachment to matter

arouses passion against nature. That's how anguish is born throughout the body; that's why I'm telling you, "Stay in harmony... If you have lost your balance,

draw inspiration from manifestations

of your true nature.

Who has ears

let him listen."

Having said that, the Blessed

greeted them all, saying:

"May peace be with you "let my Peace rise and be fulfilled in you!

Be vigilant and don't let anyone deceive you by saying:

"Here he is" or

"He is there",

for it is within you

that the Son of Man lives.

Go to him

for those who seek him will find him.

Go

and preach the Gospel of the Kingdom."

Page 9

"Do not impose any rights other than those I have testified to.

Don't add any more laws to those given in Torah,

so that they may not restrain you."

Having said all this, he went away.

The students were concerned

shedding many tears and saying:

"How shall we go to the unbelievers

and preach to them the Gospel of the Kingdom of the Son of Man?

They didn't spare his life

then why would they save ours?" Then Mary got up

embraced them all in turn and began to speak to her brothers:

"Don't give in to the worry and doubt,

for his grace will lead you and comfort you.

But let's praise his greatness,

because he prepared us for this.

He calls us to become fully human

(anthropos)." This is how Mary turned their hearts to the Good,

and they began to discuss the meaning of the Teacher's words.

**Page 10**

Peter said to Mary:

"Sister, we know that the Teacher loved you

 differently from other women.

Tell us whatever you remember

of the words he said to you,

and which we have not yet heard."

Mary said to them:

"I will tell you now

about what you have not been given to hear.

I had a vision with Teacher

and I said to him:

Lord, I see you now

in this vision."

And he said:

"Blessed are you, because my sight did not bother you,
Where is the Spirit, there is treasure." Then I said to him:

"Lord, when someone meets you

in vision,

does he see you through the soul

or through the Spirit? "

And the Teacher replied:

"Neither through the soul nor through the Spirit,

but it is the spirit that is between them

who sees me, and he who [...]"

**Page 15**

"And Lust said:

"I didn't see you coming down,

but now I see you are rising.

Why are you lying if you belong to me?"

And the soul said:

"I saw you,

although you didn't see me

and you didn't recognize me.

I was with you as if you were an outfit

and you never saw me."

Saying that

the soul walked away with great joy.

Then it entered the third climate

(sphere), known as Ignorance.

Ignorance asked the soul:

"Where are you going to?

Sinful tendencies rule you.

Indeed, you lack the ability to distinguish (between good and evil) and you are enslaved."

The soul replied:

"Why do you judge me if I don't judge?

I was mastered, but I did not control anyone.

I was not recognized

but I learned by myself

that all compound things will decay,

both on Earth and in Heaven."

**Page 16**

Liberated from the third climate (sphere), the soul continued its ascent

and found itself in the fourth climate (sphere).

This one in turn had seven manifestations:

the first is Darkness,

the second "Lust

third "Ignorance,

fourth "(lethal) Envy,

fifth "Bondage of the Body,

sixth "Intoxicating Wisdom,

seventh "Crafty Wisdom.

Here are seven manifestations of anger

which tormented the soul with questions:

"Where did you come from, murderer?"

"Where are you going, drifter?"

And the soul answered:

"What bothered me, was killed;

what besieged me, is gone;

my lust has extinguished

and I am free from my ignorance."

Page 17

"I left the world with the help of another world;

a certain pattern has been erased due to a higher pattern.

From then on I go to the Respite,

where time rests in Eternity (of Time); and now I enter Silence."

Having said that, Mary fell silent,

for it was in silence that the teacher spoke to her.

Then Andrew began to say to his brothers:

"Tell me what you think about the things

she said to us? As for me, I don't believe

that the Teacher could speak in this way.

These ideas are too different from the ones we learned."

And Peter added:

"How is it possible for the Teacher

to talk to a woman in this way?

about secrets that are unknown even to us?

Should we change our customs

and listen to this woman?

Did he really choose her and prefer her over us?"

Page 18

Then Mary cried

and she answered to him:

"My brother Peter, what do you think?

Do you think it's just my own imagination, that I came up with this vision?

Or do you think I would lie about our Teacher?" Then Levi said:

"Peter, you have always been an impetuous man and now we see that you are rejecting this woman as our enemies do.

However, if the Teacher valued her,

who are you to reject her?

Surely the Teacher knew her very well because he loved her more than us. So let us repent and let us become fully human [anthropos],

so that the Teacher can take root in us

Let's grow as he demanded from us and let us set out to spread the Gospel,

without trying to set any rules or laws

other than those he testified about.

**Page 19**

When Levi spoke these words,

everyone went out to preach the Gospel.

It was the Gospel of Mary.

**Translated by Jerzy Prokopiuk**

# From the Author

Mary Magdalene is back. Stronger than ever. She speaks to us in full voice. She is a woman so strong that she has survived for centuries, always appealing to the imagination of not only artists, but also politicians, preachers, feminist and pro-feminist movements around the world, and. most of us. Who has not heard of her?

Who was she? Who is she? How and when did she become a mirror of the eras, times and people?

Her voice was sometimes strong and sometimes barely heard. It reached people through the veils of history, penetrated through the darkness of history, often distorted or unreal, because it was adapted to the needs of the eras.

Now Mary Magdalene "more powerful than ever "no longer causes a storm, oh no! Today she is it herself! She not only intrigues, as she has done for centuries, but shows the way and fills a significant gap.

\* \* \*

Jesus followed the paths of Galilee and Judea in the company of the apostles. As the Bible recalls quite casually, "there were several women with him." We've been seen that way for centuries. As the ones that accompany men and have nothing to say to such an extent that our presence can be omitted. In the letters of St. Paul, we read about women from those times, among others, that "they are not allowed to speak, but are to be subjected, as the law requires. And if they want to learn something, let them ask their husbands at home."

Recently, we women are increasingly demanding that our presence in the pages of history be seen, and we also discover and show to the world those women, who created the history. So we get to know women placed in the so-called background, and even in more shadow, but also the largest ones, strongly influencing the shape of our common fate, for centuries omitted, whose importance was diminished or who were pushed into the background for various reasons.

I myself have listened carefully to the voices of ancient queens over the past years.

This is how the Egyptian trilogy was created: *Cleopatra's Passions, Divine Nefertiti, and Hatshepsut.* Immediately after it, a series about strong women from the Bible was born. It opened with The Queen of Sheba.

Mary Cowen, my American publisher, is the Godmother of this series. Thank you, Mary. Without you, your support, the materials you sent me, your kind words, care and gentle encouragement to work, the biblical trilogy would probably not have been created, and certainly would not have taken such shape.

When The Queen of Sheba was already in the editorial office, one night something extraordinary happened. Something that could happen to one of my heroines. But to me? In my dream I saw a bright female figure. She was floating in my direction, all in a golden glow. I didn't see her face. She stopped, put her hands on her hips. "Do you really think that some Semiramis will be before me?" "words unspoken by her appeared in my head. Any shadow of doubt who this character was, disappeared. "I'm not ready yet," I replied, equally silently. "You are". "Not yet, I'm afraid it is too difficult for me." "You can do it. I will help you".

When I woke up in the morning, there was an outline of a novel on my desk. To dispel any doubt: written with my hand. I was also sure that I would be able to handle everything.

* * *

Mary Magdalene that is present today in so-called public consciousness and pop culture, is a patchwork of several characters. She was "created" by Pope Gregory the Great at the end of the sixth century, bringing together three different women appearing in the Bible. The first is Mary of Magdala, the most faithful disciple of Jesus, the one from whom he drove out seven evil spirits, who accompanied him under the cross, to whom he appeared first after the resurrection, and to whom, after her cry *Rabbuni!*, he directed the memorable words *Noli me tangere (Don't stop me)*. It was her who announced the news of the resurrection to the disciples, and thus Jesus chose her to be the first to preach the Gospel and become an apostle of the apostles.

The second Mary from Bethany is the sister of Marta and Lazarus, whose house Jesus often visited. It was there that, when Mary was once sitting and listening to the Master's words, Marta, wanting her sister to help her at work, asked him for intervention and heard in reply: *We need so little...* Also in this house Mary anointed Jesus' feet with precious nard oil and wiped them with her own hair, as Saint John writes. Saint Luke also writes about wiping the Master's feet with the hair, but in his story it is a repentant sinner woman who does it. And finally, it was Lazarus, brother of Mary and Marta, whom Jesus raised from the dead in Bethany.

"Who among you is without sin, let him throw the stone first" "these frequently quoted words of Jesus refer to a nameless woman caught in adultery, for which she was to be condemned to stoning, in accordance with the Moses law. Mary Magdalene was also identified with this character.

In the sixth century, all these *Marie*s were combined into one by Pope Gregory the Great. This is how Mary Magdalene was created and she has been inspiring our imagination for centuries.

It was only the Apocryphal Gospels, including the Gospel of Mary Magdalene, found in the nineteenth and twentieth centuries, that made us realize who our heroine really was and how special the position she held in the world of the apostles was. Jesus called her *perfection over perfection*, said she was *blessed among women*, encouraged, *Speak openly, you whose heart is talking straight to the Kingdom of Heaven more than the hearts of all your brothers.*

In 1969, the Catholic Church entered Mary Magdalene in the official calendar of saints and recognized that Mary of Magdala, Mary of Bethany and the repentant sinner were three different characters.

For centuries, however, Mary Magdalene, the one created by Gregory the Great, has grown to the rank of such a powerful female symbol that today most of us probably know and think of her as a controversial woman with a complicated past who has entered a new path and became an apostle of the apostles because she announced the resurrection news to the world.

And without faith in the resurrection, there would be no Christianity. Yes or no?

\* \* \*

Each epoch has its own Mary Magdalene. And so does every man. Mary Magdalene is a reflection of the era that portraits her.

What is she like in our 21st century? Probably similar to us. The way we perceive her shows our vision of reality. She is also like a mirror *a mirror reflects the one who looks in it.* For the clean *everything is clean.* Who is Mary Magdalene for you, Madam? Who is she for you, Sir? Who is she for me? For you?

\* \* \*

I am grateful to Mary Magdalene for letting me write about herself. For coming to me that night and answering my doubts: "Yes, you are ready! You have knowledge, intuition, experience." And she led me step by step, gently, with kindness and tenderness.

So I thank her, and all who supported me in my writing in various ways.

Once again, thank you to Mary Cowen, for inspirations, materials, beautiful covers, long conversations across the ocean and for questions like: *What would She say about it?* Yes, Mary can really inspire!

I also thank modern priestesses from around the world who gave me their strength and spiritual power, watched over me and answered the often bizarre questions I asked them, each of them did it with patience, understanding, love, as if they had lived for centuries and by talking with me, they performed a kind of spiritual mission. These women and girls are my masters, teachers, priestesses, hemet.

Of course, as it is usually in books, any similarity of literary characters to those existing in reality is accidental and unintentional, but I am very curious if the Girls who wanted to share their experiences, knowledge and intuition with me, will find themselves in the novel...

Professor Dr. Ewa Piaskowska, who was the rector of the Upper Silesian School of Commerce for twenty years, supported me in constructing and adapting to our time the curriculum of the best women university of the ancient Egypt, that is the Temple of Isis on the Philae Island, and she has shared thoughts with me for years, not only about education.

Doctor of philosophy and psychology, Agnieszka Brzezińska from Vienna, talked to me many times about her experience gained during her travels around the world, in scientific career and spiritual wandering. Agnieszka, I could feel your view of the multidimensional reality as if ancient priestesses were speaking through you.

Jola Kurecka - a holistic medicine therapist from Antwerp - not only shared the professional literature and unusual, esoteric knowledge about my heroine with me, but also told me about the breathing that MM taught women gathered around her.

Jola Konsek, a teacher of mathematics and physics, made me realize why the sciences belonged to the divine sphere in ancient Egypt, and how in those days it was taught so effectively that the pyramids and temples built without modern tools still stand.

Thank you to Ela Kwaśnicka for the recipes for magic potions. I have the impression that nowadays we are more and more willing to use the knowledge of our great-grandmothers, also in this field, right?

The editor Maja Zawała and director Iwona Woźniak-Bagińska also deserve recognition. I am very curious in which characters from the book you will find yourself... Thank you for your wisdom, support and the creative relaxation together.

While writing, I was also supported - in various ways - by Basia Romanowska (thank you, dear, for the medieval legends about MM, for which you searched half the world), Wiesia Walkowska, Basia Kamińska, Agnieszka Kamińska and Basia Bobrowska - thank you very much, it was thanks to you that author meetings took place. Sabina Nowosielska - president of Kędzierzyn Koźle - what a strong woman she is! Łucja Kłańska-Kanarek - I suspect you paint angels with such expertise and sensitivity, because you are one of them yourself. They delight me, they are delicate and beautiful like you. Izabela Migocz - you undoubtedly also belong to this heavenly group, because every time I hear your opera singing, I feel as if I was somewhere around paradise. Really.

There are many people to whom I am very grateful. Among them are women of great sensitivity. One of them is the editor Anna Maruszeczko - the head of "Beauty of Life" - a smart and editorially beautiful magazine for women. Ania, I don't know how you do it to combine being so incredibly down to earth with the ability to function in a hard business world with a delicacy, sensitivity and strong empathy?

Bożena Walter is a TV icon in Poland. We all know her. Class, elegance, brilliance, intelligence and great social sensitivity. A precursor of modern television programs, a co-owner and founder of TVN and the Tvn Foundation "You are not alone". I dreamed to get to know her personally. Recently, I managed to realize that dream. Thank you for the warm words about my books and for the fact that the cover of the book may have the logo of the Ewa Błaszczyk's Foundation Akogo? and that one zloty from each copy sold will be donated to the account of this foundation - all this thanks to Bożena Walter. It was also her (together with A. Maruszeczko and several other people), who caused that some of my "Mary Magdalene" books are sold in the package with the extraordinary, contemplative, heavenly record "MM" by Justyna Steczkowska. I am honored.

I was able to meet Bożena Walter thanks to the First Lady Jolanta Kwasniewska. The First Lady not only supported the activities of Dress for Success in our country (this is an organization I had the honor to run in Poland for ten years), but she was and - I dare say - is and will be a mentor for me and many other women. Madam President, thank you for your extremely positive attitude to the world, openness to people, supporting those in need, passing on your beautiful energy, combining tradition with modernity, incredible class, wisdom and showing me the possible ways and positive aspects of a change, when it sometimes seemed to me, that if something ends, maybe the world will disappear. Of course it won't disappear! You can show faultlessly from which side the sun shines and make us want to look in that direction. Thank you also for reading my books and for having such nice opinions about them. Such words give you wings!

I also thank Dorota Soszyńska - the queen of the cosmetics company "Oceanic", and Grażyna Kulczyk - the queen of modern art collections and a patron of culture. Meeting both of you and cooperation over the past ten years, joint charity activities as part of Dress for Success Poland have been an honor, privilege, and great pleasure for me. Sometimes we probably don't realize how a contact with such strong and sensitive women can change our way of thinking about the world. Thank you!

While writing MM, I had the impression that there were only smart, good and kind people around me. I received support and help from so many places. I wrote to and met with many people from around the world. I consulted the book I was writing with experts, scientists and clergy. I received tremendous help from the priest Professor Mariusz Rosik - a biblist, lecturer at the Pontifical Faculty of Theology in Wrocław, a graduate of, among others, Pontifico Istituto Biblico in Rome, Hebrew University, and Ecole Biblique et Archeologique Française in Jerusalem, author of scientific books, radio broadcasts, an outstanding Bible expert. Thank you for the tips, comments and corrections. Thanks to the professor, I better understood the situation of women in the crucial times for Israel.

I would also like to thank all other priests who answered my questions with great kindness, and to Monsignor Stanisław Puchała for his openness, patience and understanding, which I have been receiving for many years.

Lots of people showed me the way, asked others to help me, dispelled my doubts, sometimes small, but important for the shape of the whole.

As always when writing, I was convinced that the book must be consistent with historical truth. I did my best to make it so.

There is a portal Roman Empire. I have been its reader for a long time. When I could not find the list of prefects of Rome in Egypt, even though I really searched all possible sources, I decided to ask the creator of the site, Jakub Jasiński. He answered me almost immediately, indicating the right place to search. It might be a small thing, but I'm really grateful.

Doctor Filip Taterka - an Egyptologist, whose help I used before for the Egyptian trilogy, showed me people who, in addition to Professor Kara Cooney from Los Angeles, can tell me about the goddesses, priestesses and the principles of Isis's temple on the island of Philae in Egypt. I exchanged letters with the whole world. Professor Jitse Dijkstra sent me to other experts, and more people showed me more friendly experts and books that I should read.

Of course, I used not only historians' help. As with previous novels, I was helped in medicine-related matters by professor Andrzej Lekston, an expert on human hearts from the Clinic of Heart Diseases in Zabrze. Thank you, Professor.

When my priestesses (including of course Mary Magdalene) went to fight, General doctor Mieczysław Bieniek, the most respected Polish soldier in NATO structures, did not refuse me a consultation. Thank you, General!

I also consulted with experts the scenes in which my heroine went insane. I especially thank my sister, Sylwia Stasikowska from Warsaw, a psychotherapist who does a psychodynamic and integrative treatment of patients, thanks to whom I could understand the difficult moments of spiritual and physical perdition Mary Magdalene experienced, and describe them in accordance with their likely clinical course.

In each of my previous books - both in the Egyptian trilogy, and now in the Bible trilogy - a cook was cooking for queens, who could miraculously transfer his skills across the centuries. Henryk Hermann, present in the novels as Enri (H)Er, this time did not appear on the pages of the book, but he was the author of the dinner at the house of Mary Magdalene's father, celebrating his daughter's return home. Thank you, Henry. The party was great, like every one you organize. I know it for sure, because you tried the dishes earlier, serving them in your beautiful palace in Krzelów, also open for tourists (just search the words "Palace in Krzelów" to find out where in Poland you can eat today a dinner from the times of Mary Magdalene).

The Bible the Old and New Testaments accompanied me all the time during the writing. That's obvious.

I also often reached for "Pistis Sophia", apocrypha, including the Gospel of Mary Magdalene. Only very small fragments have survived, I included them in the book (in Polish, of course). I also often referred to Simon Scham's 'The story of the Jews', Abraham Cohen's 'Talmud', and many other books that allowed me to feel the atmosphere of the places I visited and wrote about. Among them were: "Biblical Plants", "Fashion in the Bible" and "Biblical Geography" by Barbara Szczepanowicz.

While traveling around Israel, it was with great pleasure that I used the guides written by priest Professor Mariusz Rosik, above all the "Land of the Word".

Of course, I watched dozens of movies, paintings, historical studies, articles created over centuries, I visited hundreds of websites, and had thousands of conversations. I have also read a lot of books about Mary Magdalene, including those best known and created in recent years. Among them were "Mary Magdalene. Virgin and Sinner" by Jean-Pierre Brice Olivier, "Secrets of Mary Magdalene" by Laurenc Gardner, "Mary Magdalene Bride in Exile" by Margaret Starbird, "Mary Magdalene. Truth, legends, lies." by Amy Welborn, "Mary Magdalene. From a repentant sinner to the bride of Jesus" by Regis Burnet, "Jesus and women" by Hubertus Mynark, and finally "Mary Magdalene. The story of the most mysterious woman in the Bible" by Paweł F. Nowakowski.

The names of the heroes come mostly from the Bible. The authentic characters have certainly been recognized without mistake by the readers. Let me just add that the names of Mary Magdalene's parents, Eucharia and Syro, come from the "Golden Legend" by Jakub de Voragine, a Dominican and Genoese archbishop, who lived in the thirteenth century.

Yes, I read a lot and of course I wrote a lot, that's clear. I used to do this while traveling and on a small laptop. And somehow things turned out so that when the book was almost finished, I experienced tendonitis of the right hand, specifically, the thumb. The doctor gave it a professional name of de Qurvain's disease. I was only able to finish the writing thanks to the professional help. I underwent wonderful physiotherapeutic procedures under the guidance of the great specialists in the home-like atmosphere of the Seniors Residences in Zakrzów in the Opole region, and Dr. Mahmoud Manssour, an orthopedist from Katowice, used a type of acupuncture (my right thumb hurt and the doctor put the needles in my left foot), that allowed me to finish the book. A miracle worker.

Whenever I write, the whole family supports me. So it was also this time. The book was created in the Far East, Israel and

Poland. I thank my ever very patient and understanding Husband, who could find the books and movies I needed and get them from the other end of the world, and he listened at breakfast, if we were able to eat it together, to what happened in my dreams and what I wrote at night. Jerzy, thank you for your strength and goodness.

My Dad is with me very often. It touches me when now, as in my childhood, he makes sure I eat everything from my plate, kindles the fire in the fireplace when I'm cold, and when we make tomato puree together from the tomatoes he has grown in the garden.

Mikołaj is my wonderful son. A year ago, he graduated from the University of Shanghai in China. Many years outside Europe gave him not only a diploma of a great university, but also a huge distance to and the perspective for the matters that sometimes seem very important to us in Europe, but in general terms they are almost irrelevant. Mikołaj, thank you for your help and for the careful reading of the English versions of books, for your sensitivity, wisdom and patience. You are a real treasure.

I would like to thank Videograf Publishing Houses, especially the people with whom I had the pleasure to cooperate for Mary Magdalene: president Franciszek Leki, editor-in-chief Anna Sakiewicz, editor of the book Maria Kania. and Ewa Leśny who takes care of the publicity.

Of course, I also thank the Readers, the participants of the meetings with the author - you are really great! - all those who follow my author page on FB and www.ewakassala.com, people of the media, the bloggers, and all other women and men who support me every day, for the kind words, gestures, emails, text messages, phone calls, for the fact that we can be together thanks to common interests. Together, despite the fact that each and every one of us lives somewhere out there, often very far away, sometimes in the other hemisphere, we have all been doing the same for centuries: we are transferring the bright fire of love, kindness, support, understanding and human community from generation to generation.

Let us carry it just like those who came before us did it, and those, who will come after us, will. May the flame in our hands be even and strong.

Thank you, Mary Magdalene...

Ewa Kassala